The Dead Ringer

By Michaela Haze

THE DEAD RINGER

Originally published in the United States/United
Kingdom in 2019 by
DIRTY JEANS PUBLISHING LTD
www.michaelahaze.com
Copyright © Michaela Haze 2019
All rights reserved

A note from the author

The Dead Ringer is a standalone reverse harem romance. It can be read on its own without previous knowledge of my other books.

The Dead Ringer happens directly after the events of The Devil's Advocate, and while Mara is affected by what happened in that series, she does not appear in that novel, and you don't need to have read it to be able to pick up the story.

Unlike my other novels, The Dead Ringer is set in NYC and the surrounding areas. This is my first reverse harem (though I have written a Ménage called 'Red City.' You should check it out!)

I hope you love Mara as much as I do!

Side note:
I have included a glossary and a map of Hell, just in case! They can be found on the last page.

Love, Michaela x

Prologue

Antonio Salitari was my Spring Break.

The man known as Tony to his close friends and family was a Gangster with a capital G. He was my reward for not smarting back to my boss, Dermot Dirk, even when he made me run all over NYC cleaning up his messes.

I woke up one evening, peering out from behind Tony's eyes. His wife, Maria sat astride the middle-aged Puerto-Rican/Italian man with a pillow in one hand and a cell phone in the other. I knew who she was in an instant; Tony's memories were available for me to pluck from the dead man's skull like an easy to use search engine.

"... He's dead, D." She whispered. Her voice shook as much as the hand on her phone. "I did it. We can finally be together. That son of a bitch—"

"And you called on an unsecured line?! Maria, put down the phone right now!"

Tony Salitari was still a deafening presence in his body, despite the fact he had suffocated to death a few minutes before. I cleared my throat, quirking a brow at the distressed woman straddling my middle. As the pilot of a recently dead man, I was unable to move much. A woefully dry sarcastic facial expression was all I could manage.

The beautiful young woman dropped the pillow she had used to smother her husband and threw herself over the side of the bed with a squeak.

Her head popped over the edge, like a prairie dog. "Tony?" She hissed. *"Dio Mio!* You're awake?!"

"And alive," I added unnecessarily.

Maria stood up, her palms exposed in front of her as if she was trying to show she was unarmed. She backed away slowly, but I had lost interest in her.

I stretched out the flabby arms of my newly borrowed body and surveyed the coarse, thick hair. If I didn't know that Tony Salitari was a valued enforcer for the Gambino's, an Italian-American crime family, I would wonder why a model-pretty woman in her early twenties was with a man that looked like a deflated trifle.

"I didn't mean to, Tony!" Maria started to cry, but no tears fell. "I just wanted—"

She continued babbling as I stretched and flung my new stubby legs off the edge of the bed. I cocked my head to the side and perused the curves of Maria's body slowly.

Ever since I had come to the Human Realities, I was determined to lose my virginity. To experience touch and connection in a way that I had never experienced as an incorporeal Demon.

My sexual orientation tended to be heavily influenced by the body that I was situated in at the time. Tony was not attracted to Maria, his murderous gold-digging wife. Even though she was gorgeous.

His cock remained flaccid as I flicked through his mental directory for memories of them fucking.

Nothing.

Limp as a noodle.

Thin enough to be one too.

That made me giggle like a little girl. The sound was wholly unnerving from the throat of a middle-aged man. I quickly choked on the sound.

Tony was very gay.

That worked for me. I'd always thought that I'd prefer to be penetrated rather than do the penetrating. My gender, if a bodiless demon could have one, was of the female binary.

I had two days in Tony's body before I had to evacuate. His flabby sack of skin wasn't what I had imagined wearing when I lost my virginity, but you take the opportunities when you find them.

5

"I k-killed you." Maria stuttered. "H-how are you alive?"

I pinched the bridge of Tony's nose and snorted a tense sound of aggravation. I didn't want to rile myself up too much. I'd been told that it made my eyes turn into bottomless black pits.

"Maria, darling?" I reached into Tony's bedside table and took out his wallet, his gun, holster, and cell phone. I did not look up as I addressed the hysterical woman on the other side of the room. "Shut up," I suggested absentmindedly.

Maria's mouth popped closed. Her eyes bulged as she kept in her fear and confusion.

Muscle memory took me to the walk-in closet; I chose a silk shirt and fitted trousers. Tony's belly hung over the waistband, like a hairy grapefruit. I walked back into the bedroom, shrugging on a suit jacket as I went.

"Where are you going?" Maria demanded.

"You just killed me. I didn't think you'd care." I laughed as I turned the handle of the bedroom door and walked away to the sound of her spluttering.

I needed to get it together.

Typically, I was more careful, using the memories of the person I was riding to dictate my speech patterns and behavior. But I was on vacation. I was allowed to cut loose every once and awhile, wasn't I?

Even if Antonio Salitari's body was my boss's idea of a joke, I'd make do.

I had two days before it was back to the grindstone.

I'd placed an ad on Craig's List with a one-word title: Orgy. Then, I booked a room at the Four Seasons using Tony's black AMEX.

I'd had lots of interest in my ad, so I sat on the edge of

the divan bed, eating room service steak and waiting for ten random men to come to my room to bone me.

The room phone rang.

"Mr. Salitari?"

"Yep."

"Your guests have arrived." The attendant sounded bored.

"Awesome." I chirped. "Have you got any hot sauce?"

"I'll arrange to have some brought up to your room, sir."

"Coolios." I put the phone down and fiddled with the Saran wrap on the mega box of condoms on the vanity. I might have been riding a dead body, but I had no idea what Tony had and unprotected sex with strangers just wasn't cool.

Or so I had been informed by the sexual health clinic posters. I had slipped inside a doctor the week before to remove the record of a Politian's daughter and her abortion.

What could I say? My job was eclectic.

A knock on the door came a few minutes later. I had enough time to remove Tony's pants and shuffle to the door with my rapidly hardening dick. The peephole showed a single beanpole of a man, holding a bottle of hot sauce.

I opened the door. The bellboy flushed bright red.

"Here's your sauce, sir." The hotel attendant did not look past my collarbone as he thrust a small bottle of Tabasco into my hairy fingers.

I scratched my belly with my free hand. "Thanks, man. You want to join my friends for the orgy?"

His eyes widened as his lips thinned, trying to hold in laughter. "No, thank you, sir. I have to get back to the front desk."

I shrugged and reached down to my pants to get Tony's wallet, only to remember that my cock and balls were on display. "Let me just get my wallet." I turned around and bent over, showing the hotel clerk my butt, as I grabbed the designer leather wallet from Tony's discarded pants.

7

Even though Tony's body wasn't the greatest. Too much whiskey and not enough exercise over the years, I didn't feel self-conscious at all. Perhaps that was why the clerk was trying hard not to laugh.

I'd literally exposed Tony's winking brown star to the poor guy, and I gave zero fucks. Why would I? I'd leave Tony's body behind in thirty hours, and I'd be back on Bleecker Street wearing a new set before you could say, *'Nightmare Demon.'*

I tipped the guy a couple of hundred bucks. Enough to pay for a therapy appointment to talk about how much Tony's flabby ass had scarred him for life anyway.

I'd included a picture on Craig's List, so at least those guys knew what was up.

I rubbed my hands together, excited.

Grabbing the remote from the side, I smothered the remains of my rare steak in hot sauce and searched the pay-per-view for some hard-core gay porn.

I made sure to turn the volume up loud enough to annoy anyone staying in the rooms surrounding mine. *Heh, heh, heh.*

The men started to arrive a few minutes later. Black. White. Asian. They came one by one and shook my hand. I didn't bother to put pants on.

Someone asked if I had lube. I did.

Did losing your virginity count if you're using someone else's body to do it? I had no idea. I just knew that I had two days to enjoy myself before my little Demon self was carted back to Dermot Dirk, my asshole boss.

Everyone was shedding their clothes when someone hammered on the door. The sound was aggressive and impatient. Unlike the tentative knocks of my orgy friends.

With a bright shining smile, I pulled open the door. Tony's watermelon pregnant hairy belly sagged over his erect cock.

The flushed face of the Underboss of the Gambino crime family stared back at me. His jaw was hard, and his fists were clenched. He was alone; he looked ready to kill Tony (and by extension, me).

I flicked through Tony's memories and saw his naked back as Tony's cock plunged inside, and love-filled eyes. Mario Russo-Tailor.

His chocolate brown eyes flicked over my shoulder.

"You're cheating on me, *Caro*?" His voice was whisper quiet.

My eyes widened. I couldn't exactly explain that the man he loved had died several hours before at the hands of his unknowing wife—and that I was piloting his body.

"Umm—" I gripped the door to slam it closed. I needed more time to get acquainted with Tony's glitches and quirks. Usually, when I had a mission, I had more time to research. I'd been stuffed into Tony as a matter of convenience.

Mario Russo-Tailor pulled a gun. He pressed it between Tony's hairy moobs.

"Hey, man!" One of the more giant bears behind me held his hands out in surrender. "What the hell's going on?!"

Then Tony's secret gay lover shot me in the chest.

Chapter 1

The Four Seasons in Manhattan was a half-hour walk to Bleecker—or it would have been if I had legs.

I'd had to evacuate Tony in a hurry. The bears and twinks in the suite would have noticed their party organizer didn't die when someone shot a hole through their heart.

I didn't often play by the rules, but even *I* kept to the big Numero Uno.

Do not reveal the existence of Demons.

Because I was *sans* body, I couldn't move in the daylight. I'd had to hang about in the shadows, waiting for the night to fall. I could move at the speed of smoke, mainly because that's kind of what I was, but I couldn't just drift about on the sidewalk. That kind of thing was noticeable. Going invisible took too much energy.

Instead, I waited in the cleaning closet. Slipping inside when the cops turned up to investigate the gunshots.

When the streetlights started to flicker, and Central Park became a maze of lights in the darkness, I drifted outside. Using a garbage shoot to aid my journey.

Time doesn't mean much to Demons. I had existed longer than humans had. Living in Hell at the bottom of the rung.

I was a Drude. A nightmare Demon. We were not well respected, which sucked monkey balls. We dealt in subconscious conflicts and fear. Though I liked to add a little bit of debauchery and mischief into the mix, just to spice things up a little.

I kept to the alleyways, sliding from building to building as I made my way back to Dirk's on Bleecker.

Dermot *Fucking* Dirk.

I metaphorically dragged my heels as I made my way through the city. Waiting behind a dumpster for a crowd of people to pass, I contemplated hijacking a body to get me across town.

I could inhabit the newly dead. That was easy. Slipping into a live person was a bit more complicated. For one thing, they were already 'occupied.' It's hard to steer a car that already has a driver.

"Give me your fucking purse, bitch!" A gruff voice snarled. Scuffing shoes on the concrete and a female whimper.

I inhaled the scent of fear. Allowing the emotion to fill me and give me strength.

"Please! Don't hurt me! Here's my purse, just—"

A meaty thump as a hand met skin. Another sob.

As much as I liked fear, I didn't like people hurting innocents. The mugger stank of pollutants. Rife with Greed and Sloth.

I drifted forward, my smoky form eating up the distance between the massive brute and his cowering victim. I tasted the edge of his mind. Cloudy and malleable. I wasn't some avenger of beaten women. I was an opportunist.

I decided to hitch a ride.

I just had to remember how to push myself into a body that was awake. It couldn't be that hard.

The mugger drew his foot back to kick the diminutive woman. Her purse was clutched in her trembling fingers as she brandished it forward like both a weapon and an offering.

Here goes nothing.

I sank into his skin and wrapped myself around his mind. *Ew. Yuck.* Methamphetamine. It tasted like soap on the back of my throat. Chemicals. I ran my tongue along my new host's teeth, finding them rotting in his skull. Sharp where they had broken off in places, rough where they were blackened with decay.

I pulled the hulking body of the meth addict backward.

11

His feet stumbled as I tried to balance with the rolling cocktail of drugs in his system. It took a second for me to push his presence to the back of his skull. I raised my arms up to stretch. Feeling my limps as I filled his body and made it my own.

The woman flinched when I moved.

Shit.

"Go!" I said, but the brute's voice turned it into a snarled command. The woman did not hesitate as she scrambled away and disappeared into a crowd of people on the brightly lit street. Almost another world away from the shadows.

I wiggled my new fingers and then my toes.

The meth addict had slumped down inside his own mental prison and fallen asleep. Docile.

I reached into my pockets and perused the contents. A condom wrapper and a Metro card. Score. Though it could be empty—knowing my luck.

I caught the bus to Broadway-Layfette from Penn Station and walked the rest of the way. I enjoyed a vast amount of space, able to get a seat with little trouble as people took one look at my bald head and black teeth before moving down the carriage.

I even did a bit of man-spreading. Much to the dismay of my fellow travelers. Their annoyance thrilled me, so I kept widening my legs. Urging the old lady that sat next to me off of her seat.

Served her right. She was rotten to the core. Demons know these things.

· Moving a body that was both obese, and ravaged by drugs, was a new experience for me. The inside of my meat-suits ratty parka jacket stank of BO, and I couldn't stop clearing my throat of phlegm.

I couldn't wait to shed my new body at the first chance I got.

Dirk's was located in a Pocket Dimension. A separate reality created by a Fold in the fabric of the universe. It was a connection between the Human Realities and another place.

Sometimes Folds connected to Purgatory. The Fold above Dirk's led to somewhere else. Located above John's pizzeria on Bleecker, but non-existent to the human world, saying Dirk's was a dive was the highest compliment and an under exaggeration.

I walked past the lit-up windows of a restaurant, past the filled tables and gorgeous smells, to the black painted door to the left of the awning. I didn't bother knocking, I simply opened the door and slipped inside.

Folds only worked if someone had a connection to another Dimension. For example, a Demon could use a Fold because of their relationship to Hell. Fae could use one because of their connection to Faery, and so on. Humans couldn't see Folds. If a Human were to open the door next to John's, they'd walk into the hallway, leading to the apartments above the restaurant.

License plates on the wall, sticky wood on the bar. Cheap drinks and blood hookahs. Empty of patrons, save from a Redcap in the corner drinking a Bud and an Imp trying to find a song on the jukebox.

No-one stopped me as I walked through the door and strode to the bar. I allowed my eyes to turn to oil-slicks, consuming the whites of my host's eyes. No other Demon had black eyes. It was a Drude thing.

"Dirk wants to see you." Stan, the bartender, said as I took a stool. He didn't glance up from the dirty cloth he was using to polish an equally filthy glass.

I pouted. "Can't I get a drink first?"

"Do not make that expression while wearing that body, baby doll." He snorted but did not look up once. I wondered how he knew what face I had made.

I exhaled sharply, exasperated, as I swung my legs off the bar to stand. As I made my way around the bar to the office, I put an extra wiggle in my step.

As I rounded the corner, a stranger slipped out of Dirk's office and into the right corridor. He was built. Tall as a

13

tree and just begging to be climbed. His jaw was hard, covered in scruff, and his brow was strong. Dark hair. He walked like a man that knew what he wanted and knew how to get it. Dressed in fatigue pants and a tight black t-shirt that showed enough muscles to bench press a person.

Yum.

His eyes flicked to mine before creasing in disgust. I was mildly offended before I realized that I wore the body of an obese addict, and had allowed my eyes to turn into bottomless pits.

I rubbed my clammy hands down my worn parka. I would have liked to have met Mr. Muscles while wearing something beautiful. Like the body of Arianna Grande, for example.

Mr. Muscles disappeared around the corner. He did not look back. A curious memory and nothing more.

I knocked once on the door marked 'staff' and waited for my Lord and Master to grant me an audience. He must have been really pissed with me because he made me wait ten minutes before he called me through.

Dermot Dirk was a vague man.

Everything about him was indecisive. His body couldn't decide if it was thin or fat. His hair couldn't decide what color it was. A mixture of blacks, browns, and blondes swept into a comb-over. His eyes were beady; his belly was round, but his legs were twig-like. He moved like he expected an attack at any second. He gave the impression of a harangued father, with one foot out of the door.

The dude's energy seriously got me down.

I opened the door and slipped inside, making my way to the old sofa in the corner of the dingy office. Dirk didn't look up from his paperwork to greet me.

I tapped my nicotine-stained fingers against the grubby fabric of my jeans.

"What the Hell are you wearing?" Dirk's southern drawl cut through the silence in the room like a knife through

14

butter.

I shrugged. "All I could find."

"You couldn't even wear Tony Salitari for a day without getting into trouble." Dirk flung his arms out with a sigh. "I needed Tony to stay alive until Mario Russo-Tailor announced he was running for mayor. Which was meant to be tonight."

I rubbed my temples, right between my skinsuit's monobrow. "You couldn't have told me this?" I groaned. "You told me I was on vacation!"

"All you needed to do was pretend to be alive, Mara." Dirk opened his desk drawer and swept a chunk of his papers inside.

I didn't ask how Dermot Dirk knew that Tony Salitari was going to die before he actually did. Just as I didn't ask why Dirk would want the future mayor of NYC in his pocket.

"You're a thorn in my side, *Drude*."

"You need to give better instructions, *Fae*." I held out my hand to survey my nails.

Dirk growled.

"Who was the beefcake that just came out of your office?" I asked, affecting disinterest.

"Your next job." Dirk crossed his arms over his barrel-like chest.

"Dirk, no," I whined. "You promised me a vacation."

"Not my fault you screwed the pooch on that one, Mara." Dirk's thin lips tightened. "I can always send you back to Hell if you want?"

I swallowed the lump in my throat. I didn't want to think about what had happened to my Cluster. How my brother's and sisters—

I sunk back into my chair.

Dirk pushed his rolling chair back and swung around to reach his filing cabinet, all without his ass leaving the seat. He grabbed a file and slapped it onto his desk, the sound muffled by the sheer amount of junk.

15

I leaned forward, craning my neck to read the front of the file.

"No way." I shook my head frantically. "Nu-uh. Find someone else." I knew I couldn't say no to the job, but I had every intention of letting Dermot Dirk know precisely how much I *didn't* want to do it.

Dirk ignored my protests as he licked his finger and flicked through the file to extract a photo.

"Demon Hunters?" I exclaimed. "You're that desperate for money that you'd sell me to the Hunters?"

"Not everything is about money."

I snorted. "Rich. Coming from *you*."

"The Hunters have petitioned the Fae for help." Dirk continued as if I hadn't spoken. "Something is targeting their people. They want an outside opinion."

He pushed a glossy Polaroid across the table with his index finger. The impassive face of a beautiful brunette stared back at me.

"Frankie Gardiner." Dirk picked up the photo using only two fingers. He flicked it between his fingers like a playing card. "Twenty-two years old. Promising Hunter. Her squad was attacked. She's in a coma."

"They want me to extract her memories?"

Dirk shook his head. "She's a vegetable." He explained. "Her commanding officer was just here. Warren Davenport, leader of the East Coast branch. He wants someone to go undercover in the unit and find out what happened. He thinks it's an inside job."

"And he just happened to know you have a Drude on staff?" I bit out skeptically. "This doesn't sound like a trap *at all*."

"I suggested the possession." Dirk shuffled the papers in the file. "I might have implied that you were a 'Dead Ringer.'"

A dead ringer was a slang term for a *Mimic Sidhe*. A Fae with the ability to emulate the appearance of others. Dirk was Fae so he couldn't outright lie, but the Fair Folk were tricky bastards. They could imply, hint, and misdirect with the best of them.

"You want me to wear Frankie and get to the bottom of whatever conspiracy is plaguing the Hunters?" I summed up. "That's peachy. Except for the fact that people will notice that her body is missing."

"The plug's being pulled tomorrow. Her body won't be in the hospital anymore either way." Dirk said. "Do you want to wear her fresh, or do you want to wait for her to die?"

I rolled my head to my shoulders as I considered his question. "She'll last longer if her body is alive."

Dirk clapped his hands together. "Great." He said without enthusiasm. "Now, get out of my office—and next time you come into my bar, take a minute to shower if you're going to wear a homeless man."

I stuck my tongue between my teeth and blew a raspberry. "He's a meth addict, actually." I snapped before I spun on my heel and flounced away.

"Why does she think that makes it better?" Dirk muttered as the door slammed shut.

Dirk owned an apartment in the East Village that he let me stay in. Situated in a terracotta monstrosity of a building, on the third floor, and guarded by a dubious keypad and a housing association more concerned with themselves than looking too closely at the residents.

It was perfect for me.

Creative types were a breeding ground for dark subconscious thoughts and harrowing dreams. My building was home to an experimental sculptor and an artisanal cheesemaker. The nightmares of those two could keep me fed for weeks.

My meat-suits hands started to shake when I stepped out of the taxi, reminding me that I wore an addict, and his

17

source of vitality (drugs) was wearing off quickly. I was too tired to drift home, and getting into my building was hard without hands.

I kept my bathroom window cracked, just a hair, but it was a short jump from the fire escape, and I didn't want to risk Dirk's apartment getting burgled.

I trudged through the foyer with heavy feet, pushing Mr. Meth to the back of his mind as I struggled to keep a hold of the gurgling stomach pains and nausea that his memories told me were typical of withdrawal.

I spotted one of my neighbors from across the hall as I got off the elevator. Apartment 36. Hunched over as if his own height made him uncomfortable. Blonde hair flopped in his eyes and his cupid bow lips were always pursed. He never made eye contact. Never spoke in anything above a mumble.

I'd caught a glimpse of his face once. He was the most good-looking man I'd ever seen, and I'd met the Devil.

Well... When I say 'met,' I mean cowered from a distance as Lucifer swanned into the City of Dis.

Mr 36 left his apartment at odd hours (like me) and sometimes accepted my deliveries from Amazon.

"Hello!" I waved enthusiastically when Mr 36 stood a foot in front of me. He looked up briefly before focusing on his shoes.

His brow furrowed as his gaze zeroed back in on mine, doing a double-take.

I shrugged and kept walking as I reached my apartment. I felt my hot neighbor's eyes on the back of my bald skull as I felt along the seam of the door for my taped key.

Keeping hold of a key was virtually impossible when you didn't have a body.

I let myself into my apartment, just as my borrowed body's bowels began to revolt and sing a whale song of screaming pain and impending release.

Ugh.

The withdrawal was not fun.

Chapter 2

The next morning, Dirk's car arrived, idling outside my apartment like a flashy black shadow. I'd had the night from Hell (pun intended) and was in no mood to take the subway, so it was fortunate that my boss had decided not to take any chances. He probably thought I'd skip town instead of face the Demon Hunters.

My borrowed body was clammy and cramping with withdrawal symptoms as I rode to Brooklyn Methodist on 6th Street. Dirk's driver double-parked and dropped me off right at the doors.

I found the Emergency Dept. on the end of a red painted line through the hospital.

Demonic healing had stowed the worst of the withdrawal pains, but I still felt out of sorts. I couldn't wait to dump the body I wore and slip into something smaller and more comfortable.

I didn't bother to find out the name of my borrowed puppet, as I poured out of his skin and into the vents overhead. His substantial body dropped like a marionette with its strings cut, and hurried shouts of medical staff soon followed.

I was smoke as I drifted through the hospital, unbothered by air filters and the weaving tunnel of pipes that led me across the building.

Francesca Gardiner was in a private room on the sixth floor, with neuroscience. She was in a coma and hooked up to breathing machines. As I listened to the hiss of the equipment, I tried to decide when the best time to jump into her body would be.

Dirk had informed me that they were going to pull the

plug, but only Davenport, the leader of the NYC Hunters, was aware of that fact. Even her family didn't know.

As if my thoughts had summoned the dark, brooding beast, Warren Davenport slipped into the room on silent feet. A doctor by his side.

The commander's steps made no noise as he strode to the side of the bed and looked down at the still brunette, strung up to the machines keeping her alive.

"Corporal Gardiner." He said, his head bowed in respect, and his deep-set brow creased. "Rest assured, we will find out who or what did this do you—it might not seem like much, but it's the best I can do."

Warren Davenport pushed his fingers through his dark hair and let out a sigh. He closed his eyes as the doctor turned off the machines with care.

Fuck. Shit. I needed to jump before the body died. I didn't want to do it with a Demon Hunter in the room, let alone the Big Boss.

Frankie's heartbeat ticked down like a bomb. I waited, hanging on the edge of the vent, ready to plunge into the room like a tsunami of smoke.

"Let's step outside, Mr. Davenport." The doctor suggested.

The door had barely clicked shut before I sunk into Frankie Gardiner's skin and wrapped myself around her mind.

Step one: completed.

Now, I just had to lay in the bed until someone could take me to the morgue. Then I'd make my escape.

I hadn't thought about an outfit change when I strode to the bus stop opposite the hospital and waited for Warren Davenport to pick me up.

I was meant to be a Dead Ringer. A copy. Not the real

thing.

I had gotten a few looks from passers-by, and I had assumed that it was because the back of the hospital gown opened to expose my butt. I didn't even think about the toe tag that I hadn't bothered to remove.

Warren Davenport barely stopped. His car trailed by slowly; he honked once for me to get inside. Rolling my eyes, I skipped over the curb and sank into the passenger seat.

"Not funny." He growled. "Do all Fae have such a sick sense of humor?"

I glanced down at the horrible pattern of my paper-like gown. I supposed that it was kind of dark to dress up as someone that had just died. Davenport didn't know that I wore Frankie's body. He only thought I looked like her.

"It was all I could find," I replied simply.

"Sir."

My nose scrunched. "What?"

"You need to call me Sir." Warren's dark eyes flicked from the road. "Or Commander Davenport."

I snorted. *Fuck that.*

"Dermot Dirk told me that you would be able to perfectly mimic Francesca Gardiner so that we can lure her killer out." Warren quirked a brow. "Is that not the case?"

I shrugged.

"What's your name?" He asked.

"Frankie Gardiner." I bit out.

Warren Davenport rubbed his stubble. His jaw clenched.

"I'll try my best to be the perfect soldier." I continued in a bright tone.

"I don't need you to be perfect. I just need you to look the part."

I rolled my eyes and bit my tongue. *Make up your mind, dickweed.*

"Where's the Hunter's compound?" I asked, glancing out the window at the sea of yellow cabs.

22

Instead of answering my question, Davenport reached over and slapped the glove compartment until it opened. He fished out a black face mask and handed it to me.

"Kinky," I said, rubbing my thumb over the fabric. "What's it for?"

"Put it on." His tone brokered no argument. "You're not allowed to know where we're based."

"It'll look weird," I argued. "What if someone sees?"

"Tinted windows." He said shortly. "Do you always talk back?"

"Only on Tuesdays."

"It's Friday."

"Oh." I nodded sagely. "Then, yes. I *always* talk back."

Davenport's knuckles turned white as he gripped the steering wheel.

"Frankie Gardiner was the last survivor of Team C. Seven people are dead. She lived long enough to get to a hospital, but she never woke up." Davenport spoke slowly. "You're here to find out who did this and why. To help us find the demonic son of a bitch that did this to our Hunters and to help us put them down."

I squirmed in my seat, uncomfortable. I said nothing as Davenport continued.

"You need to tell me now if you can't do this." He glanced once at me. His voice was hard. "I don't like putting civilians in the field, but Dermot Dirk recommended you."

I licked my bottom lip. "I can do it." I was proud of the fact my voice didn't crack.

I sat one foot away from a man that commanded a group of people that were specially trained to kill me and my kin. He could end my life with the grip of his hand and a few choice magic words.

Drudes were almost impossible to kill in their incorporeal form, but I wasn't so indestructible while wearing a meat suit.

I stretched out the elastic of the face mask and settled it

23

over my eyes. Tilting my head back against the headrest.

"Wake me up when we get there," I told Davenport, closing my eyes.

He tsked but did not protest.

I used the journey to delve deep into Frankie's mind and read her. Find out her likes. Her dislikes. I watched her last moments, as her legs collapsed under her.

I inhaled sharply.

"Are you alright?" Davenport's voice drifted through the darkness.

"Never better," I said through tight lips.

He smelt like lemon body wash and something sweet that I couldn't put my finger on until I heard a wrapper. Gum. Somehow I couldn't imagine the dark leader of the Demon Hunters snapping away at a stick of Big Red.

I bit back a snort and focused on my task.

Frankie Gardiner. Skilled sniper. Almost unnaturally good. Fourteen confirmed kills. All Demons. I shivered and bypassed the memories of their deaths.

Frankie always wore gloves. I tried to locate the schema that told me why but couldn't find it. She didn't like touching certain materials. It must have been a sensory thing.

She had an older brother. Daniel. He was a medic at the compound. I wondered why he hadn't been at the hospital to see her last moments—until I remembered that Frankie's death was classified.

Her parents lived in Queens. Frankie lived at the compound. I didn't have the heart to tell Davenport that his blindfold was less than useless. I had Frankie's memories. I knew where it was.

A secret military base in New Jersey. Three hours drive from Manhattan.

Despite being alive, the owner of my body was surprisingly silent.

"Are we there yet?" I asked.

Davenport exhaled sharply. Irritated. "Are you five?"

24

I shrugged. "Bored."

"Please try and be professional." He warned. "Or I will turn this car around and tell Dirk that the deal is off."

"What deal?"

"Please just keep your mouth shut." Davenport snarled in his husky voice.

"You're the only person that knows my true identity." I reminded him. "Excuse me for sliding in a few jokes before I have to pretend to have a stick up my ass."

"Don't." His word was a slap. A harsh full stop. I'd insulted a dead woman and gone too far.

I opened my mouth to apologize, but closed it again before the words came out.

Being around Humans was terrible for my health. I was a Demon for Hell's sake. I didn't say *sorry.*

The rest of the car journey was spent in silence.

Demons, as a rule, didn't require sleep.

Somehow, despite this, I drifted off in the front seat of Davenport's armored SUV with my face pressed against the glass and drool over my chin.

Frankie's body was heavily damaged, and while I could control it, my possession wouldn't last if her body failed. The trauma would kick me out of my shell. My presence was healing her. Not that I could determine what had put the woman in a coma in the first place.

I could inhabit the living almost indefinitely. It depended on their will and my strength. Frankie had left the building. Her body was vacant and hollow. Perfect for me to control.

One of the reasons that dead bodies were easier to slide into than the living was because the deceased had no will. They were empty. Despite that, bodies carried residual memories and

25

feelings.

Watching Frankie's life depressed me.

She was good at her job. Which was basically sitting still and shooting people.

There were no memories of friends. Birthday parties. Her relationship with her brother was stilted at best. Though her parents loved her, due to work, Frankie rarely saw them.

I thought about my own family. About the red sands of Wrath, the sprawling desert, and the eagle winged Valkyries. The swampy forested Envy and the Leviathan King, as tall as a skyscraper. All teeth and golden scales. My family. My 'Cluster.' Hundreds of Drudes, spanning the Seven Circles like an undulating blanket of shadows.

I thought about their screams. Ripping from incorporeal mouths turned solid in their last moments.

I was the last one left.

My ass had gone numb despite Davenport's heated seats. I shifted my weight from one butt cheek to the next, wishing that we could have just taken the train. I took off my mask, but Davenport did not notice—his eyes were fixed on the road.

I understood that he felt that he needed all of that cloak and dagger bullshit to protect his Hunters—but if anything, I would never willingly walk into the compound. Demons would use the knowledge of its location to stay away, or at least, that was my plan once Dermot Dirk's thinly veiled plot to kill me played out.

"Your room is a single, and you'll have your own bathroom." Davenport broke the silence as we pulled up to a red light. "You can beg off most of Frankie's duties and obligations by stating that you are on leave for your recovery. However, I would like you to spend some time with the people on the base to try and be seen."

I nodded slowly, looking out the window as it started to rain. I chose an unusually large raindrop and watched it race its brethren down the glass. Winner, winner, chicken dinner.

"You'll have Frankie's personnel files." Davenport continued, rubbing his scruff. His dark eyes flashed to me before turning back to the road. "Try not to fuck it up. Put your mask back on."

"Is my job to find the culprit or to try and bait him into the open?" I quirked a brow.

He shrugged. "Both. Depending on your experience."

Which was none.

I clapped my hands and rubbed them together excitedly. Being stuck in a building with people that would kill me if I slipped up and came out as a Demon. Pretending to be a dull and uppity sniper with no friends. All the while, trying to find the person that took out seven highly trained Hunters and put one in a coma.

I would rather sink into my couch and eat my meat-suit's weight in Ben and Jerry's.

"What's the food like?" I asked as I slipped my mask back over my eyes.

If my question surprised Davenport, it did not show in his voice. "Adequate."

Groan. I flicked through Frankie's memories to try and find a boyfriend, or girlfriend, or at least someone to play with. Nada.

"Was Frankie close to anyone?"

"Corporal Gardiner did not have close friends. She was dedicated to the cause." Warren Davenport said stiffly.

"How do you guys feel about Fae?" I threw out there. That seemed like the kind of question a *Mimic Sidhe* would ask.

"We have a truce with the Fair Folk of the east coast. They police their own unless we are directly affected by the crime. They have a peaceful and quiet presence in The City and do not venture to New Jersey often. Some of our Hunters are fae."

I nodded to myself. "But, Demons are fair game?"

"We are Demon Hunters." Davenport reminded me. "You can take off your mask now. We're almost there."

27

My tongue was too big for my mouth. "Do you have any clothes I could borrow?"

He jabbed a finger over his shoulder; I craned my neck to see a duffle bag on the back seat.

I unbuckled my seat belt and wriggled into the back of the moving vehicle. Ignoring Davenport's groans of disapproval.

What did he expect me to do? A toe tag wasn't exactly this season's must-have foot accessory.

I pulled on the plain black tank and khaki cargo pants. Sans underwear. Boring heavy combat boots, but the laces undone. A hoody finished the ensemble, with a logo for *'The Davenport Halfway Camp.'*

The sporadic buildings slipped into expansive greenery, and then woodland.

The SUV handled the rough terrain and dirt road like an old friend, pulling up to a small checkpoint hidden between two large trees.

A young guy skipped out of his tiny office and saluted. Davenport handed over two laminated cards, which Skippy scanned and handed back. He wished us a nice day and waved us through the barrier.

The Hunter's compound was a campsite, with large square buildings dotted around like someone had fallen over and dumped a bunch of Legos in the middle of a forest. Circled by a tall chicken and barbed wire fence, with look-out posts every fifty yards.

The compound masqueraded as a boot camp for prisoners. I watched a group of khaki-colored commandos jog past in synchronicity as a man in a weird hat screamed behind them. It was a good cover.

"Let's head to the Mess to get some food. Lunchtime is almost over." Davenport suggested, marching ahead of me without checking to see if I was following.

I stumbled, before righting myself. I glanced up to see if anyone had spotted me. My eyes met someone's from across the clearing.

Demons had excellent eyesight, but Frankie's vision limited me somewhat. Even at a distance, the strangers' eyes were extraordinary.

Raven black hair, cropped short. East Asian, I would have to guess. Tanned skin and eyes the color of the cosmos. Light. Purple and blue. Weird.

I cocked my head to the side as I tried to taste his magic. I discreetly swiped my finger through the air and sucked it.

He tasted like birthday cake. A vanilla sheet cake with buttercream frosting and rainbow sprinkles.

So strange.

I'd never encountered anything like it.

The stranger's eyes crinkled in amusement before he turned on his heel and strode to one of the buildings.

Shit. I'd lost Davenport.

I hurried forward before someone cleared their throat behind me. I hadn't even heard them approach.

"Corporal Gardiner." A low voice grumbled. So deep that it was almost a growl.

I arranged my features in a benign and pleasant mask. A tiny smile on my plush lips. "Yes?" I spun around to the owner of the sexy grumble.

Orange eyes met mine. The color of cinnamon and dried orange peels. The stranger was a head taller, more significant than any man I had ever seen. I searched Frankie's memories but only came up with a name.

Callum Hart. Sergeant.

His hair was an odd mixture between blond and brown and was pulled back into a tight man bun. His biceps were bigger than my head.

The man must have sensed my mild confusion. His eyes flicked to my up-turned lips as if he had never seen the sight before. I let my smile drop.

"Yes, Sir?" I stuck to a simple response, using the honorific that Davenport had suggested.

29

Hart's brow furrowed as he studied my face for something. He leaned in and inhaled sharply and quickly before straightening back to his full height.

"Did you just sniff me?" I asked in horror.

"You smell like the hospital, Corporal Gardiner." He said.

"I should think so." I popped my hip and waved my hand. "I just got discharged."

Hart cocked his head to the side like a confused dog. "Perhaps you should lie down." He suggested. "You don't seem like yourself."

I struggled to maintain a casual expression as fear raced through me. "I'm on medical leave." I squeaked. "Sorry."

Hart nodded absentmindedly as he glanced over my shoulder. I followed his gaze to see Davenport using his 'murder eyes' on both of us. I ducked my head and used the chance to escape.

The mess hall was a barrage of chattering, clanging trays, and random smells. Far from the Maine lobster from *Per Se* over Central Park. My true form had no taste buds. I wasn't above hitching a ride in a dead body and using their credit card to experience all of the fine dining that NYC had to offer. It was a neat trick. Credit card companies and banks were often the last people to cancel a card due to death.

I followed Davenport's example and grabbed a tray. Dry chicken breast and asparagus. I snatched a few Jell-O cups from the counter. The evil little voice inside of me demanded that I swipe them all. I glanced over my shoulder and fisted as many of the luminous green cups as I could fit in my hoodie pockets.

Done. Evil satisfied.

Warren Davenport swanned off to a table full of Very

Important People. I made a move to follow him, but his sharp expression and pointed glance advised me to make my own seating arrangements.

Hunters, Hunters everywhere, and not a chair in sight. I hovered on the edge of the canteen. I saw someone leave, and swooped into their empty seat, slamming my tray on the table before anyone could snag the chair.

"Hello, Corporal Gardiner." A low voice murmured, barely loud enough to register.

I glanced up from the sectioned off meal tray in front of me.

"It's you!" I spluttered out before breaking out into a smile. The Hot Shy Blonde from apartment 36. My eyes widened as horror sunk into my skin. My neighbor was a Demon Hunter?

I'd kill Dermot Dirk that next time I saw him.

Mr 36 gave a muted smile as he pushed his hair out of his eyes. He said nothing.

Hugo Sinclair.

Frankie's memories whispered. I finally had a name to put to a face.

I started to cut my chicken, the movements harsh as I struggled with the dry piece of meat.

"I see Gary hasn't gotten over his grudge," Hugo said softly, gesturing to my chicken. "You just got out of the hospital, and he still feels the need to punish you for refusing to go out with him."

I smiled tightly through a bite of my food. I said nothing.

Hugo's eyes dropped, fixing on his plate. I got the impression that he didn't make eye contact often.

"I'm grounded for two weeks," I muttered uselessly, trying to make conversation. "Davenport told me that he didn't want me on the field."

Which was just as well, because I couldn't handle a gun to save my life. Even if Frankie could, muscle memory only went so far.

31

"I bet that pissed you off?" He guessed with a smile in his voice.

"You bet," I said. "I don't handle being bored well." Which was true enough.

"You should listen to Warren. He's worried." Hugo suggested. "We've all got to be on guard until we find out what took out your team." He reached out and patted my shoulder once before snatching his hand back as if he wished that he could take the small act of kindness back.

It was strange to witness grief and compassion in an abstract way. To receive sympathy for something that had happened to my host, but not to me.

Hugo glanced up for just a second. Our eyes met through the short curtain of his dark blonde hair. His irises flared pale ice blue.

I jerked back in surprise, but recovered quickly. "You're an incubus!" I hissed under my breath, glancing furtively to make sure I hadn't been overheard.

Hugo Sinclair's brow quirked in confusion.

"Are you okay, Frankie?" He whispered. "I think you should lie down."

I jerked out of my chair. The legs squeaked harshly against the linoleum. I smiled shakily. "You're right. I need some fresh air." I bused my tray as quickly as possible and rushed out of the mess hall. Resisting the urge to glance over my shoulder as I went.

The Demon Hunters had an Incubus?!

I raised a trembling hand and scrubbed it over my face as I rested my back against the pebbled cement wall of the building.

I wasn't sure if I could handle whatever it was that Dermot Dirk wanted from me.

It was only a matter of time before I slipped up. Did Hugo know that something was wrong? Had my excuses worked?

Being in peril at the same time as being around hot

men was terrible for my health.

I was a horn dog at the best of times. Putting me in a difficult situation and then presenting a bunch of man-candy was just asking for something to go wrong.

Warren Davenport with his dark eyes and severe scowl. Sgt Hart, with his growly voice and all of those delicious muscles. And Hugo Sinclair?! A bona fide sex Demon.

I sank to my butt. Tilting my head back and raising my eyes to the sky.

I was in trouble.

Chapter 3

Drudes were nightmare demons by definition. I could feed on people's subconscious terrors with little effort, but creating that fear? That took power—I hated to leak. It was a sign of weakness.

Imagine everyone in a hundred-yard radius suddenly experiencing horrific day time hallucinations at the same time, and you can kind of understand my problem.

I needed to find a way to de-stress stat. Tequila and porn would help.

Where could I find both of those things on a pseudo-army base? I sat up, fists clenched with my new mission to find alcohol, and then masturbate into a coma.

My back was ramrod straight as I left the Mess Hall and walked through the compound like I was meant to be there. I paused briefly, self-conscious, as I wondered if I was walking like Frankie.

Could people tell that I wasn't her?

I groaned. The sound was a hairball in my throat. It was so much easier when I didn't care. When my life wasn't on the line.

Someone cleared their throat behind me. Davenport. I sniffed and tilted my chin as I turned to face him.

"Yes?" I asked hotly.

His lips were pressed together in a tight line as he frowned at me. Despite that, I saw a twinkle in his eye. I amused him.

"If you're done eating, I can show you to your room, Corporal Gardiner."

I blinked slowly. "Does it have a mini-fridge?"

Davenport sighed and rubbed his hand over his face. He muttered to himself before he strode towards one of the buildings on the edge of the clearing.

"Seriously, though. I need strong alcohol. Preferably tequila. And does my room have pay-per-view? Or, like, the internet?" I wheezed as I struggled to keep up.

Frankie's body was still healing, and I could front all I liked. I wasn't at optimum captivity. Whatever had put the woman in a coma was a doozie. Even my demonic healing was taking its time.

Davenport slowed his steps to allow me to catch up. He kept pace as we walked along the trail.

"Why do you need alcohol and television?" He asked, dryly.

"Because. Reasons." I crossed my arms over my chest.

He ignored my very valid excuse and opened the door to one of the dormitories. He waited for me to pass before he followed closely behind.

Loud grunts and harsh slaps led me to pick up my pace in excitement. I hoped that it was what I thought it was.

"Last time I had an orgy, it was interrupted," I told Davenport gleefully. Bouncing on my heels as I followed the sound.

Davenport's look shot daggers. If his glare was a blade, I would be bleeding out.

"This is the dojo." He said pointedly as we rounded the corner.

I deflated. The exciting sounds had been two Hunters training. Bare Knuckle fighting. Krav Maga. I recognized the Israeli defensive fighting style.

Warren Davenport glanced at me out of the corner of his eye. "Francesca Gardiner was not the type of woman to attend an orgy. I would advise you to remain silent if you cannot think of something appropriate to say." He advised.

I snorted. "Me? Silent?" I waved a hand, dismissing the motion. "And how did you know that she didn't go to the

35

occasional orgy? It's not something that someone tends to mention to their commanding officer."

"You just did." Davenport pointed out, pinching the bridge of his nose.

I smirked cheekily. "You're not my commanding officer." I reminded him as I tilted my chin to a long corridor off the side of a wall filled with various weapons. "Is my room over there?"

"Yes." He said through gritted teeth.

"Coolio."

Davenport's expression was glacial. I held up my palms in surrender.

"I'll be cool. Chill."

He was silent. His eyes said it all. I tended to get casual and overly familiar when I was in danger. Like one of those supervillains that starts to describe their evil plot when they should just be killing the superhero.

I wondered what my evil villain name would be.

Nightmare Girl?

The Super Drude?

Davenport cleared his throat to get my attention. I shrugged, unrepentant, and followed him as he led me down the corridor to one of the suites at the end.

There was a sensor pad to the left of the ivory painted steel door.

"I need to reset the door to allow you in." He explained as he pulled a key card from his pocket.

"No need, Big Man." I stepped forward and placed my palm on the scanner. It registered as Frankie Gardiner instantly.

"I didn't know *Mimic Sidhe* could replicate fingerprints." His expression was closed off.

I didn't care to explain. I need alone time and some hard-core self-loving before I exploded in a cloud of shadows and nightmares. I wiggled my fingers in a wave as I shut the door in his face.

I had gotten wrist cramps but had finally washed the antiseptic hospital smell out of Frankie's hair when I heard a knock on the door.

If a knock could sound arrogant, it did. Harsh and demanding. I marched over, wrapped in a Terry cloth robe, and opened the door—fully expecting Davenport to be on the other side.

It was not Davenport.

I stood in the doorway, with my head cocked to the side, as the stranger wrapped his arms around me and clung to my body as if I was a life raft. I patted his back tentatively.

Ginger hair. The color of copper and strawberries. Pale skin and loose-fitting scrubs. Frankie's mental Rolodex informed me that the man was Daniel Gardiner. Her older brother.

Daniel could not have looked more different to Frankie if he tried. Frankie had mocha-colored skin, with light hazel eyes and plump lips. She was a mixture of African-American and Caucasian.

Daniel was the color of milk. It took a second for me to access the memories that told me they were both adopted by the Gardiner's as small children.

How hadn't I spotted that?

Clearly, Frankie hadn't thought much about her paternal parents. Human thoughts and feelings were complicated.

"Hey, Danny." I whispered, pulling up the nickname from a childhood playground memory as Frankie kissed his bloody knee and made a 'fairy wish.'

"I can't believe you're here." Frankie's brother murmured. "Do you remember what attacked you and your team?"

He broke away and scanned my face, searching for something. For some reason, his intense gaze made me feel

37

uncomfortable.

"No. It's all a blank." I said stiffly.

He lifted his medical bag and shook it gently, any concern was washed away and replaced by a cool demeanor. "I'm here to check you over."

I nodded and perched on the edge of the bed. "Check away, Doctor Danny."

He gave me a funny look but didn't question it as he slid his bag onto the carpeted floor.

The examination was thorough but efficient. Daniel did not speak much, apart from asking me to follow his finger with my eyes.

After he had deemed me healthy, he reached into his bag and extracted an injection.

"What's that?" I said, hopefully. Prescription painkillers? Black market heroin? Unlikely. Still, a Demon could dream. Someone in this stuffy compound had to know how to have some fun.

"Vitamin supplement." His tone brokered no argument as he jammed the needle into my arm and emptied it before I had a chance to open my mouth. I rubbed the spot on my arm. It let out a dull throb.

"I have to go." He stood up swiftly. Apart from the uncharacteristic hug at the beginning of our meeting, his behavior fit with the memories that Frankie had of him. Their relationship was cold and distant. His stilted goodbye was proof of that.

My knowledge of human emotion was limited—he could have simply been too upset to show his feelings. I wouldn't have known.

Maybe I needed a children's book or something. *This is a happy face. This is a sad face.* I didn't want to know how Davenport would handle that request, especially if he couldn't even honor my need for gay porn.

The door clicked shut behind Doctor Daniel, and I collapsed onto the bed dramatically. I was exhausted, which was unusual. I didn't even want to think about tomorrow and all the ways I could fuck up.

Chapter 4

Spread-eagled on the king-size bed, and naked as the day my host had been born, I jerked awake to the sound of frantic knocking.

I groaned and pushed Frankie's soft waves away from my face. Sunlight streaked through the window, showing that I had slept the whole night away. Which was odd.

My skin was littered with gooseflesh, indicating that it had gotten cold in the night.

Another sharp knock sounded out. Reminding me of my visitor.

I hoped it wasn't Doctor Dan. He was boring as fuck.

I slapped my thighs as I sat up, staggering. With a shake of my head, I straightened my spine and answered the door.

Warren Davenport filled out the frame. His deep-set eyes gazed into mine intensely. Another man stood behind him. Dark skinned, bald head, and even taller than the commander. His bright white teeth shone a friendly smile. I scanned Frankie's memory for him but came up blank.

"Who's that?" I jabbed a finger towards Davenport's companion.

Warren's eyes did not leave my face. "Why are you naked?" His jaw rocked from side to side as if it was physically painful for him to speak.

I shrugged and made a noncommittal sound— something along the lines of *'I dunno.'* Davenport growled in response.

I ignored him and turned my attention back to the stranger. I extended my hand and mustered a polite smile.

"Frankie Gardiner," I said. "You are?"

"Remi Weber." Remi purposefully reached over

Davenport's shoulder to shake my hand. "Specialist. Intelligence and communications analyst. I just transferred from London."

I nodded sagely as if I had an idea of what he was talking about.

"Corporal. Sniper." I informed him with a clipped tone—not inviting further description.

Remi nodded, still smirking. "Do you think you could put some clothes on?" He asked. "I'm babysitting you today, and your nudity is very distracting."

I shrugged and turned on my heel, marching into the bedroom. I pulled open the chest of drawers and searched for something to wear. Holding up each item of clothing before discarding it on the bed.

The doorway stood open with two large men on the threshold. Davenport looked furious. Remi seemed to be having too much fun for it to be legal.

I settled on a pair of jeans and a tank top. No underwear. It was restrictive and uncomfortable. If I was given a choice, I was fully embracing the commando option.

Warren Davenport pinched the bridge of his nose. "You're with Specialist Weber today. After breakfast, I'll expect you two in surveillance room three." And with that, he left.

Remi hovered for a second. He bit his bottom lip and gave a theatrical moan of frustration. "Are you wearing that?"

I cocked my hip. "You're not one of those men that tell women what to wear, are you?"

"Hell no." He winked. "I'm also not one of those men that make blatant sexual remarks to a woman that might make them uncomfortable."

I waved his politeness away. "I don't care. Be as perverse as you want."

"Dangerous woman." He teased. "I like that." His British accent turned the words into a cheeky quip. His voice made me shiver.

Remi accompanied me to the Mess Hall. Walking by my side, rather than striding off in front. He grabbed a tray for

41

me when I told him about Gary and the dry chicken adventure of my first day. Remi personally made sure to check my food, flirting with the young woman behind the counter. I got an omelet with lots of veggies.

"Can I have some hot sauce with that?" I asked, gripping my tray.

The woman looked down at the mound of jalapenos in my omelet. She directed me to the condiment table without a word.

"Like it hot, do you?" Remi nudged his shoulder into mine. I lost my balance and quickly salvaged my tray before it spilled.

"If I were trapped on a desert island, it would be the one thing I would take," I said as I grabbed the bottle and rested it on the edge of my tray. Hot sauce was the one thing I missed the most when I was incorporeal. That and legs.

Remi scanned the mess hall for somewhere to sit. "I'd take a boat. So I could sail home."

"That's cheating." I scrunched my nose.

Remi spotted someone he knew and waved before heading to the other side of the dining room. I followed on his heels like an obedient dog. Remi led us to a table in the corner.

"Hey, Hugo," I said brightly as I put my tray down and slid into my chair. "How're tricks?"

The incubus squinted, and it took a second for me to remember that Hugo knew Frankie from before and would likely spot a change in behavior.

I dove deep into her memory and straightened my spine, relaxing my expression into a 'resting bitch face.' Hugo gave me a tiny smile before he ducked back behind his floppy fringe to hide his eyes. It was exhausting to pretend to be someone that I was not.

Remi eyed me with suspicion. "Do you have a belly ache or something?"

I elbowed him in the stomach. "Shut. Up."

Remi introduced himself to Hugo; soon, they began to

talk about an event in London that Remi had done damage control for. I zoned out when they started to describe the various Demons they had seen. Remi chugged a bottle of blue Gatorade. It looked unnaturally luminous.

Raucous laughter caught my attention; I scanned the surrounding tables. A beautiful woman with deep mahogany ringlets caught my eye and scowled before turning back to the group. She said something to the woman next to her, and I got the impression that whatever it was she had said had been about me.

I turned my attention back to Remi and Hugo.

"And then the leader of the Labour party was attacked by a Shax Demon!" Remi exclaimed, stabbing a sausage link before stuffing it into his mouth whole.

"Labour party?" Hugo's brow furrowed.

"Like your Democrats." Remi supplied once he had swallowed his mouthful of food. "Anyway, Shax Demons only feed on discarded Leviathan skins..."

Hugo gasped. "No!"

Remi nodded enthusiastically. "That's right. The next Prime Minister was a Demon. A Leviathan."

I snorted and unscrewed the cap to my apple juice, downing half in one swallow. "What's the big deal?"

Remi's gaze shifted from Hugo's to mine.

"He's dead now. It was in the news." I shrugged and tipped almost the entire bottle of hot sauce onto my eggs.

I was always sad when a Demon died, but the Prime Minister had been a dick. He'd made a deal with the Devil and paid the price.

I eyed Hugo for a second. Wondering how I could bring up his demonic leanings in conversation. I swished my clean fork on the air and licked my bottom lip to try and taste the Sin. Lust. Incubus. Maybe a half-human—a Cambion.

I turned my full attention back to my meal. Famished in a way that I had never experienced before.

Someone walked behind me and bashed into my chair.

43

It skidded forward and jostled the table. I managed to catch my open bottle of Snapple before it spilled all over my food.

I looked up just in time to see a swishing cloud of dark ringlets retreat away from the table. The staring woman from earlier.

"Who's that?" I asked. Too lazy to search my mental directory.

Remi turned to Hugo, his gaze questioning.

Hugo Sinclair fiddled with his fork before delicately placing it on his tray so that it lined up with the rest of his cutlery. "That's Riley Fisher." He dropped his gaze. "She was Hambone's girlfriend." His tone was delicate. Quiet but full of censure as if I should know who she was.

I regretted not taking the time to find out. The vague memory of the bloodbath that led to my host being unplugged rushed through my head.

Hambone had been one of Frankie's squad. One of the seven that had died. Harvey Hammond, aka Hambone.

Obviously, Riley Fisher had an issue with the fact that I was alive, and her beau was not.

I watched as she bussed her tray and waved at Doctor Daniel as she left the Mess Hall. At least her grudge didn't extend to other members of Frankie's family.

"Come on," Remi said, standing up. "We've got to meet War in the surveillance room."

"War?" My nose scrunched in confusion.

"Warren Davenport." Hugo supplied helpfully. "He goes by War sometimes. It's a nickname."

"Like Maverick and Goose?" I asked excitedly.

Remi snorted. "Something like that."

Before long, Remington Weber and I began to the short walk to another one of the grey Lego block buildings between the trees. I reached down to grab one of the orange leaves that had fallen on the floor.

All of the foliage in Hell was warped in some way. Burnt. Frozen. Dead. I had never seen a fallen autumn leaf. I tried to keep my amazement to myself as I turned the fragile thing over in my fingers.

"You must know Davenport well if you use his nickname," I said, distracted by the veins in the leaf.

Remi nodded and stuffed his hands in his pockets. His breath fogged on the cold air.

"We hunted together in London." He offered no more information, but I didn't press.

The surveillance building was off the beaten track; we had passed no one on the way down the path.

A shard of fear sliced through my chest and cracked my ribs. I cupped my throat as if my hand could protect me from my vulnerabilities. I'd just met Remi, and I liked him, but I didn't know if all of this was an elaborate plan to get me alone so he could kill me.

Remi grabbed my wrist, and I jerked backward. My arms pinwheeled, and my cheeks flushed as I pulled away.

"Jesus." He muttered. "Are you okay?"

"You scared me."

"I need your hand for the scanner." He jerked his finger over his shoulder to point to the electronic pad by the door.

I nodded shakily and ducked around him to the room.

Remi did not touch me, but he came up to my shoulder.

"Are you okay, Frankie?"

I nodded jerkily. Remi studied my face for a prolonged second, and when he was satisfied, he nodded to himself. The spell was broken. We both walked into the quiet building together.

I followed Remi, who looked thoughtful rather than the mischievous puppy that I had come to see in the short time we had known each other.

I said nothing. Unable to decide if I had been foolish or prudent to expect an attack.

We found surveillance room three with little hassle.

45

Commander Davenport was watching something on the screen, standing at the desk with both hands on his hips and his legs squared.

Dude seriously needed to relax.

Warren Davenport clicked something on his tablet before he handed it to Remi. I craned my neck to watch the screen.

It was the CCTV of a warehouse. Concrete floors, metal railings, and piled boxes.

"This is the video of the attack." Davenport glanced at Remi, though his words were for my benefit as well. "See if you can spot anything before the video cuts out."

Frankie Gardiner strode in first, a large duffle bag in her hands. She sprang up the stairs away from the squad, presumably to find higher ground so she could scope her target.

A group of Hunters, dressed in black with most of their faces covered, crept forward in formation. Two at the front. Two at the side, and three at the back. With Frankie, that made eight total.

I didn't want to ask what they had been hunting—it must have been significant and dangerous to warrant that many Hunters.

The Hunters swept through the warehouse, their search economical, and their movements came practiced ease.

The camera angle changed.

"That's when camera one was disabled?" Remi glanced up at Davenport—who nodded.

One by one, each of the Hunters dropped. A dark mark flared on their forehead. It was a rune that I did not know. Not Cyclian, the language of Hell with its circular alphabet and harsh guttural slashes. Something unknown. Fae, perhaps? Ancient, definitely.

It burnt into their skin; the image too grainy to make out. The mark disappeared as quickly as it came, and I wondered if Davenport or Remi were aware of it.

The camera switched again, to Frankie on her belly.

Her gaze focused on the sight of her rifle. Her attention wholly devoted to her target. She jolted, like a spooked rabbit, and rolled over just in time for the final camera to go dead.

"Only a select few knew about the mission, but whoever attacked the squad knew their formations and where Frankie would be," Warren said. "We believe that someone might have infiltrated the base and organized the attack."

Remi looked at me expectantly, as if he wanted me to fill in the blanks. I couldn't. Frankie's memory failed at that point—so I went with the most obvious answer. The truth.

"I didn't see," I said.

Remi handed the tablet back to Davenport. "Do you have photos of the warehouse?"

Davenport clicked through the tablet until the full-blown image of Hunter corpses filled the screen. Remi hunched over and walked over to one of the computers. He logged on and began to type.

"I don't know why I'm here," I admitted, whispering so Remi could not hear. "It's not like I can tell you what happened. I wasn't there."

"Mimic Sidhe are Fae. You can identify the work of one of your kind. I believe that this wasn't just one creature. It took planning. Inside knowledge." Davenport crossed his arms over his chest and stared down at me. "Besides, You are here to lure out the culprit." He added quietly, glancing at Remi.

I rubbed the back of my neck. "I guess."

"You're being compensated for your time." Davenport leaned in. His breath smelt like cinnamon gum. "You will do as I say for the duration of your stay on my base."

His dominating attitude made my nipples hard. Which was strange because I typically hated authority with a passion.

I squirmed. "Yes, Sir."

His dark eyes sparkled; Davenport broke eye contact to watch Remi, hunched over his computer, and typing furiously. "I'll leave you to it." He said gruffly. "Try to have some suggestions for when I come back." Warren Davenport walked away, his spine rigid. He did not look back.

I danced over to Remi, leaning over his shoulder like a nosy child. "What ya doing?"

Remi laughed, showing every one of his white teeth before putting his serious face on. "Trying to recover the camera footage. I want to know if the cameras were taken out during the attack or if the footage was tampered with afterward."

I nodded. "Makes sense."

He clicked away at the keys. "Do you always let him speak to you that way?" He asked after a second of silence.

"Who? Davenport?"

Remi nodded.

"I like it." I shrugged. "Hot. Commanding. Just begging to unwind. If my life weren't on the line, I'd be on him like white on rice."

"You think whoever attacked you will come back?" Remi sat up.

Ugh. Being Frankie was confusing.

No. I wanted to say. *I am a Demon wearing one of your Hunters like meat-suit. If you ever found out, you'd kill me in a second. I might find Davenport attractive, but I can't let my guard down, even for a second.*

I said none of that. Instead, I hummed non-committedly.

Remi spun his chair around. He reached out and tucked a lock of hair behind my ear.

"We'll get whoever did this, Frankie." He said. "I may joke around, but believe me, I'm going to find whatever Demon is behind this, and I am going to rip their head off. Then I'm going to find the asshole who summoned it."

I nodded, but inside I felt sick.

Would I be forced to watch one of my brethren die? Could I sit back and let that happen? Demons didn't need a summoner to visit the Human Realities. Maybe their lack of knowledge would benefit me.

I wished that I could walk away. Just hold my hands up

48

and skip into the sunset—but I owed Dermot Dirk. He'd helped me when I needed it. He'd saved me. I owed him. He was my boss.

I just hoped that whatever plan he had was worth it.

I was as useful as tits on a chicken for the whole afternoon. Remington Weber quickly typed away on the computer. His attention focused on me with the intensity of a laser as I watched and re-watched the video of Frankie Gardiner's squad dying.

Warren Davenport came back when the sun had begun to sink below the tree line of the forest.

"Did you find anything?" The Commander addressed both of us, but his attention was on me.

I swung my legs like a child, allowing my heels to thump into the legs of my chair. "No."

Remi cleared his throat and turned the monitor of his computer around so both of us could see. He began to play the video of Frankie Gardiner's team dying.

"Notice how Team C spread out here?" Remi said, pointing to the ground of seven black-clad figures that crouched low in a V formation. "None of them are touching, so I assumed that whatever attacked them must have been able to kill without touching them."

"Like a Pure-blooded Demon." My tone was dry. Dead.

"Exactly!" Remi snapped his fingers and flashed a hint of white teeth. "But then, I noticed something."

He magnified the floor of the warehouse, just under the soldier's feet.

"I thought it was dust at first." Remi rubbed the corner of his eye. "But, it looks like smoke."

Warren stepped behind Remi and slapped him on the back. "Good work, Weber—now we just need to look into

Demons that have a smoky form."

My hands began to tremble; I stuffed them in my pocket. I said nothing.

"I've got to go." Davenport glanced at the clock over the windows and frowned. "I expect to see you at tonight's social, Corporal Gardiner. You must show your face." He gave me a look that didn't take a genius to figure out.

But I was frozen. My eyes fixed on the still image of the paused video. Black smoke around their ankles.

It couldn't be a Drude, could it?

There was no way.

I had enough time to have a shower before I heard the emerging sounds of the people making their way to the 'Social'—whatever that was.

Personal hygiene was not something I often had to worry about. Showering was an entirely new exercise. I got shampoo in my mouth. The thick goo tasted foul and stuck to the roof of my mouth. Even when the water went down the drain, the taste clung to my throat.

There were so many items that I did not understand. A pink razorblade rested on a plastic holder on the side of the shower enclosure. The presence of the blade prompted a twenty-minute unsuccessful search for cocaine after I cracked the fuchsia casing on the blade to get to the sharp metal on the inside.

I cut myself accidentally, putting my finger in my mouth to try and appease the harsh sting. Frankie's blood tasted strange, like perfumed flowers. I recognized the taste. It wasn't strictly human. A distant throwback to a hint of magic.

All of Frankie's clothes were boring with a capital B. Khaki, black and beige. She owned one pair of jeans. Deep rich indigo that fitted like a glove. The tags were still attached.

I had managed to get dressed, but my hair was still wet, and makeup wasn't an option. I sighed wistfully at the various cosmetics. If I had been in The City, I could have gotten one of those blowouts that Dirk's girlfriend Clodagh was always talking about.

I had to settle for looking like a ratty scab.

Frankie's memories told me that she placed pride in her appearance. She was neat, facetious, and pristine.

Somehow, while in possession of her body, her hair looked like I had shoved her hand into an electric outlet and then rubbed her cheeks with sandpaper.

I shrugged. It was the best I could do.

My job was simple. Lure out the potential traitor to the Hunters. Let Davenport take care of him. Return back to Dirk and resubmit my vacation request.

Do all of that without getting found out by the Hunters and killed.

Then I could finish my orgy.

The knock on my door was so quiet that I almost missed it. I leaped forward to pull the door open, eager to get my obligations out of the way. Hugo Sinclair stood on the other side of the door, his eyes widened at my exuberance. He blinked slowly, a flush rising on his cheeks as if he wanted to be anywhere by on my stoop.

"Hugo!" I clapped. "Do you want to come in? Tea, coffee? Jell-O cup?"

His brow creased. "You have Jell-O cups?"

I shrugged and rested my shoulder on the threshold of the door. "What's a Demon like you, doing in a place like this?"

"Frankie..." Hugo groaned and looked over his shoulder. "You know I don't like to talk about the... You know what."

I chewed my lip. "Why would the Hunter's even let a Demon in?" I said to myself.

Hugo looked hurt, but he squared his jaw and met my eyes. "You know why." He said through gritted teeth.

51

"Everyone here has something. Something that makes them different. Being a Demon doesn't mean I don't want to stop the ones that kill indiscriminately."

I rolled my head to my shoulder and shrugged to concede that he had a point.

Hugo sighed. "I know you hate these things, but Davenport insisted. He also told me that I had to keep an eye on you."

"Planning on putting that beautiful body in front of any bullets that might come my way?" I winked.

Hugo shifted awkwardly. "If it comes to that."

I snorted a laugh and waved Hugo Sinclair forward. He moved with a slouch like he was apologetic for his height. For such a beautiful man, his hesitance and shyness were jarring.

"You have an apartment in the City, don't you?" I asked as we stepped out of the dorms and into the brisk fall air.

"Yeah." He shuffled forward. His head dipped in a nod as his hands hid inside his pockets. "We've all been called back to the compound, though. Until we find out what took out Team C."

The social was held in the mess hall. All of the benches and tables had been moved to the side to form a square. The center of the room was bare and full of milling people. There was a beer cooler and soda.

I spotted Birthday Cake—the violet-eyed man with shiny black hair. He wore a tailored shirt and trousers. His gaze caught mine, and he saluted me with a bottle of bud.

Davenport had his back pressed against the wall and his arms crossed. He watched me like it was his job, hobby, and purpose in life. I wiggled my fingers in a mocking wave, and he scowled.

Frankie's memory provided a few names for the faces I saw, but no one approached.

I began to appreciate that Frankie Gardiner was not a social person. I didn't know how long I could keep up the pretense.

I stayed in the center of the room, ensuring that I was visible to the potential traitor.

I could see where Davenport was coming from. Thrusting a dead person in front of their murderer was going to get a reaction. It was merely a case of keeping an eye on the people around us.

Warren Davenport caught my gaze, and his jaw clenched. He communicated something with his eyes, but I had no idea what it was.

Hugo clung to my side, hovering like a shadow, but saying nothing. I could sense his discomfort.

"Don't you like this sort of thing?" I asked.

"Too many people." He murmured.

I considered that and thought of the other Incubi that I knew and the involuntary reactions they could invoke. I nodded sagely, agreeing with his assessment.

"Do you want a beer?" I jerked my finger to the cooler in the corner.

Hugo declined, but I used the opportunity to get a second to myself.

When I reached the cooler, I made sure to block the view inside with my back. I was bored, so I started to shake the cans of PBR and place them delicately back on the ice. I snickered to myself and grabbed a can of soda. I wished it was something stronger, but I had no desire to drink beer. It made me gassy.

"I saw that." Remi stepped up to my shoulder, his eyes alight with laughter.

I shrugged as I opened my can of Coke and took a swig. "Just here to liven up the party."

Remi's smile dropped after a second. "I wanted to ask, did you have an idea about the smoke Demon? The look on your face said that maybe you did?"

So, that's why I keep losing at poker!

"It's nothing." I crafted my tone to be indifferent. Apathetic. "Do you want a drink?"

"Not after I saw what you did to the cans." He teased. And like that, the conversation was dropped.

Pop music filtered through a tinny speaker in the corner, but no one danced. Hugo had crept into the corner to stand next to Sgt Hart. They were speaking in hushed tones. As if they could feel my eyes on them, they both looked my way.

I held up my red can and smiled sweetly.

"You're the computer whiz, huh?" I murmured, turning back to Remi.

"It's what I do." He smirked playfully. "Although, sometimes I go into the field. It depends on what command wants."

I nodded, and Remi snatched my can of soda from my hands, taking a long pull after he had deemed it safe. His Adam's apple bobbed; I thought about how his lips would feel.

I bet he was good with his hands. Any man that could type that fast had to be skilled with his fingers.

If I got any more excited, my eyes would turn black. Remi took another swig from my can, having commandeered it for his own.

"Can I borrow a tablet or something?" I asked. "I'm dying for access to hard-core porn."

Remi spat soda everywhere and wiped his mouth with the back of his arm. He opened his mouth to speak, but someone barged past and caused me to lose my balance.

Hugo straightened and began to cross the room towards me.

"Excuse you!" A haughty voice rang out. "You're blocking the cooler."

"And?" I said, cocking a brow as I sat up. I brushed the thighs of my jeans as I glanced up at the petite woman with a face like thunder. Riley Fisher. I blew a raspberry.

"You—" She spluttered.

"Let's dance." I looked over my shoulder at Remi, holding my hand out. His lips were pressed together, holding back laughter. The crowd parted like a slow-moving tide as we

54

made our way to the center of the room. Hugo shifted from foot to foot as he debated whether to join us.

I grabbed Remi's large callused hands and began to sway, Frankie's memory showed her doing something similar at five years old at a birthday party. Remi's one-man battle against hilarity failed, as I raised his hand and spun on my toes like a ballerina.

My neck jarred backward. My hair tore away from my scalp with sharp pain. The sound that came out of my mouth was one born of fear, a pitiful and throat tearing shriek.

Riley Fisher's dark eyes stared down at mine, her hand tangled in Frankie's mahogany waves. Anger was a fire that animated her face. Her cheeks were flushed, and her chest was heaving.

I tried to pull away but was yanked back. Her hand was still tangled in the back of Frankie's long hair. I held onto my control with a harsh grip, my inner Demon floated to the surface and demanded that I rip her apart and feast on her terror.

"How dare you!" She snarled. Spittle flew from her lips and landed on my cheek.

"It's just a cooler. Chill out." I reached behind my head to untangle her fingers, but she gripped tighter. She would never know the inner battle that I had just won. It was the only reason she was breathing.

"You're laughing and having fun, swanning around like you're Queen Bee of the base, Frankie Elise Gardiner, but your team is dead! My Harvey is *dead*."

She dragged me down to the floor; my arms flailed as I tried to break free from the tiny woman with strength like an ox. Her leg reared back; she kicked the back of my knee, forcing me down onto the floor.

"You should have done something!" She bellowed. "Harvey should be alive!"

I wanted to unleash the force of her own subconscious against her. I could taste her buried fears. Being crushed. Confined spaces. I wanted to warp her mind into a living

55

nightmare. I closed my eyes when I felt the blackness leak into the whites of my host's eyes.

I reached back with sure fingers. No longer content to allow the grieving girlfriend her moment. I gripped her hand and squeezed until I felt the bones creak.

Frankie's mind told me to make an example. She was a Private, and Frankie was a Corporal. I pulled her hand and twisted until I felt every one of her fingers threaten to dislocate. I felt numb. I opened my eyes, finally under control.

She screamed like a banshee and broke free to cradle her hand to her chest. I'd stopped short of doing real harm.

"You need to leave, Riley Fisher," I said in a low and even tone. I was very close to killing her. The buffet table was full of silverware, and it wouldn't take much to grab a knife and jam it in her eye socket.

She glanced around as if she had just remembered where she was. Her face was red; her eyes shined with tears. Someone rushed forward to rub her back and make sympathetic cooing motions. I did not care.

I'd never spent so long in one body before. I was at my limit.

My eyes darted around the room, locating the exits. I could slip into the bathrooms and leave Frankie's body behind. If I was lucky, I could be back in the East Village by tomorrow night.

Come to think of it, didn't Hugo have an apartment in NYC? He lived right across the hall from me. Maybe I could hitch a ride when he left the base.

Davenport strode over just as Riley Fisher was led away, with her head down and her diminutive figure making everyone look on in pity. The Commander did not look happy.

"You did nothing wrong." He assured me; he looked like he was chewing on nails. "But if you were Corporal Gardiner, I'd sign you up for mandatory therapy with Dr. Lee. Because of the adjustment period after your injury. And for starting fights."

56

I rolled my eyes. "I didn't start that fight."

"But you finished it." Davenport crossed his arms over his chest.

Remi had been pushed to the edge of the crowd, and he battled to reach me. "She's not going to be punished." It was a statement and not a question. If looks could kill, Remington Weber would be standing over Davenport's corpse.

"Therapy." Warren clipped. He turned on his heel and left.

Remi rubbed his bald head and scanned the crowd. "I tried to get to you, but two of Riley's team grabbed me."

I shrugged. "It's okay."

"It's not," Remi growled.

"It's over now." I nudged his shoulder. "I'm going to go."

Remi tried to protest, but I was *done*.

I'd found a cell phone in a coat on the back of a chair. I knew Dermot Dirk's phone number by heart. Still, it was a childish move to phone my boss and demand that he come and pick me up.

I was trapped in a vice. Having a body was fun for a short while, but the stress was getting to me. I was balancing too many plates at once. I didn't do well with situations where things were expected of me. Drudes had a bad reputation for a reason. We had limited attention spans. We didn't play well with others.

"Dermot Dirk." The lilting voice of the stubby Fae rang out as the phone connected. I jumped and almost dropped the small device.

Who answered a phone with their full name? How pretentious.

"Dirk, it's Mara."

He sighed heavily. "No."

"I didn't ask for anything," I argued with a pout.

"Whatever it is, no."

"Come on! Dirk! *Please*." I whined.

"What is it?" He asked, put upon.

"This is too much. I can't stay here." I looked over my shoulder as I ducked behind one of the buildings and pressed my back against the wall. When I was sure I was alone, I laid out my issues. "I'm a nightmare Demon in a compound full of Hunters. I'm wearing a sniper. I'm hours away from Manhattan and I. Don't. Like. It."

"Did you discover anything about the homicides?" Dirk sounded bored.

"Are you even listening to me?" I hissed, covering my mouth with my cupped hand, so my voice didn't travel.

"All I hear is whining," Dirk said.

"I think I have something to whine about!"

"Phone me when you've made progress." He continued as if I hadn't spoken.

"Don't hang up. Dirk. Please." I pleaded. "I swear, I'm *this close* to slipping up. Why did you think I could do this?"

It was a valid point. My other jobs had involved wearing politicians while doing embarrassing things and ensuring I was photographed. Or stealing incriminating documents. Not weeks of subterfuge.

"Mara." His fatherly tone stopped my racing thoughts. "You are the only being that could do this. There was no one else. Someone targeted Team C, and Davenport needs to know why."

"Why are you doing favors for the Hunter's?" I sniffed. Dammit. I was old as the cosmos, but I was stress-crying. I pinched my wrist when smoke began to escape out of my pores. The pain helped me to reign it in.

"Davenport helped to contain the London Fissure," Dirk said. "A lot of people owe their lives to him. Demons too."

The London Fissure had been a crack that had formed when Hell had attached itself to the Human Realities over a year ago. Numerous creatures tried to slip through. Including the ancient evil had that destroyed my kin. Hunters had ensured the speedy evacuation of that part of the city.

Dermot Dirk had a family in London. The Hunter's had probably saved their lives with their actions.

I wished someone had been around to save my kin when they had needed it. I wished that I had been strong enough. Instead, I had done what I did best. I had run.

Just like I wanted to do now.

"I've watched the video," I spoke barely above a whisper. "There's a dark shadow. It looks like smoke."

"A Drude?" Dirk jumped to the same conclusion I had.

"All of the Drudes are dead." I forced all emotion from my voice. "Something flashed on the bodies before they died. Writing, but I didn't recognize it. Not Cyclian or Enochian."

"That rules out Angels and Demons." Dermot Dirk sounded thoughtful. I hummed in agreement. "What about Frankie's memories?"

"Nothing. No pain or injury." I rubbed the center of my chest. "No scar."

"None of the other bodies have visible wounds or markings?"

"No idea. No entry or exit wounds." I said. "It could have been magic."

"Mara." The way my boss said my name was no-nonsense. "This is why I chose you. You are smarter than you let on. You just need to focus."

I groaned. "Focusing is boring as fuck."

"Mara." He repeated my name to get my attention back. "If you do this, I will shorten your contract by five years."

I inhaled sharply. Dirk laughed.

"That got your attention, didn't it?"

Chapter 5

Mandatory therapy with Dr. Lee. I fanned myself with the post-it note that had been tacked to my door that morning. A luminous green square of paper that filled me with horror and morbid curiosity.

It was early morning. For the first time, ever, my days had structure. Mess Hall for breakfast. Therapy and then rewatching the same boring video to try and unearth clues to a group of Hunter deaths.

People died all the time. It was hard to muster up any sort of enthusiasm for finding their killers. Especially when the people who had died made their living killing my kind.

But Dirk had faith in me.

Which was strange, because I was an inherently lazy and selfish creature—but somehow, having someone believe in me made me almost *want* to live up to their expectations.

I shrugged into a large and shapeless hoodie, with the *Davenport Halfway Camp* logo on the front. I managed to carrel Frankie's frizz into a messy bun on the top of her head—which had taken longer than I had thought possible.

My stomach gurgled and churned, reminding me that my host's body needed fuel. I hurried out of the room and past the dojo. People were already training despite the early hour. No one waved, and I was thankful that Frankie was an introvert because it meant that I didn't have to make small talk with suspicious people.

More people were awake than I had expected. (Did nobody sleep in?) Dogs barked in the distance, somewhere off the beaten path. I sniffed the air, tree sap and bacon from the Mess Hall. Someone called out a command. The words unclear.

Another dog bark.

Animals, as a rule, did not like Demons much. I loved dogs, even if they didn't like me. I'd made an Instagram account, so I could scroll through hundreds of cute puppy videos. I followed the sound of barking into the woods. My sneakers crunched the bracken, announcing my arrival. The snap of a twig and the rustle of a brush.

A row of kennels came into view, nestled between the trees and surrounded by a waist-height picket fence. There was a water trough. A familiar towering figure was moving in a line, pouring kibble into the metallic bowls. The sound rang out like hailstones on a tin roof.

I cocked my head to the side while I tried to remember why I recognized the bulky man in fatigues. Orange eyes glanced up and met mine. Sergeant Hart. The man that had sniffed me.

I swaggered forward and rested my elbows on the fence. "Where are the pups?" I called out.

His lip twitched before an expression of suspicion settled on his face like an old friend. "Grub's up!" Hart bellowed. The occasional barking became a cacophony as a sea of brown, black, and brindle crashed around the edge of the wooden kennel building. A red-faced man jogged after them.

"Dammit, Hart!" He scowled. "We were in the middle of an exercise!"

"8am, Skully!" Hart said, without emotion. "Breakfast for the K9."

Skully huffed and marched back around the building, muttering under his breath.

I beamed down at the sea of dogs, scrambling over their food.

"I didn't think you liked dogs." Hart studied my smile like an unknown entity.

He must have meant Frankie. My smile slipped a notch. "I love dogs. They don't like me much."

Hart hummed as he knelt down to stroke the head of a Rottweiler with an undocked tail. "Right."

I straightened. "I should get some breakfast for myself."

Hart nodded stiffly. "Okay."

A man of few words. I turned on my heel and walked away. Glancing down once at the mass of animals that were too occupied with their food to acknowledge my darkness.

The therapist's office was located behind the Mess Hall in a log cabin, with a beautifully carved overhang and a rocking chair. The curtains were drawn. My unlaced combat boots echoed against the wooden stairs as I walked to the front door.

I raised my hand to knock, but the door swung open before I had an opportunity to.

"Birthday cake!" I blurted out when the man with violet eyes opened the door. His face did not move from its expression of professional courtesy.

"Hello, Corporal Gardiner." He replied. "My name is Dr. Lee."

"Okay." I nodded, dumb. He really did smell like a birthday cake. Vanilla frosting and rainbow sprinkles. I had no idea what kind of Supe he was. I had never encountered anything like it.

He smiled politely and stepped back, ushering me into the cabin. Dr. Lee did not invite me to sit, but he did take a chair next to the bookcase. His own notepad laid on the side table, forlorn and desperate to be used.

I glanced at the neatly arranged chairs. Huge Queen-Anne backed Chesterfield's that belonged in a Gentlemen's Club. I ignored them and chose the plaid couch that was pressed against the wall. I punched the cushions and sank into the seat. I swung my legs over and rested my head against the armrest.

If I was going to do therapy, I was going to be comfortable.

The framed degree on the wall from a fancy college stated that Doctor Lee's name was Ahn-Jae Lee. Korean, I would guess. Based on the cookery books written in the Korean Alphabet, resting on the bookshelf behind his head.

He was young. Tasseled hair that implied that he cared about other things, but was somehow cute. His eyes, while gentle, bored into mine. Watching my every move.

Had Davenport told him that I wasn't Frankie Gardiner? Unlikely.

"I'm here because Davenport told me I had to be," I said. "I don't plan to bare my soul."

Dr. Lee's lip twitched. "We can talk about anything you want to talk about."

I rubbed my chin. "Can I call you Jae?"

"Can I call you, Frankie?"

"Okay," I said.

"Do you like your job, Frankie?" Jae Lee asked.

My gaze flicked over his shoulder. I focused on a particularly exciting spot on the wall. "Do you have to report anything I say to Davenport?"

Jae rolled his head from one shoulder to the over. "That depends. As my patient, I am subject to doctor-patient confidentiality. However, if something that you say implies that you will bring harm to yourself or others, I have a professional responsibility to share it."

"But, you report directly to Davenport?" I asked in a clipped tone.

"He is my commanding officer, yes." Dr. Lee confirmed. His brow creased.

"I'm not really Frankie Gardiner." I blurted out. "I'm an imposter that your boss has hired to bait the traitor in the camp into revealing themselves. I'm not a sniper. I'm not a Hunter. I'm not even a particularly good... Person." My words babbled out as I twisted my hands in my lap. "I'm the least qualified person to do this job, but my boss says that he believes in me, y'know? And even though Dermot Dirk is kind of a

Grade A asshole, I don't want to let him down. But being Frankie is exhausting." I sagged down into the couch. When I glanced at Dr. Lee, his lips had parted to form a small O. He quickly rearranged his face.

"I see." He murmured, reaching over to the side table and flicking through a file. "It says here that you got into an altercation with Private Fisher at last night's social. Do you want to talk about that?"

"Her boyfriend was one of the guys on Team C. She needs someone to blame. I'm here. So she's blaming me." I stood up and walked towards the bookcase. Pausing as I ran my fingers over the various titles.

"How does that make you feel?"

"I don't feel anything about it. Not really." I admitted. "I'm not Frankie, so it's not remotely my fault. I wasn't even there."

"So you think the attack on Team C was Frankie's fault?" Dr. Lee concluded.

"I think that something attacked Team C," I said. "Frankie lived long enough to get to a hospital. The rest of Team C died in seconds."

"That's not what I asked." Dr. Lee's lip twitched sadly.

"I don't think it's anyone's fault," I admitted. "But I don't care. I didn't know these people. You're all Hunters, and I'm...not." I tapped my pinkie against an out of place romance novel on the bottom shelf. Standing up, I pushed Frankie's hair out of my face.

"Okay." Dr. Lee nodded and picked up his notepad, flipping it open. "You said before that you don't think you're a good person?"

"I'm so not." I trilled a laugh.

"Can you elaborate?"

"No." My answer was firm. I didn't want to elude or even hint that I might be a Demon. I was confident that every word out of my mouth was going to go in a file somewhere to be perused by Davenport.

A thought occurred to me.

If Davenport was going to read my file, I might as well have some fun.

"I've had fantasies Doctor," I admitted breathily. I wished that I could force a blush to rise on Frankie's cheeks. "I dream about Davenport tying me up. Spanking me. Making me do things."

Dr. Lee quirked a brow. Amused. "Fantasies are normal. Healthy."

Ahn-Jae Lee was hard to shake. My tone got deeper. More wanton. Jae leaned back in his chair to look at me as I circled his chair.

"I want to lick him all over. In front of everyone in the Mess Hall. I want to whip him. I want to—"

"Frankie." Jae's tone was severe. "I know you're trying to change the subject."

I sighed heavily and sunk back down onto the couch. "But this is so *boring*." I moaned. "Everything here is so boring. There are no restaurants. No sex clubs. No Fae. No Sin. No crime. I want to go back to NYC."

Jae made a note in his pad. "You aren't allowed out on any missions until you have completed your psych eval in two weeks, and have been cleared medically for duty."

I snorted. "Davenport won't clear me. I'm out of the door as soon as whatever killed Team C is dust."

Dr. Lee rolled his eyes. "You always have a place with the Hunter's, Frankie." He assured me. "Even if you never return to active duty. When a Hunter is *Called*, there is no going back."

"Called?" I cocked my head to the side. "Do you guys have, like, a telemarketing platform? Like that Windows scam?"

"*Called*, Frankie," Jae replied meaningfully.

"I told you, I'm not Frankie."

"Why don't you feel like Frankie Gardiner?"

"Dude." I sat up, shaking my head. "I don't feel like Frankie because I'm not her."

"It's common to feel like a different person after a traumatic event," Jae replied earnestly.

I inhaled deeply and prayed to the Seven Circles for patience.

"What *are* you?" I asked instead of replying to his therapist's questions.

Jae turned his head to the side. I could see the cogs in his mind. Frankie would have known what he was. I could delve deep into her mind to find the answer, but her thoughts didn't just float up. I had to watch through memories. It was tedious as Angel feathers.

"You taste like birthday cake." I blurted out. "That's why I said... Earlier..."

"I'm a Nephilim." He said, studying me.

"Right." I giggled nervously. A half Angel? Fuck a duck. "Are all of the Hunters here *'special,'* like you and Hugo?"

"Some." Jae's violet eyes focused on mine. "Team P. I'm on Davenport's squad."

"P?" I gaped. "That's a lot of Hunters." A whole alphabet of Demon killers.

"P stands for Phoenix." Jar explained.

"And C?"

"Cerberus."

My eyes widened. "I've never met an Angel before." I squirmed in my seat.

"Nervous?"

My borderline hysterical laughter was the answer.

"I'm just a person, Frankie." He assured me. "I eat, sleep, and shit like the rest of us."

My nose wrinkled. "Not at the same time, I hope."

A snort escaped his nose. It was cute. He sobered quickly. "Have you had issues with your attention span since you were discharged from the hospital?"

"I've always been this way." I beamed.

Dr. Lee's intense gaze made me uncomfortable. His violet eyes looked right through me as if he knew what I was thinking and feeling. I saw the tentative emotion flash across his face as he debated how to voice something. "Frankie—"

"Not Frankie." My smile tightened and became brittle.

"Okay." He nodded, looking back down to his notepad. "You said that Davenport knows your true identity?"

I nodded.

"Do you feel like you can talk to Warren about what's bothering you? You mentioned that you have had fantasies about him—"

"I'm going to stop you there, Doc." I waved my hands in front of my face. "I have fantasies about everyone. I've imagined you naked and sticking your cock in a watermelon, and I only just met you."

"A watermelon?" His voice pitched as Jae Lee shook his head to banish the image.

I licked my lips and leaned forward, smiling in earnest. "I think about sex all the time."

"Again," He reminded me. "This is healthy. Unless you start to engage in dangerous activities, such as unprotected—"

"I'm a virgin." I interrupted. "But I want to lose my virginity soon."

"That's a big step."

I eyed him shrewdly. "You're beautiful. Maybe we could—"

Jae Lee stood up and slammed his notebook down on the side table. "Enough." He said, his lip twitched. He found me funny. I could tell. "I know what you're doing."

"What am I doing?" I asked innocently.

"You're trying to make me uncomfortable, so I will end the session."

"Is it working?"

"No." He glanced at the door.

"Darn."

"Frankie," Dr. Lee said my name like a warning. A put upon sigh. "I think you might be having issues adjusting after your accident. I think that you are a strong and brave woman who doesn't like to talk about her feelings. It is my opinion that you are perfectly healthy and mentally well. Aside from a possible ADHD and imposter syndrome diagnosis. Both of which are common for women in stressful and professionally demanding environments."

"ADHD?" I repeated, choking on air.

He nodded. "We would need more sessions for a true diagnosis. The goal of today's session was to talk about your feelings towards Riley Fisher and to resolve a possible workplace conflict. I believe we have done that."

I tapped my fingers against my thighs. Anything to keep my hands busy. I glanced at the doctor to try and gauge if he was serious. I looked away and then looked back. His expression hadn't changed.

"Really?" I asked in disbelief.

"Really."

"I clearly told you that I'm not Frankie Gardiner, and I'm basically spying on your entire base for your boss, and all you can do is rationalize." I squinted.

"What name would you prefer that I call you?" He cocked his head to the side.

"Mara." I nodded to myself.

"Mara," Dr. Lee said severely. The way he said my true name made me shiver. "You are fine. Making jokes. Feeling all of the normal things. You want to find the culprit behind the attacks. That's a human reaction."

"Do all humans rationalize like this?" I gestured to the doctor and glanced at the door, ready to escape.

I didn't know how many other ways I could tell the truth. Maybe I should have kept my mouth shut. I had no idea why I had bared my soul like that. I eyed Dr. Lee with renewed suspicion and sniffed the air again. The birthday cake smell was even stronger. The vanilla scent alone was enough to burn the inside of my nostrils.

Dr. Lee had used magic on me; I had walked straight into his trap. Whatever he'd done had made me open my trap

68

and rant away my inner thoughts and feelings—at a time when I couldn't afford to do so.

"Thanks for the help, Doc." I saluted over my shoulder as I walked to the door. "If you ever want to hear about my sexual fantasies again, I have a premium rate number I can recommend."

The erotic novel I had stolen from his bookcase was concealed in the waistband of my trousers.

I waited outside of Davenport's office, swinging my legs in the uncomfortable plastic chair as I sat next to the star spangled banner and a dying spider plant.

I watched the commander in his office through the small glass window by the door. He was talking on the phone. His face was as stern as ever as he leaned back in his chair. His eyes closed and his fingers pinched the bridge of his nose. Strangely, I felt a squeeze of jealousy; it wasn't just me that caused his exasperation. I had to work harder.

"Come in," Davenport called through the door as he put the phone down.

"You wanted to see me?"

He rubbed his temples and leaned back in his chair. "Sit down."

I did as he asked, looking around his office. There was a signed baseball on one of the bookshelves, and the screensaver on his computer was a picture of Davenport; his arm was wrapped around a good looking woman.

"Girlfriend?" I asked, gesturing to his screen.

"Mother." He clipped as he opened the top drawer of his desk and reached inside. A second later, Davenport slapped a pair of leather gloves onto the barren surface. He also grabbed a stick of gum and folded it between his lips. The way he chewed looked more like teeth grinding.

I quirked a brow in question.

"Giving up smoking."

"Uh-huh." I nodded, sniffing the air. Cinnamon. Big Red.

Davenport pressed a finger against the leather gloves and slid them across his massive teak desk. "You need to start wearing these gloves."

I picked them up and slapped them against my open palm. "Because Frankie wore gloves?"

"Yes."

"Do you know why she wore gloves?" I asked.

"No." Davenport crossed his arms over his broad chest. "But she did. Hugo Sinclair came into my office. He's worried about you—and by you, I mean Frankie."

"Did they have something going on?" I perked up. "Because I can get close to Hugo to keep undercover. Some heavy petting. Maybe some kissing."

Davenport growled. "No."

He was annoyed. I almost squirmed with glee. "You could join us, War. It would be fun. I've never been with an incubus before."

His gaze sharpened. "He's a Cambion. Half-human."

"Potato, Po-tar-to." I waved my hand dismissively.

"Hugo and Francesca were not an item. Hugo Sinclair does his best to exercise self-control." Davenport took a deep breath. "I do not recommend pursuing Mr Sinclair. Humans don't tend to emerge unscathed from *activities* with Incubi."

I snorted. "I'm not exactly human, Big Guy."

"It would also be unwise for a Fae."

I folded my hands in front of me and did not argue with his statement. The picture of innocence.

"I'll talk to Mr. Sinclair and assure him that I, Frankie, am okay," I said confidently.

"At this point, I think you would be better served staying in your room until we know more about whatever killed Team C."

I pushed myself off of the uncomfortable chair and swaggered around Davenport's desk, perching my bum at the end of it. I reached forward to grab his tie. Davenport slapped my hand away.

"War, you're so tense." I cooed.

His eyes narrowed. "You're not taking this seriously."

"I am." I patted his shoulder. "I *swear*."

"What did you do?" He scowled.

I put my hand to my chest. "Me?"

"My sister gets the same look when she has done something wrong."

I tsked. "You sound like Dirk."

Warren shook his head and rolled his eyes.

"I may have told Dr. Lee that I'm not really Frankie Gardiner." The words rushed out of my mouth on a hurried exhale.

Warren Davenport leaped from his seat. "What?!" He bellowed.

I pushed away from his desk and made a move to escape. The commander boxed me in with his body.

"Are you trying to jeopardize this mission?" His face was close to mine. His breath fanned across my lips. Mint and cinnamon.

I could see the flecks of gold in his chocolate brown eyes. The individual hairs on his scruffy chin. That's how close he was.

I studied him. By all rights, I should have feared him. The commander of the Hunters. If anyone were going to kill me, it would be him.

"Do you always act like this?" He gestured down my body with a wave of his hand. We had both moved closer. My hand rested on his chest, and I quickly yanked it back.

I blinked up with wide eyes. "It's my nature," I admitted. "I can't go against my nature."

Warren Davenport pushed forward, and for a second I thought that he was going to kiss me. I licked my bottom lip and

71

waited. My skin tingled, and I couldn't take my eyes from his.

Davenport slapped the gloves against my chest, forcing me to take them. My brow furrowed, confused, as I realized that he had only moved towards me so he could reach the item on the center of his desk.

"Wear the gloves." He warned. "I'll talk to Dr. Lee."

I straightened my shoulders and added an extra wiggle in my step as I walked away. I could feel his eyes burning into the back of my neck as I left his office.

I flipped open the leather wallet in my hands and rifled through each of the laminated cards. Boring. Boring. Boring.

Warren Davenport had a credit card, a driving license, and not much else.

I didn't know what I was expecting to find. Maybe a sober chip from AA. Or a treasure map to secret pirate treasure.

"I'm *bored*!" I slapped the wallet on the keyboard in front of me and span on the office chair—my arms were outstretched as if I was beseeching the Gods.

I heard muffled laughter. I hadn't realized that someone had come into the surveillance suite. Remi had his fist between his white teeth as he tried to hold in his hilarity. Hugo stood by his side, his cheeks pink.

"Don't you knock?" I stood up, grabbing the wallet and stuffing it into the pocket of my hoodie.

"This is my office, love," Remi said in his British accent. His voice was thick and deep, melted dark chocolate.

I turned to Hugo, thankful that I had taken the time to put on Frankie's well-worn leather gloves. "Hey, Sinclair." I wiggled my fingers in a wave, to draw his attention to the gloves.

"Hi, Frankie," He murmured.

"We were gonna order a pizza and brainstorm some ideas." Remi stepped forward, slipping his satchel from his shoulders. "You're welcome to join us."

A smile crept across my face. Slowly but no less bright, I fished the wallet out of my pocket and took out Warren Davenport's black AMEX. "Only if I'm buying."

All of the local pizza places were out of delivery range, so we hopped into Hugo's beaten up Jeep and drove to the nearest town—Maywood—about an hour from the base. I would have loved to have caught the train into NYC and stopped off at one of the rooftop bars to drink my host body's weight in Grey Goose, but Maywood was the nearest train station anyway, and I didn't have the patience to wait for my stress relief.

I sat in the passenger's side, with Remi in the back. We played a game of *I spy* to pass the time in the darkness. I guessed Remi's 'T' with ease—he'd chosen a tree and then shrugged unapologetically when Hugo and I both guessed it. I'd jinxed Hugo as we'd answered at the same time. I told him I would let him speak again if I got a kiss on the cheek. Hugo's eyes fixed on the road, and his fists tightened on the steering wheel. I did not get my kiss.

"Something beginning with D!" I sang as we drove past the town sign.

"That's a tough one." Remi flashed his teeth. "Help me out, Hugo."

"Sinclair's been Jinxed," I smirked and nudged the floppy-haired blonde. "Come on, baby. I know you like me really."

Remi cleared his throat. "Driver?"

"Nope." I popped the *P*.

"Dog?"

Hugo glanced over at me as he engaged the handbrake. "Donut shop?"

I leaned over and flicked his nose. The incubus jerked

73

back with pursed lips.

"Dick!" I shouted with a cackle, looking down to the emerging tent in Hugo's pants. "Come on, Sinclair, *hard* evidence that you like it when I tease you." I winked.

"Hugo broke the Jinx!" Remi bounced like a six-foot-four child. "We need to find a forfeit."

I opened the car door and hopped onto the sidewalk, glancing around at the shops and restaurants. There was a dive bar on the corner, *'Lacey's'* beamed a lucid green onto the curb. Remi came up to my side and rested his colossal arm across my shoulder.

"Shots!" I clapped.

Hugo slammed the car door. He glanced at the bar and then turned back to me. "I'm driving."

I waved my hand. "Remi can drive."

"What about you?" Remi argued. "You could offer to be the designated driver."

I smiled sweetly. "But then you couldn't experience the awesomeness that is Drunk Me."

"I just wanted pizza." Hugo's eyes rolled to the sky as if he was praying for God to smite him down.

"We'll get pizza after you've done your forfeit," I promised.

Remi chuckled and strode across the street to the bar. He turned back and waved us to follow. "Come on, Sinclair!" He shouted through a teasing smile. "It's this, or we order a pizza with banana and ham."

Hugo coughed a sound of disgust.

"What's wrong with that?" I wondered.

Hugo gave me a strange look. "Besides the crime of fruit on pizza, the banana makes me gag."

I snorted a childish laugh. "Nothing makes me gag."

Hugo's look turned to chastising. "Are you acting like this because I'm an incubus?"

I quirked my brow. "I'm acting like this because it's funny."

Hugo ducked his head. Avoiding my gaze.

"You shouldn't run away from what you are," I argued. "Incubus or not. Dr. Lee says sex is healthy and natural. Why be ashamed?"

I moved to join Remi on the sidewalk outside of the bar when I felt Hugo's hand grip my bicep.

"You've been talking to Jae about sex?" His eyes flashed pale ice blue. If I didn't know better, I would say he was intrigued.

I shrugged. "I'm a simple creature."

The door swung open, and the dulcet tones of Johnny Cash filtered into the street.

The inside was *sticky*. The floor, the slight sheen on the tables. Glowing signs for Bud and Coors and all of the expensive liquor was covered in a sheen of dust. The crowd were locals, I could tell because they all watched us like zoo animals when we walked in.

I slapped my hands on the pockmarked wooden bar. "I want a bottle of tequila. And lots of lemons." I jabbed a finger over my shoulder. "And a Corona for the big guy."

The woman behind the bar had bleach blonde hair with a stripe of dark roots. She swaggered over and eyed up my men like they were made of sugar, and she was the Queen of the anthill.

My teeth rolled back over my lips. My smile was fierce as I reached into my pocket and pulled out a hundred dollar bill from the folds of Warren Davenport's wallet.

She smirked, the edges of her eyes crinkled. "Right away, honey." She crooned in a Texas drawl. I would hazard a guess that she was the infamous Lacey of the big green sign.

We found a booth; I began arranging the lemon, salt, and tequila in perfect order for convenience. Remi watched as he swigged his beer. Hugo looked like he wanted to be anywhere else.

Hugo picked up one of the shot glasses and rolled it between his fingers. "I don't drink much." He said.

75

"One shot." I smooched my fingers together. "It's bad luck to break a jinx."

Hugo sighed and pushed his tiny glass forward. I opened the bottle and poured him a shot. "You lick your hand—"

Hugo interrupted my instructions by expertly licking the salt, downing the shot, and sucking the lemon like an old pro.

Remi hooted and slapped his hand against the table. "Sinclair's got skills!"

Hugo pushed his hair out of his face and rolled his eyes. "I said I didn't drink much. Not that I didn't know how to."

I smirked and downed my tequila straight down. Shaking my head and blowing a raspberry as it burnt my throat.

"Shots are done," Hugo pleaded. "Can we go now?"

I picked up the tequila and poured another two shots. "We've got the whole bottle. It'll be rude to let it go to waste."

Remi took a pull of his beer, hiding his smirk around the lip of the bottle.

"We should play never have I ever." Remi used the neck of his bottle to point at us both. My face brightened.

"Yes!" I downed another shot.

"No," Hugo argued.

"Yes." Remi shot back.

Hugo refilled my shot glass, so we were on a level playing field.

"Never have I ever... Had sex." I blurted out. Both men stared at me with wide eyes. "Go on, drink." I pushed the shot glass towards Hugo.

"You're a virgin?" He spluttered, holding the tequila but not drinking.

"Yes. Drink."

Hugo took the shot, slamming the glass onto the table with a sharp exhale.

"Never have I ever—" Remi sang.

76

"You can't play if you're not drinking," Hugo argued.

"Let me have my fun." Remi's dark eyes sparkled. "Never have I ever had an orgy!"

Remi deliberately left his beer on the table. I reached forward and took a shot. Hugo did the same.

"How can you have an orgy and still be a virgin?" Hugo asked, sucking the lemon as his nose crinkled.

Remi raised his hand like an eager school kid. "I'd like to know this story."

"I advertised an orgy on Craig's List, but then... An ex-boyfriend showed up and interrupted us. So it never happened." I explained.

Remi had taken a sip of beer and snorted at the same time. His eyes watered as he laughed and wiped the beer that had come out of his nose. "Fuck, that burns."

Hugo glanced over at his friend. "Never have I ever, stolen someone's gun and spray painted it pink."

Remi looked at me, expectantly. "I'm new to the base, and even I know this story."

"Shit!" I startled. Grabbing my shot. "Frankie—*I* did do that."

Hugo's crystal blue gaze didn't leave mine as I took the shot. Downing it with a hiss. For some reason, he was giving me an in-depth look that I didn't understand. His inability to make eye contact had been stripped away by suspicion and curiosity.

Remi broke the tension. "Your turn Frankie."

I umm-ed and ahh-ed for a few seconds. "Never have I ever been in love."

We all drank.

"Deep." Remi Weber nodded a sagely as he took a swig from his beer.

For the next few rounds, we both chose stupid shit. Like riding in a car, or eating caviar and listening to Bon Jovi. Before long, my head rested against Remi's shoulder, and my feet were propped on Hugo's lap. My combat boots had been discarded long ago, and the incubus rubbed my feet.

"You should be a masseuse." I moaned as Hugo rubbed his thumb into the arch of my foot. Remi was playing Super Mario on his phone, occasionally glancing up when one of us Drunkies said something stupid.

"Masseur." Remi corrected. "They're called a masseur if they're a man."

I wriggled and sighed as Hugo's touch made my feet feel like they were in heaven. Then without warning, Hugo dropped my legs and mumbled an apology as he ran to the bathroom like the hounds of Hell were on his tail.

"What's his deal?" I asked, putting my feet back in my shoes. "I was enjoying that!" I shouted at Hugo Sinclair's retreating figure.

Remi shook his head. "He's celibate."

I snorted.

"No, really." He argued. "Davenport told me."

"What kind of incubus is celibate?" I asked.

"He's a Cambion. Half-human. He doesn't need to feed. He doesn't like hurting people." Remi said.

My brow creased. "Hugo shouldn't go against his nature."

Remi turned in the booth to face me. He placed his phone on the sticky table, screen down. "And is what you're doing in your nature?"

"What do you mean?"

"You're a sniper. Are you lining up your shot?" Remi asked, deadly serious.

"You think I'm trying to get Hugo into bed?" I turned back in the direction of the men's room.

Remi shrugged.

"You could join us?" I suggested with a husky voice as I leaned forward.

Heat flared in his eyes. Even though what I said had been a joke, Remington Weber looked like he liked that idea very much.

I pulled away with a laugh and patted his cheek.

78

Because my host was well and truly drunk, I missed and patted his nose instead.

"Relax, you beautiful unicorn," I assured him. "Davenport would kill me if I slept with any of his Hunters."

Before Remi had a chance to reply, Hugo had come back to our table. Pink cheeks and a bit boneless.

My eyes widened. "Oh my god!" I squealed. "You just took care of business by yourself, didn't you?!"

Hugo shot Remi an exasperated look over the top of my head as I exploded in a fit of giggles.

"I think we should get Mistress Tequila here home," Hugo suggested dryly.

The corner of Remi's lip twitched. "Agreed." The huge man dipped down and wrapped his arm around my waist. He maneuvered us both out of the booth, while Hugo looked on with glassy, drunk eyes. The incubus swayed slightly, but he seemed in command of his own body.

"I wanted to bring the rest of the bottle." I pouted as we hit the cold outside air. Goosebumps raised on my arms, but I did not feel it. Alcohol was wonderful.

"She's a bad influence." Remi shook his head as we walked to the jeep.

I reached out like an infant seeking its mother, grabbing the sleeve of Hugo's shirt. "Hewey-baby, we should stick together. We're the same."

Both of the men ignored my rambling as we crossed the lot.

A can rattled across the asphalt, and raucous laughter came from behind one of the pickups in the lot. A group of men crowded in the lot. One crushed a beer can to his forehead and screamed in triumph.

Remi started to divert our path away from the group, and Hugo followed.

"Hey, Fellas!" One of them shouted. "Look what we've got here!"

"Just keep walking, Remi." Hugo murmured under his

breath as both men stared forward like the strangers did not exist.

"They're Civilians." Remi clicked his tongue against the roof of his mouth. "I'm not going to start anything." His British accent became rougher around the edges and affected a cockney twang.

I glanced over my shoulder.

"Look at that fine dose of brown sugar!" A squad man on the edge hollered. His nose was crooked; his eyes were beady.

I turned on my heel and ducked under Remi's arm.

"What did you say to me?" I called out. Striding towards the group with my chin held high. I wasn't offended. I was curious. I wanted to see what would happen if I *pushed*. Brown sugar? Did humans really care about the color of someone's skin that much?

"You're a fine piece." One of the men whistled and stepped forward. Remi grabbed my shoulder and tried to pull me back, but I shrugged him off.

I could taste their sins. They were harmless. Maybe a bit lustful, but I had met murderers and rapists—of the several men in the parking lot, none of them had the stones to do anything beyond throw a few punches.

"You want to take me home?" I stopped, cocking my hip and pouting. The men glanced at one another. I felt Hugo and Remi on each of my shoulders. Their hulking presence like dangerous coiled snakes ready to strike.

I made sure to face away from the Hunters as my eyes bled into black. My magic latched onto the drunken idiots like a whip around their throats. Their worst fears, nightmares, and regrets floated to the surface of their minds. The emotion behind them and the terror that made them want to curl into the fetal position and hideaway.

I hadn't fed in a while, and their waking nightmares fuelled me. I felt more comfortable than I had in days.

"What the fuck *are* you?" the squat man scrambled away, grasping the handle to his pick up and failing to pull open the door.

Another man sobbed and pissed himself.

"Your worst nightmare!" I said with a bright smile and an evil cackle. Hugo and Remi tried to pull me away as the redneck's car sped away from the lot with a squeal.

Two of the men that were left behind ran away, tripping like they had their pants around their ankles.

I slapped my hands together and commended myself on a job well done.

My darkness bled away from the whites of my eyes, swallowed by my pupil. I turned to Hugo and Remi—who both looked frozen.

"They're not blocking the car anymore." I said cheerfully, still a bit drunk, but full of energy. "Should we get back to base?"

Both of my men nodded robotically, and we got in the car and drove back to camp.

Chapter 6

I never got my pizza. Instead, I got a hangover that felt like someone had pushed a railroad spike through my host's skull. I pressed the heel of my palms into my eye sockets and tried to make the room stop spinning. I was going to vomit.

There was a knock on the door, but my response was a loud groan.

"Rise and shine, Mistress Tequila!" Remi shouted through my steel door, thumping once for good measure. "Got to get up, love. Boss wants to see us."

I ran my fingers through Frankie's wavy hair, too lazy to find a comb. After wiping a spot of drool from the corner of my mouth, I wrenched open the door, still clad in the wrinkled camisole and the panties that I had slept in.

I pushed my arms over my head to yawn. My jaw unhinged like a shark. The lower part of Frankie's toned stomach exposed.

Remi's eyes studied my form, traveling up Frankie's long legs, over her flat stomach and cleavage until they rested on my eyes.

Remi cleared his throat. "Davenport's office." He reminded me with a husky grunt, averting his eyes.

I stepped into the hallway and closed the door behind me.

"Aren't you going to put some clothes on?" Remi laughed, gesturing to my erect nipples.

I shrugged but did not smile. "I literally feel like canine shit. If I bend down, I will barf."

"Fair enough."

We walked to Davenport's office in silence. His PA's

desk was empty because it was so early. The sun had only been up a short while; although a few of the Hunters were jogging the perimeter, I had noticed that the admin staff didn't start until later in the day.

Hugo was already in Davenport's office. His arms flailed wildly; his cheeks flushed red under Davenport's laser point scrutiny. I wondered if Hugo was pinning the blame on me for our drunken jaunt.

I didn't get what the problem was. We were all adults.

"I'm going to get some coffee, you want one?" Remi asked, jabbing his thumb over his shoulder.

"Irish. Thanks."

Remi shook his head and chuckled. I had a feeling that he hadn't taken me seriously.

A few seconds later, when I stood alone in the waiting room, I tiptoed to the side of the door without glass and pressed my ear against the wood. Gooseflesh covered my bare legs. I rubbed the skin and groaned internally because I had forgotten that humans could feel the temperature.

I heard the low rumble of voices and found myself squished against the door until I could almost make out what they were saying.

"That woman is not Frankie Gardiner." Hugo declared hotly.

"What makes you say that?" Davenport was cool as a cucumber.

"She's so... She... She just isn't." The incubus spluttered. "She doesn't wear her gloves! She drinks, she flirts!"

"Surely, we can make allowances for Ms. Gardiner. She has just come out of a coma." Davenport's voice was low with warning. "If you have any issues with her behavior, I can assure you that she will be punished for last night."

Hugo huffed. "She's different."

"Frankie Gardiner is your fellow Hunter. She needs your support." Davenport said.

I wrenched my face away from the door and floated

83

back to my chair. Numb, my thoughts faced as I lowered myself into my seat.

Hugo *knew*.

It was only a matter of time before everyone else did. I pressed my head into my hands. *Useless. Flighty. Unfocused. Immature.* All of the words that Dirk had used to describe me in the past floated through my head until I clenched my fists hard. Feeling the bite of my nails dig into the palm of my hands.

"Are you okay?" Remi said. I hadn't heard him approach. He stood next to me, holding two reusable coffee cups. One had a picture of a witch on a broom on it, and the other had a unicorn. He handed me the unicorn.

I took a sip. No whiskey.

"I'm great," I replied.

His lips vibrated like a buzzer. "Psst. Lie."

Hugo opened the door to Davenport's office and slipped into the waiting room. He startled when he saw both of us.

"Hey guys," Hugo murmured, looking down at his shoes.

I thought about his conversation with Davenport. I couldn't exactly call him out on it without validating what he had said. Instead, I settled for a tight-lipped grin.

"What's the damage?" Remi took a sip of his coffee.

"You and I are on instructor duty for the rest of the week. Frankie has to clean out the K9 unit." Hugo glanced back at Davenport's office.

"Can I eat breakfast first?" I moaned, rubbing my churning belly. "How are you even upright?"

Hugo shrugged. "I have a high tolerance for alcohol."

My tolerance was as high as my host body, and Frankie Gardiner was not a drinker.

"This is so unfair!" I buried my head in my hands again. Willing the room to stop moving. "I feel like I am dying."

"So much for feeling *'great,'*" Remi mocked, quoting my earlier words back to me. "Just pray that Sgt Hart is in a good mood..."

Callum Hart, aka Sgt Hart, was not in a good mood. He was an evil man who had no sympathy for my pain, even after he caught me vomiting behind the kennel. He'd just glanced down at the puddle of puke and then back at my damp face, handed me a bag of sawdust, and told me to 'sort the mess.'

I didn't even get to see any of the dogs, as they were with their handlers running drills in the next field over.

After helping to clear up the poop from the enclosed grassy area, and refilling all of the water bowls, I sat on the fence and watched Sgt Hart as he threw the various dog toys littered around the grass into the chest on the other side of the fence. He hit his aim every time.

After watching him make a few nearly impossible throws, I began to cheer and whoop. His marmalade eyes turned to mine and scowled.

"This is meant to be a punishment." He sniffed.

"It's more fun to watch you."

Hart scoffed and turned around, continuing his task. He ignored me for a few minutes; I twiddled my thumbs— unsure of what to do. A few seconds passed, I looked up into Hart's scrutinizing gaze. He cocked his head to the side, like a dog trying to solve a puzzle.

He handed me a tennis ball. "Throw this," Hart demanded as he pointed at the toy chest on the other side of the yard. With a shrug, I wound my arm back and threw it. It fell fifteen feet from the toy chest and bounced off the grass.

Callum Hart's expression fell flat. He stepped into my personal space, causing me to lean back to continue to look into his eyes. I spread my knees; he advanced until he was between my legs. His nose trailed along the crown of my head, scenting me.

Arousal flared in my core; I had to close my eyes to focus on keeping the oil slick away. I felt the darkness in my chest and clamped down on it. Hoping to the Seven Circles that I had a tight reign on my nightmares.

My eyes fluttered open when I felt Hart's warmth leave mine. My fingertips tingled with the need to reach forward and touch him.

I almost did—until I caught sight of his grim expression. My hand curled in on itself as I pulled it back and gripped the fence under my butt.

"You are not Frankie Gardiner," Hart stated. His voice was anger and gravel.

I opened my mouth to speak, but decided against it. Anything that I could say would make it worse.

"Your aim is shit." He continued. His eyes pinned me to the spot. "You do not smell like Corporal Gardiner."

I blinked slowly. I was delighted that I had remembered to put Frankie's gloves on that morning. I opened my mouth to argue that I was too hungover to aim accurately, but his hand lashed out and gripped my neck before I could speak. Too fast for my eyes to track the movement. His speed was impressive. His orange eyes glowed as his fingers tightened around my throat. They did not squeeze, but his grip was firm. Enough to discourage any movement.

I tried to swallow the lump in my throat. Every instinct inside of me screamed for my magic to reign free. To wrap around the man in front of me and to reduce him to rubble. I held back. It was physically painful. A deep ache in my chest that became scores of writhing insects under my skin.

If Hart realized I was a Demon, he would kill me.

"What the hell do you think you're doing?" An angry shout came from the edge of the yard. Hart released my throat and stepped back. He blinked and looked down at his hand as if he didn't remember attacking me.

I still had not moved an inch. Frankie's heart was a runaway train, and it took all of my strength to remain still.

Locked up like a deer caught in headlights.

Davenport strode across the dog enclosure, lightning in his eyes.

"I asked, Sergeant Hart, what the Hell do you think you are doing?" Davenport repeated. His voice was dangerous.

Hart continued to blink rapidly. "I just—"

He tried to explain, but Davenport cut him off with a look.

"Go to the infirmary, Corporal Gardiner." His gaze was full of hidden meaning.

It took a few seconds for my limbs to cooperate, but when they did, I did not look back as I hurried down the path.

Dr. Dan's mop of red hair was visible over his computer monitor, tucked away from the empty beds in the infirmary. He typed away, nibbling away at a stick of celery. I almost felt sorry for the guy—eating the most boring food known to man.

"Daniel," I called out his name, so I wouldn't startle him. Though it would have been funny to see him gag on a celery stalk.

"Francesca." He turned around, looking me over from head to toe. "Have you come for the results of your medical examination?"

"Nah," I hopped onto one of the empty beds and swung my feet. "Hart went nutso and pinned me like a naughty puppy. He didn't hurt me, but Davenport sent me to the infirmary to get me out of the way."

Daniel did not rush to his feet with my proclamation of potential injury. He stood up and moved slowly to the faucet to wash his hands. When he was done, he put on a pair of gloves.

"Where did he touch you?" Daniel stepped forward. I motioned to my neck, and he tilted my chin to the ceiling.

After a few seconds, he nodded to himself. "You're

87

fine. No bruising."

"That's what I thought." My smile was cocky. "You have the infirmary all to yourself, Dr. Dan?"

The doctor's narrowed his eyes. "Daniel." He corrected. "You know I cannot abide that nickname." He studied me for a second as if we were adversaries.

"Sorry, Dr. Daniel Gardiner." I corrected as he turned his back to retrieve my file.

There was a stick up the good doctor's ass; it was a shame that the only person qualified to remove it was himself.

Dr. Dan flicked open Frankie's manila file and read a few lines. "You're healthy. Nothing to be concerned about. Some of your levels are low, so I'm going to give you a supplement."

I groaned. "I had one last time."

"It's a different supplement."

I rolled up my sleeve and waited for the needle prick. Just like last time, Dr. Dan was quick, but I was sure he left a bruise.

"If you hurry, you can still catch breakfast." Dr. Dan turned his back and dismissed me without a goodbye.

I smiled sweetly at Gary, the canteen worker, as he handed me a bottle of water and burnt bacon. He had a sadistic sort of gleam in his eyes, which I could fully get behind. I loved a bit of wrath—even in the paltry form of passive-aggressive breakfast.

My eyes swept over the various tables and benches, settling on Hugo and Remi in the corner. Hugo stared at the table as if he wanted to world to swallow him whole. Remi threw his head back and guffawed. Hugo flinched at the loud sound.

With a swagger in my step, holding my tray like a goddamn high school student, I approached the men.

"Howdy." I slid into the seat next to Remi. "How were

morning drills?"

Remi rolled his eyes. "Some of the new recruits are a bit cocky. One of the women couldn't stop flirting with Sinclair."

Hugo groaned and unrolled his silverware. "There's always one every year."

"You'd think that being part Demon would put off some of the lady Hunters." I unscrewed my bottled water and took a swig.

"Huntresses?" Remi questioned.

"No, I think the term is still Hunter." Hugo put a hand in front of his mouth as he swallowed his omelet before eating.

"No hot sauce today?" Remi pointed to my plate with his fork.

"I was running late. None left at the condiment counter." I bit into my bacon; it crumbled like black ash in my mouth.

Hugo glanced across the room, and I followed his gaze. Riley Fisher sat at a table with three bottles of Tabasco. How immature.

"Do you want me to go get a bottle?" Hugo asked.

I waved my hand. "S'okay," I said with my mouth full.

"How's your punishment going?" Remi asked.

I coughed as a piece of bacon lodged in my windpipe. I took a hearty mouthful of water to try and clear the taste from my mouth. "S'okay," I repeated, with tears in my eyes from almost choking.

I turned to the side, wiping my eyes on the back of my sleeve. "Oh, man. Gary isn't pulling any punches with his post-rejection revenge campaign."

"He'll get over it." Remi snorted.

"He'll be crying into his Cheerio's for years." I winked. "Who could deal with losing a chance at all this." I waved a hand to bring attention to my unkempt appearance. I hadn't had a chance to shower since working in the dog yard.

Hugo's look was soft. "If he keeps bothering you—"

89

"I can fight my own battles, Hewey-Loo." I gave him a chastising look.

Hugo flushed. "I didn't mean—"

"I know you didn't." I reached across the table and patted Hugo's shoulder.

Someone cleared their throat behind me. I glanced over my shoulder and was met with the massive form of Sgt Callum Hart. He couldn't meet my eyes.

I took a long swallow of my water. Crinkling the bottle when it emptied, the water tasted a bit off, but I ignored it. I said nothing and let Hart squirm.

"You need something, Sarge?" Remi asked.

"Maybe he wants to ask me on a date?" I said with a cocky smirk.

Hart looked like he was in physical pain. "Can I speak to you outside, Corporal Gardiner." His voice was calm, quiet, and polite.

Remi hooted. "You called it."

I stood up and bussed my tray with a wink and a swagger. Callum Hart followed on my heels like a chastised pet.

I didn't speak to him until we had walked off the beaten path outside of the Mess Hall.

"What's up, Sarge?" I put my hands on my hips.

"I wanted to apologize for putting my hands on you." His Adam's apple bobbed. "I treated you like one of my pack. I restrained you as an alpha. I wanted to check that you weren't harmed."

The words 'pack' and 'alpha' swirled in my mind. Any number of dog-shaped Demons, shifters, or animal Fae crossed my mind. His magic tasted like the forest. Like burning bracken.

I narrowed my eyes. "You're on Team P, aren't you?" Dr. Lee had mentioned that the entire team was 'special' in some way. I wondered what Hart's damage was.

Hart growled. "What does that have to do with anything?"

"It's okay, Sarge," I said, patting his chest. "You didn't

90

hurt me."

"All the same, I shouldn't have put my hands on you without permission." He murmured, not reacting to my touch.

"Or sniff me without my permission," I added.

Hart's orange eyes flared before he looked away.

"Its—" I opened my mouth to assure him that I really was okay. I didn't want to spend too much time around someone who was suspicious already. Hugo had already raised the subject with Davenport.

Hart's brow crinkled as I frowned and looked down at my outstretched hands. I was seeing double.

My mind felt fine, but my body had dropped. The ground raced forward. My tongue was too big. My vision died. Large arms cradled me, but everything went black.

All I could think about was how my bottled water had tasted metallic. Some fucker had poisoned me.

Chapter 7

I dreamt of the red sands of Wrath as they shifted in a breeze that would never touch my skin. I was a shadow without form. Our 'Cluster' had thrived in every circle of Hell. From the bustle of the City of Dis, with its flapping fabric storefronts and shouting vendors, to the stripped forests of Gluttony, hiding between the trees as the skeletal Purgers sought food for the King.

Drudes were little more than rodents, in the grand hierarchy of the Seven Circles. Twirling dust in dark alleys, and listening shadows.

My Cluster, my family, were hundreds.

Before *they* cracked through the surface.

An ancient evil, long since locked away, broke through the Second Circle. Wrath. They ate the smallest first. The weakest. The Drudes.

I dreamt of our screams.

I howled my brother's names. An echo in the wind. My kin became solid as their magic was stripped and consumed by the Bhakshi, hideous wyrm-like monsters—and the Shayati, their puppet masters.

The Queen of Wrath took arms and rose up to defeat them.

But it was too late.

Everyone was gone.

Their immortality stripped away and fed on without care.

No one mourned the Drudes.

No one, but for me.

For the first time in two weeks, I was completely and utterly alone. Frankie Gardiner and her memories had left the building.

The world came back slowly. The veil peeled from my eyes and sensation returned to my toes first, and then gradually spread to the rest of my body.

I blinked, taking stock of my surroundings. I was laid on a bed that wasn't mine. The room looked the same, with mint green walls and a cream comforter, but there was an open door across the room, which showed a connecting suite.

I groaned, feeling worse than I had when I woke up. Every tick of Frankie's heartbeat pressed against my skull.

"You're awake." A male voice, rough around the edges as if he didn't use it often, jerked me from the perusal of my surroundings.

Hart sat in the corner; he had been reading. He carefully folded his book shut and placed it on the small table to his right. "Do you need a glass of water? An Advil?"

"Did we have sex?" I moaned, pressing my hand against my head. "Damn, I wanted to remember my first time."

Hart ignored my ramblings. "You blacked out, your pulse was steady and breathing fine—Davenport asked me to take you to my suite and keep an eye on you."

I hummed, to indicate that I was listening. "I think I was poisoned," I said. "It must be the person that tried to kill Frankie the first time."

Hart squinted, but if he thought my referral to myself in the third person was strange—he didn't say anything about it.

"Your brother came by earlier to take some blood. He said he will run an analysis to see if any poisons come up." Hart stood up, his steps faltered, but I saw the moment that his decision was made, and he crossed the room to me. The large man sat at the end of the bed. He pressed the back of his hand to my forehead.

"What are you doing?" I asked.

"Making sure you don't have a temperature."

"Oh." I felt like an idiot, but to be fair, Demons did not get sick.

"Do you remember anything strange from before you passed out?" Hart asked, distracted by his hand on my head. He moved his fingers through my hair, feeling the wavy strands. I was too curious about what he was doing to move.

"My water tasted funny. It was sealed when I got it. Gary handed the bottle over when I got my food as there were none in the fridge."

Hart nodded as he continued to pet me with intense concentration. His touch felt nice.

"What are you doing?" I asked when he tucked a strand of hair behind my ear.

He froze, his orange eyes wide. "I don't know." His brow furrowed as he looked to the side, questioning his actions. Somehow, it just made sense for him to be close to me. Like another limb.

"I'll let Davenport know about Gary." Hart stood abruptly. The absence of his touch made me shiver.

He left the room, with a straight back and determination not to look back at me.

I flipped back on the bed and fell asleep. The sheets smelt like him. Like the forest.

Night had fallen when I woke again. My skin tingled with electricity, and the echoes of screams played in my ears like a symphony. The nightmares danced in the air.

Hart's room was empty. I was alone.

I sat up. Gliding, as if pulled by the sweet siren song of human terror. Darkness laid coiled under the surface. Flashes of images flickered through my mind. A vast gaping chasm, broken concrete, and tumbling rocks. Thousands of teeth, curved inwards—rows after rows. Monsters. Demons. Beings that I did not fear, as they had been created by the same primordial soup that had birthed me.

Hell.

I closed the door, pressing my hand flat as the latch clicked shut quietly. The hallway was dark, save for two strips of glow-in-the-dark paint that highlighted the nearest fire exit.

I followed the pained grunts and the sound of twisted bedsheets being kicked off.

Two doors down, the scent of fear and sweat grew stronger. I placed my hand against the fingerprint sensor, unsure if it would let me through. When the small electronic pad glowed red, I concentrated on pushing a small amount of my magic through it. Clouding the reading.

It took an immense amount of power, but the elicit taste of what promised to be a filling meal told me that it would be worth it.

The door clicked open, I crept inside. My hunger to sate my magic overrode all sense. The male figure tossed and turned in the bed. His room was bitter with the tang of his sweat as he shivered and thrashed among his night terrors.

Warren Davenport.

How unexpected.

My hand hovered over his body, all of the darkness drifted away from his skin like smoke, and I sucked it up. I kept going until I felt almost too full to move. Davenport stopped thrashing. His breathing grew even, and his heavyset brow relaxed into a peaceful expression.

I stared down at his hard angular face. The scruff on his chin and neck, the prominent Roman nose. In sleep, Warren Davenport looked less severe but no less beautiful.

He will kill you if he finds out what you are.

I needed to be more careful. I needed to wear Frankie like a second skin—to become her. To find whatever had tried to kill her the first time and then the second.

I was determined, but Warren Davenport made me lose all sense. His hidden trauma was a delicacy, and I was a starving Demon. My hands hovered over his body as I drew his darkness to me. Feeding. Taking his pain and making it my own. When I was done, my hands dropped, and I stepped away.

Hugo, Remi, and even Hart and Dr. Lee were tantalizing enough to make me want to stay in one place for the first time in my life.

But Drudes drifted. They rode the air currents and searched for new terrors to feed on.

I needed to solve the mystery of Team C's deaths, so I could move on.

Safe and alive.

I crept into the hallway. I didn't know where the officer's building was located, and the door had locked behind me when I had left the warmth of Hart's bed.

My thoughts of him must have summoned the stoic man because Hart stood in front of me. I had not heard him approach, which was a testament to how silent he could be when he wanted.

"You left." He said, his marmalade eyes beamed into mine. Searching for an answer that I had no idea how to provide.

"Yes?" I quirked a brow and waited for him elaborate.

He didn't. Hart growled low in his throat and strode to the door opposite. He placed his hand on the electronic pad and disappeared inside. He held open the door for me to follow.

"I have been tasked with your safety." Hart turned on a lamp and then sat on the edge of the bed. "Please do not leave without me."

I raised one shoulder and let it drop.

"Gary Putnam has been brought in for questioning, but Dr. Gardiner rushed the blood results. You were not poisoned."

"That's the most I have heard you speak." I put my hand on my hip. "I like it."

"Dr. Gardiner believes that you collapsed due to stress and dehydration." Hart continued.

"You'd know if I was stressed, believe me." I leaned back against the bedroom wall and crossed my arms over my chest.

"Where are your gloves?" Callum Hart examined me with an inscrutable expression.

Self-preservation demanded that I burst into smoke and disappear on the wind. Instead, I stepped forward, between Hart's parted legs. The same way that he had cornered me on the fence earlier.

"Maybe I don't want to wear gloves anymore," I whispered. Every word, another excuse, a lie, to make someone else believe that I was Frankie Gardiner.

If I continued living inside her body, would I wake up and one day no longer know where I ended and she began.

I never inhabited bodies for long. I did not sleep in them. I ate for pleasure but not for sustenance.

Living inside a body, using it and maintaining it, was forcing a connection that I was not sure I wanted. Something much more different than borrowing a meat suit and joyriding it through Central Park naked.

Hart reached up and tucked a lock of hair behind my ear. "You're different. Since you woke up."

I swallowed a lump in my throat. Did he know?

Heat sparked between us. The air was thick with tension. One wrong move and either of us poised to run away.

So I did something foolish.

I kissed him.

His lips were soft. His stubble scratched my chin. His tongue was tentative as if he wasn't sure that I would scarper. Our eyes were open. Close and staring into each other. I moaned as his hands reached forward and slid up the small of my back, to rest against my shoulder blades. Hart pulled me closer. I stood. He sat. He held me close and plundered my mouth. I wanted everything he had to give.

My first kiss.

Something motivated by my selfish, petty, demonic

desires, that spat in the face of self-preservation.

I kissed Callum Hart—and then I ran.

I did not sleep that night. I paced the confines of Frankie's quarters and thought about all of the ways that I had fucked up.

Was everyone in the compound utterly crazy? Or just unobservant.

I was obviously not Frankie Gardiner. It was clear that I was an imposter.

Why had no one called me out?

I couldn't even masturbate. I was too wound up. Every time I tried to think about it, Hart's face would flash through my mind, and I would remember how I had fucked up.

I had told Dr. Lee that I wasn't Frankie. All while under the influence of his therapist Nephilim magic.

Hugo knew. Deep down. He had told Davenport.

Remi hadn't known Frankie before I had inhabited her—so at least I was safe on that front.

And Callum Hart? He had been suspicious of me beforehand. He had known Frankie. Maybe they had formed a club for people with sticks up their asses and a love of using as few words as possible?

And I had kissed him.

If it weren't for Dirk's promise to take five years off my contract if I could see this through, I would have ditched Frankie's body behind and be halfway to the East Village by now.

Even the notion that Dirk had faith in me, and knew that I could do it, was wearing thin.

It was only a short jump from imposter to Demon.

I looked awful when I walked into the Mess Hall the next morning. Even though I had brushed my hair and teeth and worn actual unwrinkled clothes, Frankie had dark circles under her eyes. My lack of sleep showed. My stress was a constant thrum through my blood. An unease that demanded I bolted and leave Frankie's body on the floor. She'd die, but I'd be long gone by the time her body could be analyzed.

I had tried to read the romance novel that I had stolen from Dr. Lee but gave up after a few pages. Unable to concentrate.

None of my boys were up yet. There were a few stragglers, hunched over coffee, and looking as terrible as I did. I caught enough of their conversations to know that my power had leaked into the dorms the night before. My nightmares had infiltrated the dreams of the Hunters.

I sat by myself and poured hot sauce over my granola and banana pancakes. I drank OJ, staring at the viscous liquid and wishing that I could morph it into a mimosa if I thought about it hard enough.

I didn't know how long I had been studying my orange juice as if it had the answers to the universe when someone slid their tray in front of mine.

Riley Fisher.

Her dark eyes took in my breakfast, and her lip twisted in disgust.

I barely looked at the woman as I made a point to shove as much pancake into my mouth as possible. I did not greet her.

Riley sat down, unscrewing the top of her water bottle with a smugness that made me want to hit her.

"I saw you leave Commander Davenport's room last night, Corporal Gardiner." She said as she took a deep swig of water. "I wonder what someone of your rank would be doing in an officer's bedroom in the dead of night."

I quirked a brow and chewed. "So?"

"Sleeping your way up the ranks?" Her eyes were wide and innocent.

"If I said yes, would you leave me alone?" I asked, hopefully.

Her eyes narrowed. "Was the reason my Harvey died, because you were on a mission you weren't qualified for? A mission that Davenport put you on because you were fucking him?"

"Are you trying to blame someone that is just as much a victim as *'your Harvey'*?" I asked with genuine curiosity. The human mind was fascinating.

Her eyes sparkled with anger. "You lived. He didn't.

"Almost didn't live." I corrected her. I looked around at the hush that had fallen over the canteen. Numerous people were glancing our way and whispering. Davenport's name had worked it's way into their gossiping. I appraised Riley with a searching look. "You work quick."

"Everyone needs to know that you don't deserve your rank," Riley said, back straight.

I took a swig of my OJ and snorted. "Rank? This might masquerade as a military operation, but the Hunters are freelance. They use titles to make you think that you're doing God's work and killing all the big bad Demons, but have you ever stopped to ask why the Demons don't bite back?" I was on a roll. Riley looked at me like I had sprouted a second head. "Hunters are pests. They are weeds to Demons who are simply too lazy to deal with them—us."

"What does that have to do with anything?" Riley's lips tightened.

I leaned in and lowered my voice. "Think about it, Private Fisher. Why am I, Frankie Gardiner, back at the compound after being in a goddamn coma? Why am I not in Queens with my parents, watching crappy sitcoms and thanking the Seven Circles that I'm alive?"

She stayed silent as she waited for my answer. I spoke so quietly only she could hear.

"Davenport thinks someone in the base summoned whatever killed Team C. I'm here to lure it out, you clueless bint."

Her mouth parted before she snapped it closed. Riley

looked over her shoulders, furtively, to make sure I hadn't been overheard.

"What?" She hissed.

I gave her a look as I picked up my tray and stood. "Don't tell anyone, or Davenport will reign down hellfire on your ass." And with that, I walked away.

Remi caught up with me on the path to the surveillance suite. He jogged up the track with a natural glowing smile; he had run to catch up with me, but he was not out of breath.

"Did you catch the show?" I said scornfully, as I kept my eyes on the path.

"Riley's harmless." Remi waved his hand. "What did you say to her? She looked like her whole world was crashing down."

I shrugged. "I suppose you've heard the rumors then."

"About you and Davenport?" Remi quirked a brow. "Does he spank you and make you call him Daddy?"

"Don't forget the St Andrew's Cross." I murmured.

"For you, or him?"

"Him," I smirked.

Remi burst out laughing and darted forward to open the door for me. His hand brushed against my back as we walked inside. I shivered. Every hair on my body rose; my core throbbed.

Damn. I needed to stay focused.

"Have you had any luck on the video so far?" I asked. "Did you manage to enhance the runes that flashed on their foreheads?"

Remi's gaze zeroed in on mine. He jerked back from his computer.

"The what?"

"The runes. 3.03 minutes in." My brow furrowed.

Remi hissed under his breath. Swearing up a plethora of curse words. His fingers moved quickly over the keyboard, and he swung the monitor to me. "Point to the runes." He demanded. All hints of my happy-go-lucky Remi were long gone, in his place was an eagle-eyed commando.

I hit the space bar to pause the video, just as the strange mark etched itself onto Hambone's forehead. "There." I pointed.

Remi stared at the screen for a long time.

"There's nothing there."

I exhaled sharply through my nostrils, exasperated. I jabbed my finger at the screen again. "It's right there. Not Demon. Not Angelic. Right. There."

Remi pushed his office chair away from his desk and dialed a number on the office phone. "Come here now." He demanded, before slamming down the phone without another word.

Remi's take-charge attitude was an unfamiliar change, but not an unwelcome one.

I practically purred.

Remi stood up, pacing. "Why didn't you say anything?"

I gave him a look. "It's right there. I thought you saw it."

Remi marched over to his desk and ripped open the top drawer. He rifled through the contents until he found a pen and paper. Alive with an urgency that I did not feel, he slammed the paper onto the desk. "Draw it, please."

I sat down with a huff. I did my best, looking at the screen several times to get the lines right. It seemed a bit Arabic. More like writing than a picture. Something old. I left the last line incomplete. I didn't want to activate an ancient magic rune without knowing what it did.

Remi leaned over my shoulder and studied the drawing in silence. I took the chance to tilt my head back into his chest. He was rock hard all over.

A few minutes later, Davenport arrived with a sullen

expression and a frowning Hart on his heels. I did not make eye contact.

"What have you got for me?" Davenport asked. Remi jabbed his thumb towards my paltry drawing. I wheeled my chair back to get out the way.

"Not Cyclian." Davenport murmured. "Have you run it through the translator?"

"Not yet," Remi replied.

"Where did you find it?" The commander asked.

"Frankie saw it on the video. She thought we all did, so she didn't say anything." Remi explained.

Davenport gave me a look that could freeze water. "Is that right?"

"I wonder why she can see it, but we can't." Remi's gaze drifted far away; it looked like he was lost in a realm of possibilities.

Hart stepped forward to see the sheet of paper; I moved further back.

"Frankie," Davenport said the name of my host to get my attention. "Do you believe it could be Fae?"

It was a pretty direct question. I knew what Warren Davenport was doing. He thought that I was a Mimic Sidhe and, therefore, unable to tell a lie. I didn't think it was Fae. The writing did not look like anything that belonged to Faery.

I met his eyes. "That writing is not Fae."

If Remi and Hart thought that Davenport asking questions about the Fae language was strange, they didn't let on.

Davenport nodded. It felt nice to be instantly trusted—even if it was because he believed that I was physically incapable of lying.

The expectation was that Demons lied. But the truth was much more complicated. Demons were often very honest when the answers mattered little to them. People never believed us anyway, and sometimes being truthful was more dangerous than deception.

"I have to make a few calls," Davenport said, distracted

103

already. "Frankie, I want to talk to you later. Privately. Hart—tell Weber and Gardiner what we found."

Davenport was such a significant presence that I breathed a sigh of relief when he was gone.

"What's the news?" I asked Hart.

Hart crossed his arms over his chest. "We found both a warehouse in Queens and Maywood. Animal bones. Blood. Summoning circles. The one in Maywood was a trial run, but the one in Queens looked like it brought through something nasty." Hart's orange eyes flicked from Remi to me, as Remi put his hand on my shoulder.

"You think it's to do with Team C?" I asked around a lump in my throat.

"We didn't. Until we found the Maywood site." Hart explained with little emotion. "No reason for our Unsub to come out this far unless he was at the compound."

"Looks like Davenport's theory might be correct," Remi grunted. "At least he hadn't tried to make a move for you."

Hart zeroed in on me. "You didn't mention your collapse."

Remi's back went straight as his voice went low and dangerous. "What?"

I waved a hand to dismiss his words. "Dr. Dan said it was just stress."

"What?" Remi repeated. His tone grew more demanding.

"Frankie collapsed yesterday. She told me that she thought she had been poisoned."

Remi stood up. His fists clenched. "Gary." He spat as he marched to the door. I leaped forward and grabbed his arm.

"There was no poison, Big Guy." I squeezed his bicep. "It must have been low blood sugar or something."

Remi's eyes narrowed; he didn't believe me. To be fair, I didn't believe it either. I had demonic healing. The only way I would collapsed was if something had downed my host very quickly. Like a shot to the heart or a fast-acting poison.

I didn't say that, though. The only reason my host was still alive was because of me. That poison should have killed her.

Remi reached out and cupped my face. I leaned into his touch.

Hart shifted. "You did not mention that you were seeing Specialist Weber." He said stiffly.

I popped my hip. "So?"

Hart licked his bottom lip. "No reason." The bearded man murmured. "I have to get back to my dogs."

Then Remi and I were alone.

"What was that about?" Remi asked.

I rolled my eyes. "Hart and I kissed yesterday."

Remi's lip twitched. "Oh my." He stepped forward into my space. He was so much taller than me that his body crowded mine. "Do you like to have more than one man at a time, love?"

I shrugged but smiled playfully. "I'll take as many as I can get."

Remi's eyes hooded. "I must admit. That has always been a fantasy of mine."

"What?" I breathed.

He continued as if I hadn't spoken. "To be one of many that worship a woman's body at the same time. To treat her like a Queen as I make her shudder and moan."

His words aroused me, but they also tickled a niggling little part of me. I was no Queen. I was a Drude. The lowest on the Demonic totem pole.

I had never been treated like a Queen, not in all of my millennia of existence. Remi looked at me like he wanted to spread me on a table and eat me like a feast—I couldn't help but wonder what that would feel like.

105

Chapter 8

I burst into Dr. Ahn-Jae Lee's cabin, past the client area and Dr. Lee's office, and into his private kitchen. I leaned against the threshold and struck a pose. His beautiful violet eyes widened as he froze, caught in a trap.

Jae Lee was wearing a white gingham apron. With frills and oversized oven gloves on his hands. He was in the process of transferring a cake from the oven to a cooling rack.

"Is it time for your appointment, Ms. Gardiner?" Dr. Lee said without emotion. Straightening and brushing the front of his apron.

"I'm early." I studied the Nephilim carefully, unwilling to be subject to his magical truth juice now that I was aware of his power.

Jae huffed as he slipped his hands out of his oven gloves and placed them delicately on the granite counter.

"I was bored." I went on to say, with a shrug. "Hugo and Davenport are holed up, doing research. Remi is in the city. I'm avoiding Hart."

Jae crossed his arms over his chest and leaned back against the countertop. "And I'm the last member of Team P." He surmised.

"You're interesting. Just don't do that truth thing anymore. M'kay?"

Jae quirked a brow. His expression was placid, but his eyes shuttered. "I wasn't aware that I had been doing anything."

"It's okay, Dr. L." I raised my arms up to stretch, with a smirk. My flat stomach exposed when my tank top rose up. His violet eyes did not so much as dip from mine. "I won't tell if you don't." I winked.

Jae Lee sighed, glanced back at his naked sponge cake,

before gesturing for me to walk through to his office.

I bounced on my heels and flopped down onto the couch. Jae made a point of organizing his notepad and pen, just so, and then sitting in his chesterfield armchair. His legs crossed, ankle resting on his knee. Both his arms on the armrests. Jae Lee had delicate features, but he had a masculine aura. Something about the way he sat told me that he was entirely at ease with himself.

"Davenport spoke to me," Jae said. Breaking the silence.

I cocked my head to the side. "And?"

"He told me not to listen to a word you say."

I snorted and blew a raspberry. "Davenport's the one that assigned me therapy after I was verbally attacked by Fisher."

Jae's lip quirked. "He also told me that he only did that because it would look suspicious if he didn't."

"Right."

"Warren Davenport mentioned that you have had a traumatic experience and that I shouldn't be worried if you start acting differently." Jae Lee continued, resting his him on the meat of his palm. He did not take his eyes from mine. "Why he felt the need to tell a licensed therapist this, I don't know."

"Davenport likes telling people what to do." I bared my teeth in a jaunty smile. "It's literally in his job title. *Commander.*"

"I trust my commander." Dr. Lee said.

"As you should." I nodded as if I had the first clue as to what he was talking about.

"I trust Francesca Gardiner." He continued, his expression turned speculative. "I don't trust *you.*"

"You're getting it." My smile turned vicious. "What gave it away?"

"Apart from the fact you literally told me?" Jae's expression turned dark. "Your emotions."

My brow furrowed.

"I am an empath." He explained. "As are most

107

Nephilim. You feel too different from Ms. Gardiner. She was ice. You are not."

"You put on a good show last time." I gave a soft round of applause. My smile turned sardonic. "An ADHD diagnosis."

"My diagnosis stands." He said.

I pouted. "I can focus. I just don't want to."

Jae nodded to himself. "You taste like cinders, metal, and mischief."

"You taste like birthday cake," I replied.

"Frankie Gardiner did not taste like you." He continued.

"Do you like my taste?" I asked, genuinely curious.

"I'd like to know what you are and why you're here."

"I'd like to know why you bake cakes in frilly aprons and live in a cabin away from the rest of your team." It was a statement and a question.

"I can't live with my team. I'm an empath." He explained dryly. "I would be exhausted from all of the emotional runoff."

"Do I exhaust you?"

"No." Jae's eyes flashed.

"And the cakes?"

"My *Umma* came over to America during the Korean War. She got a taste for Western cakes when she got old."

The Korean War was in the fifties. His mother had either come over when she was very young, or Jae Lee was much older than he looked. As a half-Angel, I would guess the latter.

"*Mimic Sidhe*," I said. Two words. Not a lie, just not what I was.

"And your true form?" Jae perked up.

"I'm shy." My tone was dry.

"Davenport knows?"

"His idea. I'm here to draw out Frankie's killer. I was poisoned yesterday. We have some ancient writing on the surveillance footage. They'll figure out who or what did it, and

108

I'll scurry away back to The City. Sipping mojitos at Le Bain, in their rooftop pool."

Jae sat back. His eyes dropped to his lap. "Corporal Gardiner is dead?" His voice held no emotion. "Does anyone else know?"

I shrugged. "Just Davenport, I think."

Jae rubbed his hand over his face and swore. "Warren thinks that it was an inside job?"

"A summoning." I clarified, my smile tightened. When people said summoning, they assumed a Demon. Which wasn't always accurate.

Jae nodded as he sat back in his chair and looked at the ceiling.

"Why did you keep pretending I was Frankie in our last session, even when you knew I wasn't?"

"You're fun to annoy." Jae murmured, his gaze far away, focused above. Distracted.

I tsked. "I don't understand humans."

"Nephilim." Jae reminded me.

"Half human." I corrected myself as I rolled my eyes. "I don't know how to comfort you. I don't know what to say."

"That's okay," Jae admitted. "No one ever really does. I wasn't close to Frankie... But when a Hunter dies, it sucks."

"Yeah." I agreed, but instead of thinking of the dropping bodies of Team C, I thought of the inhuman screams of my siblings as they were eaten alive.

Strangely enough, I felt dejected. All of my men were busy with other things; I was all alone in my room with no one to play with.

I should have been happy. A sensible and smart person would be relieved that the people most likely to uncover her secret were distracted with other things.

I had never been a smart or sensible person.

I had never been a person, full stop.

I'd kept the phone that I had stolen a few days ago to call Dirk. The data was spotty at best, but I settled myself into a comfortable position and removed my trousers. If I didn't have enough bandwidth to stream porn, I'd have to settle for sexy GIFs. Anything to relieve the frantic energy in my chest that demanded I run away.

If I left Frankie's body behind, it would die, but I would live.

Davenport would be so disappointed in me. I didn't want to leave Remi. I liked Remi. Plus, Dirk would probably see it as a breach of contract and add another decade to my sentence.

I shook my head and growled. I didn't want to admit that I liked being around the Hunters. I hadn't been part of a collective in so long, I had missed it.

Do the job and go. My rational mind whispered. *Don't give them a chance to find out your true heritage. Find the killer. Find the monster they summoned. Then leave. Don't pass go. Don't collect $200.*

And suddenly, I wasn't horny anymore.

I threw the phone onto the bed, it bounced once and fell to the floor.

What was wrong with me?

I pulled the comforter up to my neck and closed my eyes. Sleep found me quickly.

I no longer wore Frankie's body. I stood, proud, skin the color of black pearls, as smoke rose and curled on the air around me. I hovered as no part of my body touched the ground.

Red sands undulated in a phantom wind that told me that my brethren were nearby.

It was a dream. I stood in the City of Dis alone.

The hustle and bustle of the market was absent. The only movement was the flapping fabric of the stained canvas storefronts. It had been so long since I had allowed myself to visualize Hell's capital city.

My form was different in the Human Realities. There, I was dust and smoke. In Hell, I had a body, though made of darkness that could never be touched.

Mara. A simple name.

I had never seen my own face.

He stood at the end of the promenade. Golden skin and floppy blonde hair. Shining blue eyes, the color of ice. A regal bearing, with an apologetic hunch to his form. His gaze darted around furtively as if he didn't want to be seen.

What was Hugo Sinclair doing in Hell?

Though he was a Demon, so I shouldn't have been surprised.

It was my dream, so I was unafraid as I drifted forward. My hand outstretched, as midnight steam rose into the air around it. In a second, I hovered in front of Hugo. Face dipped close as I studied him. My entire body moved like I was underwater.

Hugo's eyes hooded, and his stature changed.

"Who are you?" He murmured in awe.

I said nothing but drifted closer.

"Are you a dream?" He asked.

In the safety of my subconscious, I was able to reach forward and touch the side of the Incubus's face. He closed his eyes and pressed his cheek into my palm. His skin was soft. Hot.

My smoke drifted over his lips like a flower petal; he inhaled sharply. Gone was the shy hidden dream Adonis; in his place was an unsure man. His hands shook as he reached forward. The tips of his fingers brushed against my smoke.

"I can't hurt you here." He nodded to himself.

I gave him a brilliant smile.

Hugo reached forward. I squeaked in shock, finding myself slamming into a physical form that he could touch. His lips crashed down on mine, swallowed any sounds. His hands gripped my now-solid biceps.

Hugo Sinclair was a fantastic kisser. He held me still with his incredible grip as he plundered my mouth. A dam broke, and the cautious and shy Hugo disappeared to make way for the hungry demon.

His magic licked up my spine, like a phantom tongue. Feather-light touches brushed the insides of my thighs. A promise. I wanted to be so full of Hugo Sinclair that I could not breathe, move, or talk without feeling him inside me.

I broke free, with a sigh and a swoon.

"What's your name?" He whispered. "I want to—"

I never heard the rest of his sentence. I never told him my name.

The next morning, in the Mess Hall, I looked decidedly well-rested, despite my sexually frustrating PG-13 erotic dream.

I had wanted to lock myself in Frankie's room and take full advantage of having a body. Instead, I had the female equivalent of blue balls. Clam Jam? Blue Bean?

I wanted to get some petty and juvenile revenge on Remi for abandoning me to go into the City. I got a blue Gatorade from the vending machine and filled the contents with mouthwash. It looked virtually the same. I had noticed that Remi always had some sort of energy drink at meals. Maybe not at breakfast, but I was too impatient to wait until lunch.

Remi's trashcan in the surveillance room had been full of cans of Monster and Red Bull.

I got my breakfast, plain toast, which I slathered in hot sauce, and settled down on my usual table. It was not long before Remi and Hugo drifted in together, freshly showered from their instructor duties.

I hadn't bothered turning up to my punishment since

Hart and I had kissed. I figured that Davenport would write it off after I was poisoned—even if everyone else said that I hadn't been.

Remi slid his tray onto the table; I pretended to take a deep slug of Gatorade. I silently offered him the open bottle before stuffing some toast into my mouth. Remi thanked me.

He had drunk almost half the bottle before he started to gag and dropped it. Splashing minty blue mouthwash over his white cotton t-shirt.

"Really? Frankie?" Remi spluttered. "What did I do to deserve this?"

Hugo cleared his throat. "Remi, you're the worst prankster in the compound. It looks like Frankie just gave you a taste of your own medicine."

I quirked a brow and said nothing as I chewed. I hadn't known about Remi's reputation for pranks, but if I thought about it, I should have guessed. He was always laughing.

I was more surprised that Hugo had spoken up for me. Our eyes met; something passed through us. A jolt. A recognition that I couldn't put my finger on. He saw it too.

The dream.

Hugo's thumb brushed his lip, remembering our kiss. He dropped his gaze and started to fiddle with his silverware.

Had I somehow invaded *his* dream?

I was a Drude. Dreams and nightmares were my domain—and Incubi were known for being able to feed on sleeping women.

"Did you have a good night's sleep last night?" I asked Hugo as I pressed the tines of my fork against my plump bottom lip.

Hugo's ice blue eyes widened. "Yes."

"Any good dreams?" I probed.

Remi snorted. "I dreamt my teeth fell out."

"That means money worries." Hugo supplied helpfully.

"I don't have to worry about *that*." Remi smiled somewhat sadly. He reached over and stole my coffee, draining

113

the cup with a sigh.

"So, Hugo? What did you dream about?" My attention flicked between Remi and his unusually subdued expression and Hugo's flushing face.

"Smoke. Sand. Sex." Hugo muttered as he wiped his hand down his face to hide his eyes. I had been right—and that filled me with bone wrenching terror. As much as a psychopath can feel, anyway.

What had happened had been real. Hugo had seen the real me. I hoped to Hell that he didn't make the connection between the Demon in his dream and the woman at his table.

Chapter 9

Remi walked with me to Dr. Dan's office for my medical check-up.

All of the blood results had come back clean after my poisoning. I had stripped down to a paper gown and sat on the edge of the gurney, ready to be poked and prodded. Remi hovered in the doorway.

"Don't you have something better to do?" I glanced over my shoulder. An ornate brass box caught my attention. Brass was a metal known for holding magic, but the tarnished decoration looked like a cigar box. I leaned forward and poked it with my finger.

"I can see your bum, love," Remi replied with a cheeky wink. His British accent made the words coarse. My smile turned saucy; I made no move to cover it.

"Do you like it?"

"The tattoo of a fairy on the bottom of your spine." He remarked. "Not what I expected."

I shrugged. Frankie had retreated into nothingness since I had passed out and ended up in Hart's quarters. While I felt myself taking on some of her body's traits, I couldn't access her memories anymore without effort.

The mint curtain hissed as Dr. Dan pulled it along the rail. He did not look up as he entered the bay, concentrating on the chart in front of him.

"Dr. Dan," I smirked.

He glanced up before returning his gaze to the chart. "Refrain from using that name. I prefer Daniel." He said stiffly.

I jerked my thumb in the direction of the doctor. "This guy loves me," I told Remi.

"He's your brother. He has to." Remi's lip twitched.

"Adopted." Both Daniel and I replied at the same time.

Remi gave me a stern look. "Do not jinx him. I'm not driving you out to Maywood to get pissed again."

I pouted.

Dr. Dan cleared his throat. "Everything looks good, Frankie." He said, ignoring our banter. "You've recovered well. I think the best thing for you is to start physical training again." The doctor signed a slip of paper.

"She's cleared?" Remi rubbed his hands together. "Hear that, love? You can join my morning class."

I quirked a brow. "What are the rules about fraternization?"

Remi stifled a laugh but ignored my question. "We're good to go?"

Dr. Daniel nodded stiffly. I bent over and pulled my jeans on under the paper gown. Remi did the polite thing and turned his back when I pulled on my tank top.

"Mom and dad want to know if you're coming to Queens for Thanksgiving." Dr. Daniel said once I was fully dressed.

My nose wrinkled. "Celebrating millions of Native deaths with turkey? Sign me up."

Dr. Dan gave me a look. "Are you no longer a vegetarian?" He asked in a low voice.

I blinked and cocked my head to the side. "I'm... whatever. Just fancied some protein. Iron. Meat. After I got out of the hospital. It's all good."

"Iron?" Dr. Daniel repeated in a shaky voice. His change in demeanor gave me the creeps.

I glanced up at Remi to see if he had seen the same thing I had, but he was studying a poster about Meningitis awareness.

Dr. Daniel looked vaguely sick.

Did he know I wasn't his sister? Had he guessed?

I'd need to speak to Davenport soon. If everyone found out, there would no longer be a reason to live on the base.

I had to do better.

After the check-up, I handed my medical slip to Davenport's PA, Betty, and searched for the commander so I could make my excuses and avoid any sort of physical activity.

I'd found a vending machine behind the surveillance building that sold Chips Ahoy. I planned to eat enough cookies to push my host body into a sugar coma.

Remi found me trying to creep out of the back entrance of the admin building and led me through the compound with his massive arm around my shoulders.

"What happened with you and Hugo in the Mess Hall this morning?" Remi asked as we wandered towards the clearing that some of the Hunters used to train. It was an arena of sorts, surrounded by spruce trees and thick bushes. You couldn't see it from the path, but I had often heard the sounds of slapping flesh and pained grunting.

I had been optimistic that I had found a make-out spot, but was wholly disappointed when I had checked it out one morning on the way to breakfast.

"What do you mean?" I asked.

"You and Hugo had a moment."

"Jealous?"

Remi beamed. "We have tons of moments, Mistress Tequila. It's about time you shared the love."

"I had a dream about Hugo." I shrugged. "We dream-banged."

Remi's gaze shuttered. He was angry.

"What?" I demanded.

"You know that Hugo is a Cambion, right?"

"Right." I agreed.

"They can dream walk." Remi murmured. His gaze was far away. "He might of—"

"All's good, Big guy." I slapped his back. "It was very PG-13."

"Hugo doesn't use his magic," Remi explained. "He's embarrassed by it. Do you want me to have a word?"

"What?!" I gasped, outraged. "No! If you do that, he might not do it again!"

Remi burst out laughing. I blew a raspberry. He held a branch out of the way as he followed the path around a bend to the corner.

Hugo Sinclair stood in front of a group of five Hunters. His shoulders squared, his legs apart in a commanding stance. He looked in his element. Gone was the stuttering man that hid behind his hair, in his place was a soldier.

Riley Fisher stood on the edge of the Hunters that Hugo was lecturing. Another girl hovered at Riley's side, the stranger wore a messy bun on her head but a full face of makeup. My brow furrowed as I tried to pull her name from Frankie's memories, but my host's mind was quiet. Bun-girl looked at Hugo like a snack. I didn't like it.

The other Hunters were men, and they listened to Hugo with rapt attention.

"Frankie!" Hugo waved, somewhat sheepishly. "You've been cleared?"

I nodded, glancing at the Hunters in their exercise gear. The last thing I wanted to do was fight a Hunter, even if it was just an exercise. I was as physically adept as a potato.

"Warm up with Remi, and then we'll spar." Hugo turned back to the group and began to divide them into couples. Riley stood to the side and began to stretch by herself.

I followed Remi to one of the corners. Pouting the whole way.

"Come on, love." Remi laughed as he stretched his arms. "Hugo tells me that you're a Judo champion. Even if you've just been cleared, you have nothing to worry about."

I ducked my head and touched my toes. Hiding my face as I mouthed every single swear word I could think of. And

118

some more that I invented. A judo champion?!

Blue-balled tentacle-porn loving harridan.

"Did you just call me a harridan?" Remi asked.

"I plead the fifth."

He nodded, stifling a laugh. When we finished warming up, Remi led me over to the group and stood by Hugo's side.

I shot the two men a pleading look. With wide puppy eyes. They must have been immune because they did not immediately jump to my aid, and fan me while I laid on a chaise lounger eating truffles.

Bastards.

"Frankie—you should spar with Chloe," Hugo suggested, pointing Bun-girl with the jut of his chin. "Try to take it easy for the first round."

Bun-girl Chloe giggled, but her face grew severe and cold the second she laid eyes on me. The switch was jarring, like she had turned off her humanity. Was that what Hunters did?

Good thing I wasn't human.

Chloe darted forward, her left knee twitched a second before she raised her leg to roundhouse kick me. Bitch was like Bruce Lee.

Frankie might have been a judo champion, but I was not.

Instead, I closed my eyes and focused on what I did know. Moving like smoke. Fleeing. Hiding.

Being the lowest of the low meant that I had spent many years avoiding more powerful Demons. I had no qualms about crawling away on my metaphorical belly if it meant that I still got to crawl away.

I folded in half, feeling the whisper of movement in the air currents, instead of using my host's eyes.

Chloe stuck hard and fast, but I dipped and weaved. Dropping to my bum and then crab-walking backward, she raised her foot high, to use the power of the swing to aim a kick to my crown. I dropped and rolled.

Though the Hunter was tiring, Chloe didn't stop. The

rest of the matches had stopped; everyone had turned to watch as a lithe girl, half of Frankie's size, marched after me with the confidence and bearing of a Kung Fu master ogre.

I received a glancing blow of my shoulder and felt a sharp ache immediately. If I hadn't turned at the last minute, Chloe would have broken my collarbone.

Maybe I should have let her. It would have stopped the fight, and I would have been able to go and eat cookies.

Though my demonic healing would be a big flashing sign.

"Don't run away!" Hugo bellowed, hands cupped around his mouth.

"Sometimes, running away means you live!" I wheezed. Running away was the reason I was alive, and my siblings weren't.

"Someone finish it!" A hooting male called from the sidelines.

Chloe stalked towards me with renewed vigor and a cold smile. An unfamiliar feeling hit me—I didn't want to lose.

I wanted to finish the fight, but I didn't want Hugo to see me on my ass under the triumphant smirk of Bun-girl and her flirty eyes.

I reached down inside myself. Molding my darkness into a blade. I searched for her hidden fears, tasting them on my tongue like licorice. Chloe reached forward to grab me. I let her. The second her hand touched my skin, I stabbed into her mind and took control.

Piloting two people at once was worse than being split down the middle. I had enough energy to pull Chloe's hand back and form a fist. She dropped like a sack of potatoes as the woman punched her own nose. I heard it crunch. I pushed her off me. Our backs were turned. It had all happened so fast, I was confident that no one had seen Chloe's random act of self-mutilation.

I raised my hands up and whooped. Turning back to the group.

"I won!" I danced from foot to foot.

Hugo had his head in his hands, but Remi's head was thrown back in roaring laughter.

Davenport and his infamous Team P left the camp that afternoon to check out the suspected summoning spots in Maywood and Queens. I hadn't realized that every person I had gotten close to within my time at the compound was a member of Davenport's inner circle.

For the second day in a row, I had no one to tease. Even the stupidly observant Dr. Lee was part of the commander's dream team.

I had phoned Dirk to give him an update. *'Nothing has happened. Everything is boring. I want to go home.'* As usual, the Fae Lord was unsympathetic. He had made a list of potential monsters to pass onto Davenport and even went as far as suggesting that I researched them when Team P was away. I laughed down the phone for several minutes.

I was slothful and unashamed of it. Why people expected me to behave outside of my nature, I would never know.

I debated stealing a car and driving to Lacey's in Maywood to get my drink on, but drinking by myself was just sad. Instead, I used my stolen cellphone to Google: 'how to make prison wine.' I took some bread and fruit from the salad bar of the mess hall during dinner and occupied my time by trying to make my own alcohol.

It was past midnight when I felt like my world had ended.

My vision swam and shook. My stomach lurched. Every cell in my body was filled with a manic energy that demanded that I needed to RUN. To find something. Someone.

To do *something*.

I had never felt such drive in all of my many years of existence. The only thing I felt passionate about was self-gratification and getting the Hell out of Dodge when things went south.

The feeling was a fishhook in my heart, pulling me closer instead of demanding I flee. I rose from my bed, a puppet without control of my limbs. I blinked, and I was outside, dressed in my bra and panties with the cold biting September wind chilling my meat-suit to the core.

I blinked again; I stood in front of the officer's quarters. I followed the sound of frantic shouting. Grunts. And then the bone-chilling scream of someone in pain. Someone that was having their insides sliced and diced. A deep agony that had no name.

My feet slapped against the linoleum. My chest heaved out of breath, and my arms beat faster and faster as I took the stairs at a gallop.

I needed to see.

I needed to help.

I skidded to a stop when I saw a group of people gathered around an open doorway. Davenport and Hart, arguing in hushed tones. They stopped and stared as I pushed past them and burst into the room, following my gut.

Hugo Sinclair laid on the bed. Pale instead of his usual golden. His eyes screwed closed; his forehead was clammy. He was naked, black veins like charred meat spread up his legs. Smoke lifted into the air.

I pressed my hand to his shin, feeling the infection. It was pain, fire, and desire.

My heart ached. Hugo started to scream, but his lips locked shut; the sound was muffled by his clenched teeth. I swept forward and pushed my hands against his cheeks. His eyes flew open and stared into mine.

I hadn't noticed Remi, at the top of his bed. His hands hovered over Hugo's naked chest and then down over his diseased veins. Remi Weber's fingers were tipped with feathery blue lightening. Unfamiliar tasting magic that tried to push back the affliction. A witch of some sort.

I swallowed the lump in my throat and flopped to the floor beside the prone incubus. Hugo's eyes darted around wildly until I took his hand.

He relaxed.

I closed my eyes and pressed our linked fingers to my forehead.

"What happened?" I rasped.

"The same creature that took out Team C," Davenport said from the doorway. I was too drained to startle and turn around. "Hugo took a hit. It escaped before we were able to get a lock on what it was."

I nodded slowly. My eyes still clenched shut. Hugo was part Demon. He would be okay. Wouldn't he?

Remi sat back and slumped in the chair by Hugo's bedside. "There isn't much more I can do. He has to heal on his own now. I recommend we let him sleep."

Davenport nodded and gave me a look.

"I'm not leaving." I jutted my chin.

He glanced at Hugo and my clenched hands. He nodded slowly, sadly, and turned on his heel. Soon, it was just Remi and me.

"He'll be okay," I whispered. To reassure myself rather than anyone else. Out of all of the Hunters, I felt like I had most in common with Hugo. We had a shared heritage, and although he restrained his and tried to change his nature, I had a soft spot of the quiet man.

Remi tried to smile but failed. That was when I knew it was bad. He soon fell asleep, leaving me alone with a pained but unconscious Hugo.

I glanced at the door and then to Hugo's wounds. Hugo Sinclair was only part incubus, but I was 100% demonic Pureblood. Despite my low born status, I had been conceived and birthed in Hell by the threads of Sin.

I bit into the meat of my palm. Frankie's human teeth were a lot blunter than I was used to. I sawed my jaw from side to side until the thin skin split and welled with blood.

Hugo gasped in pain. His eyes shut tight, his body was rigid. Before he had a chance to close his mouth, I jabbed my bloody hand between his lips and allowed my viscous blood to coat his tongue.

I wiped the rest of my blood on the dark comforter and sat down on the floor.

Hugo would be okay. My blood would heal him.

It wasn't until the morning that I realized that wasn't all it had done.

Chapter 10

The Jade Lake of the Fourth Circle, aka Envy, was home to the Leviathan King.

Leviathan were poisonous, serpentine Demons, with the ability to shapeshift. The King of the Leviathan was taller than a skyscraper. With a golden jade scales, his body was long with frilly fins, almost like a Chinese dragon.

The Leviathan King had been around longer than any of the other monarchs. The Devil had initially lived in Heaven, as had Ba'el, the once King of the Second Circle.

My Cluster made our home in the damp caves on the edge of the Jade Lake. The tree roots were spindly cages above the water, the waterfall leading from the edge of the Third Circle, Sloth, was florescent. The Jade Lake was named as such for a reason, it looked like a milky green shard of Jade.

Drudes moved around. My kin made their home in many circles.

Demons were created when Hell had seen a need for them. The dimension was sentient in its own way. Demons were also created by those able to manipulate the threads of Sin. Monarchy of Hell, or equally powerful beasts.

I had lived many lives and lived in many places— feeding on the psychological runoff from the troubled and demonic. Sometimes I would catch glimpses of the Human Realities in the mind of a Kitsune or Baphomet-kin.

The Jade Lake was close to the City of Dis, in the center of Hell. I was able to drift through the capital and soak in the knowledge of another place, a different world with love, pain, and violence. The memories of the Human Realities seemed more colorful than Hell.

My home was stagnant. No one aged. No one died. Every day, we would feed on the diluted terror of beings that only knew about inflicting pain, but never experiencing it.

My first dream of Hugo had taken place in the City of Dis, amongst the flapping fabric storefronts. Each stall selling ancient artifacts, and Devil's Silver. Lotions and potions, and even stale Krispy Kreme donuts for the Demons that wanted to try their hand at eating human food.

The city was empty. The shouting shopkeepers were silent. No footsteps in the barren sand.

I wore my smoke. A dark galaxy, as I drifted through the ancient city.

My worst nightmare.

The world shifted; suddenly, I was in the East Village in New York City. Standing outside of the familiar door of my borrowed apartment. The shining brass number read '36'. Hugo's apartment.

Something behind the door crashed, and furniture shifted, screeching against the hardwood floors.

Every single bulb bathed the hallway in a lusty red, making the walls look like they belonged to a BDSM club.

The door was open, just a crack. I pushed against it, able to move the flimsy wood despite the fact I had no body. Stardust and nightmares.

Hugo cowered in the corner of the room, naked from the waist up, he was covered in inflamed, red scratches. Bleeding lightly. They marred his flesh like someone had tried to grab him, and he had struggled to get away. Hugo rocked with his head in his hands.

"Go away." He muttered. His voice was so quiet and without hope that it was heartbreaking.

The door to Hugo's bedroom was a wide arch with barefaced brick. The space had no door but instead seemed to be held back with a magic barrier of some kind.

Hundreds of men and women gathered in the tiny space of Hugo's room, pressed against the transparent barrier.

126

Spittle flew from screaming mouths, silenced by the blockade, fists pounded the magic until rainbow oil slicks rippled out as if the doorway was blocked by water.

Every person looked manic in their pursuit of Hugo Sinclair. Their eyes were hooded with and their movements were bestial, as if they had lost any semblance of their personalities. Fueled by their need for him.

"That's creepy," I commented lightly, stepping up to the barrier. Not one of Hugo's feverish admirers looked at me, their attention solely on the incubus.

This was not my nightmare anymore. It was Hugos.

I wasn't very powerful, but nightmares were my domain.

I stepped towards Hugo's shivering form. He pressed back against the wall as if he hoped he could disappear inside of it. His rocking grew frantic.

I held out my hand. I said his name with confidence to get his attention. It did not work.

"No. No. No. No." He whispered.

"Hugo," I repeated, more sternly.

Hugo blinked, waking up from whatever distressed trance had held him captive while the imprisoned lusty army of the damned battered at his barrier to rip his body to pieces.

"It's you." He said in awe.

It took a second to realize that I wore my own form, the incorporeal smoke. Not my Frankie Gardiner meat-suit.

"Come with me," I commanded, stopping myself from glancing at the rabid crowd.

Hugo stood, unfolding his leonine body. He looked over his shoulder at the lusty zombies. "What about them?"

"Who are they?" I asked.

He shrugged. "When I get too close... To excited... That's what happens."

I nodded to myself. I had suspected as much. Young incubi, especially ones from Pureblooded lines, were hard to control. They did not feed on humans as a general rule, not until they had millennia of experience and control under their belt.

One of Hugo's parents was a Demon. A powerful one. And an old one, if he or she had been able to sleep with a Human and not drive them mad.

Hugo's tentative, delicate manner made sense. If every time he showed the slightest interest, it made someone a lust-filled crazy, I could see why he would be hesitant.

"They don't matter." I waved my hand, taking control of his nightmare. With barely any effort, I turned every single person into a traffic cone.

Hugo's eyes widened. "How did you do that?"

"I eat my vegetables," I replied smugly.

The walls melted away; the empty City of Dis returned.

While I could manipulate dreams, I couldn't do much about my own.

Hugo's fingers squeezed mine. I hadn't realized that we were holding hands.

"Where are we?" He breathed in wonder, staring at the sun, shining a bright beam through the faraway peaks of the Greedy Mountains.

I smiled sadly. "My home."

Hugo drank in the sights. The harsh, jagged lines of Cyclian, the language of Hell. The fluttering breeze that would never be felt. The twirling sand of the wastes. The path was worn to nothing by hundreds of thousands of Demons over the years.

"This isn't Earth." He said.

"You're right. This is *Dis*." I gestured around us with a sweep of my free hand. Hugo's touch felt strange. Intense. My true form existed in the planes between worlds. Somehow, Hugo could touch me when no one else could.

Maybe it was because it was a dream.

He would never see my true form in his waking world to find out.

"Who are you?" He breathed. "I have seen you before. In my dreams."

"They call me Mara," I said. "I am the last of my kind."

"I'm Hugo."

"I know." I smiled sadly.

"Do you know what I am?" He asked, his fingers loosened as if he wanted to take his hand back. I did not let him.

"Yes."

"Then you know what I can do." Hugo spat, disgusted with himself.

I couldn't help but laugh. "Hugo," I said, not unkindly. "You are young."

"My first girlfriend—" He interrupted himself to swallow the lump in his throat. "She killed herself after we... You know."

"Why?" I cocked my head to the side, mildly curious.

"She forced me. I wanted to take it slow. I wasn't ready. I stopped her halfway through. I'd only put it in. Just a little bit. Then I stopped." His voice gathered momentum. Manic as he was caught in his memories. "I hadn't paid attention to someone like that before. She was crazy. Slumped. Like she had been drugged. I almost killed her."

I patted his shoulder. Silent.

"I broke up with her. I couldn't risk getting close to someone. I didn't know what I was yet. She killed herself the week after I did it. She blamed me in the note."

I could have spouted a human platitude about it not being his fault, but Hugo didn't need to hear that. Maybe the girl would have committed suicide later in her life after some other event had triggered her. I didn't know. I wasn't powerful enough to see the future.

"Did you know what you were?" I asked gently.

Hugo shook his head frantically. His eyes were wide with panic. "I didn't. I swear."

"You are half-human," I said. It wasn't a question. "Who sired you?"

"My Demon parent?" He closed his eyes and inhaled deeply. "My father."

129

"His name?"

"*Eadwald.*" He whispered, clenching his fist. His body tensed as if he worried that speaking the name would summon to Demon.

"You're safe here," I assured him.

"Are you a Demon?"

"Yes."

"You're like me?" Hugo sounded hopeful.

I smiled but said nothing. I knew his father. I knew Eadwald by another title, but I knew him none the less.

Eadwald. Asmodeus's second son. Prince of Lust.

No wonder Hugo had problems.

"You choose to be celibate," I noted. "Because of her." He had not told me his first girlfriend's name.

"And the others."

"The first time I killed someone, I ripped into their mind and stole a bevy of information," I told him. "I did it because someone told me to. Because I was afraid and alone. Tired and on the run. I wanted to be safe."

"How does killing someone make you safe?" Hugo reached up to touch a loose tendril of my starlight smoke.

"I needed shelter. I needed protection. In exchange, I do things." I said, without emotion. Describing my complicated relationship with Dermot Dirk in as few words as possible.

As soon as I thought about my last hours in Hell, the sky turned black. The dust kicked up. I turned to Hugo.

Horror made my chest swell as my nightmare grew wings, and the ground buckled.

"You must wake," I demanded. My voice echoed through the empty market.

"What?" He called over the howling wind.

"They're here!" I shouted. "Go! Wake up! Leave!"

"Come with me!" He bellowed back, wrenching my arm, so my smoky form laid cocooned in his warmth.

The ground cracked. The fissure in the bedrock spread like a glowing vine.

130

Their magic was dark. Ancient. More powerful than anything I had ever felt.

The Bhakshi and the Shayati.

The creatures below the surface of Hell. The beings that had stolen my family and eaten their magic.

The shadowy form of the Shayati rose up, like a cloaked specter from the expanding chasm. I stepped backward, stumbling as if I had suddenly been made flesh.

A single bony finger pointed at me.

The Shayati were not Demons. They were a force. An idea that God had made flesh and given power. All they wanted was to feed.

Hugo tugged me backward, and our feet flew across the sand, skidding as plumes of dust exploded.

"Is that what killed Team C?" He called, shielding his mouth.

I shook my head. "That's what killed my family."

A hole opened in the sand, rapidly expanding until the circular edges looked like an hourglass. Before I could stop my feet, Hugo and I toppled over the edge.

We kept falling and falling, tangled in thick black vines like the ones I had seen on Hugo's lips as Remi had fought them back with magic.

"Where are we now?" Hugo asked in the darkness.

"This is your nightmare," I informed him. The dream no longer felt like mine. I felt control pour back into my body, and I sagged with relief.

The lights flickered on, Hugo and I stood tangled in the rotten rope. The floor was covered in wax chalk.

Hugo straightened his shoulder. "This is where I was attacked."

I shrugged a shoulder. My eyes focused on the bastardized version of a Cyclian rune and ancient Arabic meshed together. I should have known.

I sighed heavily and chuckled.

"What?" Hugo demanded. "Do you find this funny?"

131

I shook my head. Floating above the crime scene, I looked down on the entire circle and the scattered animal bones.

I wish. I wish. I wish. I wish.

"I know what did this," I whispered. "It was a—"

Chapter 11

I woke up with my body wrapped around Hugo's unconscious form. I quickly wiped the corner of my mouth with the back of my hand. I had drooled all over the beautiful golden chest of an injured Cambion.

That wasn't the most difficult part.

Hugo had seen my true form twice. He had seen my worst memory and my deepest fear. He had seen how I had run away instead of standing and fighting for my family.

If he were smart, he would put it together.

The only thing I was good at was running away. Being a coward.

Not that Hugo would ever put it together. Mara, the Drude, was a wholly different being from Frankie, the Hunter.

I felt a connection with the half-incubus.

Something deeper than Sin. Something threaded into the fabric of my being. Something that I wasn't worthy of having.

I was temporary. My time with the Hunter's had a countdown; now I had a solid clue about the creature that had attacked Hugo at the scene of the crime, I was one step closer to my lonely existence in the City. Piggybacking on the newly dead or horribly drunk. Stealing their moments and savoring the sensations their slowly decaying bodies could feel.

I liked being in Frankie's body too much. I had become too comfortable.

I hated my compliance in Dirk's scheme. Even though he had offered me early freedom with my contract, and I had jumped at the notion—I didn't know what I would do if I were free.

The Bhakshi and the Shayati were gone. Dead. I was safe.

Could I ever go back to Hell? To my home?

Was it still my home, if my family was gone?

Hugo stirred; I pushed myself slowly into the chair at his bedside. Gooseflesh raised on my arms and legs, making me aware of how little clothing I wore. I leaned over and rummaged through one of Hugo's drawers, finding a shirt that smelt like cotton fabric softener, and Hugo's spicy signature scent that wasn't a cologne. It was part magic and all Hugo Sinclair.

Remi had gone in the night; his chair stood empty on the other side of the bed.

I reached forward to brush Hugo's dirty blonde hair away from his closed eyes. The blackened veins were gone. His skin was no longer pale.

He would live, thanks for my blood and Remi's witchy magic.

I thought about our hidden truths and shared secrets. Admitted in a dream that neither of us thought the other would remember.

I placed my hand over his heart.

Ready to say my own personal goodbye.

My one and only moment of closeness that I would allow myself to have with the jaw-dropping Hugo Sinclair.

His skin grew hot under my palm; I jerked my hand away. Eyes wide, I watched as lines burnt into his pectoral muscle. Like a snake eating its own tail. A circle within a circle, a harsh slash through the middle.

I knew that rune.

The scar faded to silver as if it had been there years instead of seconds.

It was the mark of a Soulbond.

Hugo Sinclair was my soulmate.

No.

No. No. No.

I pushed open the door, head down, as I wove through

the hallway. Determined to get back to the safety of my locked room. My warm bed.

Not mine. Frankie's.

I hissed as if I had been struck in the gut. I was a parasite. I lived inside of a body that wasn't my own. I had *marked* someone I could never have. A Hunter of all things.

Even if Hugo wasn't a Hunter, he was descended from royalty, from the Court of the Seventh Circle. I was a Drude, the only one of my kind left.

"Whoa there!" Someone grabbed my biceps and held me still before I slammed against their hard chest. Remington Weber. He did not wear his signature smile. Instead, he studied my face.

"What's wrong?" He demanded. His featured were shadowed, his skin a dark contrast against his straight white teeth. He glanced over my shoulder. "Did something happen to Sinclair?"

I couldn't speak around the lump in my throat. I shook my head frantically.

"Are you okay?" Remi's deep espresso eyes studied mine.

I tried to summon a smile, but it wavered.

"I..." My mouth was dry. "I think I know what killed Team C. What attacked Hugo."

Remi's gaze grew even more intense. He squeezed my shoulder and maneuvered himself behind me. His hand was on the small of my back as he started to stride with purpose. I almost tripped over my feet.

"Where are we going?" I asked.

His answer was simply, "Davenport."

A minute later, up the stairwell and into the officer's quarters, Remi hammered on a nondescript door at the end of the corridor. Davenport greeted us. His hair stood around his head like a mussed-up crown of raven feathers. His scruff was denser. He looked alert, but wan.

"Talk to me," Davenport demanded. He stepped aside

135

to let us both through and then closed the door behind him. He glanced at my bare legs. "What are you wearing?"

I crossed my arms over my chest and tapped my foot.

Remi gestured to me with a brief wave. "She knows what killed Team C."

Davenport's eyes zeroed in on mine, like a predator scenting his prey.

I glanced from the commander to the bald-headed hacker. Gauging how much I could say without revealing the truth of my identity.

"Hugo... Projected... While he was unconscious." I murmured, hoping they wouldn't pick up on my hesitation as I chose the right words. "I recognized the summoning circle."

Davenport crossed his arms over his chest. Remi cleared his throat. "What is it?"

"And how do we find it and kill it?" Davenport added unnecessarily.

I breathed a sigh. Finding the truth incredibly tricky.

"You are looking for a Wish Demon. A spirit called an Ifrit."

"Wishes?" Remi glanced at the commander. "Like a genie?"

"Not quite." I winced. "Wishes can be both 'good' or 'evil.' There are celestial beings known as Djinns. They are coincidence. They reward good people by manipulating certain events. They do not have a body. For example, say, a single mom can't afford a present for her kid's birthday—and then she wins a scratch card for fifty bucks? Dijinn love setting that shit up."

"And Ifrits?" Davenport sounded like he was quickly losing patience.

"Ifrits are the other side of the coin. They are primarily death spirits. They are karma for murderers and such."

"Isn't karma a good thing?"

I shrugged. "Whatever harm you wish on someone comes back thrice. Ifrits are big on paying back dark wishes.

136

Wishes that people don't even realize they are making."

Davenport pinched the bridge of his nose. "You saw the summoning circle in Sinclair's mind?"

I nodded. I hadn't wanted it to be a Demon. I wanted it to be some other beastie. A Fae or even a human. Something inside of me wanted to protect my kin. It drew a line in the sand between them and me. I was a creature of Hell. They were Hunters. They killed my kind.

Ifrit were beings of flame and dust. They were dark wishes given form. Revenge Demons who feasted on murderers, rapists, and the most dismal of Human Kind.

"Could someone have wished for Team C to die?" I asked. "Or do you think that they were just in the wrong place at the wrong time?"

Remi shook his head to imply that he didn't know. I thought about the offensive lines of the summoning spell. A shackle around the neck of a Demon. A blood scented rag to lure a dark wish to a victim.

My heart ached for the Ifrit, but I knew I was the only one that cared.

"The circle was surrounded in Cyclian runes, but they had been mixed with ancient Arabic, Sanskrit, and Enochian. The combination made it almost impossible to decipher." I explained.

"But it's an Ifrit summoning circle?" Davenport asked.

I nodded and shifted from foot to foot. I didn't want to explain that the Ifrit was under someone's control. Admitting that a Demon could be summoned and then leashed like a dog felt like a betrayal of the secrets of my kind. Still, for some bizarre reason, I wanted to help the Hunters.

Was I suicidal?

Davenport narrowed his eyes, his expression grew shrewd. "Remington, I need to speak with Corporal Gardiner alone."

It was a subtly worded command. Remi opened his mouth to argue, but something in Davenport's gaze told him

137

that wasn't a good idea. Remi shot a look at me, one that told me he would be listening behind the door if I needed help. I blew a raspberry and rolled my eyes to try and alleviate his worry.

Davenport stepped into my personal space the second the door clicked shut. I had thought his eyes were black. They weren't. They were the darkest blue. Ink. His pupils dilated. He smelt like cinnamon gum.

"How does a Mimic Sidhe come to know about summoning circles?" He asked delicately.

"You said yourself that I would have knowledge that you do not." I cocked my hip.

"But to be familiar enough with a circle, to recognize it under several layers of foreign graffiti and bastardized spell extensions? That's more than a glancing knowledge." Davenport licked his bottom lip.

"What are you getting at?" I asked heatedly. I almost wanted him to say. To admit that he knew deep down that I was Hellspawn and that he wanted to kill me.

It would be a damn sight better than the intense look in his eyes, torn between throwing me on a table to either subdue me or fuck me.

My chest heaved; my nipples tightened against my cotton t-shirt. I wanted to squirm, but I squared my shoulders and met his gaze head-on.

Davenport exhaled slowly, and the wound-up tension drifted from his shoulders. "A Hunter becomes a Hunter only after they are *'called.'* They could be an average person on the street. Human. Fae. Part Demon. Part Angel. It doesn't matter. If they have a glancing blow with real evil, and that evil marks them, the *balance* will 'call' them to be a Hunter."

Zealots had called it the balance, once upon a time. The Threads of the world were every emotion, every action, reaction, and thought. Demons fed on the threads of Sin. The balance was the force that held it all together.

"The Balance tries to equalize the world by calling a

Hunter to do good after they have been touched by evil." I clarified.

Davenport nodded. I tapped my chin, in thought.

Evil was relative. By definition, I was evil. I was a nightmare demon. I fed on the deep subconscious fears of Humans and Demons alike.

But I did not create those fears, I only exploited them.

Just as most Demons did not create or encourage Sin. They just fed on it.

"Why am I getting a play by play of the Hunter initiation rites?" I asked.

"Have you been touched by evil?" Davenport's voice was soft and coaxing.

"Pretty baby," I cooed, reaching up to pat his chest. Unable to stop myself. "I've bathed in the stuff. If evil were a glitter bath bomb, I would have thrush and the complexion of a disco ball."

Davenport's eyes widened, surprised, as he took in my words, trying to make sense of them. His lips tightened as if he struggled to hold back laughter. My admission was forgotten in the presence of graphic imagery and harmless joking.

"What I meant to imply, *Sidhe*, is that if you have been touched by Evil, you may be called to become a Hunter." The commander said, once his mirth melted away.

I gaped. "Me? A Hunter?"

He shrugged. "Stranger things have happened."

Davenport had been presented with the evidence, but he had gone down the wrong garden path. It was just as well. Why did I continuously flirt with revealing my true nature? How did the male Hunters manage to delve past all my barriers?

"Coolio." I backed away slowly. "Just drop the welcome packet off at my room, and I'll let you know." My hand fumbled for the door as I made my escape.

Davenport did not move. "You will know if you are *'called.'*" His voice followed my retreating figure. "You will have to make a choice."

139

Nervous laughter burst from my lips, "You're Fruit-Loops, Big Guy!" I called out as I walked away.

Over the next few days, I avoided the guys. I ate in the Mess Hall, took painfully embarrassing physical training with the rest of the Hunter newbies, and thought about Hugo Sinclair's mark.

Soulbonds were rare.

So rare, in fact, that finding your true mate was a legend. I had never met anyone that had found their other half before.

You could Bond with someone through a ceremony. Which Demons rarely ever performed. The Bond allowed you to access the powers of your mate, read their intents and thoughts once it had solidified.

If you were to die, your Bonded would weaken. They may even wither and perish from the loss of the connection.

But a True Bond?

A Soulbond, a mark that had formed on its own? That kind of thing just didn't happen.

Was Hugo Sinclair, my true mate? The mark on his chest certainly implied that he was.

My first reaction had been to run. To keep the bond a secret and hope that Hugo would live a full life without ever knowing that the universe had placed us together for its own nefarious idea of a joke.

Hugo was a Hunter. A half-demon, by blood, but he had been *'Called.'*

My own mark was a single silver line across my collarbone. Over my left breast. If I focused my magic, pulling the threads of Sin towards me –in the same fashion as if I was aiming a mental blade at someone—then I could make the mark fade.

The scar on my chest was not the same elaborate

Cyclian rune as Hugo's. It was only part of the word. A syllable grunted, but not the true meaning.

I had finished sparring and ducked out of the way when Riley Fisher had swanned up to me to strike a conversation that would no doubt dissolve into insults. I escaped down the path and found myself sitting on the fence surrounding the K9 enclosure. The dogs were all lined up and eating from their bowls. A few tails wagged excitedly. I found myself smiling. I swung my legs, content to watch them at a distance.

"What are you doing here?" Hart asked brusquely. I jumped, pressing my hand against my chest as I wobbled from my precarious seat on the fence.

Hart ducked forward, his orange eyes rolling at me as he gripped my shoulders and righted my balance.

There was too much saliva in my mouth. Human bodies were so weird.

Hart was looking at me strangely. I wondered why.

"Well?" He demanded.

Oh. I hadn't answered Hart's question.

"Bored." I shrugged.

Hart crossed his arms over his chest. "Okay."

My eyes narrowed. "Do you have a problem with me?"

His lips tightened. "No."

"Is it because we kissed?"

Hart closed his eyes, inhaled deeply, and whispered a soundless prayer to a Dead God. "Jesus, Frankie."

"Is it?" I pressed. Mildly curious.

"You hate me." Hart murmured. His orange eyes darted away. "After the Blood Sidhe incident in Queens, a year ago, I thought you *wanted* me to transfer from Team C."

I didn't want to ask what had happened. Blood Sidhe were ruthless bastards. They could rip someone's blood from their bodies through their pores. Kind of like vampires, but they were Fae. They didn't feed on the blood they stole from their victims. Their power came from the magic in the blood. Making

141

amulets and potions from it. Blood Sidhe were the natural enemies of the Mimic Sidhe.

"That was ages ago." I smiled gently. Affecting the most generic response that I could think of, I said, "Did we have something going on before...?"

Hart looked horrified. "No."

"Sorry." I shrugged and plastered a gentle but self-deprecating smile on my face. "The coma has left my memories kind of fuzzy."

I had tried to reach into my host's mind to extract what I needed, but there was a clear pool of nothing in the back of my mind. Frankie was still alive. At least, her body was. The coma had pressed her down into a locked box.

"It was my fault the Blood Sidhe attacked you and Daniel. It's the reason he no longer goes on field missions." Hart explained. His face creased as if it pained him to do so. "I ignored a direct order and entered their suspected lair and left the rest of the team behind. If I hadn't, you wouldn't have been outgunned, outmanned..."

I quirked a brow. "I can fight my own battles, you know."

"Snipers are best at a distance, and your brother is a doctor, not a fighter," Hart growled. "I shouldn't have left you behind."

"But, I'm alive," I stated blithely.

Hart blinked.

"So, I assume that the Blood Sidhe were taken care of?"

He nodded slowly.

I slapped my hands together and jumped from the fence, landing with my knees bent and arms outstretched. Perfect dismount. Olympics here I come.

"What's fun around here?"

Hart was speechless.

"Are you glitching, Marmalade?" My nose scrunched.

He shook his head to free himself from his stupor.

"Marmalade?"

I popped a hip and waved a hand. "Your eyes."

Hart opened and closed his mouth a few times before he cleared his throat. "We could go to the range?" He suggested. Eying my face like I was some newly found creature.

"Not bad," I said. "Let's do that." I skipped forward and looping my arm through his. He stood stock-still for a few seconds looking down at where our arms linked. I shook him. Laughing—I realized that Hart was growing on me.

"You're just a big old teddy bear under there." My smirk was smug. "A softie."

Hart raised a brow and said nothing.

"Still not a big talker?" I chattered away as he directed us down the path. "That's okay, Marmalade. I can talk enough for the both of us."

Halfway down the path, Callum Hart had to take control of the route as I had no idea where I was going. He said nothing, but his lip tightened.

Hart had been on Frankie's team over a year ago. I hadn't known that. Her memory had only supplied a name. He had been closer to her than any other Hunter, apart from Daniel. Even though it was a professional relationship, it was evident that the Sarge knew my host, and he knew that her behavior was strange.

There wasn't much I could do at that point. Typically, I retained access to my host's mind, but Frankie was gone gone gone. I couldn't autopilot and let her mouth do the talking while I hitched a ride. That had never happened to me before. I was well and truly on my own.

Hart opened the door to one of the grey Lego block buildings that I had never entered before. As soon as I stepped onto the worn linoleum, the harsh snap of gunshots and the smell of gunpowder burnt my nostrils.

I had not spent much time around firearms in my life. I was intrigued by them. Humans used bang sticks to kill each other. Demons had no use for such things. Hart strode over to

143

the sign-in sheet. His massive body moved more gracefully than I could ever accomplish while wearing a borrowed flesh suit. He signed a piece of paper; the man behind the desk gave us ear defenders, guns, and bullets.

"Booth thirteen is free." The soldier behind the desk grunted. Hart nodded and took the heavy box before I could make a move to help.

I wondered if I would be able to shoot a gun while wearing the thin leather gloves that Davenport had instructed I wear. I had been religious about donning the items, it was almost second nature to wear them.

Hart pushed open the door to an enclosed booth and held it open for me. I danced through, excited. I had never been to a gun range before. I had seen various TV shows, so I knew what they looked like.

A paper target on the end of a long run, with a reinforced concrete wall behind.

Hart placed the box of bullets and the gun onto a shelf and handed me a yellow set of ear defenders.

Hart did not ask if I had ever used a gun before. Frankie Gardiner was a sniper, and firearms were her bread and butter.

I closed my eyes and took a deep breath, allowing the barest hints of my host's muscle memory to guide me through loading the gun. I hooted in triumph when I succeeded the first time.

Hart gave me a questioning look.

"I haven't held a gun in a while," I lied with a grin. I cheered like my team had just won the Superbowl when I emptied the chamber into the target. The ear defenders meant that I couldn't regulate my voice correctly, so I had shouted. I mouthed an apology and turned back to the targets.

Frankie's body remembered the gun. I was able to arrange myself to hold the weapon, adjusting my meat suit's limbs one by one until it felt right.

We stood in silence, the only noises were the quiet

pops of the guns discharging. I was able to hit the target, but barely, even though Frankie's eyesight was better than any humans that I had been inside before.

The gloves had long since worn away in the joints of the fingers, which made pulling the trigger easier than I had expected. My hands sweated, and I wondered, not for the first time, why my host insisted on wearing such horrible garments.

I smiled brightly, feeling genuine happiness at being able to do something right for a change. Even if the skill had been honed for years by my host, and I had little to do with it.

Hart slammed his fist on the button above my head; the paper targets raced towards the gallery.

Hart took off his ear protectors and gestured for me to do the same. "Haven't lost your touch." His lip twitched in the first sign of warmth I had seen from the man since we had kissed in the middle of the night, while I was high from feeding on Davenport's nightmares.

"Thanks," I pushed Frankie's hair out of my face. Noticing that my forehead was damp. Shooting a gun was more physically demanding than I had expected. Frankie's stomach muscles ached slightly.

"I'll get us some water." Hart's orange gaze softened as he placed my target on the shelf in front of me. All of the red zones had holes in them. Frankie's skill had won against my inexperience. Her aim was second nature.

I glanced over my shoulder as Hart strode to the vending machine, and quickly removed the glove on my right hand. Wiping the clammy skin against my cargo pants. I wondered how it would feel to hold a gun without the cumbersome gloves in the way.

The metal was skin warm. I'd heard the man at the desk say the gun was a 'Luger.' Small compact and dark. I wondered what kind of weapon Frankie usually used. All of the snipers from various films I had watched used long guns that mounted on weird triangles on the sand.

I locked my legs and turned to the new targets, forcing

145

Frankie's instincts to the front of my mind and aiming the gun.

"What are you doing?" Hart's voice was a whip-sharp crack behind me.

I exhaled and bent over at the waist, placing the gun on the shelf once I had engaged the safety. "Seven Hell's, you scared me."

Hart's eyes had darkened, alive with thunder. All softness had drained away. He stepped forward into my space, his palm rested on my hand as I released my grip on the Luger. His jaw rocked from side to side, angry and grinding his teeth.

I stepped back before I could help myself. "Callum?" I asked hesitantly, using his first name. "Is everything alright?"

"You're touching metal. Without your gloves." Each word was carefully measured. Painful for him to say.

I frowned. "Yes?"

He closed his eyes and exhaled, stepping back abruptly. It took a second to realize that he had pulled the guns away from the shelf and away from where I could reach them.

"Who are you?" Hart asked delicately. "Because you sure as hell aren't Frankie Gardiner."

Horror bloomed in my chest and squeezed my heart. My face flooded with color. I forced my lips into a tight smile and trained my eyes to his. Every tick of my heartbeat grew louder and louder until the roar was like hummingbird wings. My fingers tingled; my leg muscles locked, preparing my body to run far and fast.

"I don't know what you mean, Hart." My words held a bite as I grabbed the gloves from the side, the smooth leather was still warm as I yanked them on as fast as possible.

"You're different," Hart said accusingly.

"Almost dying does that." I lied through gritted teeth. I squinted as I took in the familiar gleam in his eyes. I licked my bottom lip to taste it. Guilt.

"You're attracted to me." I reasoned. "But you weren't before." My realization was like lightning through parted clouds. "That's why you're so pissed at me all the time."

146

Hart clenched his fists. "Who are you?" He repeated. "Corporal Gardiner is allergic to steel. She can't touch it without getting a painful rash."

I held up my gloved hand and surveyed the worn leather. So that was why Frankie wore gloves? I thought it was because of poor circulation from having a heart made of ice.

"Have you seen me naked before?" I asked, cocking my head to the side. I had to stop myself from asking if he had seen 'Frankie' naked.

Hart raised both of his hands and brushed them over his already tight man-bun. He nodded hesitantly, and I did not ask how or why he had seen Frankie in his skivvies. I could only assume that changing into tactical gear for a mission wasn't a private affair.

I turned around and hooked my fingers under the hemline of my tank top.

Hart's lips popped open. "What are you doing?"

He made a move to stop me, but I quickly whipped off my tank and crossed my arms over my chest to cover my breasts. Right on the bottom of Frankie's spine, between the two dimples above her buttocks, was a Tinkerbell. Shoddily drawn and lucidly colored. A trashy tattoo for a very untrashy woman.

Hart's eyes fixed on the splodge of ink, a cascade of emotions played over his face. Shame. Lust. Anger. Denial. Acceptance.

He stepped forward, the heat of his body rested against my bareback. I shivered. His calloused hands wrapped around my biceps. He was so tall that he could have rested his head on my crown with no effort. His large frame cocooned my own, and Frankie was by no means diminutive.

"I've seen that tattoo before." He said softly. Hart's voice was muffled by my hair.

"Yes." My answer gave him no leeway. I tried to hold onto anger, but I couldn't. Some deep part of me was happy that he saw through my guise. That he could differentiate between my host and me.

147

On the other hand, what if Hart was the one that had summoned the Ifrit to kill Team C?

I couldn't imagine it. I had watched the bulky bear of a Hunter, with his long mountain-man hair tied back in a bun, I had seen the way he loved every dog in the canine unit. Especially Dixie, the blonde Labrador that kept demanding extra food and trying to push her soggy plushie against his leg when he hadn't paid her enough attention.

He kissed like a coiled maelstrom. Like a gentleman that would turn into a deviant if you managed to break through his hard shell. I wanted that so badly.

I wanted to tell him. To spread the truth free like open wings and scream about my true nature from the rooftops.

If I did that, he'd kill me.

For the first time in my life, I felt something like a squirming worm inside the core of my being. Guilt. Uncertainty. I hated that I had grown close to Hart, Hugo, Remi, even Davenport, and Dr. Lee, and none of them would ever know the true me. They would never know my true nature.

Part of me wanted to let my mask slip, just a little, to see what they would do.

But not yet.

Hart's body was warm. I tilted my chin back until my head rested between his pecs. I buried myself in his embrace and closed my eyes.

I hadn't felt safe in so long.

I didn't think I had ever been held like that before.

Sharp pain sliced through my forehead and down my brain until it rested at the base on my skull. Images flashed past my closed eyelids. Frankie's memories, through her own eyes.

Callum Hart covered in blood, staunching the bleeding from Frankie's middle. Daniel, her brother, rocking back and forth in the corner. The headless body of a Blood Sidhe ripped clean in two, laid prone next to my hand.

Callum was pale white, panicking.

"For fuck sake, Hart." Frankie's bitter voice was cold. "Don't

148

touch me."

"I'm so sorry, Gardiner." He whispered, placing gauze on the healing wound.

"Get off me, you dolt!" Frankie waved him away.

"I didn't mean to—"

Frankie pushed him away and stood on shaky feet. She marched over to her adopted brother and gripped his arm, pulling him up to her side. She called Daniel's name a few times, he continued to shake, and his gaze was fixed on the dismembered Fae corpse.

Frankie slapped him. Her hand a whip. Daniel's head jarred to the side.

"We don't have time for this." Frankie eyed her brother, meaningfully. She limped away from the scene.

Callum Hart lowered his head. His fingers glistened with blood, both Frankie's and Blood Sidhe. His eyes glowed as he looked down at the floor.

I slammed back into my body quickly. It felt uncomfortable, like a poorly tailored suit. Frankie had shown me something. I did not know why or what it meant.

Callum had taken her brusque manner as a rejection. A scolding.

But Frankie's wounds had healed incredibly fast. Too fast for a human. Was that the reason she had pushed Hart away?

I stepped out of Hart's embrace and ducked down to snag my top again, pulling it over my head with a swift movement. I looked down at my pebbled nipples and thought about possibly wearing a bra.

I shrugged when I decided against it. It made me too happy to make people uncomfortable. The outline of a nipple through a cotton t-shirt was a good way to fuck with people with minimal effort, even if it impossible to run anywhere without getting slapped in the face.

"I'm hungry," I said brightly, to change the subject.

Hart cleared his throat and scooped up the guns. Dumping them in the same box as the bullets. I caught a glimpse of his hardness, pressing against his distorted zipper.

I squirmed with happiness.

I wasn't allowed to indulge in any sexcapades with the Hunter's. Giving Hart blue-balls was as far as I could go.

The soldier at the desk had abandoned his post, reminding me that the Hunter's compound was pseudo-military at best.

Hart reached into his pocket and produced a keycard. He led me through the gate to the side, and we walked into the armory.

Every type of weapon imaginable greeted us. Walls of swords, from samurai and rapier. Tasers and some sort of whip. It reminded me of the weapon's masters of the City of Dis, touting their wares.

I whistled in appreciation as Hart led us down the correct aisle to deposit the guns and the bullets. Halfway down, my neck prickled, and I stopped walking.

Hart turned; his brow was quirked. "What is it?" He asked.

I pointed to a box on the side. Something about it made my skin crawl. "What's that?"

Hart gave me a funny look. "They're the new bullets. The ones that dissolve on contact. Devil's Silver. For Demons."

My eyes widened. Devil's Silver was enchanted metal that could scar a Demon. If the bullets melted, then it could very well kill one too.

I swallowed the lump in my throat.

"How did you get a hold of Devil's Silver?" My voice was tight with fear.

"We don't have a lot." Hart frowned at the box. "Still in testing."

I nodded and gave him a relaxed smile. Inside, I wanted to burst from my skin and flee.

I tried to see Hugo Sinclair that afternoon. Affecting an air of nonchalance as I walked past the officer's quarters, my face was hidden by the hood over my head as I sat on the wet grass outside the dull grey building, weaving the thin green blades into a braid. I could feel the Cambion, like a second heartbeat in my chest. The closer I got to the building, the stronger that heartbeat was.

Muddy combat boots stepped into my vision. I glanced up at Davenport. His arms were crossed over his chest, his inky eyes studied me from behind his thick brow.

"What are you doing?" He asked. His entire presence made the question a command that I wanted to answer like an eager dog.

I held up my small grassy braid. "It's a tiny noose," I informed Warren with enough glee to rival a small child.

Davenport pinched the bridge of his nose. "Sinclair is resting. He has asked me to deter any visitors."

I tried not to let my disappointment show on my face. "I'm just making daisy chains, Daddy Davenport."

Davenport grunted; he eyed the ground with distaste and to my surprise, eased himself onto the soggy grass.

"It has come to my attention that you are spending a lot of time with Weber, Sinclair, and Hart." Davenport's gaze zeroed in on mine and pinned me to the spot. "I feel I have to remind you to act with the conduct of a Hunter while you are in the compound and to not do anything that Corporal Gardiner would not do.

"Relax." I breathed a laugh. "I'm not about to proposition anyone for sex."

I had standards—standards that didn't include people whose job it was to kill my kind. No matter how at home I felt with them. Or how attractive I found them.

"I'm gone in a few weeks anyway." I reminded him.

"You've gotten close to some of my Hunters," Davenport said gravely. "I don't want to see them led astray."

My eyes widened. "By one of the tricky, slippery, Fair Folk?" I said, playing along with my mask as a Mimic Sidhe.

"Exactly." Davenport's eyes narrowed.

"You're not just saying that because you're tempted, commander?" I asked with a hint of a condescending smirk.

"You'd know if I was tempted, Girl." Davenport's voice rumbled. The sound traveled straight to my female parts. Delicious.

"Jealous?" I suggested with a purr.

His eyes hooded, but he stood up abruptly and straightened his spine. "Maybe another time." He suggested. I protested when he turned to leave but Davenport smiled softly. "Show me your real face, and I'll show you mine."

I wondered what he meant by that.

That evening, still paranoid from Davenport's rejection, I stepped under the scalding spray of the shower and scrubbed my host's body until my skin turned pink.

Davenport had implied that he wanted me. The real me. My personality. Not the face I wore.

To his knowledge, I was wearing a mask. He didn't realize that if I slipped out of my shell, I would be nothing but smoke and nightmares.

I grabbed the shampoo and poured enough into my open hand that the silver goo dripped from my fingers. I swore and looked down only to find that the water had gone red.

Horror made my head swirl. I reached out and gripped the shower curtain. I was bleeding? I searched my legs for cuts but found no injury. Demons didn't bleed. There weren't many weapons we couldn't heal from immediately. Adding to the fact that I didn't have my own body, which made the slow fat droplets of blood on the porcelain more surreal.

I reached between my legs. My fingers came away

152

crimson.

"I'm dying," I whispered. Wiggling my fingers. "*Seven Circles! Shax Shit! Devil's dirty underwear!* Fuck!" I wailed, staggering out of the bathroom, still naked, dripping water and blood onto the tiled floor and then the carpet. I grabbed a white towel and pressed it between my legs.

I was going to bleed to death.

Had something broken inside my host? Was it the poison? Or maybe whatever had put Frankie in a coma had messed up her insides? Was I going to start vomiting blood next?

A cramp built in my lower stomach and spread to my lower back. I swore loudly.

Someone knocked on the door. Hunched over, crying like a kicked dog, I waddled to my door and pulled it open.

"Can you keep it down in there?" Riley Fisher flicked her mop of curly mahogany hair over her shoulder. Her gaze traveled over my naked state before resting on the towel between my legs.

"What happened to you?" She gaped. "Are you okay?"

"I'm dying!" I howled. Ripping the towel free, I brandished it at her. "Look!"

Riley flinched. Her eyes rolled to the heavens. "Have you lost your mind?" She pushed past me and slammed the door shut. "Get in the shower now."

"I'm bleeding," I told her. My hysteria failing and slowly being replaced with glum acceptance.

"Yes. You idiot." Riley shot me a look. "You're on your period. You've probably had one a month since you were thirteen."

"A period?" I repeated slowly.

"Riding the crimson wave. You're on. Aunt Flo is visiting." Riley waved her hand. "Get in the shower. I'll go and get some supplies from my room. You owe me."

My eyes were wide as I watched the petite woman disappear in a flurry of movement. I did as she said because she

153

honestly scared me a little. When I came out of the shower, my bed was covered in pink and blue boxes.

"There," Riley growled, throwing a packet at my head. I turned the box over in my hands.

"I'm all for weird sex acts. But this is chocolate, it's not going to help with the bleeding." I frowned.

Riley sighed. Exasperated. She tugged the chocolate from my grip and tossed it on the bed. "What the hell is wrong with you? What *happened* to you in the hospital?"

My lips tightened. "This is a normal human thing?"

Riley gave me a long look. After explaining the fine art of tampons and sanitary pads, Riley said that she would talk to Dr. Daniel. She then left. I was more confused than ever. I had never been in a meat suit long enough to experience anything like this before.

The other bodily functions were standard. Breathing. Eating. Peeing. I had never thought about the concept of menstruating before. Demons were created, not born.

Drudes did not have physical relationships. They did not take a single partner, preferring to be part of the Cluster—belonging to all and none.

I had set myself apart from my kin long ago. More interested in other realities, magics, and stories than others of my kind.

I had never experienced a physical relationship. Or a meaningful one.

I had never had to think about reproductive cycles. Though I had read something in Frankie's report about a contraceptive implant. Dr. Daniel had looked aghast when I had asked him what that meant.

I stuffed the Hersey bar into my mouth, barely pausing to swallow. My head hit the pillow. I fell asleep as soon as my eyes closed.

I stood on the top of a three-story building, watching the empty streets below. The edges of my vision fuzzed and blurred if I moved my head too quickly, telling me that I had stumbled into someone else's dream.

A lone dark figure ran through the streets, pausing at the dead end of a dark alleyway, and scrambling backward like a trapped rat. Dressed in black trousers, ripped in various places, Hugo Sinclair hugged his chest. Pressing his hands against the slowly leaking wounds on his arms and back, he curled over as if he wanted to make himself as small as possible. The cuts looked like nail marks.

The mob rustled, their sound like an approaching hoard of chittering roaches. Pouring from the various buildings in the dream-scape.

Hugo clasped onto the fire escape of my building, just as the group of people with feverish lust and devotion started to follow. Their arms outstretched as the incubus hung from the iron railings, his feet dangling as he pulled himself up.

Golden skin, ashen in the dim moonlight. Blonde hair pushed back, streaked with dust and sweat. It was criminal for someone to look so delicious and disheveled.

Hugo's ice blue eyes widened. The streetlamps cast an orange glow over his face, his long eyelashes drew long spider leg shadows down his cherubic face.

"It's you." He whispered reverently.

I looked down, only to find that my human suit had dissolved, and I stood in my true form. Hollow eyes. Tendrils of darkness and starlight. I nodded but said nothing. My gaze fixed on the Soulbond mark craved into his chest, above his heart.

"You're here." He murmured, stepping forward. His hand was outstretched.

I ignored his tentative advance and glanced down at the baying group of admirers.

I recognized the streets. It was my neighborhood. Our apartment building was just across the block, located in one of

155

the red-brick townhouses.

With barely a thought, the raging mob vanished. Becoming dust and drifting away on the wind.

"What are you?" Hugo's demanding voice caught my attention. Now that his raging admirers had vanished, I caught a glimpse of a backbone that I wasn't sure had existed.

"I am a Demon. Same as you," I replied simply.

Hugo blinked slowly. Surprised that I had answered, he blinked slowly. "I know that." Despite the wide stance, his voice was delicate.

"I am Nightmares. You are Lust." I explained, deliberately vague.

"And this is my dream?"

"It's not mine." I shrugged as much as a demonic cloud of smoke could.

Hugo pressed his hand against the Soulbond mark on his chest. "Do you know what this is?" He asked as he stepped forward. One of my tendrils reached forward, like a wayward limb, and brushed his cheek before I could stop myself.

If I had worn a human form, I would have been shifting on my feet and searching for an escape with frantically darting eyes. Instead, I hovered.

I did not want to tell him.

"Please." His husky timbre was seductive. A crack in his voice told me that it was a tone that he did not often use. Based on his dreams of uncontrollable mobs, I could see why. He would cause a riot if he broke out those sexy vocal cords in the Mess Hall.

I wanted to rub against him like a cat in heat. Hugo spent so much time hiding away, hating the way he looked because of his heritage. I had known hundreds of Seventh Circle Demons. All he needed to learn was control.

I stepped forward and placed my hand against his chest. Marveling at the feel of his warmth. I had never been able to experience physicality with my true form—but our combined dreamscape had different rules. Ones that I was fully willing to take advantage of.

I had made an unsaid pact with myself. To not get involved with the Hunter's. To keep a respectable distance, no matter how attractive I found them.

But I was a Demon. We were not known for our self-control.

The world shifted. From the apocalyptically quiet East Village to the hunched over and crooked glass of the Prideful City in the First Circle.

Every surface was a reflection. The clouds were a harsh churning grey, and fluttering snow and ash rained down in a lazy dusting. Every building reached into the sky like gnarled fingers. Hundreds of reflections stared back at me. Hugo's cherub face, and his full, scared ice blue eyes.

In the distance was the Ice Palace, once home to the Devil and his Consort. I had heard that the very floor was made up of the frozen blood of traitors and adulterers.

Hugo glanced at me, expectantly to ask where we were, without words.

I did not answer. Instead, my eyes were drawn to the circular lines of Hugo's Bond mark again. Sorrow and elation churned inside of me, like two oceans fighting for dominance. He was a Demon, that was true, but Hugo had been *called*. He belonged to the Hunters more than he belonged in the world I had come from.

I drifted forward. Silent, as I reached out and cupped the Incubus's cheek. He closed his eyes and leaned into my touch. Seeking comfort from a creature that only ever created terror in the deep of the night.

"Who are you?" He whispered. In awe. His eyes still closed tight.

My chest and throat were too tight. I couldn't bring myself to answer. Hugo knew my real name, but that would be all he ever knew. I could only visit him in dreams, and even then, I knew I should stop.

I was putting myself in danger.

157

I hadn't fled my home, and left the rotting bodies of my family in the chasm, only to die at the hands of the Hunters.

I pulled myself away from the dream. I did not say goodbye because I knew I was too weak to mean it.

Dr. Jae Lee caught me the next morning, stuffing blood-stained sheets into the laundry shoot, with enough fury to power a dozen suns.

I had pummelled the comforter through the metal hatch, swearing up a storm. Jae stood, his shoulder against the threshold. Wearing a white shirt and dress pants, the sleeves rolled up to his elbows. His lips twitched as he held back a mischievous smirk.

I couldn't help but compare Remi, with his bright and carefree laughter, to Dr. Lee, and his wicked glint.

Jae looked as cute as a button, but his insides were jagged like broken glass. His violet eyes seared straight through me. Deep down, I knew that I couldn't bullshit the doctor. Our time together was limited, by design. Jae knew that I was not Frankie. He was also an empath, with the ability to sense other's emotions. Keeping secrets around someone like that would be almost impossible.

"Frankie," He teased, glancing over his shoulder at the empty hallway before he pushed away from the doorframe. "Have you killed someone? Getting rid of the evidence?"

I popped a hip. "Women bleed," I informed him. He was a man, he probably didn't know. "You should be scared of a creature that can bleed for several days without dying."

"Clever." Jae tilted his chin.

"I read it on a t-shirt." I gave my comforter one last push, before slamming the metallic hatch shut. I slapped my hands together, congratulated myself on a job well done; then I turned back to the doctor.

"Did you need something?"

Jae's expression sobered. "You missed your appointment."

I hitched a shoulder and let it drop. "I've been busy. Therapy is a farce anyway."

"Busy?" Jae's gaze was intense.

I waved my hand towards the closed shoot, where my bedsheets had been moments before. "I took a few personal days. Everyone's been on a manhunt in The City. I'm not needed." I rested my hip against the laundry cart.

Jae leaned back against the wall. He crossed one ankle over the other. "You don't like feeling useless." He guessed.

"Is every word I say going to be psychoanalyzed?" I rolled my eyes. "Because I can tell you about the time I got drunk and stole a penguin from the zoo."

"That didn't happen." Jae narrowed his eyes.

"Okay." I held my palms up in a disarming motion. "It might have been a box of doves from a wedding in Central Park."

I had sold them to the Leviathan that worked in the DMV on 25th Street. He had most certainly eaten them.

Jae ignored me. "Riley said that you might need more chocolate—Hart and I are going into Maywood for a supply run, and wondered if you wanted to come."

If I were a dog, my ears would have perked up. "Chocolate?"

Jae glanced at the laundry shoot. "I've heard it helps with these things."

My brows raised as I considered that. "If Riley said I should get chocolate, I'm going to get chocolate." I nodded sagely.

"Decided to mend bridges?"

"She hasn't told me to die this week. I consider that progress." Plus, she'd given me tampons and thrust an instructional leaflet in my hands when I had asked for a demonstration on how to use them. I felt like she had welcomed

159

me to the Woman Club™.

Jae nudged my chin with his knuckle. "Hart's waiting." His violet eyes grew soft. He whispered a word in Korean, but I had no idea what he had said. I considered asking, but Jae had already turned to walk away. He beckoned me to follow.

Ahn-Jae Lee was short by Western standards. Almost exactly Frankie's height. Our steps matched perfectly. Hart stood in the entranceway to the dorms, watching two men spar in the dojo. His shoulders were squared, and his gaze was impassive. If I didn't know better, I would say he was bored.

Dressed in a flannel shirt and worn jeans, his tied-back hair made Callum Hart look like a lumberjack.

"Where's your ax?" I asked as a danced to his side, followed by Jae.

Hart gave me a hard stare that said more than any words. I could almost hear his voice in my head. *'You think you're a comedian? Don't give up your day job'*.

"I know I'm funny." I pouted.

Hart grunted but said nothing as he palmed his car keys. Jae stifled a snort.

I scowled. "Aren't you meant to offer words of kindness and support, Dr. Lee?"

"There, there." Jae patted my shoulder without sympathy.

We walked to the edge of the car park, Hart unlocked a Dodge Ram. The truck was so muddy that I couldn't discern the color.

I called shotgun and leaped into the passenger side with the enthusiasm of a child. As soon as my butt hit the seat, a loud wheezing squeak filled the cab. It was coming from my ass. I wriggled, and the disembodied groan slipped out from beneath my thighs. I reached between my legs and pulled out a yellow rubber chicken. Its red beak was rounded in the perfect O face.

I brandished it at Hart as he did his seatbelt up. "Dixie." He explained without embarrassment. Naming his favorite pup from the K9 unit. I didn't know that he was close

160

enough to them to let the dogs in his car, but as I looked, I caught little signs here and there. Dog treats in the cupholder. A dog leash in the footwell. Even the air freshener was a paw print that smelled like cherries.

"What supplies are you getting?" I turned to Dr. Lee in the backseat.

"Costco," Jae said the one word like it was an explanation. I'd heard of the store but had never been. It sounded like a gluttons paradise.

The road out of the wood was rough and jarred my shoulder against the seatbelt. I had to hold the handle above the door to stop moving so much. Pretty soon, we were driving through a winding snake of concrete, divided by a wall of trees.

"I didn't know you two were friends," I commented lightly. "Both of you seem like loners."

"I resent that." Jae winked. "I'm good in small groups. Not too much with crowds. Emotional overload."

I nodded. "And you?" I glanced at Hart.

"He's just antisocial," Jae answered for him. "He prefers his dogs to people."

"Hey!" I turned around and slapped Jae's arm. "Dogs are better than people."

"Agreed," Hart grunted.

"Besides," I smirked. "Callum isn't antisocial. He was very attentive on our date yesterday."

Jae quirked a brow. "Oh?" His gaze darted to Hart. The big man squirmed and looked away.

"We went to the shooting range. Together. It wasn't a date."

I rolled my eyes. "You hear this, Jae?" I pouted. "He won't acknowledge our undying love."

"Oh my." Jae snickered.

"Would you stop it?" Hart pleaded.

I flicked my hair over my shoulder. "It's okay, Big Guy. Even if you don't admit it, I love myself enough for the both of us."

161

Hart shot Jae a look in the rearview mirror. It was full of meaning.

A shadow moved out of the corner of my eye, "Hart!" I squeaked, pointing at the windscreen. "Slow down!" Callum drew his attention back to the empty road, as a large black mass darted from between the trees and rolled over the hood.

I gripped the dashboard. Adrenaline surged, and my heart fluttered like hummingbird wings. I gasped.

My reflex had been to vacate Frankie's body. I could *die* while wearing a meat-suit. Somehow, I had the presence of mind to not become smoke and burst out of her skin in the presence of two Hunters, but as the car skidded, I held onto my control. Barely.

"What the fuck was that?" Jae demanded, sitting up in his seat. Hart grabbed my shoulder, pulling me forward and wrapping his tree-like arms around me. I opened my mouth to protest as he pressed me to his chest and hunched over the center console. My argument was swept away when a series of pops hammered the passenger side window. Bouncing off the protective glass.

"Do you have your gun?" Jae hunched over, covering his head as he used the driver's seat as a shield.

"I thought we were going out for toilet paper. I didn't think we'd be dodging Demons." Hart grunted. His hand was tangled in my hair, pushing my cheek against his pecs.

The wind howled outside of the vehicle. Bending the trees almost in half. Red glowing eyes moved in the darkness. The car smelt like cinders and old dirty coins.

It smelt like *wishes*.

If I had to choose a way to die, it was not in the burning carcass of a Dodge Ram.

"Drive! Drive! Drive!" I batted Hart away, as the glowing eyes in the dark forest blinked out. He did not need to hear me twice. His foot stepped on the gas as he did a U-turn in the middle of the road and sped back to the compound.

Hart pulled up and went through the careful motions of parking his SUV and collecting his sidearm from the glove compartment. Jae was silent in the back, alert, as the air around him shimmered. It wouldn't be hard to imagine the doctor with huge golden wings.

"Was that what attacked Team C?" Hart's orange eyes pinned to mine. I nodded silently. He turned to Jae. "We can do two things after we report this. We can go back to the dorms and sleep. Or, we can go to Jae's cabin together. Safety in numbers."

"I'm not scared." I scathed with narrowed eyes. I was immortal. I was nightmares given form. A little predator in the forest didn't scare me. I clenched my fists. My hands were shaking. I sat on them. Damn traitorous body.

"I've got wards on the cabin, but we might be able to catch whatever it is on camera," Jae suggested. "If we split up, it might not follow."

I heaved a sigh. "Do you have WiFi?"

"Yes?" Jae said it like a question.

I did a happy dance in my seat. I could use my stolen phone to watch YouTube. And porn. Lots of porn.

Hart unbuckled his seatbelt. "Watch my six." He handed me the gun. I was almost shocked before I remembered that Frankie was a damn fine shot. Hart jumped out of the SUV and went to the trunk, he popped it. Lifted the fabric lining and somehow pulled a shotgun from the bowels of his vehicle. I turned my wide eyes to Jae.

"Let me guess you carry throwing knives?" I guessed sardonically.

"We *are* Hunters, Mara." He said dryly.

"Why did you ask if Hart had a gun in the car then?" I popped my hip.

Jae rolled his eyes. "Because guns are loud. Normally

the noise is enough to scare off a predator."

Hart opened my door and helped me out of the vehicle. I had almost forgotten that Jae knew that I wasn't Frankie.

I ran down the list of people on my head.

Davenport and Jae thought I was a Mimic Sidhe.

Hart had his suspicions that I was not Frankie, but he was in the dark.

Hugo had seen my true form, but there was no way to link that to my host.

Remi was a new addition to the team. As far as he was aware, I wasn't acting strangely. Mainly because he hadn't known Frankie before the coma.

Dr. Daniel and Frankie had little to no relationship. He hadn't seemed to have noticed a difference in behavior. As a doctor, he would have submitted me for testing if he had suspicions.

All in all, I just had to keep my form inside of Frankie's body for the time being.

Easier said than done when bullets were flying, and I liked living very much.

Jae disabled the alarm and set up an air mattress in his office. Hart took the couch.

I was ashamed of how fast I fell asleep, as I snuggled up to the scent of Jae on my borrowed blanket.

Vanilla birthday cake with sprinkles.

Demons did not need sleep, but my host did. As soon as I closed my eyes, I found myself thrown into someone's dream. A starlight shadow, moving soundlessly through the dense forest.

The trees were tall enough to block all sunlight. They bristled and creaked as if they were alive. My movements make no sound as I drifted. Smoke on the wind.

At first, I thought that I had been thrown into Hugo's dream again, but the flavor was different. The landscape of Hugo's dreams was very urban. Central NYC. His apartment. The current dreamscape was so far into the wilderness that I couldn't see evidence that humans had ever walked through the space between the giant redwoods.

A howl broke through the lullaby of the forest. Shattering the illusion of peace.

It was a cry of pain. Battle.

I slammed into an unseen barrier, thrown back into the center of a small clearing. The howling wolf began to whine. I turned on my heel and found the beast by my side. Cowed and trapped by the same invisible cage.

The canine had russet fur. Shaggy in places. The glowing orange eyes that I had only ever seen on a Hell hound, but the wolf was the wrong color. His paws were dipped in white. His teeth were bared, and his ears flat against his skull. The wolf's attention flicked from the invisible walls as it felt them press in.

"Who are you?" I wondered, looking down at the beast. He ignored me as the walls crept closer.

The beast dropped to his belly and let out a whine that broke even my cold dead heart.

The walls began to ripple. I glanced up.

Callum Hart stood, naked, banging his fists against the invisible barrier that separated him from the wolf. Desperate. Frantic. He did not notice as his knuckles began to bleed, smearing the boundary until the wall became visible with his blood.

I looked from the wolf to Hart.

They had the same eyes.

I jerked awake, the bird song of the early morning filtered

through the window. Callum Hart laid on the air mattress, his fists clenched, and his face screwed up as if he was in pain. Still caught in the throes of his nightmare.

I was not a creature made to nurture and comfort. I reached down and placed the palm of my hand against Hart's bare shoulder, hoping to soothe him, even if I did not understand what the dream had meant.

The second my skin made contact, Hart's face relaxed.

Was Callum Hart a wolf?

I had once thought that Hunters were human zealots that had a hard-on for killing things they didn't understand. That clearly wasn't the case.

Davenport's words ping-ponged around my mind. How Hunters were people touched by evil and Called away from it. To ensure a balance.

Good and evil were constructs.

I couldn't deny that I had felt a small spark of pleasure, of belonging, when Davenport had asked if I could be Called.

But then, Davenport thought I was a Mimic Sidhe. Not a Demon.

He would feel differently if he found out I was 100% Hellspawn.

Hugo was half-human. He straddled two worlds, belonging to both and neither.

I had been shunned from Hell. Running from my home with my tail between my legs. The cowardly Drude.

I had never felt so far apart from those around me.

Hart grunted again, my fingers jerked. His pained expression had come back the second I had broken skin contact.

Before I could think too heavily about it, finally happy to have found something I could actually *do*, I slipped off the sofa and onto the air mattress. Snuggling up next to Hart. His muscles relaxed, and his arm slung over mine.

I laid awake and looked at the Edison bulb, caged in a geometric copper cage. Very industrial. Jae had good taste.

As if my thoughts had summoned him, I felt eyes on

166

my face. A sweeping tingle. I pushed myself up onto my elbows. Hart moaned, disheartened at my movement, but he rolled over, and his breathing evened again.

Jae stood in the doorway, his shoulder pressed against the dark frame. He wore low slung jeans and a loose fitted cotton t-shirt. The sleeves were long, and they covered his hands. His thumbs poked through self-made holes in the wrist.

He crossed his arms over his chest. Jae glanced at Hart before his eyes settled on mine again.

"Nightmares?" Jae stepped forward, his violet eyes flicked to the lamp on the small table near his therapist's chair. It flared on without being touched. Magic.

I nodded silently. Unwilling to betray any more information.

Jae ignored the sofa, and the chesterfield chair, and instead dropped down onto his butt next to the air mattress. His legs sprawled out. So at odds with the earnest therapist mask, he wore when I first met him. I realized quickly that it was a barrier, a shield between him and the people he could read.

"Callum's latent." Jae smiled softly, but it did not reach his violet eyes. "A bit of wolf. Bit of Hell hound. Mostly human."

"Latent?" I understood the word, but not the context. Latent: to exist, but undeveloped. Hidden or concealed.

My nose scrunched in confusion.

"Callum can't shift," Jae said. Hesitance in his voice, as if he wasn't sure with his decision to tell me. "He's closest to his dogs, but he can never run with them. He is Kin, but not."

I turned to watch the sleeping man with newly found sympathy and respect. "I can't imagine," I whispered. Thinking about being unable to move through the wind, dust, and sky with my brother's and sisters. Watching their shadows but never being able to be one of them.

I felt the heartbreak of their loss again. Hart must have felt his own version of heartbreak every single day.

As if he could sense us talking about him, Callum Hart

choked, in pain, in his slumber.

"He's dreaming about his wolf," I said.

Jae nodded. His eyes studying mine. "What are you doing?" He asked, blithely. So innocent and unaccusing that my mind did not place it as a question.

I blinked. "Huh?"

"What are you doing, Mara?" Jae repeated the question. The burn of vanilla touched my lips as his magic twisted the air around us. It disappeared as soon as I noticed it. A slip in the Nephilim's control.

"I'm gone the second that the Ifrit is dealt with." I pulled a stray thread from the edge of my trouser pocket. "I'm not here to make friends. I'm not one of you."

"Callum doesn't 'do' people." Jae's voice was full of longing sorrow. "He avoids others. He does not bond easily with Humans. He is hurt the most by callous words and aggression. Though you would never know it. He does not get close to people. But you..."

"We aren't close," I argued. "Him and Frankie probably—"

"Hart moved to Team P because he could not stand to look into Corporal Gardiner's eyes every day and know that he had failed her. She refused to let him administer first aid. She refused his apology. Frankie called him pathetic. A mutant mutt. She was horrid."

"Maybe there was something there, under the surface—" I argued, before being interrupted with a single look. I imagined a biology professor being told that evolution didn't exist would have a similar expression. Patient but superior.

"There was nothing there. Not then. But now?" Jae quirked a brow.

"He thinks I'm her."

"He knows, deep down, that you're not." Jae rebuffed.

My brow furrowed as I stared down at my hands. Hart's uncomfortable look when he had seen the tattoo raced through my mind. He had accused me twice of being someone

168

other than Frankie Gardiner. He was adamant. When he had seen the tattoo, he looked blindsided.

"What do you hope to achieve?" I asked bitterly. "I can't stay here. I'm temporary. You'll never see my true face. I could walk past you next week, next year, and you would never know it's me."

Jae smiled softly and shook his head. "Mara," He chided. "We'd know it was you."

I pouted. "Unlikely. I'm a master of subterfuge."

Jae snorted. "Right."

"Seriously."

"Of course."

I reached over and tugged the blanket over my shoulders. Turning my back of the Nephilim. I closed my eyes.

Jae pushed himself onto the now-vacant sofa and got comfortable.

After a moment of silence, I spoke. "I've noticed your bookshelves are looking a little bare..." I allowed my words to trail off.

Jae swore under his breath. A Korean curse that I did not know, but I recognized the tone of a dirty word when I heard one. Hart shifted in his sleep.

"You're the one that's been stealing my erotica?" He hissed. Keeping his voice low.

I hummed but did not answer.

Something hard dug into my back, and the skin under my ear tickled. I reached up to push my hair away from my face, only to encounter a mass of russet strands that did not belong to my host's body.

Callum Hart's hair had fallen out of his ponytail holder in the night. The poker straight locks tumbled around his shoulders. I was envious of the quality of his hair. Frankie's was wavy, but when I had tried to brush it, it had gone out of control.

Some of the products in her bathroom had worked, but it had been a case of trial and error. Even following the instructions, my host's hair did not look as good as the beautiful black women on the bottles.

Hart looked more peaceful than I had ever seen him. His rosy lips parted in sleep.

I wriggled, feeling too hot, as I kicked off the comforter. It took a second to realize that someone had come up behind me, cocooning my body with their warmth. Jae had slipped off the couch in the night and had joined us. I was sandwiched between Hart, tucked into his large body, and pressed against the leonine, more feminine frame of Jae. And Jae's erection was pressed against the small of my back.

Jae had reached over in the night, his hand rested on Hart's. Their entwined fingers told me that it wasn't the first time they had slept in the same bed. My brows raised. I had not expected that. Though Jae and Hart were similar if I really thought about it. Somehow their intimacy both intrigued, aroused, and warmed me.

Jae shifted. His breath tickled the hollow of my ear. Deep and slow. Still asleep.

My eyes fluttered as I debated whether to go back to sleep. The sunrise had cast the room in dim light. My sleep had already been erratic. Thrown from many dreams.

My eyes met Hart's orange ones. He was awake. His expression was soft and vulnerable in the morning light. Far from the stoic man I typically saw.

We were close enough to share the same breath. I couldn't have said who had moved first, but Hart's lips pressed against mine. His stubble tickled my chin, his tongue pressed against mine tentatively, as if seeking permission.

Hart rocked his body into mine. The evidence of his arousal pressed into my stomach. I raised a leg and hooked it around his waist. Feeling his hand pressed against my hip, still entwined with Jae's.

I squirmed as the kiss grew more profound. Our heads tilted. Our chests pressed together. Disturbed, Jae began to wake. His hardness pushed into my back and reminded me of his presence.

The two men shifted, pressing against me.

A light brush of fingers moving my hair away from my neck. A fluttering set of lips pressed against the seam of my jaw. The physical sensation was too much. I was lost in it. The taste of Hart's lips. The tingling of the soft skin of my mouth and his divine taste. The undulating press of Jae's magic, as it rolled down my body. No words needed. Hart and Jae untwined their hands. Hart reached up to grip my cheeks. To position my head where he wanted. His touch loving, as if he did not want to let go lest I dissolve into nothingness.

Jae's fingers spread until his hand spanned across my flat stomach. With a jarring oomph, he pulled me back into his body until there was no room between us.

Slowly, his finger teased the waistband of my trousers.

"What is it that you want, *my love*?" The endearment was said in Korean.

Nae Sarang.

내 사랑

I broke free from Callum Hart's kiss to take a breath. The large man moved his lips to the column of my throat. Laying laboriously slow kisses along my pulse line.

"I want to be touched," I admitted. Closing my eyes as I revealed the most profound truth. "Touch me. Don't stop touching me."

I was drunk on the slow, sliding, feeling of Jae's rough fingers as they explored my soft skin. Dipping under the waistband of my cargo pants, but not removing them. The tight press of another man against my front, combined with the confinement of clothes, meant that Jae's movements were restricted. Somehow it made the light brushes of his tentative touching all the more elicit.

Jae rose up, bending over until his lips pressed to mine. I craned my head back to meet his mouth. His taste was different from Hart's. His kiss felt different too. Hart was deep and tender. Jae was an unleashed, raw, clacking of teeth. A fiery passion. Needy and frantic.

Hart's fingers dipped under the hem of my cotton t-shirt, bringing the fabric up my torso until it rested on my collarbone. My nipples were already hard, but the cold air and their exposure made them tingle and throb. Begging to be touched.

Hart's warm mouth wrapped around the stiff peak, his hand gripped my other breast, and his callused hands tweaked my nipple. Making my body jolt and core tingle.

The realization that I was bleeding from my vagina like a wounded soldier was enough to break through the fog of my lust. Making me flush in embarrassment. I had never been touched in a way that set my soul on fire before.

But was I really being touched?

It wasn't my body sandwiched between two men that had escaped death with me the night before. It was Frankie Gardiner's.

They didn't know the true me. The real me.

The flames of my arousal were doused with an ice bucket of realization.

As much as I wanted them. Hart, Jae, and Hugo. It could *not* happen.

I gripped Jae's wrist. Halting his teasing motions, pulling it free from my waistband. I kept my eyes down as I broke away from the two men. Shifting to the edge of the bed without a word. I righted my clothes.

"Frankie?" Hart sounded adorably confused, his words tinged with worry for me. Jae held out his hand, halting his friend's movement towards me.

"It's okay," Jae assured me. "We can stop."

I nodded, the movement frantic with my need to run.

My eyes darted to Hart's and then back to Jae's.

Jae got the message. "Callum, could you step outside for a minute?"

The mountain man opened his mouth to argue, before deciding against it with a solemn nod. He smiled tightly as he stepped out of the room.

"Are you alright, Mara?" Jae scooted forward, decidedly not touching me. He used my real name for the first time in the whole evening, I noticed. He had not called me Mara in front of Hart. A fact I now realized I was grateful for.

I blinked slowly. My tongue felt too big for my mouth. "It's not *my* face," I whispered, pressing the meat of my palms into my eye sockets and rubbing until I saw a dancing kaleidoscope of colors. "You're touching me, but not *me*."

Jae nodded solemnly. Slow realization dawning on his face. "You're wearing a disguise. Someone else's face." He noted.

"Someone that you both knew." I spat.

"That isn't what this is about," Jae said softly. "This isn't about Frankie."

I wanted to believe him, but I couldn't. It was the same story, but with another man. We sat in silence, the distant sounds of kitchen cabinets opening and closing could be heard from the other side of the cabin. The crash of a mug and a grunted curse word.

A few minutes later, Hart returned, a strange expression on his face. He rubbed the wrinkled material of his shirt, right over his heart. Scratching his chest, like an irritating scab.

My chest filled up like a lead balloon.

I couldn't have marked another man, could I? Bond marks didn't just happen. Soulmates didn't just happen. Monogamous pairings were rare. I knew only of one triad pairing. Had I done something? Had my desperation for contact, and affection, somehow tied my lifespan to two different men? Two Hunters?

173

I didn't have a chance to ask.

The front door of the cabin burst open. Hugo rushed through, his gaze frantic before settling on mine. When he saw that I was whole and healthy, his whole body relaxed. Davenport stepped through a few seconds later. He surveyed the rumbled clothing, the air mattress and the scent of sex, with no emotion on his face. Davenport crossed his arms over his chest.

"Watchtower reported your vehicle returned last night, in tatters." Davenport gave us all a look that could freeze water. "Why was I not informed?"

Chapter 12

After we were called into Davenport's office in the main building, Jae and Hart leaped into an explanation about the car crash, the dark shadow, and the invisible attacker.

I couldn't exactly explain that I had smelt *wishes*. That the metaphysical concept of a wish had a tangible effect on my senses. Old coins and dying flames. The scent conjured the mental image of a burning pile of blood-stained ancient coins, each one with dead ruler stamped into the metal.

Davenport had waved away the explanation and demanded that Dr. Lee and Sgt Hart get back to work. Davenport's dark gaze was inscrutable as he watched the two men leave.

I struggled to maintain eye contact when I remembered the previously forgotten warning that the commander had issued. A thinly veiled demand that I retain distance from his Hunters.

Davenport tented his fingers; his elbows rested on the lip of his desk. He pressed his lips to his clasped hands and inhaled deeply. He closed his eyes for a long minute. I waited in silence, but it was as if I was not in the room.

"Was there anything you wanted to add?" Davenport asked. His eyes remained closed.

The sound I made sounded like a cross between a gurgle and a question mark. It must have been my lack of a father figure because the gravitas that Davenport welded—the unsaid command of every part of his body and existence—made me want to roll on my belly and call him Daddy.

"Was there anything that you could not say in front of Dr. Lee or Sgt Hart?" Davenport clarified. His words held no inflection.

"It smelt like wishes," I explained.

Davenport made a thoughtful sound. The statement was vague enough to belong to a Fae. The Fair Folk had brilliant senses. He didn't need to know that I could *taste* magic.

"You're certain?"

"Yes." I cleared my throat.

"After your first session with Dr. Lee, it has become apparent that he is aware of your identity." He continued as if I hadn't spoken. "Unless Corporal Gardiner had suffered a psychotic break, it was unlikely that she would have changed so abruptly. You have forced my hand. Not to mention that you also told the man outright."

"You think that Jae could be behind this?" I could not keep the incredulous hitch out of my voice.

Davenport shot me down with a look. "That is beside the point."

"You put me in *therapy*." I hissed. "What did you want me to do?"

"I do not have to justify my decisions to you." Davenport leaned back. The picture of calm serenity. "We need to maintain appearances for the sake of the entire operation. Please refrain from telling anyone else. You, as a *Mimic Sidhe*, one of Dermot Dirk's mercenaries, should be capable of that."

I huffed and blew a lock of hair away from my face. Davenport reached into his filing cabinet and produced a document. He slapped it onto the desk and opened it up at a page of a crime scene.

"Tell me what you see."

I rose off my seat to look down at the various photos. A blood-stained crime scene. Burn marks. Salt and dead animals. No markings. I remembered the motivational posters on the walls of the tiny office, a computer and a desk that must have belonged to a long-defunct company.

"I don't understand." I breathed, flicking through every single photo. "I saw the markings before. Hugo projected the image of the crime scene. The summoning circle was right *there*."

"Wax chalk." He explained. "Invisible once activated. To all eyes. Except those with Demon Blood."

A roll of sweat ran down my forehead and then my cheek. I restrained the urge to wipe it away with the back of my hand. I locked my muscles. Beating down any urge to squirm or shift.

Did Davenport know?

Did he suspect?

My eyes darted to the exits before I could control myself. I licked my lips. They were dry.

"Hugo is a Demon," I said without emphasis. "I saw his memories."

Davenport nodded as if confirming something, shutting the manila file. He stood up, placing the sleeve of documents back into the filing cabinet. The metallic door closed with a soft snick.

Davenport turned to face me, resting his hip against the side of his desk. "Have you thought more about what I've said?"

I cocked my head to the side, confused.

"About becoming a Hunter?" Davenport elaborated with a patient smile.

I blinked a few times. My mouth parted in an O. "No."

Davenport bent at the waist until our faces were only a foot apart. His eyes burned into mine as he took in every aspect of my face. "My team could use someone like you."

"Someone who can be anyone?" I spoke delicately to hide the hurt I felt. "Wear any face?"

Davenport continued. His words were soft and carefully measured. A rebuff. "Someone with knowledge of Demonic rituals. Someone loyal to my Hunters. Someone who doesn't crumble under pressure." He listed. "Hart told me that you didn't panic when you encountered the Ifrit. You didn't start screaming or try to escape. You didn't draw attention to yourself. You identified the threat immediately."

177

I'd never heard of my proficiency at fleeing described as a positive attribute.

"Hart mentioned that your aim was also particularly good," Davenport said.

My heart sank. That skill belonged to my host, not me.

"Would I have to follow orders?" I asked sweetly. "I don't think I would be too good at that."

Davenport's lip twitched. "My Hunters are not slaves. They have some discretion when it comes to following the chain of command. That said, following orders helps everyone."

"I don't think I could follow orders." I pouted.

"Then, you might be punished." His gaze darkened. His face was so close to mine that I had a front-row seat as his eyes turned to ink. Dark and deep.

"I'm not a Hunter. You can't punish me." I replied. My hands gripped the armrests of the chair. I had twisted and moved closer to Davenport without realizing.

To an outside audience, Davenport sat casually against his desk, I was positioned in front of him, on the chair. Somehow, it felt a lot more intimate than that.

"I'm certain I could punish you. If I were so inclined." Davenport murmured, his knuckles gripped the edge of the desk, firmly in place.

"Hmm." I hummed. "Really, Daddy?"

Davenport licked his bottom lip. His eyes sparkled. The height difference began to bother me. That, or the intense stare-off. I stood up, but that brought my body closer to his.

Transfixed, we focused on each other. Davenport reached out. His fingers brushed against my arm, and then my waist, leaving a trail of heat racing through my body.

"Are you certain that you don't like to be punished?" Davenport asked quietly. "Sometimes, people require discipline."

"Do you punish all of your Hunters like this?" My brows rose as I plastered a sickly sweet smile on my face.

His eyes darkened. "No." He said. "Put both of your hands on the desk. Palms flat."

178

I swallowed deeply. Unable to think of a single reason why I shouldn't do what he had said. I *wanted* to. There was something dark, sexual, and twisted about being his to command. Something about his darkness, his strong confidence, that told me that he would take good care of me. I could be his possession. His to position and play with as he saw fit.

I took two steps past the chair and placed my hands flat on the desk. Swiping his files away and onto the floor in the act of childish rebellion. Davenport pushed his tongue between his teeth. Surveying the scene. His baring had changed slightly. He stood, moving with a swagger that he had not had before, as if he had slipped on a persona that fit him like a glove. I had heard the term before. Domme. I wiggled, unable to control my apprehension.

Davenport placed his hand against my rump. Following the curve of my bottom with an appraising stroke.

"Mara." He said my name like the crack of a whip. "Do you want this?"

The words themselves were innocent enough, but they felt like a cliff's edge.

"Do your worst, commander." I teased. "Give me your punishment."

Davenport gripped my waist and pulled my bottom into the curve of his hips. He leaned over, his larger hands rested on the outside of my own. "As you wish." He purred. His hardness pressed against the crack of my ass for just a second, before the air charged and I waited with bated breath for the swing.

"There's someone here to see you, Commander Davenport." A tinny voice broke through the tension. "Andrew Jarman, from the armory."

The commander cleared his throat. "Thank you, Betty." He replied, pressing the button on the intercom.

I flushed from head to toe as I straightened. Embarrassed and angry with myself. I had almost done what I had sworn I would not do. Get involved with a Hunter. With

179

someone that would never see or accept my true self.

Losing my virginity didn't seem important anymore. When I had added sex to my 'to do' list, I hadn't thought about what that meant. Using a human host and having a meaningless orgy had seemed like a good idea at the time. A way to sate my curiosity and lust for connection. Frankie Gardiner's soul had left the building. If I evacuated her body for any reason, she would be dead. I was a pilot to an empty vessel. Finders keepers, right?

But I didn't want to sleep with someone that could never accept me.

I was a Demon. A fact I told myself often to comfort myself. Demons were strong. Demons were powerful. Even if I was the weakest type of Demon, the pitiful Drude, being the lowest of a strong race was better than being the strongest of a weak one.

I ducked under Davenport's arm and escaped the room, with my cheeks flushed and my eyes forward.

The Mess Hall was bustling with the morning breakfast rush, as I weaved through the crowd and joined the end of the line for food. My mind drifted as I thought about what I had almost done. I was walking a path that was already razor-thin.

The line moved, and I shuffled forward, only to trip on someone's heels and end up with a mouthful of hair. I spat it out, tasting the plastic residue of whatever product had been in the strategically shaggy blonde mop.

"Frankie." Riley glanced over at Chloe, who's hair I had almost eaten. She said my host's name as a greeting. An acknowledgment. Aloof and cool. Something I could never hope to achieve.

I wiggled my fingers. "Hey, Riley—still planning my death?"

She rolled her eyes. "Obviously."

"God, she's such a freak." Chloe slapped Riley's arm as if I couldn't hear her. Shooting a glance my way, she bestowed her benevolent wisdom unto me. "Look where you're going." She hissed.

I cocked my head to the side. "Why would I do that?" I asked innocently. I covered my mouth and leaned in as if I was letting her in on a secret. "Your hair smells like coconuts."

Chloe shivered and turned away, flicking her hair over her shoulder. She uttered one last *'idiot'* remark, but no more.

I gave Riley a toothy grin. "Thanks for the save the other day."

She surveyed her nails. Bored. "Uh-huh."

Maybe we weren't going to be besties. Which sucked. She had anger and nice hair. I wanted to be Riley Fisher when I grew up. But, you know, without the dead boyfriend.

The line shifted again, and Chloe moved with it. I stepped forward, but a hand clasped my bicep.

"What did you mean when you said they think the attack came from one of the Hunters?" Riley whispered, so low that I had to strain to catch the words.

I surveyed our surroundings to see if we would be overheard. It looked clear.

"It's a Wish Demon," I replied simply.

Riley swore. "And?"

"And someone has to actually make the wish for it to be granted." I licked my bottom lip.

Riley looked around as if seeing her fellow Hunters in a new light.

"Did Hambone have any enemies?" I whispered.

Riley shook her head but paused during the motion to think about it. "One of the guys had an abusive ex. She was a civilian though. She wouldn't know *how* to summon a Demon." Riley murmured thoughtfully.

"You'd be surprised." I quirked a brow.

"Greyson Marsh." Riley ignored me and continued.

181

"There was a Fae on the team. Conrad Neilly. I always thought that you two had a thing..." She allowed her words to trail off.

"I'm asexual." I lied.

Riley snorted. "Babe—I've seen you with men. You're as asexual as a dolphin pumped full of Viagra."

"Dolphins *are* oddly sexual creatures." I tilted my head to the side. "Would Viagra even work on a dolphin?"

The line shifted, luckily Riley and I remained on the end of it. Alone.

"Conrad was Fae. Fae don't typically work with Demons." I said.

Riley shrugged. "Gary from the canteen? You were pretty harsh when you rejected him a few months ago."

I narrowed my eyes at the hairnet wearing mouth breather behind the hot food trays on the other side of the canteen. He continued to spoon out green beans, unaware he was the subject of our conversation.

"Gary." I spat his name like a curse.

Riley laughed, before slapping her hand over her mouth, shocked by her reaction.

"Or Callum?" Riley suggested. "You and he had this weird hatred, unspoken enemies going on for a while. Honestly? You were kind of a bitch."

I rolled my eyes to the ceiling before remembering that I did not pray to God. Frankie had not been a pleasant person to work with, it seemed.

Chloe turned around, finally realizing that Riley was not by her side. Chloe hissed her friend's name until it got the petite Latina's attention. Riley gave me a look of sympathy before she swanned off to join her friend.

I chose a chocolate bar and a banana for my lunch, not trusting the green beans after Gary caught my eyes from across the room. I specifically picked up a blue energy to taunt Remi with. I had noticed that he had been avoiding them since my mouth wash prank.

Hugo and Remi sat alone on a table in the corner.

Heads hunched over in private conversation. When I was halfway across the room, I realized that maybe I should not disturb them. My fear evaporated when Remi glanced up and waved me over with a bright smile. Despite my insistence on keeping some distance between myself and the Hunters—I found myself poking the hornet's nest.

I danced over, placing my bright blue Gatorade on the table in front of Remi. His hand reached out.

"Mine." I sang, snatching it away.

Remi widened his eyes, affecting a puppy dog stare. "Frankie..." He coaxed with his deep voice. Molasses and the lowest piano note. "Want to trade?" Remi pushed a reusable coffee mug in my direction. Steam curled into the air. Caffeine was hard to ignore—especially when it came in a form that wouldn't turn my tongue blue.

"The coffee machine is out of order." I narrowed my eyes.

"Brought this from home."

I plucked the plastic mug from the table. Pushing the blue energy drink in Remi's direction. I peeled my banana and ate it slowly. Winking when Remi caught my eye.

I felt eyes on the crown of my skull. I glanced up at Hugo. The incubus stared down at his food, awkwardly pushing a tater tot from one end of his tray to the other. "Hewey-loo." I beamed. "I haven't seen you in ages."

Remi gave me a look that informed me that my aloof attitude was coming off as anything but. Did Hugo know I had spent most nights outside his dorm, straddling the desire to talk to him? To claim him as my mate and reveal all my darkest secrets, all while battling my inner coward. The little voice that demanded that I run far and fast—possibly stealing as much as I could on the way.

I'd once spotted a small armored tank in the parking lot. I didn't know what I would do with a tank, but I could think of something.

"Frankie," Hugo nodded stiffly and did not meet my

eyes.

My brow scrunched. "I thought that you'd been cleared after the attack?"

Hugo hummed non-committedly. His attention was elsewhere. A shard of hurt nestled itself between my ribs. Hugo had seemed so awed when he had danced with my starlight. Tangled with my darkness as he had shown me his own troubled past.

I wondered if I had done something to upset him—it took a few moments before I realized that I was Frankie at that moment. Not the Mara that Hugo knew.

Hugo stood up, gave a half-hearted wave, and a whispered goodbye. His head ducked down as he bussed his tray and walked away.

"Hugo is quieter than usual," I noted thoughtfully.

"I wouldn't worry about it." Remi shrugged. "Apparently, he's been having some side effects from his run-in with the Ifrit."

"Like what?" I demanded. Thinking of the blood that I had given Hugo and all of the ways in which that had possibly gone wrong.

Remi's gaze turned uncharacteristically shrewd. "Incubus dreams." He squinted. "Why? Do you know anything?"

I shook my head, my lips pulled into a false smile. I did not think he bought it.

"He'll be right as rain soon, love." Remi patted my head, messing up my hair with a gruff chuckle. "I've only just met the guy, but I can tell he isn't an arsehole. He'll be back to your friendly Sinclair in no time."

I shifted in my seat, turning back to my meal. "Whatever." I lifted my coffee and blew the steam away from the top, I took a deep slug and turned back to my food.

I paused. The coffee was odd. Different. My eyes widened, and I gagged. A metallic taste filled my mouth as blood pooled in my throat and made it hard to breathe.

"Ha! Got you!" Remi jumped up, pumping his fist. "I went against my British roots and went for the old salt in the coffee trick that you Americans love much—" He rambled.

My chest heaved, and the tight press of my lips spluttered. A mouthful of blood dripped from my teeth. The spittle flew across the table and marred the faded cream table surface.

Remi's face fell. He darted forward. "Frankie?" He whispered in horror. "Oh my god. Frankie?!"

My esophagus was burning with the fury of a thousand papercuts. Blood continued to pour from my lips. Demons and salt did not mix.

For a second, I had believed that I had been poisoned again. Instead, it was a prank gone wrong. A joke that would reveal my true nature. I scrambled back, fight, or flight instincts battling against one another.

Darkness edged around my vision. I reached forward to grip the table as the world tilted sideways. Remi cradled my body, whispering frantic and rhythmic magical words.

He swore under his breath. My eyes struggled to focus. I felt a warm drop on my face. A tear. I reached up to touch Remi's face. Staring into his impossibly dark eyes, I passed out.

I woke up, wrapped in a scratchy blanket. Swathed in the scent of disinfectant. Moaning, I brought my hand to my mouth. My throat constricted, causing me to wince. Salt restricted Demon magic. If the pain was anything to go by, my accelerated healing had been compromised.

My eyelids felt heavy like two little gnomes had decided to set up camp on my face.

The faint smelt of burning plastic, tinged with sage and lavender, hung on the air. Like an out of date air freshener.

"Frankie?" Hugo whispered gently when I opened my

mouth to test my facial muscles. The shock of his voice made my eyes open wide.

The incubus sat in a visitor's chair in the corner. He glanced over to the closed curtain. "Remi just stepped out," Hugo informed me as if I had asked a question. "He's been using too much magic."

Hugo Sinclair looked anywhere but in my eyes. In fact, he seemed to be deliberately avoiding them. Too many possible reasons fluttered around my mind, like chaotic butterflies.

"Do you want some water?" He asked, already moving to the jug on the bedside cabinet. Hugo did not wait for a response before pushing a Styrofoam cup into my hands, awkwardly sloshing water over my hand.

I reached out, as if on instinct, and gripped his sleeve with my free hand. The connection, a tugging hook under my third rib, flared to life.

Hugo jerked back.

"What's wrong?" I whispered, unable to speak at a reasonable volume due to the damage in my throat.

Hugo swallowed before closing his eyes and exhaling. "We're friends, right?"

I cocked my head to the side and stayed silent. Deciding to save my voice.

"We went out once. As friends. To a bar. You tease me. You smart off. You've completely and infuriatingly changed since you came back from the hospital, but still—" Hugo's cheeks flushed pink as he stopped his sentence mid-word. He clenched his fists and took a step back. "Remi told me that you came to see me after I was attacked. That you were wearing..." he waved a hand and made a pained noise. "Almost nothing."

I quirked a brow. I'd once bent over and shown a bellhop the ball sack of a middle-aged Italian gangster. Nudity meant less than nothing to me.

Hugo continued. "You've been hanging around the officer's dormitories. Trying to see me. The cameras show that you've been there every night. I would like you to stop."

186

I didn't understand the point he was trying to make. "Why?"

Hugo rubbed his hand over his face. "I am an incubus. I have had this problem time and time again. It's not *you*. People get enamored. They follow me. Start to obsess."

My nostrils flared as I held back laughter, confident that my nervous giggles would not be taken well due to the situation. My own *mate* didn't want me around?

"You want me to stay away from you?" I asked carefully, as the gravity of the situation sank in slowly. Hugo Sinclair was rejecting me.

I felt sick.

Hugo's ice blue eyes flicked to mine before focusing on a spot above my head. "Whatever this is. It can't happen. Everything is different now. I've changed. It's all changed."

"Changed?" I repeated back.

Did Hugo realize that he was my soulmate? Was he going to deny the claim? Deny fate, the universe, and his heritage?

"I'm mated now." He pulled his t-shirt down, ruining the collar by stretching it to reveal his silvery scar. The Cyclian rune that connected his soul to mine.

"Right," I said without emotion. Unsure of where the conversation was heading.

"I'm attracted to you, sure. But you're not the one for me. You have to get over this obsession. My mate is the night sky, dreams, beautiful and wise. Immortal. Everything I want. You're... not."

My mouth opened to correct him. To tell him the truth. That the unrealistic being he was describing was me. The same person he was rejecting. I wanted to scream that *I* was his mate. That he was mine and always would be.

But the words died in my mouth. Burnt down to ash.

"She's a demon?" I asked. My voice croaked, and I was unsure if it was due to my injury or the conversation.

Hugo nodded.

187

"And you're a Hunter." I continued.

"Yes."

"You'd accept her?"

"She's mine." Hugo was full of conviction.

"It won't work," I said, bitterly. "You might be a Demon, but you've cast your lot with the people that kill them."

His eyes flashed with anger. "My mate will understand."

"Understand that you turned your back on your own kind so that you could 'redeem' yourself?" I bit out, fisting the blanket. Unable to control my mouth and not meaning any of the words that pushed past my lips. "A baby incubus who can't control his lure. Who won't even try? Your Demon half is starving, Cambion. That is the reason you cannot control it."

Hugo shook his head and stepped back. His expression twisted in pity.

"I'm sorry." He whispered. "I didn't realize that I had used my magic on you. Remi told me about the dreams..."

I pinched the bridge of my nose. "I'm not enthralled," I said, exasperated. "Go on. Reject me. That's what I want. You're too much hassle. I don't have time to hold your hand anyway."

When I looked up, Hugo was gone.

Something tickled my cheek. I reached up, and the pads of my fingers came away wet. I turned my hand over and studied it. Unsure of what was happening. Was I crying?

Hugo had done me a favor by walking away.

It gave me an excuse to stay away while I was in the compound. To play the wounded ex. The spurned suitor.

I had told myself that I would not accept the claim. That I would leave after Davenport found his snake in the grass. Hugo wanted a perfect mate, and I certainly wasn't that.

When my cluster had died... My world had ended.

I wouldn't survive the loss of the one soul that the universe had tied to mine.

Silent tears continued to roll down my cheeks, and

before long, the salty water dried and stung. My breaths became pathetic hiccups.

I wasn't even sure why it hurt so much. Why it felt like I was dying from an invisible gaping wound.

I had been inside of Frankie Gardiner for too long. I was beginning to forget who and what I was.

Remi found me an hour later standing on top of my bed, pretending to surf. My arms outstretched and eyes closed. He pulled the curtain back, carrying a few of the erotic novels that I had stolen from Jae. He had a change of clothes slung over his arm.

I was stir crazy, my skin itched like a swarm of fire ants were crawling over my skin.

Being taken out by a few tablespoons of salt had done a number on my reserves. I needed to *feed* asap.

Unfortunately, the sun was still in the sky, and I could not sense any sleeping people around. I was going out of my mind. Manic energy charged through my body, trying to push my true form out through my pores. My skinsuit felt ill-fitting. Too tight and too loose at the same time.

"Frankie, honey?" Remi said tentatively as he approached my bed with cautious steps. "Are you feeling alright?"

My eyes darted to his. My lips lifted into a jaunty crooked smile. "Never better, old friend." I mimicked his British accent.

"Are you sure?"

"Just hungry." I sat on my bed, bouncing once before crossing my legs.

Remi's guilt was a tangible heaviness. It tasted like chalky love-hearts candy.

"I'll go get you something to eat." He suggested. "I promise to check it for poison."

I stifled a laugh. They thought I had been poisoned? At least they didn't know the real reason I had been puking blood. "Hugo was just here," I said, feigning disinterest. "Apparently, you told him I was stalking him."

Remi's guilt intensified. "To be honest, I thought he would be flattered."

"Right." I picked at the skin of my thumb. "He joyfully informed me that he never wanted to see me again."

Remi's gaze darkened. "He said that?"

"More or less." I shrugged. "It's okay. I'll be gone soon, and he can go back to his pitiful existence. Waiting for his Soulmate."

His brow quirked. "He told you about the mysterious woman that's been visiting his dreams?"

I scratched my arm, about to burst out of my skin. "Uh-huh."

"You don't think she's his mate?"

"He's got the mark." I chewed my bottom lip, worrying it until I drew blood. Unable to contain myself, I pushed away from the bed and began to pace. Remi held out his hands; he made a *'Woah'* sound, like someone in a movie if they wanted to calm a horse.

"Are you sure?" Remi looked dubious. "I thought you hadn't been enthralled, but now I'm not sure."

I exhaled sharply. "It's not that," I mumbled and threw my hands up in the air. Frustrated and full of energy.

Remi stepped forward. He gripped both of my hands and held my eyes. "Frankie, you're all over the place. Take a deep breath."

I closed my eyes. My teeth gritted. Remi wrapped his arms around me. Holding me tightly. Giving me comfort. I found myself relaxing into his embrace.

"Am I still crying?" I asked.

"Yes." Remi laughed.

"Damn."

"I'm sure Hugo didn't mean to hurt your feelings." Remi stroked my hair. "He doesn't know what he wants."

I hummed but did not argue.

"He was the first one here. When he heard that you'd

collapsed..."

"Remi?"

"Yes, love?"

"Shut up."

His chin rested on my head. I gripped his shirt. It was wet with human tears. Drops of water that I could not control.

"Don't worry, love." Remi murmured. I wanted to hold onto him forever. It would be so easy to reach back and press my lips against his. To feel his hands against my skin. To roll in the sheets, high on touch and laughter.

I glanced up through tear-stained lashes. Remi brought his palm up to my face and rested it gently against my cheek. Caught in each other's orbit, I wanted my Remi. He made everything better. My only constant.

Was I greedy? Yes. *Hello*. Demon.

I hi-coughed. Remington Weber pulled away, holding my shoulders so that he could survey my face.

"I'm going to get the doctor." Remi stood. His tone brokered no argument.

My head bobbed in a parody of a nod. "Yeah. Maybe something to eat as well? I'm *starving*."

At least that was the truth.

Remi stepped backward; he glanced back once—reluctant to leave. I gave him a sad smile before I began to pace again. The electric energy in my chest was back.

I wanted to reach out with both hands. Tell Hugo that *I* was his soulmate. Tell Remi that he belonged to me—that I had his back. To hug the stoic Hart and tell him that his latency didn't matter. To look Jae in the eye, and tell him that I saw *him*—not just the genteel therapist, but the wicked and cheeky man underneath.

And Davenport...?

What was the problem? I wondered. Oh. Just the tiny little fact I was masquerading as a Hunter, wearing someone's skin-suit to try and catch a murderer while simultaneously falling for several of the men around me.

I screeched to a halt.

Falling for them?

That couldn't be.

Abandoning one mate to save both of our lives was one thing—my mind flashed to Hart, scratching his chest after we had almost slept together. I couldn't have more than one mate, could I?

Demons only had one Soulmate, as a rule. But every rule has exceptions.

Baphomet-kin were twins but had one soul split between two bodies. Naturally, they would mate in a triad.

Demons were not monogamous. Drudes did not engage in physical relations at all, it wasn't possible. Our relationships were entirely platonic. Our cluster was a cloud of demons, ebbing, and flowing in number.

It was rare for a Drude to break away from their cluster. I was abnormal by those standards.

Hugo was an outsider, like me.

Callum Hart was latent. Without power. Without a home. Like me.

I rubbed my hand over my face.

I couldn't do it anymore. It was too much too soon. I wanted to abandon Frankie's body and go back to my life in the city.

Wearing various humans. Doing pointless jobs for Dermot Dirk and eating in luxurious restaurants every night. To hover in the corner of strip clubs and bars, watching the world unfold.

I wanted to pour hot sauce on pancakes and not have to answer questions.

My hands began to tremble. My teeth started to chatter.

I needed to do something before my eyes turned to black oil slicks, and I attacked the first person I saw, flowing through their tear ducts and ripping their mind apart to get to the juicy subconscious underneath the tedium of their personality.

The window was easy enough to Jimmy open. Hidden by the curtains, invisible to the rest of the ward, I made sure to be as quiet as possible. I climbed out, with difficulty. The cold air rushed up my back and reminded me that I wore a backless paper gown.

Best to end an adventure in the same way it started. Dressed like a hospital patient. The only thing missing was a toe-tag, but the second I reached the City, I'd abandon Frankie Gardiner so hard that her body would have road rash.

I didn't bother to escape through the woods. I had no survival training in the Human Realities. I occupied a body that needed to eat, drink, and shit. I did not fancy my chances of survival in the wilderness.

I bypassed the watchtowers with my shoulders pulled straight. As if I had all the time in the world, and I was right where I was meant to be. The confidence must have worked because I was unaccosted as I walked the worn dirt road through the forest. My feet bled, torn apart by tiny rocks and pieces of gravel. Every step was accompanied by a wince. I did not care.

It took a few hours to get to an actual concrete road. Boxed in by trees, I recognized the single lane that led to Maywood.

I stood on the edge of the road, hopping from foot to foot as I waited for a car to pass. I had been walking for an hour when a large semi roared around the bend. I stuck my hand out like I had seen people do in movies.

The sun was setting. I didn't want to have to go back to the compound with swirling rage and hunger rolling about my body. The semi pulled to a slow stop twenty yards away from my position.

I did not hesitate to scramble across the verge to hop inside. I had clicked my seatbelt on when I looked across the cab at the driver.

"Where are you heading, ma'am?" His lips curled up in what was meant to be a reassuring smile. The semi had already pulled away and was rumbling down the road before I had even

193

said a word.

"New York." I blinked, cocking my head to the side to survey the middle-aged man.

Yellowing eyes, the signs of a heavy drinker. A nose with a lump that told me he'd broke it more than once. He was slim, but his arms sagged in a way that told me it was from genetics and not any effort on his part.

The cab smelled like stale cigarettes. The trucker tasted like Lust and Wrath. A combination that would not play out well for any young woman.

At least he had picked me up and not someone else.

"I'm heading to Staten Island, myself." He reached over to the ashtray and fished out a lone cigarette. Creased in the middle. "What's your name?"

"Frankie." My fingers trembled. I glanced out the window, unsure of how long I could keep a handle on myself.

"Duane." His smile showed every one of his teeth. The front one was cracked, but Duane appeared to have good dental habits. "What brings a pretty little thing like you to the middle of the garden state?"

I shrugged.

"Running from an ex?"

I shot him a look, and Duane let out a dark chuckle.

"Why else would a woman be hitchhiking nowadays?" He lit his cigarette and carefully blew the smoke out of the crack in the window. He did not ask if I minded. His eyes flicked down to my trembling fingers.

"Or rehab." He suggested. "You've got the twitches, missy."

I stifled a snort. That was an understatement. "Just drive."

"No need to be rude." Duane chided softly, but his questions stopped. The sun set slowly; the trees growing long shadows across the road before darkness fell.

We did not pass Maywood, but continued to the freeway, merging with the traffic and sitting in comfortable silence. I watched the signs for NYC and made a note of the miles.

"So, there's this guy," I said, my mouth forming my life story without being able to stop. I had been silent for weeks. With no one to talk to about my dilemma. No one knew my true nature. "I kind of like him. He's hot, but he isn't a player. His name is Hugo. We were getting on well, and then suddenly, he's like 'boom! Actually I like this other girl.' And I'm like... 'Oh okay.' But that other girl is me, and he doesn't know that."

Duane gave me a long look. "Uh-huh."

"So, I got pissed that he rejected me." I rambled, manic, with the need to consume sin and terror. "But he didn't really reject me if you see what I mean?"

My fingernails dug into my thighs through the thin fabric of my hospital paper gown.

"Not even a little bit, missy." Duane smiled, the hairs on the back of my neck rose. "Are you talking about one of those online dating profile things?"

"Is there a motel around here?" I asked with a crack in my voice. Motels meant sleeping people. I could feed easily and without hurting anyone.

Duane chuckled darkly. "That's what I was thinking, missy." He pulled over to a layby. The locks clicked home. I did not move. "How do you suppose you're going to pay me for driving you all the way to New York?"

"We've been driving for an hour," I said dryly.

"Payment in advance."

I gave a long put upon sigh. Pinching the bridge of my nose. "I'm giving you a chance to turn around and stop whatever it is you've got planned."

Duane gripped the back of my neck. His other hand fumbled with his zipper. "I've got a knife right here. You suck my cock real good, and we've got no problems."

I narrowed my eyes. "You've done this before?" My tone was mildly interested as best. Duane answered by forcing my head nearer to his semi-hard penis. A wave of male musk, old cheese, and sweat hit my nostrils and made me gag.

My eyes turned black. My power bubbled to the surface, pushing smoke through my pores and lashing out with terror. My magic speared his mind like a blade, tearing apart the soft outer layers of his personality. Pulling the screaming subconscious to the surface. Nightmares did not have to make sense, they just *were*.

Blood began to leak from his eyes as I purged his mind, churning the fertile ground with my hooked claws.

A car horn drew my mind back from the frenzy. Duane, the creeper was slumped back against the driver's seat. His own blade plunged into his chest. He must have killed himself to get away from his own darkness.

That wasn't my fault.

I had given him a chance to stop.

I clicked my neck and rubbed my hands together. Already feeling more comfortable. I hadn't been thinking clearly, but now that I had fed, my mind was a crystal clear lake that I could see to the bottom.

The sign by the layby stated that the nearest town was two miles away. The glowing lights of a gas station were visible from the concrete stretch of the freeway.

I grabbed Duane's bony shoulders and stood up, neck bent against the roof of the cab, as I maneuvered his corpse to the passenger's seat. I looked down at my hospital gown, splattered in blood. I ripped it off and used the material to clear the pool of blood from the driver's seat.

I found some spare clothes under the seat, wrapped in a grocery store bag.

I'd never driven before. Hell didn't have roads, and only the insane, rich or the perpetually late, drove in NYC.

I turned the key in the ignition until it clicked, eying the gear stick with resignation.

It was two miles. I could drive two miles. The semi lurched forward, stalling. I swore under my breath and restarted the truck.

196

The blood on my face had started to dry and flake. The enormous wheels of the truck bounced against the curb when I pulled off the freeway and into the gas station.

If the police came, I was dumping Frankie's body and running. Screw Davenport. Screw Dermot Dirk. Screw Hugo and his damned Soulbond.

The truck was so large that I didn't even try to park it properly. The vehicle stretched across three lorry spaces, like a lazy cat.

I pulled on Duane's spare clothes, wrinkling my nose in disgust at their strange smell. Cheap detergent and nicotine. The front of the ratty t-shirt bore the message, 'my favorite food is pussy.'

I hopped down from the cab, using the back of my hand to rub the tiny blood spots from my face. All of the pumps were empty. A lone clerk sat by the till, his attention laser-focused on a magazine. He did not look up when I walked in, even though the obnoxious bell alerted him to my arrival.

I'd taken some coins from the ashtray, so I grabbed an energy drink and marched up to the till, counting out the dirty quarters.

"Can I use your bathroom?" I asked the teenager.

He did not look up when he replied. "Customers only."

I placed the can in front of him, in the center of his *national geographic*. With a heavy sigh, he turned around and grabbed the bathroom key. There was a paddle of wood attached.

The teenager did not look at me once.

I slapped my open palm with the paddle and held back a snigger as I thought about spanking. Then I felt sad. I closed my eyes tightly and shook my head to try and erase the image of Davenport that floated in front of my eyes.

The bathroom wasn't as bad as I was expecting. It smelt like urine, and the soap dispenser looked empty, but it was better than some of the Bodega bathrooms I had seen.

I gripped the edge of the sink and leaned over, bringing

197

Frankie's face closer to the mirror. I surveyed her pores with scrutiny and the blood splatter from Duane's untimely demise.

The lights flickered. I eyed the bulb shrewdly. The hairs on the back of my neck rose. Gooseflesh peppered my skin. The air changed, it felt charged. Like I was seconds away from a lightning strike.

Plunged into darkness for a few moments, I did nothing. I felt no fear. I had been born of darkness. I feasted on terror. No matter what horror movie had decided to follow me into the bathroom, I would walk away laughing.

When the light came back on, my eyes struggled to adjust. A small child stood in front of me. She couldn't have been taller than four feet. With waist-length white hair, and the complexion of an albino. Her eyes were entirely white, with no iris and no pupil.

She was not a ghost. Nor a demon or an angel. She was too much. Her magic crackled the air around us; my chest constricted. I was sure that if I were human, I would have lost the ability to breathe. I wanted to bow down and worship at her feet—I also wanted to cower and shield my face. I had only had that reaction to one other person before, and that was the Devil, King of Pride and Lies.

"I don't know *what* you are." I rubbed my chin thoughtfully as I surveyed the little girl. "I'm digging the routine, though. Are you going to trap me in the mirror?"

The girl's wide eyes fixed on mine, like a predator surveying it's prey. Her neck cocked to the side at an unnatural angle.

"Mara." Her voice was clear. Hundreds of souls layered over one another, chiming in time. I shivered. My brows raised in confusion.

"Who are you?" I asked.

"I am everything." The girl said simply. "I am *The Balance,* as your Hunter friends call me."

My eyes narrowed. "You look familiar."

The girl's expression was blank. "I am everyone and no

one."

"Why are you here?" I asked. "Not that I'm not flattered, but I'm not exactly the most interesting of creatures."

"I disagree."

There was no room for argument with that statement. "Okay." I sounded the word out slowly. Popped my lips and slapped my thighs. I pointed to the door.

"I should get going." I smiled brightly.

"I have come to warn you."

"Oh?" My hand paused on the door handle.

"You can only run for so long before your destiny finds you." The little girl said ominously. "I have taken care of the dead body for you." She added, waving her hand as if she was talking about the weather.

I turned, my lips parted to ask what the Hell she meant, but I was alone again. She had vanished.

"That was so cool." I danced on the spot and back into the gas station.

The Balance was true to her word. The cab of the semi was clear of corpses and blood. I didn't know how she did it, but I had long ago learned not to question powerful beings.

I turned the keys in the ignition, but the engine clicked and did not start. I threw a few choice curse words about, before stepping out of the semi and kicking the door on the way out.

I had no phone. No money. A can of Red Bull, and a truck that did not work.

I looked to the bright blinking lights of the sky and then down to Frankie Gardiner's bare hands. It was time to say goodbye. I could ride the wind currents home. Stowaway in a passing car. It wasn't often that having a body hindered my movements.

"I need to go," I whispered. Closing my eyes and

exhaling softly.

"Why?" A male voice replied. The tone was innocently curious, I recognized the rough timber immediately.

Warren Davenport.

Feigning nonchalance, like he hadn't just given me the jump scare of a lifetime in a gas station parking lot, I rested my elbow on the door of the semi.

"What are you doing here?" I tried to stay calm even though my heart was racing.

Davenport gave me a long look that seemed to ask if I was mentally sound. "I tracked you."

"I went for a walk." I waved my hand to gesture to the empty pumps. "I wanted to stretch my legs. See some sights."

He sniffed the air. "You smell like blood."

"I've got eight pints of it," I said. At least I thought that humans had that much. Duane had certainly bled a lot.

Without another word, Davenport strode past me and threw open the door of the truck. He sniffed the inside of the cab; his eyes were narrowed and his expression severe despite not finding anything suspect.

I silently crossed my fingers and thanked *The Balance* for cleaning up my mess.

Davenport turned back to me, he leaned over until his nose was an inch from mine.

"Tell me the truth." He commanded in a brusque tone. "Why did you leave?"

I avoided his eyes. "I wanted to."

"Why?"

I shrugged.

"That argument would work if you were twelve. You're not. Try again." His jaw rocked from side to side in anger.

"I could be twelve." I joked.

His eyebrow twitched.

"I'm not, though." I offered a lame smile.

"Mara..." Davenport said in warning.

I exhaled deeply and took a step back, turning to face

the roving headlights on the freeway. "I haven't done anything. I'm stuck with your Hunters until we find out who is behind the attack, but there hasn't been any progress. It's boring. Tedious. I wanted to go back home. I just wanted a moment's peace!" I hissed.

Davenport rubbed his hand over his face, his shoulders deflated. "It wasn't because of what we almost did?" The question was surprisingly innocent.

I batted his question away. "Please."

"Mara, we have made progress." Davenport's hand dropped to his side. "We've identified the Demon responsible. We've got patrols in the City, Queens, and Maywood. Circling the warehouses that we think the killer used to summon the Demon." He implored. "We've been interviewing every Hunter in the compound. I have personally interviewed over a hundred people."

My lips parted. "Oh."

"You are an asset. You're not trained. You're not a Hunter. Your job is to be visible and to try and lure the Summoner out."

I rubbed my thumb against my bottom lip. "I *know* that."

"Somehow, you have also found time to grow close to some of my best Hunters." Davenport continued with a wry smile. "If you wanted a more active role in the investigation, you just had to ask."

Davenport's soft look faded and returned to the stern dark expression I was used to.

"Is that the only reason you left?" He queried delicately.

I decided to go as close to the truth as possible. "I had to eat."

"And what, pray tell, do Mimic Sidhe feed on?" His brow quirked.

It felt like a test. I searched my brain. Dead Ringers were rare, but not an unknown breed of Fae. "That's private," I said.

He grunted and looked down at his watch. "Dermot Dirk requested a meeting. He wanted an update on your progress in person." Davenport informed me. "If you want to withdraw, I'm sure he could send another mercenary."

A petulant part of me wanted to stamp my feet and throw a tantrum about being replaced. I had run away, hadn't I? In my starving haze, I had come too close to tearing into the Hunter's and releasing chaos. To hurting someone and leaving a trail back to my demonic leanings.

Maybe it was for the best.

"There's a motel on the edge of town. We can stay there for the night and set off in the morning before traffic gets bad." He suggested, somewhat distant.

I shifted from foot to foot. "Traffic in the City is always bad." I stifled a laugh.

"You chose to live there." He shrugged.

I bit back a smile. "Yeah."

"Come on," Davenport unlocked his SUV. "Let's get a few hours of sleep before I deliver you back to your boss."

We got some food from the Drive-thru, which Davenport hadn't let me eat in the car. I had to wait, forlornly glancing at the bag as the burgers got cold.

The motel wasn't the worst, but you couldn't have paid me to look at it under a black light. Some things are better left unknown.

Davenport had requested two rooms, but the motel only had one twin left, leaving us in a dated room that belonged to the seventies. With A TV that didn't work, and a shag carpet that belonged in the Mystery Machine.

I crawled onto the bed and made 'gimme' motions with my hands—like a grasping toddler—until Davenport handed me the greasy bag.

I ripped into my burger like a hungry wolverine. The commander looked intrigued if a little disgusted. I wiped a bit of ketchup from the corner of my mouth with the back of my wrist.

"How did you become a Hunter?" I asked, after I had swallowed a mouthful of food.

"How old would you say I am?"

"Don't change the subject." I chided.

"Seriously. Answer the question." Davenport rested his hip against the writing desk.

"I don't know? Thirty?" I took another bite of my burger. "Do you always have to lean?" I gestured to his position with my burger.

He rolled his eyes. "I'm over two hundred years old."

I gave him a faux round of applause. My food-laden hands dulled the sound.

"How old are you?" He asked.

"Rude, much." I pulled out a pickle from my burger and placed it in the wrapper. "I don't know how old I am. Older than Yeshua—you call him Jesus. I lost count a while ago."

"You lost count?" He repeated back dully.

I stuffed a handful of fries into my mouth. "Uh-huh."

"Don't speak with your mouth full," Davenport said, his brow creased in thought. "How did you come to work for Dirk?"

"I'm a refugee." I wiped my hands on a paper napkin, before easing myself back and rubbing my belly. "Aren't you going to eat anything?"

Davenport took a single fry and chewed it.

"Were you from *Tír na nÓg* originally then?" He asked after a moment.

I rolled my head on my shoulders and made a vague hand movement. I couldn't tell him the truth, so I gave him the best answer I could. "I'm from all over. My family liked to move around. Never settling."

"What happened to them?" Davenport walked over to the other twin bed and removed his shoes methodically before climbing on top of the comforter.

"They died." My voice was hollow.

"I'm sorry."

I shrugged. "I'm the last one left. I escaped into the Human Realities. I was clueless then. Dirk took me in, gave me a job. Fed me."

"And you can't go home?" He rested his head on the pillow and looked straight up.

I did the same. "When they were killed..." My eyes stung. "No one cared. No one *did* anything. The Queen of—" I had been about to say Wrath, but I stopped myself. "The Queen did nothing until the same evil threatened her Court."

"Queen Titiana of the Summer Court?"

I hummed. I wanted to scream my truth. *No! Dahlia, Queen of the Second Circle--Wrath. Home to Valkyries, Demons, and beautiful red sand deserts.*

"I don't know if I can go back. To look into the eyes of the same beings that let my family die, and didn't care until it affected them."

Davenport was silent. The only noise was the muffled sound of someone watching Sesame Street in the room next door. Proving the walls were paper thin.

"Why do you kill Demons?" I asked. Studying the sweeping plaster on the ceiling. The pitted patterns and yellow staining.

"My parents were Hunters," Davenport whispered. "My family line are guardians. It's what we are born to do."

"Born to kill a race of people?" I echoed without emotion.

"Mara," He said my name in a way that demanded my attention. I glanced over to see that he had rested his head on his elbow. "We kill those that upset *The Balance*."

His words had more meaning than he knew. The Balance was a real creature. More powerful than anything I had ever felt. She was light, darkness, and the cosmos in the form of a creepy child.

"There is good, and there is evil." He argued. "There must always be both."

204

"Demons aren't always evil," I said.

"And Angels aren't always good."

"Would you kill an Angel?"

Davenport rubbed the stubble on his chin. "If I had to."

I let out a large yawn, an awkward gurgle came from the back of my throat, and I hoped that Davenport didn't notice.

"You're old," Davenport noted after he watched me tuck myself into bed.

"And?"

"I followed that truck off the freeway." He laughed. "You've been alive for over two thousand years, and you can't drive for shit.'

"Hey!" I argued, sitting up. "I'm an excellent driver."

I was not.

"If you say so." He laughed.

I gave him the stink eye as I flounced back down under the covers.

I never thought to ask how he had tracked me. I should have.

Chapter 13

I stared up at the water-stained ceiling, with my fingers threaded together and my hands resting on my stomach.

I couldn't sleep. I did not know why.

Davenport's breathing had evened out a short while ago, and I listened to the rhythmic sound of his lungs filling with air.

The muffled conversation of a man and a woman drifted from the wall behind my headboard, and the room on the other side had started watching SpongeBob.

Warren Davenport jerked in his sleep, and the image of burning flames slashed across my vision so quickly that if I blinked, I would have missed it. Coupled with a short but shrill human scream inside my skull, that was abruptly cut off when my vision cleared, I realized that Davenport was having a nightmare.

I had two ways of feeding. One lacked control and happened when I was starved. I ripped the nightmares from the subconscious, dragging them to the forefront of a person's mind.

A mind is a terrifying place, and many people don't truly know what beasties lay nestled behind their benign dreams about hair loss and flying.

I could make someone experience deep fears that they never knew they had.

I could also remove those fears altogether.

Another burning scream roared in my ears, bouncing around the inside of my skull.

Davenport must have been powerful to be able to project like that. He had called to me before; something scarred the man. Something no one else could see.

I swung my legs off the bed and padded over to the commander's jerking and fidgeting form. Asleep, his dark brow lifted, and his lips choked in pain.

My hand hovered over his face, brushing my fingertips lightly over his Roman nose. The images rushed over me in a cascade, dragging me under.

Warren Davenport stood in a world of flames. A Hell unlike any I had ever experienced. Burning souls. Fire. Cinders. Ash. Red. Red. Red. A lone figure in a wasteland.

I wrenched my hand away, cradling it to my chest, as my lungs fought to swallow as much air as I could. My mouth burnt with smoke damage, the heavy taste of destruction and death on my tongue.

What was that place?

I had scoured every inch of Hell, from the Greedy Mountains that had once been home to the long-dead Dragons, all the way to the hidden city made of tunnels, in Lust. I had never experienced anything like that before, but only one word could describe it. Hell. The like of which I had never seen. An unknown world.

I closed my eyes as my heart rate slowed, no longer banging against my ribcage in fear. The emotion was foreign to me. I did not like it.

Smoke drifted from my pores as I climbed onto the bed, deciding that I needed access to Davenport's mind to be able to heal him. I swung my leg over, straddling his deep sleeping form. He did not twitch, still caught in a Hell of his own making.

My hands boxed his ears, as I leaned in close enough to feel his breath against my cheek.

I focused on the darkness inside of him. It called to mine.

It felt like stretching taffy. Removing every tendril of a nightmare was complicated and required control. I allowed the sticky mass to wrap around me and dissolve into my skin. With a contented sigh, I wiped the sweat from my brow and rocked back.

Davenport's obsidian eyes stared back at me. My lips

pressed together as I tried not to laugh when I realized that I was straddling the man.

I lifted my hand and wiggled my fingers in a shy greeting. "Hey."

His eyes hooded. "Hello."

Davenport moved so quickly that I had no time to react. He bent at the waist, sitting up and cupping my body towards his. His hand wound in the back of my hair, holding my head in place. His lips met mine, my eyes were open in shock. His expression was desperate. In pain. But not from the nightmare.

He wanted me badly. I could taste it in the fevered and hard press of his lips. I could feel it in the clasped grip that I could not escape. I wanted him just as badly. Moaning into his mouth, I melted as his cinnamon tongue brushed against mine.

I broke free with a gasp. "We shouldn't do this—" I was interrupted by another kiss. My objections disappeared into the ether, like dissolving pop candy.

I wanted to ask about the fire. His dreams. But to do so would reveal too much.

Every part of his body was hard. My hands reached up, fingers pressing into the fabric of his shirt and holding onto it for dear life.

I found myself rocking, seeking something, anything, to ease the aching throb between my legs. He tasted my lips. One hand in my hair and the other on my hip, as his distorted zipper rubbed against the thin fabric of my sweatpants.

My fingers flew to his crotch, and I quickly discarded his trousers. Pulling them down around his muscular thighs before rubbing my hands over the long pipe stretching the fabric of his black boxer shorts. His cock twitched. Davenport cracked his neck and looked up at me with such unhurried confidence that I wanted to slap him.

My hand skimmed the edge of his hard cock, separated by only a thin piece of cotton. "It looks like you want something?" I guessed. His manhood twitched as if to answer

208

my question, and I tapped my chin with thoughtful innocence. "I wonder what that could be?" I smiled wickedly.

Davenport's eyes narrowed. "You like to play games, *Sidhe*?"

Pain ricocheted around my chest and rippled across my face. I jerked back as if an icy bucket of water had doused my entire body, reminding me that Davenport did not know *me*.

All emotions drained from my face, and I pushed myself away from the bed like a cat faced with a bath.

"Mara?" Warren sat up, he reached out to me, but I flung my hands up to ward him away. I refused to look him in the eye.

"It's nothing," I whispered. "I'm tired."

His look darkened as he sat up, pulling up his trousers. His obsidian eyes flashed in anger, and I flinched.

Warren's jaw rocked from side to side. Was he upset that I had rejected him? He looked ready to hit me. I didn't know what to do. He was the leader of the Hunters. If he saw my true nature, if I defended myself, he would hunt me to the edge of the earth to bring me down.

I was used to being abused. Taken advantage of. Lower Demons had numbers, but not power. I had taken my fair share of licks.

I locked my body and closed my eyes, preparing for the blow.

"Mara?" Warren Davenport's tentative voice broke me from my rapid thoughts. "I'm not going to hurt you."

My eyes fluttered open. I tilted my chin, confused. I said nothing.

Davenport clenched his fists "Has someone... In the past... Has anyone?"

I blinked slowly, unsure of where his question was heading.

Davenport growled and rubbed the scruff on his chin. "Has anyone... Hurt you?" He bit out the words as if they tasted foul.

"...Yes?" I was utterly bemused by his question. I had no idea why he wanted to know.

Davenport inhaled deeply. His eyes closed. It looked like he was counting to ten in his mind. "Sexually?" He did not open his eyes when he asked the question in a flat impassive voice.

I laughed, relieved. "No. I've never had anyone like that. Sexually. Romantically. It's just not been my thing." I wanted to explain that the ability to touch and feel things was new to me, still a novelty, but I *couldn't*.

I hated that I had to censor so much of myself. It fucking sucked.

"But you've been hurt in other ways?" he asked.

I shrugged. I was old. Remembering past tortures became tedious after a while. Many of my enemies were dead. Ba'el, the once King of Wrath, had prided himself on collecting Drudes and experimenting on them inside of his fortress in the middle of the desert wastes. My kin never returned when they had been taken by Ba'el, but he had been too powerful to argue with.

Drudes shared pain. They were a hive mind. I had felt their screams, just as I had passively experienced the deaths of my family. Feeling their strength drain away as they were eaten alive piece by piece.

Thankfully, Ba'el was now dead. As were the Bhakshi and the Shayati.

Warren Davenport had gone stock still. I wanted to make a joke or tease him, but somehow it didn't seem like the right them to do. He looked ready to blow.

Then the fire alarm rang. The sprinklers whirred to life, dousing the room in a thick mist of water, slapping me in the face. I wiped moisture out of my eyes, glaring up at the infernal device.

Davenport strode to the hotel phone, with a rigid set to his shoulders. He barked into the handset for a few seconds, before slamming it down onto the ancient device.

"It's just our room." He said. "We should pack and get on the road while we're up. We can get breakfast before we go to see Dirk."

The suspiciously timed alarm was ignored as I jumped on the spot and clapped. "We should do Lil Frankie's. We can drink prosecco."

Davenport gave me an expression that I had come to know as his signature *'look.'* It said more than words could, and right that second, it seemed to say:

There is so fucking way I am drinking sparkling wine over English Muffins.

"But I want prosecco." I scrunched my nose and met his stare. His look continued and grew darker.

Eat whatever you want, but don't expect me to follow suit.

I crossed my arms over my chest and let out a loud hmph. His gaze melted into something smooth and decadent. My chest fluttered. Davenport liked it when I was bratty. I smiled wickedly. I could almost feel the burn of his palm across my bare ass. I squirmed, and he seemed to read my thoughts.

Instead of bending me over the bed and giving me the belt, the commander swung his duffle bag over his shoulders.

"Let's go." He said without room for argument. I took solace in the fact he rearranged his trousers discreetly, as he opened the door for me.

I liked his dark side.

Everyone knew about Lil Frankie's in the East Village, but I had never gone inside.

Brunch wasn't high on my list of priorities, and the people that Dermot Dirk made me wear often made appearances at the Opera or Political rallies, not the kind of people that would go for inexpensive Italian food.

Warren managed to find a place to park a few blocks

away. A marvel in itself.

Dressed in my borrowed 'pussy is my favorite food' shirt, sweats, and too large sneakers, I looked like a homeless person compared to Davenport—who had changed into a pair of dress pants and a white shirt. He had offered to find a Target so I could get a change of clothes, but I wanted to get the day over with as quickly as possible—it would be painful enough to see Dirk and tell him about the situation.

The thought of leaving the Hunters filled me with unfamiliar emotion. My eyes welled up, and I struggled to breathe. Seven Hell's, I needed a slap.

I thought about my men. Each one different in their own way. Each friendship offering something that I hadn't known I needed.

I had felt like I had been missing pieces of myself for so long. When I had seen Hugo's Bond mark, I had felt whole again, even if just for a second. I could see myself with each of the Hunters I had grown close to. Remi, Jae, Hart, and even Davenport, though there was no guarantee that they were mine.

The idea of tying myself to someone else frightened me. I liked knowing that I could escape a body at a moment's notice and borrow someone's life for a short while. Experience new foods, new feelings, and memories. Every human experienced things like taste, pain, and love differently.

What would happen if I was Bonded?

Could I be tied to one person for my entire existence? No. But all of them? The idea seemed to tear the fabric of my soul in several directions. I wanted so badly to belong to them and to claim them.

If only they weren't Hunters.

I did a double-take as I walked past the beige wall covered in generic painted landscapes and photos. Davenport's hand brushed my waist as he led us to our seats.

"Did you tell Remi that we were coming here?" I asked, cocking my head to the side as Warren continued to lead me to the other side of the restaurant. "Why aren't we sitting

212

together?"

Remington Weber sat under a row of mirrors, alone at a table for two, with his head dipped behind a menu. His lips were pulled down, and he looked troubled.

I wondered if Remi was angry at me for escaping out of a window. I couldn't see it. Remi was too sunny to hold a grudge.

Warren continued to lead me away, even when I tried to turn. He swore under his breath as the host showed us another table.

I craned my neck before I raised my hand to get Remi's attention. Davenport gave me a look, and I slowly folded my fingers into a fist and rested it against my chest.

"What?" I quirked a brow.

Davenport shook his head and clicked his tongue against the roof of his mouth. He plucked a menu from the side and began to peruse it.

I put my hand on the laminated sheet and lowered it to the table. "Do you not like Remi or something?"

Warren gave me a withering stare.

I sat up. "I'm going to say hi." Before the commander could make a sound of protest, I was out of my seat. I had walked past two other tables when I slowly stopped. My heartbeat grew louder under all I could hear was *'whump whump whump,'* drowning out all other sounds.

A beautiful redhead, in a summer dress covered in red cherries, but with a body that belonged to an exotic dancer and a swagger to match, joined Remi at his table. He stood up, and they kissed cheeks before he pulled out her chair. She said something. He laughed.

I wanted to wring her neck until it popped off her spine and then spit on her face.

A hand wrapped around my shoulder. Tentative. Gentle. So unlike the Davenport that I knew.

"Let's eat," Warren suggested softly.

I swallowed the lump in my throat and the urge to find

213

a waiter and bribe them to spit in the redhead's food. I sat down. My movements robotic.

"I didn't know Remi had a girlfriend," I said stiffly. My inner goddess wanted to backhand the shit out of me. Where did all my chaotic evil go? Was I going soft?

"Fiancée," Warren corrected tersely, his eyes darted from mine to survey the couple across the restaurant. "He didn't tell you?"

I shook my head, cheeks flushed. I thought about all of my interactions with Remi. There was something there. I wasn't insane.

"Her name is Alicia Greenlea." Davenport folded his menu and placed it in front of him. He knotted his hands together and watched me with guarded eyes. "She's a Witchling. Connecticut family. Goes to Columbia."

My lips twisted into a sardonic smile. "Yippee for her."

"Remi transferred from London to NYC because she is here." Davenport continued as if I hadn't spoken. "The Weber family are well respected in Europe, but their magic will dim if they do not breed into diversity and power."

"An arranged marriage then?" The waiter came, and I ordered three mimosas and two espressos. No food. Davenport ordered a frittata. The waiter left. "What is a Witchling anyway?" I asked.

"Considering your age, you should know this." He said.

"Please," I snorted. "Never shame a lady for her age."

Davenport arranged the salt and pepper shakers, and then his silverware, taking a second to collect his thoughts.

"Angels get their magic from God. Demons from Sin. The Fae, as you know, are more unique. Witchlings, however, use their own life force to power their spells. Their magic is finite. Burned away with each spell."

"So if Remi uses too much magic, he'll die?" The thought made me a little sick.

"Witchling power is a Devil's bargain gone wrong. Once Remi turns thirty, he will not be able to use his magic

214

anymore. If he does, he *will* die. Until then, every spell is a gamble."

"And Alicia is a Witchling too," I concluded.

"Yes."

"And they plan to make cursed babies and live happily ever after in her family's Connecticut mansion." The waiter brought over our drinks, and I necked two mimosas, holding one in each hand.

"I didn't realize that you and Remi were..." Davenport's face had cleared of emotion.

"Jealous?" I laughed harshly. "Don't be, he's getting married."

"I'm not jealous." He said softly. "What you have with Remi does not affect what you have with me."

I wanted to ask about what *we* had, but I couldn't bring myself to say the words. Thinking about the way Davenport's lips felt, and his hands tangled in my hair, made my entire body burn.

"Remi loses his value as a Witchling in several months, but he can help his family maintain their status by having children with another prominent Witchling." Warren reached into his pocket and produced a pack of Big Red. He folded a stick into his mouth and chewed.

"What's up with the gum?" I wondered. Davenport carried a hint of cinnamon with him, but he didn't seem like the type of guy to chew gum habitually.

"Giving up smoking." He explained.

I glanced at Remi's table out of the corner of my eye. Alicia flicked her shiny hair over her shoulder and let out a peal of laughter.

"Is Alicia a Hunter?" I asked.

"She is a film studies student."

My lips pressed together to hold back laughter. "Definitely not a Hunter."

Davenport laughed before he caught himself and rubbed his hand against his stubble. "Unfortunately, the

Greenlea's have foisted their daughter onto me, to keep an eye on Remi. She will be staying with us for a few weeks."

"Good thing I'm leaving then." I chirped as I lifted my remaining mimosa, but my smile was fake.

"Yeah." Davenport echoed. His voice was surprisingly hollow. "Good thing."

After finding Davenport's armored SUV with a bright yellow ticket under the wiper, we decided to take the subway to Bleecker. As Warren had reasoned, getting a ticket was probably cheaper than paying for parking.

It was early afternoon by the time we stepped into *Dirk's*, above John's pizzeria. The unusual warmth that blanketed the fall air disintegrated as soon as we stepped into the Fold between dimensions and into Dermot Dirk's bar.

Dirk's was the same as always. Rusted license plates, a Jukebox playing 'What's New Pussycat,' and an entire bar of empty seats save from a Redcap drinking away his sorrows.

Stan, the bartender, was in the exact same spot I had seen him weeks before. Polishing a filthy glass.

I sauntered up to the pockmarked bar and slid onto a stool. I ordered a shot of Tequila.

Stan did not move. "Boss is expecting you." He grunted, looking over my head at Davenport.

The Hunter nodded, his arms crossed over his chest, radiating masculine energy. Warren waited patiently for me to disembark from the stool with a heavy sigh. I dragged my feet as we walked through the corridor that led to the backroom.

Davenport knocked on the door. Unlike when I did it, Dirk called him straight through. I scowled and eyed the door with disdain.

Dermot Dirk sat in his office chair, his potbelly hidden behind his desk and his spindly arms folded in front of him, resting on the polished wood. He smiled at Davenport and did not spare me a glance. "Commander." He oozed the charm that he reserved only for clients. "Thank you for heeding my summons."

Davenport tilted his head. "You needed an update on Mara's progress?"

Dirk leaned back, his gaze darted to mine and back again. "Yes and no."

I cleared my throat. "Can I speak to you alone, Dirk?"

Davenport narrowed his eyes. "I'd prefer to stay."

"It's private." I insisted. "Just a minute."

Though he clearly didn't want to leave me alone with my boss, Davenport patted my shoulder and left the office.

It was a few moments before either of us spoke. The Fae stared at me with pale watery eyes.

"I haven't got all day." Dermot Dirk raised both of his eyebrows, affecting an attitude of innocence.

"I'm trying to organize my thoughts."

"That shouldn't take long." His lips curled up in a teasing smile.

My fists clenched. "I don't want to do this anymore."

"We've been over this." He sighed.

"I was poisoned with salt. I've Marked someone. It's only a matter of time before I'm found out." My fingernails bit into the palm of my hand. Drawing blood. "We're no closer to finding the Summoner. I'm less than useless as anything but bait. You can put a real Mimic Sidhe in the compound in half a second. Why me?" I tried to keep the whine out of my voice but was unsuccessful.

"I've told you. I believe this is your chance to shine."

My eyes narrowed. I wanted so badly to believe that. His kind words and praise; that I was someone to seriously consider, not just an impulsive and powerless Lower Demon. I should have known better; Dermot Dirk was not a kindly man. He was not a father figure to dole out advice and encouragement.

217

"Bullshit," I said through gritted teeth.

Dirk exhaled. His face flushed red. "Fine." His tone mirrored mine. "A few months ago, someone contacted me claiming to be Warren Davenport. He said that he needed someone to help broker a deal with an Ifrit."

"And you helped?" I scoffed. "From the kindness of your Winter Fae heart?"

"I owed Davenport a favor." He said, his teeth grinding.

"You didn't check if this man was actually Davenport?" I laughed harshly. "You just, what? Attached a PDF of the correct ritual to summon an Ifrit?"

He did not look me in the eye.

"You didn't?" My anger gave way to disbelief. My eyes widened until they were in danger of popping out of my skull.

"I couldn't send a true Mimic Sidhe. They wouldn't be able to deal with a Demon." He continued as if I hadn't spoken.

"You could have told me all this from the beginning." I pointed out.

"Mara." Dirk chided with a chuckle. "Please. You have the censorship capabilities of a four-year-old."

I rubbed my eyelids with the pads of my fingers before resting my hand on my lips. I tasted the blood from the tiny crescent wounds my fingernails had left behind.

"The true Warren Davenport visited shortly after Team C was murdered. He asked for my assistance." Dirk admitted. "It did not take long to realize that someone had, indeed, summoned an Ifrit."

"But you didn't tell Warren your part in it?" I closed my eyes and counted to ten.

"I offered my assistance. I also alluded to the fact that one of his Hunters must have been behind the attack." Dermot Dirk cleared his throat. He looked contrite. "I offered your services. Confident that you would find the Ifrit and free it."

I thought about the bastardized markings I had seen in Hugo's mind. The numerous languages layering over each other.

I had not recognized many of the words because they belonged to the Fae Lords. A language that predated Cyclian and the language of Hell.

"I can't do this." My voice hitched. "I want to go home."

"To a world without taste, smell, touch?" Dirk asked bitterly. "I allow you to *live*."

I didn't know how to explain that I felt terrible for deceiving the Hunters.

I knew what guilt felt like—the emotion was a hollow crater in my soul, whenever I thought about my Cluster.

Demons did not side with Hunters. They did not *love* them.

"Don't make me do this." I pleaded. Thinking about Hugo's Soul Bond and his rejection. Remi's fiancée. Davenport's nightmares of a world of flames.

Dermot Dirk's eyes flashed, and his eyes narrowed. "You've changed." He noted without emotion.

I shook my head but said nothing.

He studied Frankie's body with a dispassionate eye. His gaze rested on the blood I had smeared on my lips by accident. He sat up in his chair. "She's not human," Dirk stated. With no context, I had no idea what he was talking about.

"No shit, Tinkerbell."

Dirk gave me the stink eye. "Your host is not human. Perhaps that is the reason the Ifrit could not kill her."

"Except that there were plenty of non-humans on Team C, and they all died." I put my hand on my hip.

"Leave the body was a second," Dirk commanded. "I want to see."

"She'll die," I argued.

Ice began to bloom on my exposed skin, a thin layer of frost. I saw my breath fog in front of my face.

"She won't die." The Fae's voice had no room for argument.

I slumped my shoulders and poured from Frankie

Gardiner's mouth, a thick plume of black smoke. Dermot Dirk stood up and moved around his desk, his thin limbs made the movements jerky and inherently suspicious. He waved a hand as if I was a bad smell, and I drifted to the corner of the room. Resting near the ceiling like a spider in a web.

Without a body, the Human Realities seemed drab to me. Without texture. I eyed Frankie's blue-lipped still form with a sense of possessiveness that I was unused to.

Dirk lifted her hand and turned it over, running his thumb over the newly healed wounds. His look was contemplating.

He did not acknowledge me, but I felt self-conscious of my form regardless. I distracted myself from the emptiness of being without a body and followed Dirk's ministrations as he studied Frankie Gardiner's body.

Neither of us heard the door open.

Warren Davenport had enough of waiting, it seemed. As he stood in the doorway, I realized what he must have seen. Something that could not be explained. A frozen and motionless body and terrifying undulating smoke with tentacles and deep hollow eye sockets. My true form. The wide gaping maw, simulating a human scream. The floating darkness, stretching and reaching.

Davenport's entire body stiffened and went on alert. His muscles bunched, and his nostrils flared. He did not spare my true form another glance, as he looked at Dermot Dirk with contempt.

"Explain," Davenport demanded.

Dermot Dirk could not lie.

As one of the Fae, he was physically incapable of it, but as he stood there, stock-still, with his mouth gaping open in shock, I would have expected Dirk to at least come up with *something*.

Davenport's shoulders were squared as he held his ground. His towering presence took up the entire doorway.

I zipped forward, moving as quickly as I was able, as I

220

went for the door. I had one avenue of escape, and I planned to take it.

Davenport reached for my incorporeal form, his eyes glowed the same deep red that the evilest of demons wore on their irises. I knew he couldn't touch me. I just had to get past him.

I focused on the open door with laser-like precision. My only goal was to escape. My mind layered Davenport with the shadowed figure of the Shayati, as they rose from the cracks in the world to devour my kin. I didn't want to die.

Warren Davenport's hand connected with my bodiless form, slamming me backward, I hurtled back into Frankie's body. A writhing mass of black worms. Dirk leaped forward, and frost spread across the walls so quickly that it cracked audibly. Dirk's form shimmered, and his true visage showed for a blink. A tall regal Winter Fae, stood behind his desk, instead of the vague and watery-eyed businessman.

The commander of the Hunters gripped Frankie's still body as I dissolved into her pores. I felt my possession turn her eyes to oil slicks—the only physical marker of my presence. Davenport waved a hand, and Dirk slammed back against the wall. The Fae's ice melted as my boss passed out with a line of blood down his face from a nasty looking cut on his forehead.

Warren gripped my wrists and held them in front of my chest, disabling me. My head swam with the sudden, forced, inhabitancy of a body. Taste, smell, and touch roared to the forefront of my thoughts, and my eyes blinked hazily as I struggled not to vomit.

"Who are you?" Davenport shook me. I reared back like a spooked horse and tried to upend myself from Frankie's body. I was stuck tight. Shocked, I gaped at the Hunter as his dark eyes flashed.

"What did you do?" I whispered. His grip on my wrists began to burn with more than just skin-on-skin friction. It felt like his hands were on fire.

I blinked my demonic eyes away as I began to panic. I

221

struggled to pull away, but he held me still.

"Who are you, Demon!?" He shook me again as he snarled in my face.

My face pulled into an ugly expression. "Fuck. You." I spat.

The room grew too hot. My chest struggled to pull in air.

"Wrong answer." Davenport put his hand on my forehead, and suddenly the world was on fire.

Chapter 14

Flames as tall as skyscrapers roared and crackled, their bright appendages reaching ever higher in the search for material to burn. The sky above was black with thick plumes of smoke, a drape over the landscape battered back only by the never-ending fire as far as the eye could see.

The back of my throat burned. The smell of burning rubber made me move my feet, only to discover that I had left behind the melted sole of my sneakers.

Davenport was nowhere to be seen. The hissing growl of the fire blocked out all noise. Cracking and popping as I continued to walk.

My skin felt tight as the heat began to penetrate my borrowed body. I continued to move as if the Hunter would emerge behind me at any second.

I tried to escape Frankie's body, but I was stuck fast. My lungs labored, unable to find anything breathable in the smoggy atmosphere. The air tasted like ashes and pain.

I didn't want to die.

Davenport would kill me. I was certain. I knew too much about the Hunters. I had seen their compound. Learned their names. He would never let me live.

What had I been thinking—hanging around with a group of killers, eating up their attention and friendship like a starved child? I had been foolish.

I kept moving, even when each breath became tight against my ribs, and my lungs seized and cramped.

I didn't want to die.

Drudes had a collective memory. I had felt the desolation and hopelessness of my kin as they felt their skin

223

harden and their essence drain into the ground, gobbled by the writhing mass of ancient wyrms.

I had managed to break free. I had managed to escape the Bhakshi and Shayati. I would be damned if I allowed a Hunter to take me.

But it seemed like the effects of the fire would drag my host's body into the sweet embrace of death before Davenport would ever find me in his own fiery Hell.

Perhaps that had been the plan all along.

The bare soles of my feet blistered.

I winced with every step.

Just as my foot lowered to make a connection with the cinders on the ground, the world slipped away, and I fell on all fours. The chilling feel of concrete was a refreshing relief to my burned palms.

I gulped air like a person dying of thirst and rolled over onto my back as I felt my demonic healing wash over my body.

My clothes hung from my body in tatters, turned to sludge by the flames.

My eyes took the longest to heal, blinded by the fire, all I could see were rainbow spots and dark blurs.

When my vision finally focused, Davenport stood in front of me. His arms crossed, and his legs shoulder-width apart. He looked like a man that would not be moved for anything. Still dressed in his shirt and trousers, his sleeves were rolled up, and his scuff had grown enough to mark the passing of at least a day.

My teeth were bared. I stepped forward only to find myself knocked back by a line of salt. I growled, low in my chest, a sound that should have not have been possible from a human voice box.

"Who are you?" Davenport asked in a low and dangerous tone. His dark eyes focused on my own, coated with contempt that told me my host's eyes were black with my inner Demon.

I cocked my head to the side. "And who are you to

224

demand my name?"

Davenport laughed without humor. "Do you have any self-preservation?"

I seriously considered the question.

"I will not allow you to kill me," I told him.

His eyebrows raised, and Davenport's look said everything that he did not speak out loud.

I stopped you from escaping your host. You really think you could stop me if I wanted to kill you?

I narrowed my eyes but bit my tongue against all of the deliciously horrible insults that ran through my mind.

Instead, I reached out with my magic—attempting to latch onto the fear and turmoil that all humans kept below the surface. I honed my magic into a blade and reached for the Hunter. I would not go down without a fight.

Davenport waved me off.

My heart stuttered, and my mouth popped open. My magic was flawless, immune to all attacks and defenses, and yet, a trumpeted up Hunter with BDSM tendencies had the cajones to actually stop my magic in its tracks.

I couldn't fight well, but I would find out if my survival instincts were enough to keep me alive. I'd go for the balls and hope for the best.

Damn. I should have gotten that printed on a t-shirt.

Davenport had stepped forward while I had been distracted, his Italian leather shoes almost touched the salt line.

"I have no plans to kill you, as of yet," Davenport said. "But that may change if you do something stupid."

I liked to think that I had gotten to know Warren Davenport in the weeks I had spent at the Hunters compound. He was a man of his word. A man that would walk on Legos to ensure he did not break a promise.

Despite my survival instincts screaming in my ear, and the residual memories of my kin's deaths making me want to bite, claw and chew my way out of my salt prison, I decided to trust him.

For now.

Davenport left shortly, and I spent my time surveying my surroundings.

The walls were made of seamless concrete, with no pipes or door in sight. The circle was large enough that I could lie down, but not much else. The space around me pointed to a warehouse floor, stripped of machinery. Cavernous. Strips of lights ran overhead, the strange foreignness of fluorescents bathed the concrete in a grey glow.

I reached forward, studying Frankie Gardiner's callused hand. With little thought, I was able to push my darkness out of the pores to shroud her fingers in a haze of smoke. I breathed a sigh of relief. Whatever Davenport had done had only worked when he was touching me. I wasn't doomed to spend the rest of my life in an aging body.

The salt line would keep me in place for a while. I could leave Frankie's body behind, but I still wouldn't be able to pass the barrier unless I could find a way to break the continuous line.

Still clad in the burned remnants of Duane's stolen clothes, my feet started to protest after I had been standing for an hour. Boredom was not a good state of mind, and I felt myself ping-ponging back and forward in my own mind. Desperate for stimulation of some kind.

I started to sing to myself. Under my breath at first, but then loud enough that my shouting echoed off the concrete and back to me.

After I grew bored of Carly Rae Jepson and my loop of *'Call me Maybe,'* I took off my oversized sneakers and did all the actions to the *Cha Cha Slide*, using each of the fun dance moves to test the circle for weak spots in power. I found one next to the rune for Imprisonment. *H'caryhkut.*

A previously unseen panel shifted and slipped into the floor, revealing the inscrutable figures of Warren Davenport and Remington Weber. Both of their faces were devoid of emotion.

Davenport strode in first, stopping at the edge of the circle. Remi leaned against the back wall, a spectator, he tilted his head and did not take his eyes off mine.

"Dermot Dirk put a *Demon* in my compound," Davenport stated, speaking to Remi as if I wasn't there. "It seems that the Fae are attempting to start a war."

I tapped my lip with my fist, but said nothing.

"The question remains. A war between the Hunters and the Demons, or the Hunters and the Fae?" Davenport added as he paced the line of my circle.

I gave him a bright disarming smile and a shrug. "Above my paygrade." The commander scowled but ignored me as if I hadn't spoken.

The salt ring began to glow, infused with magic that smelt like burning plastic. I winced, even though the magic didn't seem to be affecting me. If Witchling magic was the result of a Devil's bargain, it made sense that it couldn't harm me.

Drudes were so low on the totem pole of power that most magic did not recognize our existence, so we were immune.

"That body belongs to Frankie Gardiner," Davenport said.

"I'm just borrowing it."

"So, she's still alive." He narrowed his eyes.

"Not really," I admitted.

He was silent as he contemplated my words with a heavy frown.

"Why would a Demon be working for a Fae Lord?" The commander's voice held no emotion.

I looked like my hand had been caught in the cookie jar. The magic whipping around the trapping circle grew heavier.

While Davenport's demeanor hadn't outwardly changed all that much—he was still the same no-nonsense man

227

with an inherent quality that made you want to roll your belly and obey him—Remi's disposition was very jarring. Seeing the typically jovial prankster as a stern and unforgiving Hunter was a sight I should have been prepared for, but wasn't.

"I'm a mercenary," I explained. "Dirk asked me to help solve the murder because he owed you a favor for London."

"True." Remi sniffed and wiped his nose discretely against his sleeve. It came away stained with blood. Worry nestled into my chest like a burrowing insect.

"You've seen our compound," Davenport noted gently. "What should I do with you?"

I licked my bottom lip. "You could let me go?"

"Ask her what kind of Demon she is." Remi piped up.

"I can hear you."

"Answer him," Davenport demanded.

"A Drude." I shrugged.

"Never heard of it." The commander glanced at Remi, who shook his head.

Damn. That was embarrassing.

"Show us your true form," Remi demanded, his typically relaxed face was carved from ice.

"No, thanks." I rolled my eyes, remembered Davenport's previous look of disgust at my incorporeal self.

"Make her." Davenport turned to Remi and stepped away from the edge of the circle. I made a move to follow him but stopped when my toes hit the salt line.

"Wait, what?" I asked, panicking. I reached inside of myself and fastened my darkness to my Host's skin like a sea urchin to a rock. My eyes darted wildly as I stepped away from the edge of the circle like a cornered animal.

Remi closed his eyes and waved his hands, the taste of burning plastic dominated all my other senses. I gagged.

But his magic did nothing to me.

Blood began to ooze from Remi's nose, and even though his face creased in pain, he continued to chant. Davenport's previous words echoed in my ears like an airplane taking off. A dull roar that grew louder and louder. Remi could *die* if he used too much magic.

I might have been a Demon, but I loved Remi in my own twisted unrequited way. He had been the first person to treat me with kindness when I had gotten to the compound. To joke with me and make me feel seen. I didn't want him to get hurt because of my stubborn magic immunity.

I hunched over and pretended to wheeze. I held my hand up. "Uncle!" I cried, hiding my face behind a curtain of frizzy hair. I exploded out of Frankie's body, letting her dead form drop to the ground with a harsh whack. Both men winced.

My smoke spindled to form a human shape, the whorls of curling shadows rose from my silhouette like steam. I hovered, a mermaid made of the night sky, underwater.

Remi stepped forward, reaching Davenport's side, they both looked up at me.

"That's a goddamn nightmare Demon," Remi whispered, in awe. Warren spared him a glance.

"What Circle do they reside in?" The commander asked, unconcerned as he turned his back to me.

Remi shook his head at a loss.

"What is your Sin, Demon?" Davenport asked.

I floated there. My mouth opened to speak, but only a rustling sound came out—brittle fall leaves skittering across the concrete. I had no voice as a Drude.

Warren gave me a look that could kill.

"I don't think she can speak." Remi offered, his demeanor had softened since seeing my true form, which I had not expected.

"No red eyes." Davenport finally turned to study for my form, he stepped around the circle. His gaze never leaving mine. "Call for Sinclair. He knows more about Demons."

My form struck out in all directions, bouncing off the salt barrier as I tried to escape. I didn't want Hugo to see me. He'd know.

I did not have a plan, besides getting out of the circle.

Proving my innocence would have been nice, but I was realistic. Once Davenport had done his 'due diligence,' I fully expected to be banished back to Hell at best or shot with a Devil's Silver bullet at worst.

Davenport and Remi turned to the door to wait.

I spread myself thin until I was invisible to the naked eye. Nothing but a shadow. If I had a human skin, it would have been the equivalent of curling up on the floor to hide. I had no shame when it came to survival.

Remi's magic couldn't touch me, but whatever Davenport had done in the office *could*.

What the Hell was Davenport anyway?

Behind the lines of the circle, I was safe but trapped.

A few minutes passed, but they seemed like seconds, as the seamless concrete slipped down to reveal the entrance. Hugo Sinclair strode through, the hunched over and tentative set to his shoulders was gone and in his place was an eagle-eyed Hunter. He looked competent. Dangerous.

"You called, Sir?" Hugo asked, eyes straight on Davenport.

The commander finally looked back to my circle in the center of the room. Only to find I was no longer visible.

He swore. His dark eyes flashed, and he turned to Remi.

"Where did the Demon go?" He enunciated each word through his clenched jaw.

"She's still in there." Remi glanced at the salt circle. Hugo's eyes followed his. The incubus stepped back, he touched the mark on his chest without conscious thought.

Davenport rubbed his hand over his eyes. The first crack in his armor since he had walked into Dirk's office.

"Frankie Gardiner is dead." Davenport's statement was said without emotion. "She did not make it back from the coma. That—" he waved his hand in my direction, "—is the Nightmare Demon that Dirk masqueraded as a Mimic Sidhe. The slippery Fae bastard put a Pureblooded Demon in my compound, and I didn't even know!"

The dam had broken on Davenport's reserved manner, he began to swear again. He pushed his fingers into his dark wavy locks and tugged the strands.

Hugo turned slowly. His expression was unreadable. "Why did you require a Mimic Sidhe?"

Davenport explained his plan to lure out the summoner.

Hugo's face grew harder and harder. The incubus looked down at Frankie's immobile form, sprawled out across the jagged lines of the circle, then to the space above. I hovered, invisible to the naked eye.

"Frankie Gardiner didn't come back from her last mission." Hugo echoed back. He stepped up to the edge of the circle. His steel-toed boots hovered on the line that separated my invisible form from his.

I was in a vacuum, without sensation. But somehow, I could feel Hugo. His thoughts, his emotions, and the undulating dark chocolate of his magic. Bitter, but still smooth and sweet. The connection lived inside of me, a bond that I had denied and tried to escape, pulled taut without Frankie's body to act as a buffer.

"What is her name?" Hugo asked. His fists clenched.

"She called herself Mara." Davenport sneered. "But Demons are known to lie."

I scoffed. That was patently untrue. Demons were actually very truthful creatures—though our truths differed from small-minded Human ones. My sound of derision was unnatural.

"Mara?" Hugo stepped closer to the circle. "I know who you are." His voice was soft, and I realized that all of his anger that had been simmering under the surface was directed to Davenport and Remi. "We won't hurt you." Hugo held up his palm, disarmingly.

Davenport's shoulder barged Hugo out of the way. Scuffing the incubus's shoe against the edge of the circle, disturbing the pristine line. "What are you doing?" Warren snarled. "A Demon is a threat until we can collar it and determine its motives. You're talking to it like a stray cat."

My smoke spun slowly, becoming visible piece by piece. I hung two feet above the ground, curled over so the numerous limbs of my darkness could test the edge of the circle. Gone. The magic had dissipated. No one had felt the loss.

Hugo stood his ground. "You will not hurt her." He rose up to meet Davenport's face. Hugo's ice blue eyes glowed.

Remi stood between the two, his hand slipped into the small space between their two hard chests as he tried to push them apart. Neither man moved.

"And why's that?" Davenport asked dangerously, and it was clear that he did like being told what to do.

Hugo's magic leaked from his skin. Davenport's trousers tented, and the room grew hotter. Remi flushed and pulled away, fanning himself with his collar but looking away.

"Control yourself, Sinclair." Davenport snarled, his own eyes glowed like embers. I was impressed with the amount of magic slipping out of Hugo, I would have expected even the most dominate man to spin on his heels and present like a dog in heat.

"No." Hugo dared.

"You want to go to bat for a Demon. A spy for the Fae?" Davenport mocked. "We have a duty to The Balance."

Hugo's palms lashed out, slamming against Warren's chest, forcing the commander back.

"She's my mate!" Hugo screamed.

They stared over Hugo's shoulders as I rose, blanketing the incubus in the smoothing darkness of the night sky. I unfurled myself behind him, free, tendrils outstretched like a black pair of wings.

Chapter 15

When Davenport stopped threatening Hugo, I slipped back to the circle, docile like a well-trained puppy.

The commander's eyes immediately found the broken circle. "Fix that." Davenport barked. Hugo stepped away from the edge of the circle as Remi bent over and pulled a canister of salt from his utility belt.

"It *is* you." Hugo's eyes were wide. His gaze clouded when he looked down at Frankie's dead body. "Why didn't you tell me?"

"She can't speak in that form." Remi put his hand on Hugo's shoulder.

"But—" I knew what Hugo had been about to say before he had interrupted himself. He had heard my voice in Hell. But dreams and nightmares obeyed a different set of rules. Drudes were silent, never touching. Never interacting with the world. Carried by the wind. Feeding on hidden terrors like a dog looking for scraps.

"Who else knows?" Hugo demanded.

"Dr. Lee knew about the Mimic Sidhe plan." Davenport pressed his fingers against his head. Discreetly massaging his temple, I hoped he was getting a headache. "Only the three of us know she's a Demon."

"Then we don't tell anyone," Hugo said, pulling his attention from my spectral form. "We can let her go."

"Then how do you catch the killer?" Remi asked. "Because using Frankie as bait was the only plan we had."

"You were perfectly fine using a recovering woman as a target for a Demon." Hugo pointed out. "Mara is a Demon too. She can handle it."

"Hugo..." Davenport stepped forward.

"No." The incubus waved him off. "She's my mate. I trust her."

"She's a *Demon*," Remi said softly.

Hugo flushed, hurt slashed across his features. "So am I." The force of his emotion was heart-breaking.

Davenport looked stricken. He turned back to the reinforced circle. "Mara, can you return to Frankie's body so we can talk to you?" Davenport was reluctant to step closer to the circle; I wondered if it was because he remembered how close he had gotten to *an untrustworthy Demon*, that night in our hotel room.

With a sigh, I drifted as petulantly as I could (which was a feat for a being made of shadows) and poured myself into Frankie's body. The sweet taste of decay clung to her throat, and I coughed as I sat up—if I left her body again, I wouldn't be able to go back inside. Frankie's eyes turned black before I blinked the oil slick away. I stood, awkwardly arranging my limbs. As I stumbled like a baby fawn, Davenport reached forward to help me, before catching his hand at the salt barrier. Hugo watched the exchange with a shrewd expression.

The world returned slowly. Taste, smell, and touch. I felt the heat of the room. Hugo's magic was a rolling drumbeat against my borrowed skin. The scent of burning plastic hung in the air from Remi's Witchling spells. My joints ached. The rush of sensations was almost too much to bear, and I struggled to focus.

"Are you involved with the Ifrit?" Davenport demanded.

My brow quirked. "Drudes don't really interact with other Demons."

Davenport rolled his hand to indicate that I should hurry my explanation. I cocked my hip.

"That's a no." I snarled. I didn't mention that Ifrits and Dijinn were *way* above me on the power scale. My only advantage was that I didn't have a body they could kill.

"And you work for Dirk?" Remi chimed in.

I rolled my eyes and nodded.

Davenport waved Remi and Hugo over to the side, away from the circle. He glanced at me over Hugo's shoulder before turning away.

"We can't let her out." Davenport murmured.

Hugo looked ready to burst. "She's not a prisoner." His arms crossed over his chest as if daring for someone to argue with him.

"Hugo..." Remi seemed reluctant to speak. "She lied to you. She hid her identity. She knows too much about the compound. We can't..."

"Do not finish that sentence," Hugo warned.

"I can hear you!" I called out theatrically, with my hands around my mouth to amplify my voice. "Look, guys. You can let me out. Seriously. I'm very trustworthy."

"You stole Warren's credit card." Remi pointed out dryly. "And made me drink mouthwash."

"So?" I laughed. "It's not like I murdered anyone." Apart from that creepy trucker—but they didn't need to know that.

Davenport turned to me. "This conversation does not concern you."

"Really?" I tapped my chin with my finger. "Because I think it's very concerning, *Sir*." I blew him a kiss.

"What is she talking about?" Remi bit back laughter, despite his efforts not to.

"Tell them I know what you taste like," I whispered with a conspiring wink.

Hugo's fists clenched. "Don't tell me..."

Remi held up his hands and stepped between the incubus and the commander. "Lads. Calm down." His voice sounded rougher and even more English if that were possible.

Davenport gave everyone his signature look. "Out." He pointed to the Hunters, and he ignored me as he marched out of the room.

235

Remi looked back and smiled for the first time since he had found out I was a Demon.

I couldn't physically touch the salt while I was inside Frankie's body—it burnt my skin and did not heal quickly—but I also couldn't vacate Frankie's body without risking being unable to get back inside.

So, I was stuck in one position. Standing rigidly in the center of the Cyclian rune for Imprisonment and trapping.

I drifted in my own mind for a while, as I thought about everything and nothing.

I didn't know how long I stood still before Remi and Davenport came back. Instead of Hugo, Dr. Lee had decided to join them.

"I thought we weren't telling anybody?" I said happily, pretending to be calm and comfortable when it was a struggle to stand.

Davenport said nothing. I turned to Dr. Lee. "Hey, Birthday Cake."

The Korean man smirked. "Mara."

Davenport cleared his throat and addressed Remi and Jae, ignoring me.

"Your guard shift starts now." The Commander told them sternly. "Do not let her get under your skin." He gave me a dark look before marching away.

"You really bother him," Jae noted, he seemed to take a wicked sense of delight in the notion. Jae glanced at Remi before he stepped forward.

"In my defense, I was left unsupervised," I said harmlessly. "I'm normally much better behaved."

"Really?" Remi chuckled.

"No." I winked.

"Your emotions make sense now," Jae replied. His

hands were in his pockets, just shooting the breeze like two old friends. "For a Demon, you seem remarkably balanced."

"I prefer the term, Chaotic Evil."

Remi sat on the concrete floor and crossed his legs. He yawned and stretched, closing his eyes as he rested his head against the wall.

"Hey!" I pouted. "Aren't you meant to be guarding me?"

Remi did not open his eyes. "Try and get past that circle. I dare you."

Jae's eyes sparkled with delight. He stepped back.

My fists clenched and I gave Remi the stink eye. "I'm an evil Demon!" I stamped my foot. "Take me seriously, dammit!"

Jae hid his smile behind his hand. "Mara..."

I was trapped. There wasn't much I could do. They could keep me in the circle until they decided to kill me. I wasn't sure Hugo would be able to stop them. Still, I had pride and absolutely no impulse control.

My magic became a blade. It raced across the room and sliced into Remi's brain with the careful precision of a surgical scalpel.

"You're scared of spiders?" My brows raised. "Really?"

Remi's eyes flew open. "How did you know that?"

My magic affected the mind. I couldn't physically create spiders, but I could draw his nightmare to the surface of his mind. Remi yelped, like a dog with a trodden tail. He stood up and raced to the corner. Jae and I watched with detached curiosity as the bald man began to brush the unseen insects away from his body. Jumping around like he stood on hot coals.

Jae snickered.

"Help me, you sadistic winged bastard!" Remi barked at Jae as he tried to shake the insects off of his body.

I allowed the spiders to melt away, buried deep in his nightmares. He was unhurt, although Remi seemed on edge as he jumped and slapped his arm even after the arachnids were long gone.

"Do me!" Jae urged, with an enthusiastic clap.

I rolled my eyes and searched his mind for his fears. I pulled my magic back into my body, shocked straight. I shook my head frantically.

"No way," I muttered. "You freak."

"Coming from you, that's high praise." Jae mused.

"What?" Remi demanded, curious.

I eyed Jae critically. "You're messing with me."

Jae shrugged. "You'll never know."

There was no way that the Nephilim had a phobia of *yogurt*.

Remi covered his mouth as he yawned again. It was then that I noticed the dark circles around his eyes. "I'm going for a piss." He told Jae. "Watch her."

When Remi left, Jae turned to me. "How long have you been in that circle?"

I shrugged because I did not know. His violet eyes stormed at my non-verbal response.

"Are you hungry? Thirsty?" He asked and I realized that his anger was because he cared about my wellbeing.

I rolled my head on my shoulders and took inventory. "I think so."

Jae shook his head. "I'll get you something to eat when Remi comes back."

My brow creased. I had expected Jae to joke about it with me. To make fun, and to take my mind off of my situation. I hadn't expected comfort.

"Why are you being nice to me?" I asked suspiciously.

Jae smirked his crooked grin. "I've been in your shoes."

"Davenport put you in a circle for days?" I asked dryly. Somehow, I couldn't see it.

"No. My *Omma*." Jae admitted casually. "She was a cold woman. The only time she ever smiled was when she cooked. She would lock me in the closet when she went to work. Paranoid that I'd cause mischief when she was away."

238

I stared at him in disbelief.

"I was seven." He added.

My mind conjured up the distressing image of a tiny boy with a bowl haircut slamming his fists into the shuttered door of a closet and crying.

"Demons don't harm children," I said.

"There are many ways to harm that aren't physical."

I hummed my agreement. "Is that why you became a therapist?"

Jae considered my question. "I thought I was a psychopath for a while."

"Really?" I asked excitedly.

Jae gave me a hard look. "I felt like I was mimicking emotions. I wore a mask constantly. Smiled at the right times. Said all the right things."

I had seen his therapist mask. That blank and earnest innocence that was so far off the mark it was almost funny.

"I experienced everyone else's emotions all of the time, and I struggled to identify my own. I realized that it was okay to be an introvert. I like my space. I only interact with a few people at a time. I was depressed for a long time." Jae continued.

"Why are you telling me this?" I cocked my head to the side like a confused puppy.

"I was lost until I found my place with the Hunter's." Jae gave me a meaningful look. "I think you're lost too."

I started to consider his words as the door slipped down, and Remi entered again.

"Did I miss anything?" The Witchling asked, not looking at me.

"A riveting game of Charades." Jae lied with a bright smile.

A few hours later, Davenport brought in a cot for Remi, as Dr.

Lee swapped over with Hart. Hart brought a bottle of water and a greasy bag filled with burgers and fries. Not the healthiest, but my stomach felt like it was going to devour itself. Human hunger was different from Demon hunger. More sluggish and painful. I didn't like it.

Remi had curled up and gone to sleep in the corner of the bare room, as Hart stood to attention by the door. I wolfed down my burger, wiping the residue of my meal from my face with the back of my bare arm.

"How long has it been since you last ate?" Hart did not look at me as he asked the question. His arms were crossed as he stood sentry.

"The morning we went to NYC." I sucked Coke through a straw. The ice made my teeth ache.

"But you need to eat?"

"Only when I'm in a body." I clarified.

"Why don't you just leave?" He asked.

I waved a hand to gesture to the salt line on the floor and quirked a brow.

Hart shook his head and clicked his tongue against the roof of his mouth. "I don't believe for a second that you're actually trapped."

"Believe it," I grunted. "My ass is numb from standing for so long."

Remi stirred in his sleep and rolled over. He did not wake.

"Why is Remi here? The shift changed over already."

"His magic is warding the circle," Hart informed me.

Guilt twisted my stomach. Apart from the salt line, Remi's magic couldn't touch me. I hated that he was wasting his life force on something so trivial.

"Davenport thinks I'm a big threat, huh?" I laughed bitterly.

"You're not worried he's going to kill you?"

"If anyone could, it would be Daddy Davenport." I admitted. I turned to Hart and appraised the burly man with

240

curiosity. "You're talking more than usual."

"I honestly thought I had gone insane." He gave me a dirty look. "I'm glad you aren't really Frankie. It's been fucking with my head for days."

I nodded. "You're not angry."

Hart shrugged. "Jae explained."

"Ah. Jae." I wiggled my eyebrows.

Hart ignored my statement. Remi let out a breathy laugh in his sleep. It was very cute. I wanted to see what he was dreaming about, but that would take more energy than I had.

"I think that Remi is trying to avoid Alicia anyway." Hart followed my eyes to land on the sleeping man.

"She's here already?" My heart squeezed painfully like someone had gripped it in their fist and twisted.

"Another team got attacked," Hart said. "We believe it was the same Demon that took out Team C."

"Damn." I breathed. "Did anyone survive?"

"Two people lived longer than the rest." Hart's tone was dead. "They did not have any visible injuries. All of their levels were normal. Nothing out of the ordinary."

"But the rest of the team were fried on the inside?" I stepped to the edge of the salt circle. "Which team?"

"Team G," Hart said. "All fried, apart from two."

The strangeness of the homicide whirled around my mind. Why not just kill them all the same way? If I was a murdering Demon, that's what I would do.

Unless I knew the terms of the summoning, I could not accurately say if the Ifrit was acting under the complete control of its summoner. Was there a significance in the different types of death?

"Thinking too hard gives me a migraine." I moaned.

"And feminists everywhere weep." Hart deadpanned.

I narrowed my eyes and stuck out my tongue. "I'm a Demon. When I concentrate, bad things happen."

Hart exhaled. It almost sounded like he was laughing at me.

241

"I need the bathroom," I added. Fairly certain that I also stank to high heaven. Humans did things like sweat, even when they were doing nothing.

Hart glanced over at Remi, and with a sigh, he used his foot to break the pristine line of salt. He marched over to the door and only looked over his shoulder once.

"Are you coming?" Callum asked.

I stumbled over the salt circle, with unsteady legs, as the Sergeant continued on without me. Confident that I was following.

I used the two seconds alone to bite my thumb and swipe the bloody digit on Remi's bottom lip before I hurried after Hart. I couldn't have explained my reasoning, even if I tried.

My blood would heal Remi, and hopefully, negate some of the symptoms of his excess magic use. I had never seen the vibrant man so rundown.

Hart stood in the utilitarian corridor. He tapped his foot before he glided to the end of the empty hallway and opened a door, ushering me through.

The bathroom was a shower and toilet combination. I eyed the soap with Lust and Envy but made no move towards them. Hart guarded the bathroom, content that I would not try to escape.

"I could have left Frankie in the bathroom and be halfway to NYC by now," I said brightly when I had done my business.

Hart licked his bottom lip. "Doubt it."

"Why's that?" I stopped walking and cocked my hip.

"I have a theory." Hart turned to face me. His marmalade eyes bored into mine. "Dirk owes Davenport for London, but I think you owe Dirk. You're not going to leave a job half done, and screw over your boss."

"Maybe I'm just horny for Hunters." I joked, but it fell flat. A little bit too close to the bone.

"Say what you want." Hart was smug. "You're in this

242

until the end."

We walked back to my prison cell. The salt circle laid broken, as we had left it, but Remi was no longer on the cot.

He had rolled onto the hard concrete floor, his hands around his throat as he gasped on a silent scream. Huge choking breaths escaped his lips, and his eyes bulged.

Hart rushed to his side immediately. He shifted Remi into the recovery position.

"What's wrong?" Hart's tone was steady. Calm in a crisis.

"My skin. Burns." Remi wheezed.

Hart whirled around, paying attention to me for the first time since we had walked into the room. My back was pressed against the concrete wall.

"Could it be the Ifrit?" Hart demanded.

I gestured helplessly. "I think so." I hated that my voice was weak as I watched Remi grunt in pain.

Hart gripped Remi's khaki cotton t-shirt and ripped it down from the collar to the hem in one swift and short movement. I was too worried to even make a joke.

Circles and lines marked the space over Remi's heart. Inflamed red, before they melted to silvery faded scars.

My mouth went dry. I wanted to run far and fast, but my feet would not move.

"Did the Ifrit mark me?" Remi's voice pitched as he looked down at his bare chest. His fingers sought the markings like a blind man reading braille.

Hart looked at me for clarification.

"Not quite," I admitted sheepishly.

Chapter 16

Remi was pulled out of the room by Hart and taken to the medical ward. I was left alone with my broken circle and an uncomfortable canvas cot. I tried to sleep but found myself unable to.

Hours passed before Davenport came to my cell. I sat up immediately, before arranging my expression into an uncaring mask.

Warren Davenport held out his hand. A silver collar hung from his index finger.

"You must have some powerful friends," Davenport said, his eye twitched. "The *Higher-ups* have officially petitioned for your release."

I blinked slowly and waited for him to continue to speak.

"I seriously considered just killing you." He admitted.

I smirked. "But I'm so likable."

"This is an F-Status collar." He informed me, even though I did not ask. "Feral shifters use them to prevent the change into their other form. I believe this will lock your magic into that body, so you cannot leave it."

My lip tightened. "You want me to stay in this body?"

"Until whatever it taking out my Hunters is found." He didn't sound too happy about that. Davenport's eyes swept over the remnants of the broken salt circle, but he did not say anything.

"Is Remi okay?" I asked tentatively.

Davenport's gaze darkened. "He appears to have recovered."

I nodded to myself and looked down at my hands. Existence was more comfortable when all I cared about was eating gourmet food and getting plowed.

I pulled my legs to my chest and wrapped my arms around them.

Davenport perched on the edge of the cot. He held out the collar. I eyed it with disgust but made no move to take it.

"I don't know what I did," I admitted in a small voice. "Demon matings take *days*. There's rituals, an orgy, and a Scribe to oversee it all. It doesn't just happen."

"Remi is your mate?" Warren's eyebrows arched in question. "What about Hugo?"

"Him too," I admitted.

"Hugo informed me that a Soulbond is a very private and intricate thing," Davenport said lightly. "There are almost no instances of a Soulbond forming on their own."

I lifted a shoulder and let it drop in a half-assed shrug.

"You're now a temporary member of Team P," Davenport said, changing the subject. "It will allow us to keep a closer eye on you."

I pasted a smile on my face. "Yay to not being killed."

Davenport gave me a look.

"Right." I rearranged my face into a stern and stoic expression. "This is my professional face."

Davenport rolled his eyes and motioned for me to follow. I rose but snapped out my foot using the element of surprise to kick Warren behind the knee. He grunted in pain and whirled around. His eyes wide with shock. It was cute. He was like a hurt puppy, unused to being the victim.

"What was that for?" He barked as he straightened to his towering 6 foot 1 height.

I shrugged, eying the silver collar in his hand with disdain.

"I'm a Demon. You didn't make a bargain. You issue orders and assumed I would follow them." I told him. "I don't have to pretend to be Fae anymore."

Davenport looked like he didn't know if he wanted to rip my head off or bend me over his knee. He would have

245

probably enjoyed both equally.

"You want to make a bargain?" Davenport asked delicately.

I nodded earnestly.

"You believe that you hold enough power to enforce a bargain?" He scoffed.

All amusement drained from my face and was replaced with a dead mask. "It seems that I have the backing of your *Higher-ups*." I reminded him.

I didn't know who his bosses were, but I would hazard a guess that The Balance had greased the wheels.

I held out my hand and called up the innate connection to Hell that I often squashed. All Demons could bargain. They seldom did it because it was tedious, and there wasn't much that was interesting enough to trade for. The Devil used contracts to broker souls. I had never called one forth, but a length of vellum unfurled in my hand like a skin-colored dahlia.

Davenport watched the display with suspicion.

"Do you have a pen?" I gave him my best *fuck you* smile.

Yeah. He definitely wanted to spank me—and judging by the rigid set of his gritted teeth, he hated himself for that.

I didn't put the collar on until the contract was to my satisfaction.

I was to be released from the collar and from any obligations, penalties, or punishments that the Hunters may want to bestow on me the second that I found the Ifrit and its Summoner.

Davenport had tried to include a tidy monetary bonus for taking care of the problem, but I was realistic about my abilities.

I could challenge the Ifrit and break the Summoner's

hold on it, no problem. Handling someone that could trap a Demon? Not so easy when you didn't know what to expect. So, I made no promises. They were Hunters. I didn't feel bad for warning Davenport that I was going to scram if the going got tough.

I wasn't big on the whole sacrifice thing.

Yes, I thought about my kin's death, every single day, and prayed that I could have saved them—but at the end of the day, I knew that I couldn't. I was just a tiny cog in the machine of Hell. The problem of the Bhakshi and the Shayati had been taken care of by the Queen of Wrath, which proved my point.

I might be mated to two Hunters, but I would drag them away from the battle with me rather than putting myself in danger.

Almost dying was a flavor that I did not like. Davenport's flame world had assured me of that.

I was put in a new suite in the officer's building. Between Hugo's room and down the corridor from Hart. Remi shared a connecting suite with Hugo, and Davenport was on the end. I had never asked why Hugo bedded down in the executive suite, but it made sense. The rooms were more separated than the other dorms, and Incubi did tend to project into dreams.

Maybe Davenport was trying to hoard all the erotic night time fun for himself.

I thought about asking him just to see the look on his face.

I scrubbed my skin until it turned pink, and then scrubbed some more. Someone delivered food to my new room when I was in the shower, and I ignored the silverware to scoop fistfuls of hot mash potatoes into my mouth. My cheeks bulged like a hamster, and I covered myself in gravy in my haste—which resulted in the need for another shower—but I did not care.

The brief lack of sensation, coupled with being dragged through an unknown fire landscape and being trapped with Hunters, meant that I was desperate to eat, sleep, and *live*.

247

A hard, impatient rap broke me from my internal ramblings. I whipped my hair back like a dog and pulled on a robe. I debated flinging open the door in all my nude glory, but I was exhausted and emotionally spent. I could barely bring myself to care about my own wellbeing, let alone sating my mischievous desires to make people uncomfortable.

"Remington Weber." I stepped back and studied his sodden form. It must have been raining outside. I hadn't noticed.

Remi looked better than he had in days. The dark circles were gone from beneath his eyes, and he was no longer writhing in pain—which was a good thing when it came to humans.

"Can I talk to you?" He sounded devoid of life. I was concerned which was strange to me.

I stepped back to allow him to come into my room. He hesitated for a second before disappearing inside. Remi did not take a seat, he began to pace.

"I don't like that," I told him. "You're making me nervous."

Remi stopped as if he had been caught in quicksand. He fisted his large hands and forced them down to his side.

"Warren said that you are aware of my engagement," Remi stated blandly. "Can you tell me what happened?"

I took a deep breath, fingering the silver band around my neck. "You looked tired. I gave you some blood."

"You gave me some blood." Remi echoed back.

"Demon blood heals humans. It feels better than heroin, apparently." I winced at the analogy. "I wanted to help."

Remi stared at me. His expression was inscrutable. "You weren't enthralled by Hugo. You mated yourself to him."

"Not on purpose." I pointed out.

"And this mating thing? It's permanent?"

I rolled my lip between my teeth.

"Mara..." Remi chided when I did not answer.

"I'm just trying to figure out how much to tell you."

248

My voice was quiet. "I never wanted a mate. Let alone two."

"Mara," Remi repeated my name to get my full attention. "It's me. You can tell me."

"It's not you!" I waved my hand in his direction, snapping. "You're acting all strange!"

Remi sighed, finally perching on the end of my bed. He folded in half, putting his head in his hands.

"My family has signed documents." The sound was muffled by his hands. "This marriage will bring prestige to the Weber family after my father ruined our reputation when he knocked up my mum. I can't do this."

"Do you want to marry Alicia?" I asked tentatively.

"I want to save my family." He replied.

I nodded. I could respect that. "We can't break the Soulbond, but we can ignore it. Distance helps."

I didn't add that a bond made it very difficult to *want* to stay away from someone.

Remi's entire frame relaxed, the tension melted away. "Really?"

I smiled tightly. "Just try not to get killed. Your life force is tied to mine."

Remi's chocolate eyes shuttered. "What does that mean?"

I waved away his concern. "You die. I die."

His frown could have been carved from marble. "Right."

I sat on the edge of the bed, careful to keep my distance. I swung my legs as I tapped my fingers against my knees. "So... Alicia's here."

Remi sighed. "She's a powerful Witchling."

"Of course." I ignored the spearing pain, it felt like a vital part of myself was being torn apart.

"You'd like her." He offered. "She likes Tarantino and Chinese food."

My lips pinched like I had tasted something foul. Tarantino and Chinese food? Everyone liked those things, they weren't a marker of good taste.

Remi roared with laughter at my facial expression.

"I just want you to be happy." I reached forward and placed my hand on top of his before I could stop myself.

Remi's eyes sparkled. "Strange thing for a Demon to say."

"Sorry, what I meant was, I just want to sever your spinal cord and then dance naked around your paralyzed body." I rolled my eyes.

"Oddly specific."

"Lucifer once punished an ex-prima ballerina that way." I snorted. "She'd beaten out her competition by staging an accident during rehearsals—Pride's punishments depended on Lucy's moods."

"You met the Devil?" Remi asked.

"Cowered in fear as he strutted around the City of Dis like a peacock? Why, yes, Remington. I have." I tilted up my nose as I affected a fake-British accent.

Remi chuckled softly. My hand still lingered on his. I tried not to focus on how large his hand was compared to mine.

Remington Weber was destined to marry another Witchling. A cursed human, with a preferred bloodline. I was only meant to be a temporary part of his life before I flitted away to another body and another mission. Another life to experience.

"Are you scared of me?" I asked, keeping the emotion out of my voice.

Remi quirked a brow. "I've seen you fight. You couldn't punch your way out of a paper bag."

"You've seen my magic." I reminded him with a pout.

"You have a problem with people underestimating you, don't you?"

A smile lit up my face, wicked and full of mischief. "Go on!" I clapped and bounced on the bed. "Underestimate me. It'll be fun."

Remi's smile was a sunbeam. "Too cute." He whispered, shaking his head, the words were so quiet that I

250

didn't think he meant for me to hear them.

I hadn't realized, but somehow, we had moved closer like two magnets unable to deny the thrumming vital connection between us.

I could see every individual eyelash and the almost indiscernible dilated pupil in the center of his warm chocolate irises. His lips were plush, a rose color, his cheekbones were sharp. Remi was a beautiful man.

He was studying me just as intensely.

"We shouldn't do this." He breathed but did not move.

"Relying on a Demon to exercise control is a foolish move on your part."

"I'm talking to myself." Remi chuckled before his smile fell clean off his face. "I'm sorry." He stood up and moved towards the door before I could process what had happened.

My lips tingled as I thought about what his kiss would have felt like—but I knew Remi, he would be faithful, even if it cost him his Soulmate.

My muscles felt worse after a full night's sleep than they had done when I had been walking about. My gait resembled the Tin Man from the Wizard of Oz as I dressed and headed to the Mess Hall to eat my weight in Tabasco soaked pancakes.

Gary had attempted to start a conversation with me, but my face was set in a fixed frown as I moved down the queue to get my breakfast. Every movement made my spine throb, I hadn't realized how long I had been stood in the salt circle, unable to lie down for even a second.

Wasn't that against human laws or something?

I began to shovel food into my mouth when Hugo slid his tray into the seat opposite mine. He did not say a word as he silently began to eat. The incubus seemed content in my company, and I did not want to ruin it with a barrage of questions.

Had he accepted me at his Mate? The confrontation in the warehouse pointed to yes. But I hadn't seen him since. He hadn't actually spoken to me.

Hugo was half-human—a species with emotions too complex to fully understand. He had been raised with Humans. If Hugo were Cyclian, a denizen of Hell, I would simply walk up to him and bite his lip until it bled. Any incubus would view that as a green light. Blood was an aphrodisiac for Demons.

A few minutes later, Jae and Hart greeted me and sat down at our table. I felt warm and gooey because Jae greeted me with a dirty joke as if nothing had changed, and Hart swatted him with the back of his hand.

Someone cleared their throat over my shoulder, I ignored the sound as I took a tentative sip of my coffee.

"Frankie," Dr. Daniel drawled in a bored voice. My eyes widened as I affected an air of innocence.

"Dr. Dan!" I acted as if I hadn't heard him.

His lip curled. He hated the nickname, his discomfort made my heart sing. Dr. Dan did not address my use of his disliked moniker.

"It's Thanksgiving tomorrow." He stated blandly.

I turned to my men, eyebrows raised in a questioning expression. Jae shook his head and shrugged, clearly unaware of where the doctor's thought process was heading.

"Yes." I nodded sagely. "And ducks have corkscrew penises."

"What?" Daniel spluttered, my comment breaking through his empty mask.

"I thought we were stating facts." I sipped my coffee around a benign smile.

"If you remember, a few weeks ago, I reminded you of our parent's invitation to Thanksgiving dinner." Daniel glanced at Hugo and then Jae and Hart. "You said that you could make it."

"Did I?" I tapped my chin.

Hugo made a strange noise with his throat to catch my attention. "We'd love to go." The incubus chimed in pleasantly. "What should we bring?"

If Daniel was shocked by Hugo inviting himself, he did not show it. "Bring dessert." Then the doctor turned on his heel and walked away. I watched him go, trying to catch a peek at the obvious stick up his ass.

If he and Frankie were both ice cold, dull, and mean, I didn't want to meet their adopted parents. There must have been a reason for their personalities, and I was willing to bet that it started at home.

"Why did you say that?" I hissed under my breath, confident that Hugo could hear me.

Hugo flicked his hair away from his face and looked to Jae and Hart for assistance.

I clicked my fingers to draw his gaze back to me as I waited for his response.

Hart must have taken pity on the incubus because he started to offer an explanation—unwilling to let delicate Hugo squirm.

"The Gardiner's are famous Hunters. If Frankie did not come to Thanksgiving, they would likely come to the compound." Hart said.

"Which would be dangerous, because of whoever is targeting the Hunters." I realized.

Jae snapped his fingers. "Ten points for Slytherin."

"How dare you assume my Hogwarts house." My hand fluttered to my chest, offended.

"I'm in Slytherin too." Jae winked. "It's where all the cool kids are."

Hart tsked, but did not interrupt.

"Such a Hufflepuff." Jae murmured, digging into his omelet.

"Anyway..." Hugo interrupted, blushing when our attention focused back on him. "We can use the opportunity to follow one of Remi's leads."

"Remi has a lead?" I perked up.

Hugo nodded solemnly. "There's a club in Queens called Fool's Gold." He said.

A smile spread on my lips. "I've been there!" I said excitedly.

"So it's a Demon hangout." Hart's voice was dry.

"Don't discriminate." Jae chided seriously.

"One of the Ifrit symbols was spotted on the security cameras, on the brick wall of the alley by the club." Hugo elaborated.

Finally, a clue.

Somehow, Dr. Dan had found my new room assignment and posted a very in-depth itinerary to my door. I found the laminated A4 document as I left my room with a duffle bag of Frankie's clothes on Thanksgiving morning.

Hugo startled when he spotted me, but the movement was falsely casual as if he had been waiting for me. His greeting was stilted as we walked together, and I wanted to ask him what bug had crawled up his ass. Somehow, I behaved myself and stayed silent.

Dr. Dan had left the day before, driving to Queens to spend the night at his parent's house. Hugo and I decided to drive down early the next morning.

We rounded the fence and ambled to the SUV in silence. Jae and Hart were leaning against the vehicle looking calm, each with a duffle over their shoulders, sporting matching *'Davenport's Halfway Camp'* t-shirts.

"What are you guys doing here?" I wondered as Hugo popped the trunk for our bags.

Hart ignored the question and ducked into the backseat. Jae rolled his eyes.

"Did you think we'd let you both go to *Fool's Gold*

254

without us?" Jae's violet eyes sparkled. "Besides, Remi's in Connecticut with Alicia and Warren has a conference call with the West Coast."

Hart poked his head out of the open window. "Jae didn't want to be alone on Thanksgiving."

"I thought you were Korean? Do they even have Thanksgiving." Hugo wondered as he returned to my side.

"His Omma is Korean." I reminded him. "You were born in the US, right?"

Jae's cheeky smile melted into a genuine and confused one. "You remembered."

I shrugged, distracted by the empty passenger seat. I bounced forward and wrenched the door open while calling shotgun.

No one argued with me.

We made good time to Queens and were greeted by Daniel on the porch of the wisteria-covered baby blue house. The flower beds were perfectly tended, though the mailbox was dented. Matching the neighbors on either side, which implied that teenagers had vandalized the local area.

Hugo had briefed me on the Gardiner's before we got out of the SUV, but his knowledge of the subject was formal. Two ex-Hunters, Elsie and Andrew Gardiner. They had two adopted children, Frankie and Daniel. Raised in Queens, away from the compound, both children had been the victims of attacks from otherworldly beings that resulted in the loss of their families. Both children later went on to become Hunters, like their adopted parents.

I had expected stoic and stiff people, like Daniel, but on steroids. Instead, I was swept away in a flurry of floral perfume, the grip of a full-body hug from a tiny woman, and a kiss on every surface of my face.

255

"Mom..." I spat out, feeling guilty for some reason, but unable to identify the source. Maybe it was because I was wearing her adopted daughter like an overcoat, and in a few weeks, she'd be standing on the same porch and hearing about her daughter's death.

... Yeah. That was probably it.

Elsie Gardiner gave me a strange look in response to my greeting, and I soon figured out why when she lovingly introduced herself as 'Momma G' to Hugo, Jae, and Hart.

Andrew Gardiner did not look up from his newspaper once. Daniel had disappeared.

The house was stuffed full of knick-knacks and unique furniture, a mixture between IKEA and old-world antique. The air was thick with the delicious smell of Thanksgiving dinner, and before long, I found myself seated at a dining table.

Sandwiched between Hugo and Hart, I stared at the glistening and crispy skin on the turkey. I hadn't realized how hungry I was.

Momma G made us hold hands and say grace. Jae did the honors with aplomb, switching to his bright-eyed gentle therapist persona. I wanted to laugh, and Jae definitely caught the curl of my lips as I restrained himself, because he kicked me under the table.

Dinner didn't get interesting until we were all on our second portions, and the subject of 'The Calling' was brought up—surprisingly by Frankie's father, Andrew.

The mild-mannered man asked about some of the most recent takedowns and then began to reminisce.

"I lived in Iowa. Cornfields for miles, and suddenly I hear a baby crying. Crazy, right?" The man took a sip of his beer. "You didn't go into cornfields at night. It just wasn't done, but that baby was howling. I followed the noise."

"Bubak." I supplied helpfully. Andrew nodded sagely in my direction, which gave the impression he had told Frankie the same stories many times.

"That's right, honey." Andrew agreed. "They lure their

256

victims in with a cry and then eat them. Gluttony demon. Fifth circle."

Hart cleared his throat. "I was working as an animal handler for the New Orleans zoo. Caught a Shax Demon trying to mate with one of our Komodo dragons." Hart's eyes sparkled with laughter.

"What about you, Jae?" I asked.

"I had just qualified as a therapist when one of my clients went completely catatonic." Jae shrugged. "It's not an interesting story, but I was able to pull her out using my empathetic abilities. Next thing I knew, I had the three stars."

Hugo must have caught my desire to ask what the three stars were because he brushed his shaggy blonde hair away from his left ear and showed the formation of three white scars that looked like stars in a perfect triangle. My hand reached behind my ear to the raised skin behind Frankie's ear, having not noticed it before.

Momma G glanced at Daniel, who was focused intensely on his plate. Food laid forgotten.

"Does anyone want more green beans?" The short woman asked brightly.

Daniel Gardiner pushed away from the table. His chair made a harsh screech on the wooden floor as he burst from the room like the hounds of Hell were on his tail.

My brows raised in question.

Momma G tried to smile, but it did not reach her eyes. She gripped her husband's hand and turned to him. "Maybe keep the *Calling* talk to a minimum, honey-bun. Daniel doesn't like to be reminded that Frankie was called, and he wasn't."

The rest of the dinner was eaten in silence.

Every time I looked at Daniel's empty seat, I wanted to burst out of my skin with questions.

The guys had gone to the guest rooms to shower and dress before the club. Daniel had not come down after dinner, not even for dessert.

I lingered in the hallway, studying the various happy photos that lined the hall like they contained the answers to the universe.

Momma G caught me brushing my fingers against a framed photo of a red-headed Daniel, with a similarly afflicted woman stood behind him. The happy smiling human had her arms wrapped around the grumpy child like he was the key to her happiness and the only thing she had ever needed.

"Daniel told me that he joined the Hunter's to follow you." Momma G had crept up on me when I wasn't looking.

I hummed but did not look away from the photo.

"He wanted to find the Blood Sidhe that killed his birth parents, but he also wanted to protect you." She added.

The Blood Sidhe that killed his parents? A few months ago, a Blood Sidhe had attacked Frankie and Daniel while on a mission. That couldn't have been a coincidence.

Blood Sidhe could pull blood from people's pores with a thought. They used it for pointless purposes. But they were smart and compelling. They did not target indiscriminately.

"Maybe try to be kinder to your brother, Franny. Hmm?" Momma G patted my cheek and slinked away upstairs.

Hugo and I were sharing a room at the end of the house, across the hall from Jae and Hart. The incubus was tucked away in the bathroom, using the ensuite to shower.

A folded pile of fabric caught my attention, placed lovingly on the pillowcase on my side of the bed. I brushed my fingers over the dress, holding the delicate fabric as if it was priceless. Letting the shimmering darkness slide over my skin like water.

"It reminded me of you," Hugo said, his voice startled me, and I whirled around, hugging the dress to my chest.

Hugo had changed clothes in the shower. He wore a pristine, slim-fitted black shirt. The top button had been left open to show a flash of golden skin.

"It's for me?" I clasped the dress tightly.

Hugo blushed. "If you don't like it, I can return it."

"No!" I protested, tightening my grip around the dress. "I love it."

It looked like starlight, twinkling distant planets and darkness too deep to comprehend.

"It's beautiful," I whispered.

"We need to talk." He sat on the end of the bed, his expression grim.

I stopped my casual perusal of his body and gave him my full attention.

"Why didn't you tell me who you were to me? That day in the hospital?" His tone was even and without judgment.

I felt nauseous. My eyes drifted to the corner of the room.

"Mara..." Hugo said softly to get my attention. "I'm not mad. I'm not hurt. I'm confused. I want to know what you're thinking and feeling."

I blinked rapidly. "You rejected me."

"I rejected Frankie because I had found my true mate."

"You should have recognized me." My voice was tiny. Weak. I hated it.

Understanding blossomed over Hugo's face. He pushed his bangs out of his eyes.

"I didn't want a mate." I continued. Ignoring the pain that flashed through Hugo's eyes. "But every night, I'd visit your dreams, and you'd see mine, and I felt like I *knew* you. You belonged to me. I didn't want to see you hurt. I wanted you safe, even if it meant that you weren't with me."

Hugo nodded in understanding, silently urging me to continue. I stared at the beading on the edge of my dress, so I

259

did not have to look into his eyes.

"I told myself that I was safer alone, but I found myself standing in the cold and wet outside your window. Just to see if you were awake. Healthy. Healed." I laughed bitterly. "And you used that weakness as an excuse to reject me."

"I thought you were an enthralled human," Hugo explained. I waved my hand to dismiss his words.

"I know it's not rational." I pleaded. "Everything you did was because you wanted to be *my* mate. Everything I did was because I didn't want the Hunters to find out what I am."

"They wouldn't kill you." He said strongly.

"Hunters kill Demons. They're celebrated for it." I shrugged. "You're a Cambion. You can't tell me that you've never been treated differently because you're part hellion."

Hugo shook his head. "Hunters only hunt evil."

"Who decides what evil is?" I asked.

"I don't know." He admitted, before turning back to the door. "You should get ready. We have to go soon."

Fool's Gold was located in an abandoned and then refurbished department store on the border of Queens and Brooklyn. The first floor of the club opened up to a massive sprawling central staircase that was cordoned off with velvet tape. As far as I knew, the upper floors were inaccessible to humans.

Fool's had made an unpopular choice in the otherworld community, by refusing to hide in one of the Folds between worlds, and instead the club rested entirely in the Human Realities.

While it was known as a predominantly Demon club, I had been once or twice and had noticed an abundance of Fae as well.

Fools was tacky, with a side of bad taste. The walls were carpeted shag in a lucid purple with neon green piping. The floor was concrete, painted into tiger stripes. Every inch of the place was designed to insult your senses and the tiny part of your mind that took life too seriously.

We took a cab, which dropped us off in Ridgewood and we bypassed the queue at the club—much to the grumbled protests of everyone in line.

Jae hung back, his violet eyes were dim.

"Are you okay?" I asked, stopping at his side. Hugo and Hart slowed down and turned to us both to see what was happening.

"I'm fine." Jae swallowed deeply.

"You're not." Callum Hart stated. "You're around too many people. You've got limits, Jae."

Anger flared in the Nephilim's. "I'm fine." He repeated, sounded out the words.

I glanced at the bouncer, as an impatient and perplexed expression implied that our welcome would be taken away if we didn't get a move on.

Hugo had obviously had the same idea. "Jae, Callum, go over to that diner over there. We'll text if we need back up."

Jae exhaled reluctantly and opened his mouth to argue. He turned to me and nudged my shoulder.

"Don't start any fires," Jae warned.

I pouted. "Why doesn't Hugo get a warning?"

Instead of answering, Jae smirked as Hart pulled him across the road to the glowing lights of the *Soup Spoon Diner*.

The Human bouncer at the door waved us through, and we did not encounter trouble until we reached the VIP lounge at the very top of the sprawling staircase.

Hugo moved gracefully, but sensually. Every shift of his hips was an invitation. My incubus spent so much time hiding, it was a marvel to see when he was switched *'on.'*

A Leviathan, a Demon belonging to the Fourth Circle, Envy, was manning the velvet rope to the third-floor private area.

Hugo and I allowed our eyes to flash, mine black and

261

his ice blue, to show our inner Demon. The Leviathan unclipped the rope and ushered Hugo through, but placed a hand on the center of my bare sternum to push my body back into the hall.

"Hey!" I protested loudly, rearranging the thin straps of my dress.

"No." The Leviathan shut me down. "Only one Drude has ever walked through these walls, and good things never follow."

I popped my hip to one side. "It was one bottle of Grey Goose."

"Into the mouth of a teetotal player for the Yankees." The Leviathan pointed out, baring his teeth. "We did not need that bad press."

"Dirk made me do it." I fluttered my eyelashes. The Leviathan remained unaffected.

I pleaded with Hugo for help, over the spindly man's shoulder. Even though it clearly pained him, the incubus stepped back.

A wave of Lust clouded the air, a subtle incense. The Leviathan straightened. Hugo reached forward and ran his index finger down the lapel of the man's cheap orange uniform blazer.

"Can you let her in?" Hugo purred. "As a favor for me?"

Even I felt myself getting sucked in. He was good. I was almost jealous.

The Leviathan swallowed profoundly and leaned forward, lips puckered as if he wanted nothing more than to French kiss the living hell out of my Mate.

I gripped Hugo's shoulders to pull him away, darting into the VIP area, I shouted a quick thank you over my shoulder before the Envy Demon could stop us.

"You've been practicing," I noted proudly. My chest heaved, and my eyes sparkled with the residual effects of his magic.

Hugo smiled weakly. "A certain person told me that only young Incubi had so little control."

"I'm sorry." My smile slid away. "I wanted to hurt you because I was hurting. I shouldn't have said that."

"I needed to hear it," Hugo said as he reached out with tentative hands, and pulled me into his embrace. My head fit between his pectoral muscles perfectly. He smelt like expensive cologne and magic.

"I'm still sorry." My voice was muffled against his chest.

After a second, Hugo let go. I lamented the loss and turned to the subdued VIP section. The walls were polished dark wood paneling, the opposite of the horrendous decor that swathed the floor below. Soft and delicate music weaved through the sparse chatting crowd. Cigar smoke and wind chimes. An odd combination.

"Who are we looking for?" I leaned over and gripped Hugo's bicep as I surveyed the crowd. I recognized a few faces from my covert wanderings, but they would not have known who I was.

"Ryn Cole," Hugo said out of the corner of his mouth. I groaned. "Do you know who that is?"

I quirked a brow and gave him a look that screamed, *'are you serious?'*

"I was raised human," Hugo spoke so quietly that he barely moved his mouth. "Help me out here."

I turned away from the crowd and tugged the incubus to the dark corner, nestled between the empty chesterfield and a dusty bookshelf.

"Is he over there?" Hugo asked, craning his neck to look past my shoulder. My curly hair smacked him in the face as I whipped around and glanced at the room.

"Brown hair, in a low ponytail. Drinking scotch by the fire." I tilted my jaw in the direction of the man.

"And?" Hugo whispered.

"Ryn Cole is Mammon's, the King of Greed's Second in Command," I said in a deep breath. "He's dragon-blooded."

"He's a dragon?" Hugo hissed.

263

"No. He's a Fae. Enslaved. Cursed by dragons, the original Kings of Greed. That ownership and curse passed down to Mammon when the dragons left Hell."

"How do you know all this stuff?"

"Basic Cyclian history." I shrugged.

"How do we get his attention?"

"Greed likes unique things. Ryn hunts rare items for King Mammon. Did you bring anything?"

"Yes. Let me just get this one of a kind Fabergé egg out of my pocket." Hugo remarked dryly.

I snapped my fingers. "Love it. Love the sarcasm. Love the energy here." I said, genuinely. "Maybe, let's think outside the box instead of shitting on it, okay?"

Hugo had the decency to blush, chastised.

"I can't think of anything." He bit his lip before his eyes widened. "Wait! You're a Drude."

"Yes." I rolled my eyes. "A Drude is not a rare item. We're..." My mouth slammed shut. I had forgotten my pain for a brief second. Being around Hugo had led to the longest time without thinking about my family since they had died. I wasn't sure how to feel about that.

"You're the last one left." Hugo finished the sentence. His eyes were soft. "Rare." He raised his hand and cupped my cheek. Staring down at me like I was the beginning, middle, and end of his world.

"How do we get his attention?" I asked.

Hugo's eyes darted around the room. "Leave that to me."

Ten minutes later, Ryn Cole remained by the fire. Hugo and I had not moved from the shadow of the bookshelf, but every other person in the room had been stripped of their inhibitions (and clothing) and decided to partake in an orgy.

The floor was a carpet of writing bodies. Demons, Fae, and the occasional human.

I grabbed Hugo's hand and stepped over two stunning men who were discovering each other, and continued until we had taken a seat the abandoned couch opposite the Fae.

Ryn Cole swirled his drink and stared into the fire. He stayed like that for a long time before he pulled his attention away from the roaring flames. The Dragon-blood's face was impassive as his gaze swept across the orgy and then settled on mine. He took a leisurely sip of his scotch. Unconcerned.

"Mr Cole—" Hugo leaned forward, but Cole put his hand up to stop him. The Fae finished his scotch and placed the tumbler down on a coaster.

Cole shifted in his seat, folding his hands over his lap. "A unique way to ask for an audience." His voice was a dangerous purr.

Hugo cleared his throat.

"I wasn't talking to you. Cambion." Run Cole stated without emotion, not sparing Hugo a glance.

I smiled weakly and waved. "Hey."

Ryn Cole's eyes were the only thing that moved.

"Drude." Cole scoffed, turning back to the fire. "Such a shame. What happened to your kin. Did my floral wreath get lost in the mail?" Cole spoke with a strange accent. A mixture of British and American, with dropped syllables.

"I heard that King Mammon did not join the fight against the Bhakshi and the Shayati." My voice was hard. "Your King hides behind treasure, but will not rise to save his home."

Ryn laughed. "A strange way to ask for a boon. To insult my King and bait me."

"Everyone knows you hate your King," I winked.

"Except, perhaps the King of Greed." Ryn smiled sadly, his eyes did not leave the fire. The flames were reflected in his gaze.

I stayed silent, the occasional pop of the burning wood, and the low husky moans of the copulating people behind us were the only sounds.

"Ask your questions," Ryn said gravely.

It took a second for the words to sink in.

"There is a symbol, burnt into the wall behind your club," Hugo said. "When did you first notice it?"

Ryn narrowed his eyes. "Three months ago."

"Do you have the security footage?" the incubus pressed.

"Gone." Ryn's lip twitched. "Your questions are rather tedious."

I examined his words. Fae could not lie, so he was truthful. The issue was that we had to find the right questions to ask before his generosity ran out.

"Do you know who put the symbol there?" I asked.

"No." Ryn licked his lip.

"Who do you *suspect*?" I reworded my question. He smirked, amused like a giant watching an ant.

"You might find this interesting, Hunter." His eyes bored into Hugo's. "Mr. Davenport, your commander, arrived to collect his usual shipment of Devil's Silver bullets. Shortly afterward, the rune had been burnt into my wall. Just dreadful. Vandalism is just so petty, don't you think?"

I didn't answer his question.

"Was there anything odd about Davenport's behavior?" Hugo asked, his voice somewhat strangled.

"Yes."

"*What* was odd about his behavior?" Hugo clarified with a growl.

Ryn Cole was having too much fun playing with us. I could see it on his face. "Davenport placed the order over the phone, as usual, but changed his mind when he arrived. Instead of Devil's Silver, he requested a shipment of Iron bullets, coated in Devil's Silver, and spelled to dissolve after impact."

"Fae killers," I whispered, staring down at the hands of my host.

"Verily." Ryn Cole smirked.

266

"And you gave them to him?" I asked

"Of course." The Fae shifted to stand. Hugo and I moved to our feet, determined not to put our backs to the dangerous creature.

"It's been a hoot." Cole doffed an invisible hat. "And I don't often mean that."

I smiled tightly. Hugo looked more wound up than I had ever seen him.

"I wish you the best in your Hunt." Cole adjusted his lapels. "If you are ever in *Avidity*, do stop into the Palace of Greed. Mammon would love to add the last of the nightmares to his stable."

Then Ryn Cole folded into the space between worlds and disappeared.

Hugo and I did not speak until we had sat down opposite each other in the Soup Spoon Diner. Jae and Hart had ordered coffee and pie, and I followed their example.

Hugo looked ready to burst, and his questions rushed out of his mouth before anyone could ask us how our little interrogation had gone.

"What did Cole mean by stables?" Hugo whispered, keeping his head low.

Hart cleared his throat. "Pimps often refer to their collection of workers by the term stable."

I grabbed a fork and swiped a piece of Jae's blueberry pie. "That's not it," I spoke with a mouthful of pie.

"What was he talking about?" Hugo repeated his question.

"It's not a big deal." I hedged. "Let's just put a pin in it, and talk about what we learned." Look at me, being all responsible and shit. "Daddy Davenport has been ordering Fae-killing bullets."

267

Jae shook his head and spooned pie into his mouth. Hart was fixated on something outside the window.

"I need to get this straight in my mind..." I mumbled, holding out my hand so I could tick things off on my fingers. "Someone, claiming to be Davenport, emailed Dermot Dirk three months ago and bartered for information on how to summon and trap an Ifrit." I folded down a finger. "Team C is attacked. The team is taken out by the Ifrit—but Frankie managed to escape before she fell into a coma. I remember the pain in her memories. She could have been shot."

"There were no wounds in Frankie's medical files," Hugo stated.

I snapped my fingers. "Exactly! Want to bet that Frankie was shot with a dissolving bullet by accident, but she didn't die because she wasn't Fae?"

Jae sipped his coffee. "All of her levels were normal. There wasn't any excess iron in her blood, and there would have been if Corporal Gardiner was hit with a Fae killing bullet."

I blew a raspberry. "Bear with me." I swiped his coffee and took a sip. The waitress was taking ages to bring out my order. "Warren Davenport then contacts Dirk and requests a Mimic Sidhe to play the part of Frankie. He wants access to another Fae, to kill them. I was poisoned, remember?"

Hugo winced. "It's a stretch." He looked to Jae and Hart for support.

I recited all of our questions to Ryn Cole, and then the answers that he had given us.

"I'd rather know about the original email that Dermot Dirk received," Hart said. "Is Remi aware of it? Has he been able to track it?"

I sunk down in my chair. "No," I said sullenly.

"No, he's not aware of it? Or No, he can't track it." Hart's eyes shot to mine.

I picked up a fork from the table and pressed the tines into the pad of my thumb. "He doesn't know."

Hugo's eyes widened. "Mara..."

"I hate it when you say my name like that."

Hart pulled a smartphone from his leather jacket and held it to his ear. It took awhile to connect.

"Yeah?"

"Dermot Dirk received an email, supposedly from Warren, three months ago, asking for instructions on how to summon an Ifrit," Hart explained economically.

"You want me to trace the email?" Remi replied.

Hart glanced at me and asked for the email address. I rattled it off from memory.

"Why would Dirk tell someone how to summon an Ifrit?"

"Why do the Fae do anything?" I shrugged.

"Remington?" A female voice screeched on the end of the line. *"It's rude to take phone calls during dinner."*

"Just a sec, Ally," Remi replied, there was silence as he waited for her to leave. *"Sorry about that."*

"How are the new in-laws?" Jae asked with a smile.

Remi cleared his throat to smother a laugh. *"I'll text when I manage to get to a computer."*

"Remington!" Alicia shouted. *"Get off the phone. Daddy wants to talk to you."*

"Thrilling." I drawled.

"Bye, guys!" Remi said, ignoring me. *"See you Monday."*

"She sounds as fun as hemorrhoids." Jae deadpanned.

"I know, right?" My nose scrunched. I couldn't help it, I sounded jealous, but Remi belonged to *me*.

I could be patient. It might drive me insane, but Remi's lifespan was tied to mine. He was the nearest thing to immortal as he could be. He'd marry Alicia, and then when she died, I would swoop in.

I just had to control myself in the meantime. Thinking about Remi and Alicia touching, kissing, fucking, made me want to hurt someone.

The flimsy fork bent and snapped between my fingers.

"It's Davenport. He sent the email. He ordered the bullets. Done deal. Let's get ice cream." I said with a bright

269

smile.

No one moved or acknowledged my words.

The waitress finally came over with my pie. I asked for a new fork.

"I wonder if Cole was lying about the video footage?" Jae stole a piece of my cherry pie. I swatted his hand but allowed it when he showed me his cheeky smile.

"The Fae can't lie," I said, adding sugar packets to my coffee.

"Warren wouldn't do this." Hart shook his head, disappointment crossed his features and hit me right in the chest. "Apart from a Mimic Sidhe, what creature could wear another's face?"

Hugo glanced at me out of the corner of his eye. "Are you sure that it's a Wish Demon?" He asked, tentatively. "There was smoke on the camera footage of Team C. It looked like your true form."

Hurt flashed across my face, but I hid it quickly. "Why would I want to kill Fae and Hunters?"

Hugo reared back. "I meant that it *could* be another Drude."

Pain ricocheted through me.

I put my fork down and pushed my plate away. "I have to go to the bathroom," I muttered, rushing from the table as fast as possible.

I had done my business and was washing my hands when I caught the washed-out face of my host in the dirty mirror.

I didn't really believe that it was Davenport. It couldn't be him. It just did not compute.

The guy's reactions had mirrored my inner thoughts, but I had tried to get a reaction—for fun—and I regretted it.

I splashed some water on my face and adjusted the neckline of my starlight dress. I left the bathroom, ready to finish my coffee and go back to the freshly laundered sheets at Frankie's parent's house. Momma G had promised waffles for breakfast. I planned to eat until it was hard to move.

My steps slowed to a stop when I saw a made-up, coiffed blonde in a tiny skirt hovering over the edge of our booth. Hugo looked like he wanted to be anywhere else. Hart couldn't care less. Jae's benign mask was entirely in place, but even I could see the unfurling irritation behind his violet irises.

I sauntered over to the table, and hip-checked the blonde out of the way. I slid in next to Hugo and used my shoulder to wriggle under his arm. Hugo got the message and rested his arm over my shoulders in a possessive move.

"Who's the girl, honey?" I asked Jae sweetly.

Jae flashed his teeth. "This is Melody."

I blinked and looked up into the stranger's beautiful face. "Hello, Melody."

Melody ignored me. "We're about to head to the club. My friends over there made a bet that I couldn't get you one of you three stunning men to join me."

I snorted.

"No, thank you," Jae said politely.

"We're with someone." Hugo murmured, unable to make eye contact.

"All three of you?" Melody's eyes finally met mine. My smile looked like a cat that had eaten the canary.

"All of them," I said proudly. "Sometimes at the same time. Hurry along now."

Melody looked mortified, and a tiny bit intrigued. She scurried away back to her table to friends, and only looked back once.

"All of us?" Jae asked.

"At the same time, apparently." Hart smiled; he seemed to find my declaration amusing.

Chapter 17

Hugo's eyes were closed as he laid next to me on the bed, but I had no idea if he was asleep or not.

I was unable to sleep. The distance between our two bodies felt like a gulf. I wanted to reach out and touch him, but at the same time, I was scared.

Hugo Sinclair was my *mate*. My SoulBond.

The pressure to be with him was stifling. He wore a mark that declared our relationship was not a possibility, but a certainty.

My heartbeat roared in my ears. It was difficult to breathe.

A low moan drifted through the thin walls between our room and Jae and Hart's.

A low mumble, and a louder groan filled with pleasure. Jae and Callum must have been getting intimate. I squirmed, closing my eyes tightly, as the imagined visions of the two men, writhing, thrusting, and kissing, raced through my mind.

"Are you awake?" Hugo asked softly.

I looked up to find his ice-blue eyes on mine. His lips pulled into a timid smile. I found myself returning the expression, despite the turmoil boiling in my chest.

"What gave me away?" I quirked a brow, turning my upper body to face the incubus.

The sound of the bed frame knocking against the drywall drew Hugo's attention for a split second.

"Does that bother you?" I asked.

Hugo gave me a questioning look.

"Sex." I clarified.

"I'm an incubus." He said, amused.

"A celibate one."

Hugo winced. "Yeah."

I didn't need to ask. Hugo had already shared his background. Intimacy was something that couldn't be afforded when every touch, word, or kiss could lead to obsession.

I twined my fingers together and placed them on my stomach. "The first body that I possessed was a beauty pageant contestant," I said, changing the subject. "Dirk gave me a job. Wear Elissa-Mae for two hours. I had to lock another contestant out of their dressing room."

"What happened?"

"I did the job."

Hugo must have sensed that there was more to the story.

"I had just escaped Hell, thrown through the fabric of dimensions. I landed in Dirk's bar. Scared. Alone. My family was gone. I'd have done anything for that man. He saved my life." I explained. "I hung around after I left Elissa-Mae's body. It was like watching one of those machines where all the parts look random, but they all come together like dominos. You know what I mean?"

Hugo nodded, his attention solely on me. Jae and Callum were forgotten.

"When Harper, the other contestant, couldn't get into her dressing room for a final touch up before the last round— she snuck into another room and used someone else's cosmetics. She was allergic to something in the blusher. She went into anaphylaxis. Died."

I closed my eyes. "I killed her."

"I'm sorry."

"I'm not," I admitted. "Death is temporary. It's circular. I lived in Hell for many millennia. Souls would come. Redeem. Recycle. Repeat."

"Death isn't the end," Hugo whispered.

I exhaled a relieved breath. "Yeah."

An especially loud moan took my attention for a

second.

"The second that I took over Elissa-Mae, my world was colorful. Touch. Taste. Smell. I'd never been able to do any of those things before." My voice was tinged with the same wonder that I had felt that day, and every other, when I allowed myself to think about it.

Hugo's lip tightened, and I gasped when I realized where his thoughts had gone.

"I don't want to have sex with you." I blurted out. "Well, I do. But I don't. If that makes sense?"

"Thanks?" Hugo stifled a laugh.

My cheeks burnt hot. "*Seven Hell's.* I am the epitome of articulation. Marvel before my wordliness."

"Is wordliness a word?"

"Yes." My chest puffed out in pride. "I just used it."

Hugo grinned, unable to keep his amusement from his face. "You were explaining why you didn't want to sleep with me?"

I sobered, shifting until my back pressed against the wooden headboard. No more sounds drifted through the walls.

"I'm not in my own body." I looked down at my hands. "I don't have a body."

Hugo reached over and twined his fingers with mine to stop me from picking at the cuticles. "You don't need a body."

I was conscious of how immature it would have been to have stamped my foot and loudly proclaimed how I wanted one, even if I didn't *need* it. The brief periods of greyscale between possessions were getting harder and harder to stomach.

Dirk lined up easy targets, but unless someone was comatose like Frankie, wearing anyone for an extended period of time was almost impossible. Dead people rotted. Drunk people sobered up. Eventually, the owner of whatever body I was in would manage to push me out.

"I don't want to be *with* you while I am wearing someone else," I explained. "It just doesn't feel right."

Hugo pushed a tendril of hair behind my ear. I placed

274

my hands over my eyes. I sunk down slowly until my head hit the pillow.

"Roll over," Hugo suggested, pulling the comforter up high to cover body of us.

"Why?"

Hugo's response was a sharp look.

I did as he said with little protest.

Hugo's arms slipped around my chest, pulling me into the arch of his body, like a big warm spoon. I felt swaddled and safe. I never felt safe.

"Will you meet me in my dreams?" Hugo asked sleepily. I did not have a chance to answer before Hugo's breathing grew heavy.

Soon mine followed as I fell asleep in his arms.

The dream began like it always did.

The red sands of Wrath shifted with the invisible breeze of our presence. My Cluster rolled and danced across the expansive wastes, rattling the brittle trees and throwing the sand into the air in blood splatter bursts.

A chasm, on the edge of the Valley of the Valkyries, was our hunting ground. The eagle-winged women, souls of vengeful spirits too powerful to punish, flew high in the grey clouds. They were the Queen of Wrath's army. The most powerful of warriors, and the most damaged of souls.

My kin and I would feast on the nightmares of the Valkyries. Trying to offer them relief from their pain, and selfishly fill our metaphysical bellies too.

Abuse of all kinds at the hands of men birthed nightmares borne of reality.

The chasm was far away enough from the Valley that my kin would be undisturbed and unchallenged. We drifted over the edge of the sheer crimson rock face and flowed like water until we reached the bottom in a plume.

Something was wrong. We all sensed it as one.

My kin and I tried to rise, to escape from the chasm. Danger turned the air thick and hindered our movements, but magic locked us and turned our shadows into solid flesh.

Our screams were piercing. A keen of a dying animal.

I had a body. For the first time in my life.

The sand burnt into my dark skin, the dim light seared my eyes. I reached out to connect with my kin. My Cluster. But found nothing.

My legs shook as I clawed my way along the rough rock, pressed close. I did not want to be out in the open, the walls made me feel safer. I was able to see all around and to protect my back. I tried not to look at the ground. The hundreds of pitch-black bodies, hunched over, solid and screaming.

Every step was pain, but I made it.

I felt my kin die, one by one, like candles being snuffed. With every death, I grew faster and more determined. I would survive.

Hairline cracks broke through the sand, and the ground began to rumble. I stumbled along. Every step cut across my new flesh. Touch was pain. Feeling was agony.

The further away I got from the chasm, the less it hurt. I felt my flesh turn to shadows once more. I slumped, head down, relieved to the point of tears, and unable to hold back my despair.

Then I looked back.

A Bhakshi slivered through the dying bodies of my kin. The huge wyrm had razor-sharp teeth. Rows and rows, curved inwards. Dripping. Snarling. Hungry.

My instincts hammered against my mind. Warning me that the Bhakshi would devour all in its path.

I turned back as I ran. The Balance sat on the edge of the cliff face. A hundred feet above me. Her childlike legs swinging as she watched how my life had ended, and my family had died.

276

I looked up to where the Bhakshi had been, it was gone, along with the corpses of my family. When my gaze dropped down to my surroundings, I found myself staring into the shining silver eyes of a little blonde girl.

"Do you know who created the Bhakshi, and their masters, the Shayati?" The Balance asked delicately, her eyes scanned the chasm with indifference.

I shook my head, still reeling from the trauma of experiencing the worst event of my existence.

"Have you heard of God?" She wondered.

My brow quirked. The Balance sighed.

"Wait?" I shook my hand to try and alleviate some of the tremors left over from my fear. "Are you God?"

"No."

I eyed the little girl, shrewdly.

"In the beginning, I created two children. Life and death." The Balance continued, ignoring my studying look. "Nova—all that is life—named herself God of all, and grew her own kingdom. The Summerland."

I knew about the Summerland, it was basically heaven.

"Nova created her Chosen. Angels."

"And your other child?" I asked.

"Death created a home. A wasteland, where all that perished would eventually go." The Balance looked sad. "If Nova was the stars, then Death was the darkness in-between. Vast and necessary."

"Not to be an asshole..." I stated. "But what does this have to do with those massive worms?"

"Death was happy in their domain. They took in all souls that were not Pure enough for Nova. Death rehabilitated them and recycled them." The child continued speaking as if I hadn't said anything. "Nova grew jealous of Death. Of their world. Life has no power over Death. No power over the creatures that Death held most dear. Nova created monsters that had no desire but to devour all in their path. She released them into her sibling's home to strip Death of what Nova believed to

277

be her power."

"Did it work?"

The Balance shook her head. "The Bhakshi and the Shayati did as they were meant to do. They ate their way through all of the souls that Death had in their care. Death's creatures, Demons, were devoured. Few were left." The world around us melted away, as The Balance manipulated the landscape around us.

We stood once again on the red sands of Wrath, high on the towering dunes, watching a battle between golden-winged angels and great hulking beasts. I could smell the metal in the blood. The rotting meat of the Bhakshi's foul breath.

"Nova believed that she could simply take Death's world, but she could not. Nova's creations were too powerful. Her only available action was to beat back The Devouring and trap them beneath the sands."

"But they got out."

"Powerful things tend to do that." The child smiled sweetly. "Several millennia after Nova razed her sister's home, the Demons came back, slowly but surely. Hell flourished once more, but without Death to watch over it, the beasts once again rose to the surface."

"What happened to Death?"

The little girl's eyes bored into mine. The silver irises had disappeared and been replaced with glowing white. Every color and none at all. Every question and answer that could possibly be pondered waited behind those eyes, like a sleeping tiger.

"Who knows?" The Balance shrugged.

My fists clenched. The Balance seemed very cavalier over the fact that her two creations—her children—created, played with, and destroyed world's as if it was nothing.

I had never wanted to wake up from a dream before. The world before waking was *my* domain. Being faced with the physical manifestation of the universe was enough to make me tuck my tail and admit that I wanted to be as far away from possible from a being that could crush me like an ant.

"Thanks for getting rid of that body for me," I said. My mouth was dry. I licked my lips.

The universe turned away. "I simply asked one of my Hunters to dispose of it."

"What?" I was horrified. The mental cogs of my mind were sluggish as I pulled a conclusion from the dregs of my mind. "The only Hunter around was Warren Davenport."

The universe said nothing.

I had so many questions that they threatened to burst from my lips like vomit. Had The Balance made Davenport clean up the corpse? When he had found me, had he known that I had just killed a man?

I forced calm over my face and chose carefully, hoping that Little Miss Wikipedia was feeling generous with answering questions.

"Who summoned the Ifrit?" I asked.

The little girl waggled her finger, the movement, surprisingly, looked like it belonged to a small child. "It is not the destination, but the journey." She said. Sage advice in a squeaky falsetto voice.

"Send that shit to Hallmark." I crossed my arms over my chest. "You might make a buck or two."

The Balance shook her head indulgently. "Mara, be patient. When you find the end of this puzzle, you will find yourself."

I opened my mouth to argue but found myself jerked backward, my world twisted and turned as the dream changed.

I had hoped that The Balance would tell me who had summoned the Ifrit, and how to defeat the damn thing. The ever-present issue was tedious. What was the point of being friends with an all-powerful being if they couldn't make your life easier?

"Boil the rice, Ahn-Jae." A soft but stern voice said in Korean. "The foundation of the dish must be strong. Rice is the foundation of Bibimbap. If your foundation is not strong, your

279

house will fall."

"Yes, Omma." A tiny voice responded.

The kitchen was made of cheap linoleum and the kind of kitsch accessories that implied poverty, and not style. Tiny touches, a pizza flyer, and a mayo jar on the side, both written in English, told me that even though the older woman and her son were obviously Korean, they lived in an English speaking country.

Hunched over, with ebony hair pulled back in a neat ponytail, the regal but dainty woman must have been Jae's mother. She had no lines on her face—but it was from her stern and unsmiling disposition, not from her age.

"Have you cut the beefsteak, Ahn-Jae?"

"Yes, Omma."

The rhythmic sounds of Jae's mother washing the starchy rice were comforting. The small boy was barely taller than the countertops. His vivid violet eyes were so unnatural that they were always the first thing that caught my attention. Set in a cherubic face with floppy hair, the same color as his mother's.

I stepped forward. My fingers brushed against the sticky plastic of the cheap card table, with two rickety chairs on either side. Young Ahn-Jae Lee came up to my hip as he stood at the countertop and arranged the ingredients for his mother. She hurried around the kitchen, a petite maelstrom, only stopping to question Jae when she required something.

I hovered, an unwilling but curious spectator to the activity. Mother and child moved with familiarity, decidedly separate, as they orbited around each other. I had observed few parental relationships, but there was a cold indifference that lurked on the air and within Ms. Lee. I did not know what it meant.

"Mara!" Ms. Lee snapped. "Get the Kimchee. Ahn-Jae, get the eggs."

The beauty of dream logic. No one ever turned to a stranger in a dream and asked why they were there. No one questioned the floating nightmare. Instead, I was swallowed by the dream and expected to participate.

Jae opened the fridge and took out a carton of eggs. He turned towards his mother and began to walk across the kitchen. His knuckles were white around the container. The leg of the chair seemed to move on its own, slamming into the young boy's shins. He dropped the eggs. Each one smashed, like gooey fireworks on the checked tile. He winced with every sound.

Ms. Lee stiffened by did not turn around to the source of the sound. She made no noise as she reached to her left and picked up a wooden spoon, set apart from the other utensils. The curved wood at the top had a large crack down the center, stained brown at the top with something I could not identify.

"Ahn-Jae Lee." Mrs Lee said delicately and without emotion.

Dream-Jae had shifted, becoming his adult self. Still wearing the same Danger-mouse t-shirt that his younger self had been wearing. His face had drained of color as he stared down at the shattered eggs and refused to look up.

"One for every egg, Ahn-Jae?"

"Yes, Omma."

Jae moved to the spindly kitchen chair and gripped the back. He tilted at the waist, his mother's arm drew back as she moved to strike her son. One hit for every egg. I closed my eyes, unable to move. Unable to put myself between them.

Useless.

When I opened my eyes, there was nothing but a wall of trees. Their shapes were a silhouette in the darkness. The only sounds were the panting breaths of a man, and the cracking twigs and rustling bracken as the forest floor gave way to his clumsy footfalls.

Callum Hart broke through the space between two towering redwoods. Naked from the waist up, strips of blood across his torso as if he had been clawed by a dozen animals. His hair was shorn close to his skull, his orange eyes darted furtively. Surveying everything quietly, as if he expected someone to jump out and attack. I had never released that part of Hart's silence was because he was always on guard.

Wolves howled in the distance.

I followed after Hart as he took off at a sprint. Only on the cusp of his teenage years, his body was large but without muscle. All awkward angles.

Hart staggered and fell into the undergrowth. His knees gave out. He slammed his fist into the soft rotting leaves.

"Shift!" He snarled at himself, hitting the ground. Hart's shoulders began to tremble. "Shift!" His voice broke. "Dammit. Why won't you come?! Why is my wolf so fucking weak!" I pressed my back against the rough bark of the nearest tree, as I watched Callum Hart, stoic and silent, break down. He curled into a ball, shivering and bloodied. Tears mixed with snot as they ran down his face.

The wolves grew closer, their hungry snarls were loud and feral. Hart's pack. His family. They were hunting him.

The scrawny teenager had changed into his adult self. Shoulder length russet hair, bulky with every muscle honed for strength. He had changed so much, but in his dream, he was still a little boy. Cowering from his own pack because he was defective.

I opened my mouth and stepped forward.

The Balance stood in my way. Her head cocked to the side.

"You have chosen damaged men." She observed, her language was formal, but her expression was curious in the same way that a child's would be. "Do you plan to fix them?"

My fists clenched. "They don't need to be fixed. There is nothing wrong with them."

The Balance waved her hand towards the curled up man on the forest floor and quirked a brow as if to say *'see?'*.

"Everyone has a past," I said.

"And you?" The Balance cocked her head to the side. "Can you put yours away, and become what you need to be? Like they have?"

I didn't have a chance to answer before I jerked awake.

282

My heart pounded, residue from the nightmares.

"Stupid god's and their stupid riddles." I punched my lumpy pillow to rearrange the down inside and laid back down. Hugo's heat seeped into my skin, and I found myself relaxing against the incubus.

I stared into the darkness, thinking until the sun leaked through the floral curtains, and Hugo woke up. I smiled brightly as if I had slept peacefully. The lie fell easy off my tongue.

I wondered why the Universe's empty platitudes filled me with dread.

At breakfast, Momma G rushed around, making pancakes and bacon for everyone. She asked Jae to fetch the eggs from the fridge. I watched as he did as she asked without a hint of the past trauma that he had endured in his mother's kitchen.

The Balance had been wrong. My men weren't damaged.

If there was hope for them, there was hope for me.

Chapter 18

The next morning, the drive to the compound was made in silence. My thoughts raced around my head and stole my ability to speak. I didn't even have the heart to tease Jae and Hart for their loud sex the night before.

I didn't want to admit it but seeing the guard booth, and then the Lego block buildings nestled in between the trees, felt like coming home.

My nails dug into my palms, as I wondered how my Bonds with Remi and Hugo would endure once I went back to NYC.

I had met The Balance twice, and I hadn't been *called* like the other Hunters. Why would the most powerful force in existence want a Drude on their side? Every Hunter I had met had something to offer, even the humans. What could *I* offer?

My skills included borrowing bodies, being able to taste random hidden ingredients in gourmet food, the attention span of a toddler on sugar (I could admit that about myself, but Hell would fall before I would let someone else say that about me), and a talent for fleeing to save my own skin.

Hugo reached over and linked our fingers when we got out of the car. Jae and Hart walked ahead, with a few backward glances that told me that both men had noticed that my mood had plummeted.

"Are you okay?" Hugo's ice-blue eyes were worried. "Did our conversation last night upset you?"

I shook my head, my teeth worried my bottom lip. "It's nothing."

"Because I can wait," Hugo assured me. "I belong to

you."

I reached up and cupped his jaw. "I'm not worried about that," I assured him.

Hugo didn't look like his believed me.

"Come on.," I urged, nudging his shoulder. "Let's go accuse Davenport of killing a bunch of Fae."

"Mara..."

"I'm joking!" I danced away, down the well-worn path, and towards the office building. "Or am I?" I wiggled my fingers and made spooky ghost noises.

Jae and Hart were already inside when I reached the door. Hugo held it open for me, ever the gentleman.

Davenport stood, pacing behind his desk like a stalking tiger. His muscles were bunched, and I would not have been surprised if he lashed out, unhinged his jaw, and swallowed me whole if I said the wrong thing.

Remi sat in the corner with a tablet on his lap, he did not look up to greet me.

Hugo followed on my heels.

"Now that we are all here," Davenport began, glancing at Remi. "Can someone tell me what is going on?"

I opened my mouth and closed it, deciding how much information I wanted to share if Warren Davenport could potentially be our killer.

"Someone hacked your business email and used it to arrange several ventures," Hugo spoke with confidence, as he stepped in front of me as if to protect me unconsciously. "The Summoner gained the knowledge to summon the Ifrit by trying to cash in on your favor with Dermot Dirk."

Davenport narrowed his eyes but allowed Hugo to keep talking.

"They then requested Fae Killing bullets, dissolving, like our Devil's Silver ones, from Ryn Cole."

"I had no idea that my standing was so high amongst the Fae," Davenport said dryly. "They seem to be bending over backward to supposedly accommodate my requests."

I shifted from foot to foot. When he put it like that, it did sound suspicious.

"The Summoner must have already summoned the Ifrit when they contacted Cole. They wore your face to the meeting." Hugo concluded.

Davenport glanced at me. "Could it have been a Mimic Sidhe?"

"Are you accusing Dermot Dirk of trying to start a war against the Hunters?" I countered. "Did *you* kill those people?"

"No," Davenport said through clenched teeth. I preened like a peacock as I smirked. Happy that I had gotten under his skin. He turned to Remi, dismissing me. "What do you have for me?"

"The email trail leads back to a coffee shop in Maywood. I phoned and asked for their security footage, but they don't have cameras." Remi did not look up from his tablet. "I've sent a team to get a statement."

Davenport turned to Jae. "Keep a feel out for any residual guilt, pride, or general nerves." He ordered. "I want you eating in the canteen, and around people as much as you are able until we find the Summoner."

"And me?" Hart asked.

"Keep your eyes open to any suspicious activities. Anyone acting differently." Davenport said. "Dismissed." Everyone turned to leave, including me. "Mara, you stay."

I turned back, just as Davenport stepped around his desk, resting his hip against the wood and crossing his arms. He studied me to a few seconds, with a mix of exasperation and arrogance.

"Was it easier to believe me capable of murder, than admitting what you feel for me?" He asked gently, eyes boring into mine.

"Hugo told you?"

"Yes, little Demon."

I swallowed the lump in my throat that made it difficult to speak. "You scare me," I admitted, the words were pulled from my mouth. Beyond my control.

"It wasn't me." Warren's eyes flashed. "But should I be flattered that a Demon thinks I'm capable of killing so many people?"

I winced. "I've never killed anyone."

Davenport's lip twitched. "Right."

"I've never killed an innocent." I corrected. My cheeks flushed with anger (at myself) and embarrassment when I remembered that Davenport had been the one to clean up my mess. At least he wasn't asking questions and calling me evil. I couldn't read his expression. I had no idea what he was thinking, and for that, I feared him.

Davenport gripped my shoulders and pushed my back against the rough concrete wall. He towered over me, his frame shielded the rest of the world from view. When he spoke, his breath brushed the shell of my ear and made me shiver.

His fingers danced across my flat belly. I forgot that I was just a passenger in someone's body. All I wanted was to experience his touch. His warmth.

His hand dipped under my waistband and slid into the front of my panties. Dipping inside me for a second before retreating.

His lips pulled into a predatory smile. Anyone would think he was the Demon.

"Your fear is the reason you're wet right now," Davenport smirked. "I arouse you, as much as I scare you."

He leaned in and pressed a tender and slow kiss to the seam of my jaw. I arched my neck, groaning.

"Besides..." He purred. "You only fear me because I can hurt you. Not because I will."

Davenport pulled away. I felt lost, empty, and fragile without his body in front of mine. Touching me. He tapped my nose.

"We all have our secrets." He smiled.

My eyes narrowed, but before I could argue, Davenport had walked away.

I was unashamed to say that I ogled his round, muscular ass as he went.

After I calmed down my inner thirsty bitch, I went to the Mess Hall, determined to eat something, and then go to bed. I had only been away from the compound for a day and a night, but something had shifted, and I couldn't put my finger on it.

I caught Riley's eye as I turned to the tables with my tray in hand. She lifted her hand to wave, before catching herself and offering her typical glare instead. Chloe sat next to her, her hair back in its signature bun, as her arms flailed wildly as she told a story. My eyes had already moved away when they doubled back, stopping on the beautiful redhead at their table. Wearing a kelly green wrap dress, and high gladiator heels, Alicia, Remi's fiancée, was a beautiful flower in a sea of khaki.

Remi stood away from the tables, talking to Hugo. Their body language implied that an interruption would not be welcome—I was proud of myself for deciphering the markers of human behavior.

I waved at Dr Dan and got a perplexed expression in return. If being uncalled in a sea of Hunters bothered Frankie's brother so much, I had no idea why he stuck around.

Then again, I was a Demon who ate nightmares—I was one to talk. I continued to stay at the compound even though it was severely harmful to my health.

The silver collar on my neck chafed, but it wasn't Devil's Silver. I could destroy it if I wanted to. It was more for Davenport's piece of mind that I kept it on.

There was an empty table in the corner, so I sat down and started to eat my Thai curry. It was spicy enough that no hot sauce was required.

The back of my neck prickled; someone was watching me. My spine stiffened, and my fist clenched around my fork. I froze and waited, but the feeling drifted away.

"Do you mind if I sit?" I looked up to find Remi, smiling down at me. I grinned, even though it felt like a hand had wrapped around my heart and squeezed. His dark eyes sparkled, but it hasn't escaped my notice that he had not looked at me once in Davenport's office.

The bond between us snapped tautly. The rest of the world fell away. I could sense his concern radiating through our connection, like an itch at the back of my skull.

"How was Queens?" Remi pulled out the opposite chair to mine.

"It was my first Thanksgiving," I said, stabbing a piece of chicken. "There was stuffing. Pie. Momma G had Jae running around her kitchen like her own personal sous chef."

Remi chuckled. "Bet he loved that."

I shrugged. Remi's smile fell as he studied my face for a few seconds.

Reni leaned forward, he dropped his voice so that only I could hear him. My heart took flight like a pair of hummingbird wings. He smelt like laundry detergent. I found myself moving toward, drawn into his space.

"Mara, what's wrong?"

I jerked back. Shaking my head, I forced a mouthful of curry into my mouth and used that as an excuse not to say a word. My smile tightened.

Was I the only one that felt our Bond?

"What were you talking to Hugo about?" I asked, swallowing my food. "Picking up some handy tips for your wedding night from the resident sex expert?"

Remi snorted. "You think I'd need help in that department?"

Jealousy stabbed my insides, turning them to hamburger meat. "Hugo's an incubus. I've seen his dreams. That man knows things you couldn't even imagine." I embellished.

Remi's eyes hooded. "Is that so?" He purred in his British accent.

289

My expression turned saucy. "He's good with his mouth." That wasn't a lie. Hugo and I had kissed, Remi didn't have to know that was all we had done. I enjoyed the tangible reaction that I got from the jokester. Intrigue. Teasing. Daring.

I had been so absorbed in a silent standoff with Remi, that I hadn't noticed that someone had approached our table.

Alicia Greenlea.

She looked like she belonged on the cover of Vogue, not in a Demon Hunter's compound.

I had never had a body to dress before. Style was part intuition and part study. It did not come naturally, in my experience. I was lucky that Frankie had a wardrobe already, as I couldn't bring myself to care about what I wore. Mainly because in the past, it hadn't mattered. Looking at Alicia made me feel awkward. I didn't like it.

"Remington, aren't you going to introduce me to your friend?" Her lips were smiling, her eyes were not. Both her hands rested on her narrow hips, as Alicia Greenlea looked at me with a sort of smug superiority that I had only seen on the faces of Hell Sovereign.

I wiped my hand on my shirt and offered it to the redhead. "M-Frankie." I stuttered, as I almost slipped up and said my true name. Remi's attention had thrown me through a loop.

Alicia looked down her button nose, her expression grew even more sickly-sweet. "I thought y'all used rank here?"

My brow furrowed at her use of the word *y'all*. I turned to Remi. "I thought she was from Connecticut?"

Alicia gripped Remi's shoulder. "Have you been talking about me, Remington?"

Remi forced his own smile on his black cherry lips. "No, Alicia."

"Are you on Remington's team?" Alicia asked, decidedly not taking a seat at the table.

"Yep." I did not elaborate.

"So, you're who Remington has been spending his

290

nights with?" Her laugh was a confident tinkle. Her words had been pointed in a way that I did not understand.

I glanced at Remi. "Yes?" I answered. Remi had kept me company in my cell for many nights. I assumed that was what she was talking about.

Remi smothered a laugh, putting his hand over his mouth.

Alicia's hand, still on Remi's shoulder, tightened enough to strain the fabric. Remi's expression went blank.

"My Remington is such a friendly soul. He doesn't realize that it gives people ideas." Her eyes flashed.

"Okay." I nodded, but my expression broadcasted *'wtf.'* Her words said one thing, but I had the feeling she meant something else. Whatever she was trying to say was lost on me.

"Mara is just a friend, Alicia." Remi reached out and patted the hand on his shoulder.

Alicia shot him a glare. "Remington." She hissed his name as an admonishment.

I pushed my chair back, unable to finish my food. "I'm going," I announced, but neither Remi not Alicia paid me any mind. The female Witchling was too busy laying into Remi as I walked away.

I found Hart in the fenced area next to the kennels. I leaned back against a tree, as I watched the typically silent and expressionless man throw a tennis ball for a golden retriever. The dog yipped with excitement, rolling over in her haste to reach the ball. Black lips peeled back over her teeth as she tried to catch it in mid-air.

Hart let out a whoop when the dog finally picked up the ball and trotted back to his side. Hart rubbed her head, kneeling down to the dog's level and cooing like a proud papa bear.

I stepped forward, approaching the fence to let myself be seen. Callum Hart straightened, his hand in the cookie jar expression melted away, barely a glimpse, before his impassive stare was back.

"Is that Dixie?" I asked, tilting my chin to the sitting dog. Her thick tail swished from side to side, kicking up dust.

Hart nodded.

I wiggled my fingers at the golden retriever but stayed behind the fence.

"You can come closer if you like. Dixie loves everyone." Hart winced at the awkwardness of his own words.

"Nah." I waved my hand dismissively. "Dog's don't really like Demons, so..." I added, dropping my voice so I couldn't be overheard.

Without another word, Hart marched to the gate and stepped through. He tugged my sleeve. "Come here." He ordered, moving back to the enclosure with me in tow. Dixie sat, still smiling a beaming doggy-smile, and wagging her tail.

Hart deposited me in front of his dog. He held out his hand and reminded Dixie to *stay*. "She won't hurt you."

I twisted my hands together. "I don't want to stress her out."

"She's fine." He assured me.

I swallowed the lump in my throat. My voice cracked. "But—"

"Mara." He warned. "Pet the damn dog."

"Seven Hell's, you're bossy," I grumbled, kneeling down to Dixie's height. "I think I liked it better when you didn't talk, Marmalade."

Hart rubbed his face. "Look, if you're scared—"

I blew a raspberry. "Please." I whispered under my breath as my trembling hand outstretched to rub Dixie's furry head. The beautiful girl vibrated with excitement. Hart once again commanded her to *stay*. I couldn't believe it. I was close to a dog. She wasn't freaking out. The whites of her eyes were normal, she hadn't lost it and tried to bite me. Dixie nuzzled into

292

my hand, and let out a bark.

"Beautiful girl," I whispered in awe.

Dixie took my words as encouragement. Leaping forward, she placed her heavy paws on my shoulders and pushed me backward. Slathering my face with kisses, I looked up to see Hart's smug expression.

"She likes you." He told me. For some reason, that felt vital. Like I had passed some sort of test.

I laid back in my bed, eyes closed tightly as I tried to sleep.

When I wore my true form, I existed in the world between reality and dreams, there was no bridge. Wearing Frankie's body had dulled my sight, but it was a small price to pay for the ability to interact with the world.

I couldn't seem to differentiate between Frankie's body and my being anymore. I had grown roots.

A jolt of electricity twanged through my body, a discordant note of arousal. I sat up; the comforter fell around my waist. I looked down at my pebbled nipples, hard enough to cut through glass.

"What in the Seven Hell's...?" I wondered out loud as I pressed my lips together to stop my whimper. It felt like a hot and slippery tongue had traced the edge of my nipple. A warm hand on the span on my ribs. My eyes fluttered closed as pleasure coiled inside of me like a waking beast.

Two bonds hung in my chest, hooked to my center. My soul. One vibrated with pleasure. Desperate need but with restrained and delicious feeling. A spider in a glass jar.

One of my Soulbonds was enjoying themselves. I kicked off my bedsheets and stood up. My knees knocked together, as I struggled to reign in the spiraling beginnings of an orgasm.

Was it Remi? Were he and Alicia getting to know each

293

other together at that very second? Images flashed across my eyes. Creamy pale hands raking red nails down a dark, muscular back. Bile rose in my throat. I was going to be sick.

Coupled with the building orgasm, unfurling and ready to strike at my throbbing core, I staggered to the door. Fumbling, like a drunk, I managed to find Hugo's door first. My hands shook as I knocked and waited, my arms wrapped around my chest as I gasped. I shuddered, and then like a switch, my orgasm died.

Someone fiddled with the deadbolt on the other side. Struggling for a second before they pulled open the door. Hugo's face popped around the crack, his cheeks flushed bright red, and his eyes glazed and shifty.

I barged past him, and then looked down to the prominent tent at the front of his pale boxer shorts.

"What are you doing?" He stammered as I ripped his underwear down, watching his cock slap his toned stomach. His ice-blue eyes were wide with disbelief.

"Were you masturbating?" I demanded, swiping my thumb over the head of his cock.

"Hello, Mara, nice to see you." Hugo's sarcasm stuttered as he closed his eyes and suppressed a groan. I loosened my grip, suddenly aware that I had been holding his cock.

He straightened when he saw my panic. "What's wrong?" He gripped my shoulders.

I kept my eyes on his. "I felt you."

Hugo Sinclair flushed a deeper red. "Oh." His lips parted adorably. "*Oh.*" He inhaled sharply, and I stretched onto the tip of my toes until my lips pressed against the corner of his mouth.

"You *felt* me." He repeated, his hand tangled in the back of my hair as he reverently held my body to his. I melted into his hold as he tasted my lips with slow precision. His erection pressed against my stomach, peeking out from the top of his underwear.

My hand brushed his stomach, and Hugo began to walk backward until he sat on the edge of the bed. Still kissing, I stood between his legs.

My chest heaved when Hugo broke the kiss and brought his forehead to mine. We simply looked at each other without a word. Sharing the same breath.

"Give me a minute," Hugo whispered. Closing his eyes as if he was in pain.

"Thank you," I replied, meaning the words from the bottom of my heart. Hugo knew that I didn't want to go too far in a borrowed body. "There's always dreams," I suggested, winking salaciously.

He chuckled. The sound was husky with arousal. His eyes remained closed as I slowly stepped out of his embrace, unpeeling myself reluctantly. His warmth was too addictive. Stepping away from our connection—which felt like puzzle pieces finally slotting into place—was physically painful.

My fingers knitted together as I stood and began to pace.

"When you knocked on the door, you had this look on your face..." Hugo murmured.

"When I felt *that*...I thought Remi and Alicia were..."

The side door opened, and I blinked, surprised as Remi poked his head through the gap. Hugo grabbed a cushion from his bed and used it to hide his erection. Remi did a double-take.

"Was Remi here this whole time?" My question trailed off as my eyes narrowed. "Was he the reason you were so..."

"No." Hugo vehemently protested. "We have a double suite, remember?" He shot Remi a look, pleading for the man to agree.

Remi's eyes gleamed with mischief. "Are you denying our love, Hewey?"

Hugo stomped off, muttering to himself as he bustled over to the chest of drawers to grab a shirt. The incubus glanced over his shoulder as he grabbed his phone and left the room. Remi and I were alone. My fist clenched. *Damn you, Hugo. For*

295

making me address my problems.

"Wait?" Remi blinked slowly. "Did I interrupt something?"

"No." I licked my dry bottom lip, still twitchy from my stolen orgasm. "But I think I did." I tried not to slump with relief that Remi was alone, and not with Alicia.

"I felt something." Remi glanced at me before turning away. My hand fluttered to my chest as if I could claw our Soulbond from my being.

"Hugo was having some alone time," I smirked. "You probably felt it come through the bond."

Remi looked thoughtful. "I didn't realize it was so powerful."

My body twisted away from Remi, towards the door, and he noticed my unease.

"You'd tell me if there was something wrong between us?" Remi asked, surprising me with how serious he was. His body angled toward mine, without him noticing.

"It's not your job to worry about me," I told him as I shifted uncomfortably Marriage meant almost nothing to Demons. Hell was full of adulterers, but I didn't want Remi to become someone he wasn't.

"We have a Bond." He scratched the back of his neck. He swallowed as if in pain. "I know it's not ideal, but I have to do this for my family."

"I get it," I said, and I meant it. "I'm okay." If I kept saying it, maybe it would become true.

Hugo's muffled voice came from the other room before he walked back into the bedroom with a phone to his ear.

"The scouts found something in Maywood," Hugo informed us. "Davenport wants to check it out."

I went back to my room and dressed quickly, before rushing to

296

the front of the officer's quarters to find the rest of Team P. Hugo's entire being relaxed as he saw me, the golden aura that he hid for fear of enthralling the populace shone for just a second when he looked at me. Jae quirked a brow as I bounced to his side, forcing my way between him and Hart.

While the rest of the team were dressed in black tactical gear, Hart wore a plaid shirt and worn jeans. His thumbs were in his belt loops as he studied the trees like he expected an ambush any second. His marmalade eyes flicked to mine as he greeted me with a lip twitch, his version of a smirk. Remi stood on the end, arguing with Davenport in a low, hushed tone—everything about their body language screamed *secret*.

The commander was unmoved. I quickly realized the subject of their conversation when Alicia Greenlea sidled up to Remi, and both men immediately stopped talking.

Davenport greeted Alicia with her surname and a curt nod. Remi's smile was strained.

"What's she doing here?" I lowered my voice so only Jae could hear me.

"Alicia is a talented Witchling. Having two on the Team will prevent any nasty surprises." Jae explained.

"Right." I was skeptical. "Witchlings are liabilities. Every spell puts them closer to death. Why would she even want to come?"

Hugo put his arm over my shoulder and pulled me into his side. "Jealous, nightmare?" Hugo kissed my forehead.

"You wish, wanker." I winked.

"Have you told Remi that his life force is linked with yours?" Hugo asked softly, glancing over to Alicia as the redhead clung to Remi's side.

Jae blinked, and a slow smile lit up his face. "Remi joined the immortal club?"

"He doesn't know," I said. Craning my neck to try and hear Remi and Alicia's conversation. I was nosy, and I felt no shame about that.

"Miss Greenlea is accusing Remi of cheating on her,"

Callum Hart informed me. When I eyed him in questioning, he tugged his earlobe to draw attention to his werewolf hearing.

"Remi came to America for her." I arched a brow. "He's marrying her."

"Mr Weber decided to stay at the compound, with an acquaintance, rather than join Miss Greenlea near Columbia University or her family's estate. What does that tell you?" Hart's rumbly tone was full of chastisement.

"It tells me that humans are complicated." I was put my hand on my hip. "Don't ask *me*. My knowledge of human reasoning is as big as Tinkerbelle's dildo."

Jae snorted. Hugo blushed. Hart rolled his eyes. Davenport stepped forward, putting himself between Remi and Alicia—whether it was subconscious or on purpose, I would never know.

The commander clapped his hands together once, and the team silently began to file into one of the matte black armored trucks at the end of a row of cars. Alicia and I trailed at the end of the line, unaware of the choreographed movement.

"It's Frankie, right?" Alicia moved daintily, looking down at her feet when she walked. I would too, if I was wearing heels on uneven terrain.

I tried to make my smile as genuine as possible. "Corporal Gardiner, at your service."

Jae snickered, but he did not turn around. I reached forward and punched him between the shoulder blades. The Nephilim did not react.

"So which of the guys are you with?" Alicia whispered as Hart moved to the doors at the back of the truck.

My eyes flicked over the men of Team P, everyone was something *other*, they could hear the redhead even if they pretended not to. Only Remi seemed blissfully unaware as he climbed into the passenger seat, next to Davenport, and fired up his laptop.

"That's a difficult question." I hedged.

Alicia's head cocked to the side. Her face turned

shrewd. "How so?"

I caught Hugo's eye on the other side of the truck as we all settled in our seats. Two ledges ran vertically down the carriage, separated by a large steel trunk in the middle of the vehicle. The driver and passenger seat were set apart with a thick mesh. Hugo made a movement to get up when he saw how uncomfortable I was. Hart put his hand on Hugo's chest, and I gave the werewolf the stink eye.

"I'm with all of them," I said coyly.

Alicia's eyes widened minutely. Her neck flushed, but her face did not change color. "All of them?" She repeated, her voice steady.

"I'm on their team." My words were slow. Sounded out. The redhead looked like she had received a blow to the back of the head. "I'm with Team P." I clarified.

A few seconds passed as the truck began to move. I bounced up and down before I buckled my seatbelt across my chest. Everyone else did the same.

There was utter silence as I wordlessly pleaded with one of the men on the other side of the vehicle for help.

Then Alicia Greenlea surprised me. She threw back her head and roared with laughter.

"Oh!" She parted her lips, her eyes were childishly wide. "You meant that you're *on* Team P! Not that you're *with* them." Her hand rested on her chest, and she relaxed. She turned away. I had already been dismissed. I opened my mouth to clarify when Hugo cleared his throat and shook his head.

Fine. I could play nice.

I was wrong. I was going to kill the woman and leave her body for the black bears.

We'd parked around the back of the coffee shop where the email had initially been sent, but the workers of *Beanies* had directed us to the person that rented the apartment above the shop.

The name on the lease was a dead end. It was obviously fake. Remi's online search had stalled, so Team P had gathered to continue the investigation in person. A team had already swept the apartment, and they had found something interesting enough to call in Davenport.

We hadn't even stepped over the threshold before Alicia decided to show off.

"Come *on*." She nudged Remi's shoulder with her own. "Let's set up a protection spell. With the two of us, it will be easy."

"I don't think that's a good idea." Remi glanced over at us. "Maybe an anti-Demon ward? A salt line over the threshold should work."

I didn't like that Remi looked so unsure of himself. I thrust my hands into my pockets to avoid flipping her off.

"Remington, you have to use your magic. A Witchling is worth nothing if they can't do spells." Alicia chided.

"Alicia..." Remi warned.

Alicia's eyes turned conniving, but her smile was fixed. "We need to test the compatibility of our magic." She argued. I thought that she was going to stamp her foot, but was pleasantly surprised when she didn't.

Davenport stepped forward. "Perhaps test your magic another time." He suggested gently, but there was no room for argument. "Remi, up here with me. Alicia, stay in the van. Rest of you, follow behind."

Alicia opened her mouth to argue. Davenport shut her down with a look.

The apartment was empty and cleared of all dangerous magic, but every man prepared differently as we walked up the steps. Remi's fingers spread as if he was readying himself to fling a spell. Davenport slid a gun from the chest holder under his fitted dark jacket. Jae's eyes glowed, and Hart stiffened.

Hugo sidled up to my shoulder, as Davenport pushed

into the residence and strode in like he lived there.

"Why bring Alicia if you're just going to leave her in the car?" I asked Davenport as we poured into the hallway.

"The Greenlea's have demanded that I watch their daughter and keep her safe. They also stipulated that the large donation they made to my compound was conditional on the amount of time Alicia spent with Remi." He explained in a dry tone.

"It's about money, boss?" Jae sauntered up to us. His hands were in his belt loops as he rocked on his heels.

Davenport glanced at Jae. "How else would I pay you enough to sate your addiction to erotic novels?" Davenport's lip twitched.

Remi hooted. "He's got you there, Jae." He said as he clapped him on the back.

"Mock me all you like." Jae's eyes twinkled. "I'll just tell everyone about that book you borrowed from me—"

Remi slapped his hand over Jae's mouth and pulled him back into the room as Jae's protests were muffled by Remi's fingers.

Davenport pinched the bridge of his nose. "I expect this sort of deviant behavior from the incubus—"

"Hey!" Hugo straightened.

Davenport continued as if he hadn't spoken. "Hart. Make sure they don't kill each other."

The solemn man dipped his head and followed Remi and Jae into the living room.

"Deviant, huh?" I teased.

"Don't start," Davenport growled and marched away. I held up my hands in surrender despite his retreating form.

"You get under his skin." Hugo murmured, brushing a lock of hair behind my ear.

"I do, don't I?" I preened.

The living room of the apartment looked like a typical rental. Beige walls. IKEA furniture and a cheap polyester carpet. The only thing that was slightly out of the ordinary was the longest wall was completely papered in various photos, connected with red marker and scribbled notes. I squinted as I stepped forward, my fingers paused before they made contact with the grainy black and white picture of my host. Frankie Gardiner's face was circled a dozen times. The eyes were completely scratched out.

"Do you think it's a stalker?" I wondered. "I once wore a stalker for a day. His name was Finley Ryan. He'd masturbated on some sorority girl when she was asleep. Her dad was an important actor or something."

Hugo was horrified. "Tell me he was arrested."

"It wasn't a crime in NYC at the time. The court found him not guilty." I explained.

Every other Hunter was sweeping the room, but their heads tilted to me as they pretended not to listen.

"He got away with it?" Hugo rubbed his mouth. "Shit. Damn."

I ignored his swearing. "He was found not guilty. But it was so random—" I injected sadistic cheer into my voice. "He walked right into the Hudson. Didn't even leave a suicide note."

"He deserved to go to prison." Davenport stepped up to my side.

"He wasn't a nice person," I said darkly. In fact, Finley Ryan had been a fan of Rohypnol, and not taking no for an answer. The Seventh Circle would have fun with him. Asmodeus, the Queen of Lust, enjoyed taunting rapists in creative and horrific ways.

Remi perched on the armrest of the couch and began to type, glancing up at the photos on the wall sporadically.

"I've checked our database. Every person who's picture is on this wall was Fae." Remi informed us. "Except Frankie."

"We don't record that." Davenport stiffened.

"I cross-referenced every person here with their latest

302

physical. Not one person had iron in their blood." Remi explained. "That means Fae."

I did a little dance. "I was right?"

"No one likes a braggart." Davenport gave me his signature look. I stuck out my tongue.

"Only a third of the people that were killed are on this wall." Jae stepped forward, his fingers brushed the face of one of Team G. "No one that was taken out by the Ifrit is on here."

"Collateral damage." Hart nodded, scratching his bearded scruff thoughtfully.

A flash of platinum blonde hair caught my eye. The Balance stood in the doorway to the bedroom, her presence was eerie. She had appeared so suddenly that I physically jumped, drawing the attention of the entire team. No one else turned to look at the child; it was as if she wasn't there.

"Let's check out the bedroom?" I suggested. Davenport took out his gun and walked right through *The Balance* like she was a reflection staring back from a pond.

When Davenport returned, he was holding a white business card.

"Do you know anything about this?" His voice was light, dangerous. The commander flicked the card in my direction. I grabbed it out of the air and turned it over in my hands. A translucent snowflake shone on one side, but the rest of the card was blank. Expensive card stock.

My gaze turned questioning as I moved the card, so the tiny metallic snowflake caught the light.

"That belongs to your boss," Davenport growled. "Dermot Dirk."

I slumped down in the IKEA armchair but slapped the wooden armrest in frustration when the damn seat threatened to spit me onto the floor if I adopted the brace position.

I couldn't deny that my boss was a shady character. He played his life like a game of blackjack, only Dirk knew the cards before the dealer had even pulled the first one.

The Fae Lord's bar straddled Tír na nÓg and NYC, but

he had a dozen mercenaries. It would not have been difficult to enlist an Ifrit to help his killing spree.

"It doesn't make sense," I whispered to myself. "What courts do the Fae victims belong to?"

Remi, perched on the edge of the couch, pulled up the files again. "It doesn't say."

Davenport's face was made of stone.

"What?" Jae turned away from his intense study of the photo wall. "Your emotions just went sub-zero."

"Dermot Dirk could be taking out the majority of my Hunters. Our verbal agreement stipulated that he would help me." Davenport pressed his fingers to his temples, massaging his forehead as if he was getting a headache. "The Fae are tricky. He could be killing my Hunters. Helping by ensuring I have fewer people to look after?"

I snorted. "You asked for a favor after the first Team died." I pointed out.

"How does that explain his card?" Davenport spat, his demeanor shifted as his calm mask slipped. I stood up, staggering as the flimsy chair pitched to the side when it lost my weight.

I stepped into his space, but the top of my head only reached his chin. "The Summoner asked Dermot for help by pretending to be you."

Davenport's face twitched as he realized something. He swore, as he fished his wallet out of his back pocket.

"Looking for something, boss?" Jae asked rhetorically as Warren Davenport began pulling out cards from his wallet and stuffing them back into their folds.

Hugo and Remi watched on, both alert.

"It's gone." Davenport snarled, rearing back, he threw his wallet across the room. Taking out a cheap paper lamp and making the bulb shatter with an almighty crash.

Hugo's lips pinched. "What's gone?" His eyes flicked to mine, silently asking if I had taken anything.

"I put it back." I cocked my hip to the side, referring to

Davenport's shiny black AMEX that I had used to treat the guys to tequila at the bar (one time).

Warren held out his hand for the business card that I was still twirling around my fingers. "I had a card in my wallet. It's gone." He said.

"You think that's the card?" I asked.

Davenport did not answer my question, but he didn't need to.

Remi's laptop snapped shut. "I'm still trying to pull the names of the warehouse owners where the ritual sights are, but it looks like we're back to square one."

Hugo reached forward and twined his fingers with mine, squeezing my hand.

It looked like I would be around a bit longer. As Remi packed his things away, his eyes hooked on mine for just a second. Our Soulbond vibrated like a guitar string.

Chapter 19

The next day started with breakfast in the Mess Hall and swiftly moved onto training in one of the clearings with Hugo.

I took my time, circling the makeshift arena, before joining the group of young Hunters. Everyone was a suspect. Someone had stolen Dirk's business card from Davenport's wallet. In the wrong hands, it was deadly.

I trusted my team—Davenport, Hugo, Hart, Jae, and Remi—but I could fit the number of other people that I had spent time with at the compound inside of a thimble.

I watched Riley doing press-ups, as Bun-girl Chloe chewed her thumbnail while texting instead of counting her friend's reps. The two young men traded blows, my head tilted to the side as I tried to remember their names. Chad and Brad or something.

Hugo stood with his legs shoulder-width apart, shouting out commands in short bursts. I watched the group shift without argument and kicked away from my seat on the fence, so I could join in the exercise before Hugo reprimanded me in front of his other students.

I jogged over and was paired with Riley. I slipped on some boxing pads as the petite woman bounced on her heels. Her curly hair was pulled back into a tight ponytail, but a few wisps had managed to escape by her ears.

I held out my hands, and we fell into a comfortable rhythm as Riley's blows crossed over and hit each pad evenly.

"You need to watch out for Alicia." Riley did not look at me as she spoke.

"Why?" I was genuinely perplexed.

"She thinks something is going on with you and Remi."

The sound that escaped my throat was strangled laughter. Riley pulled back, her eyes narrowed and her nose scrunched as she studied me.

"Holy shit!" She hissed, glancing over her shoulder with a wince when she realized her volume. "Something is going on!" Riley kept her voice low.

I shook my head, as I noticed that Chloe had perked up like a meercat looking for danger.

"You don't get it. Alicia will kill you. You're acting like you don't care." Riley tugged on my sleeve and led me away from the group.

"Acting?" I quirked a brow. That was insulting. I genuinely didn't care. Witchlings got their magic from a Devil's bargain. It had been proved that it could not affect me.

Riley gave me some acute side-eye. "Don't say I didn't warn you."

I responded with a chilled out smile. She clicked her tongue against the roof of her mouth.

"God, you're strange," Riley said, rolling her eyes.

"Looks like we have something in common then, don't we?" I replied joyfully.

Someone cleared their throat behind me. I turned to find Hugo. His brow was furrowed—an attempt at chastisement—before he relaxed into a floppy grin. Riley slammed her fist into one of the pads, and I staggered back, unprepared for the blow. Hugo gripped my shoulders. "Making friends, I see." He laughed.

I huffed, blowing a tendril of hair out of my face. "I am the picture of strength and grace. Riley is a slacker."

Hugo craned his neck and glanced at Riley.

"Don't believe a word she says." The Latino woman said dryly. Hugo chuffed a laugh and looked over his shoulders before he swooped in for a quick cheek peck. Unexpected and sweet, my face broke into a wide grin. Hugo did not look back as he sauntered over to the other Hunters to assist with their sparing.

I raised the pads and turned back to Riley.

"Hugo too?" She appraised me slowly before letting out a low whistle.

"The more, the merrier." I winked.

Every muscle hurt as I dragged my feet back to my room. I unlocked the door with Frankie's fingerprints and flicked on the light. As I stood on the threshold and studied Frankie's meager belongings, I noticed that every drawer had been turned out, and the contents littered the floor. The long-dead smartphone I had stolen weeks before laid cracked on the floor. My room had been ransacked, or the maid service had seriously gone off the deep end.

I cast my eyes over the damage with a veiled sense of detachment. It wasn't *my* things that had been carelessly dropped to the floor and then ground into the carpet. I shouldn't have been bothered. But I was.

The Disney snow globes that had been moved over from Frankie's old room had been swept off the chest of drawers, their jagged broken edges dulled by wet glitter.

The brief memories that I had experienced when I had taken over Frankie's body had been joyless and strict. But the snow globes had been a small sign of whimsy. Each one had a note from someone called MG, who I recently found out to be Momma G.

The more I thought about the damage, and the memories that had been washed away, the angrier I became.

Every inch of my body drew back, taut, like a crossbow ready to fire. My eyes bled into black. Darkness swallowed the whites, and I closed my eyes, pressing my thumb's into the corners to try and rub away my slip in control.

I shouldn't be upset. I told myself. *None of these are my things.*

My fingers wiggled as I tried to lift a magical signature from the room. The faint taste of burning plastic clung to the back of my throat, but nothing else. No residue, which meant it would be pointless to appeal to Davenport and ask for him to fingerprint Frankie's room.

I rolled my head on my shoulders, grabbing a cracked pair of Raybans from the floor, I slipped them on to cover my eyes and decided that I needed to get as far away from the mess as possible before I stabbed someone.

I knocked on Hugo's door, but he hadn't made it back to his room yet. Instead, I decided to walk around for a little bit to try and calm down. Which was awe-inspiring personal growth.

I was circling the K9 pen like a shark, huffing, and puffing as I wrung my hands around an invisible thief's neck when Hart found me. The first words out of his mouth were said with his blunt candor.

"Why are you wearing sunglasses? It's dark outside." Hart shut the gate behind him as he moved closer.

Blinking, I removed the glasses and stuffed them in my pocket. "I'm a douche that likes to wear sunglasses at night."

His lip twitched. "Douches don't call themselves douches."

"The first step to solving a problem is admitting you have one." I waved my hand helplessly.

"Very sage."

"I read it on the back of an AA pamphlet," I confessed. "I found it in the dumpster behind my local rec center. On Tuesdays, they teach a French cooking class."

"You cook?" He looked pleasantly surprised.

"I'm an Avant-Garde chef." I hedged. "I boil and burn. My skills are in tasting."

"Don't you eat hot sauce with every meal?" Hart broke into a full smile, enjoying our banter.

"Hot sauce improves every meal."

"If you say so." He chuckled.

I looked away, into the darkness of the empty pen

309

surrounding the kennels. I wanted to ask about Dixie and how his day had gone. Boring human stuff. Somehow, opening up in that way felt like I was giving away another part of myself.

"What's been bothering you?" Hart asked, his impassive mask was back.

"Who said that anything's been bothering me?" I put my hand on my hip, putting on my cheeriest smile. He did not fall for it, not even for a second.

"Come on," Hart gestured over his shoulder to the kennels. I followed on his heels as Hart led me to a tiny office around the back. A calendar hung on the wall with bright shining Labrador faces beaming back at me. There was a poster that had the words *'you don't have to be mad to work here, but it helps!'* It looked older than Betty White.

"Sit." Hart pulled out a chair. "What's wrong?"

I took a deep breath, ready to inhale my secrets back into my lungs, where they would fester and rot, which was unlike me. As usual, I found my lips moving as I regaled Sergeant Hart with the state of my quarters and how angry it had made me.

"There wasn't anything *demonic* in your room, was there?" He asked when my mouth finally stopped rambling.

I gave him a look that could curdle milk.

Hart picked up his office phone and called housekeeping for me. In a few seconds, he arranged a sweep and a clean of my room. I was grateful, I hadn't known that I could do that.

"Stand up," Hart said, pushing his chair back to make room in the center of the pokey office. I did as he said, as he arranged the furniture and then sat in the middle of the floor with his legs crossed.

"What are you doing?" I couldn't help but laugh like a hyena. I held my ribs as I watched zen-master Hart close his eyes.

"Meditating." He said shortly. "Try it."

"No, thanks."

"Afraid?" One of his eyes opened, just a hair. I sank

310

into my haunches.

"I'm going to reach enlightenment before you." I goaded as I assumed the same position as Hart. "Bring on nirvana," I mumbled as I tried to empty my mind.

We sat in silence, my mind was a dark pool lapping at the edge of a beach of black sand. I drifted away, and before I knew it, I was standing in the ether between dreams and reality.

I turned on my heel, taking in my dream-scape. "Coolio!" I fist-pumped. I had never been able to access the in-between while awake and wearing a host before. Hart stood on the horizon, a tiny dot. A thought brought him to the shore. He looked around wildly, unsure of what was happening. I had managed to pull him into the dream with me, but I couldn't begin to explain how I had done it.

"Hey." I wiggled my fingers.

"You're meant to be meditating." He scowled.

"I am!" I beamed proudly. "I'm so calm that I'm practically horizontal."

Hart turned and eyed the black water. "Mediating is about nothing and everything. It's about finding your center."

"Do you do it because you're trying to find your wolf?" My voice turned gentle.

Hart smiled sadly, his marmalade eyes did not stray from the lapping waves. "I don't have a wolf."

I reached forward to grab his hand, finding my own appendages were starlight and shadows. My true form. Hart had not even reacted. Something inside me splintered.

"You have a wolf," I said adamantly as the scenery around us changed. We were back in the forest, with redwoods so high that they swallowed the light. Bracken was dusted with hoarfrost, and the forest was silent as a bronze flash darted through the trees. A flash of color and nothing more. I spun, dragging Hart with me.

"There he is!" I danced excitedly.

"Mara..." Hart sounded so scared, the same little boy that had huddled on the cold forest floor all those years ago. I

311

ignored his fear and continued to drag him after the blur as I caught snatches of his wolf. A tail darting behind a tree. A flash of orange eyes.

We hiked for hours but did not tire. Such was the nature of dreams.

Hart was crying. Huge gulping silent sobs, but he held my hand tightly and followed. "He's not here." He whispered, after a few hours. "Please stop."

I continued to pull his protesting body to the edge of a clearing. We were so close, I could feel it.

"There he is..." I whispered in awe. The russet wolf stood, taller than me, even on all fours. His tail swished from side to side, and he ducked his head as he approached slowly.

Callum looked up. His eyes widened, and he cried out in pain, dropping to his knees. Swearing, I raced forward with my arms outstretched to catch him, only to find that I was alone.

It took less than a thought to swim back to the waking world. Hot breath moved my hair away from my face, the ground was hard behind my back, and I realized that my head was throbbing as if I had been thrown backward. I opened my eyes slowly and found myself staring into Hart's marmalade orbs, fixed in the face of a beautiful majestic wolf.

There was a *werewolf* on my chest, pinning me to the floor. No humanity stared back at me—which wasn't unusual. New shifters typically took a backseat to their animal for the first few shifts. Callum Hart had been pushed back into the passenger's seat, and his wolf had finally reared to the surface.

Hart's wolfy black lips pulled over his teeth, and a string of saliva stretched between his top and bottom canines. I shifted backward slowly, but his huge paws reminded me of his weight.

The office was a mess in the wake of his transformation. It must have been painful enough that Callum had flailed because a smashed frame laid face down on the floor with glittering shards of glass surrounding it like a halo. A smattering of pens and a mess of papers joined it.

312

I cleared my throat. "Hart..." I whispered. My voice broke and croaked; I wet my lips to try again. "You need to step back. You're hurting me."

The wolf hunched forward, his forehead against mine. He panted and let out a small whine.

I pulled my hand out from behind my back, squished to the floor, and reached out to pet his large canine head. "It's okay," I assured him as I turned my palm over. I had cut my wrist on one of the glass shards that littered the floor. Though the wound had healed, a smear of blood wrapped around my wrist, still wet.

Hart let out another whine as he nudged his head against mine. "You want snuggles, don't you?"

His entire body wiggled, and I realized that his tail was wagging. His dark tongue swiped across his lips as he snuffled. I protested as Hart nudged my bloody hand.

"Don't you dare," I warned as I tried to pull away. The wolf growled at me. I rocked from side to side to try and free myself from the three hundred pound wolf. I was unsuccessful. With a frustrated snarl, the wolf huffed and licked my wrist. A concerned whine left his lips.

I put my head in my hands, finally free, when the wolf began to howl. His scream of pain was a shrieking and gut-wrenching cry that sounded like metal being torn apart. I tried not to cry when the shivering form of a russet wolf curled over and transformed into a naked man.

What had I done?

Hart did not wake up straight away. I waited, pacing in a small section of the office that was not littered with debris, and chewed on Frankie's fingernails. When it began to look like I had actually killed the man, I reached for the office phone—seeing that Jae was number one on speed dial, before Davenport even.

How would I explain to Jae that I'd killed his boyfriend? My hand shook as I waited for the line to connect. I pinched my forearm, allowing the pain to pull me from my terror.

I managed to bark a shaky command at the Nephilim, demanding that Jae come to Hart's office before I slammed down the phone. I pushed my bloody hands through Frankie's thick dark locks and resumed my pacing. My eyes fixed on the motivational poster on the wall, never leaving the jaunty smile of a man in a straight jacket.

Jae took hours to arrive, but it must have been seconds because he was out of breath, and his hair was wet from the rain outside.

"You're not wearing a jacket," I told him, noticing the collar of his pale blue shirt was soaked.

Jae's eyes were feverish with panic. "Where is he?" He scanned the destruction before finally spotting Hart on the floor. Naked and still. Jae crouched down and pushed his hand under his head, cradling the much larger man. "Callum?" He whispered, repeating Hart's name over and over to try and wake him.

"He's breathing," I said, without emotion.

"What did you do?" Each word was measured but accusatory.

I felt the bond begin to unfurl in my chest, like a blooming flower. An unbreakable string made of gold.

Callum would be alright. He had Jae. He'd be fine. I stood robotically. Detached. It felt like I had left my body behind and was floating about in space, looking down.

But I was firmly rooted inside of Frankie Gardiner. I could not tell where she ended, and I began.

I turned on my heel, determined to leave as quickly as possible.

The downpour rushed over my head, but I did not bother to try and shield my face.

I had made it three steps away from the building, and into the pouring rain before Jae called my name. He roared it, his voice was a harsh crack of thunder.

With my spine ramrod straight, I kept walking.

"Mara!" He bellowed as he caught up to me. Jae

314

grabbed my shoulder and slung me around. I threw my arm back to try and dislodge him but was unsuccessful. My eyes were trained downwards, unable to look him in the eye.

"You're running away?" Jae's voice vibrated with barely suppressed rage.

I slumped but did not look up as I nodded.

"You're running away." He repeated in a dead voice.

"I'm sorry." The cold rain began to seep into my clothes, and I shivered. "I didn't mean to. I know he's yours... I'm so sorry, Jae."

Jae let go of my shoulder and took a step back. "You think I'm angry because I'm jealous?" He asked through clenched teeth.

I nodded, glancing up once before looking down. I could feel the undulating waves of his magic. The vanilla scent was so strong that it burnt my nose. My eyes watered with the potency of his power. I waited for the hit—I steeled myself not to flinch.

Jae did not move. "You've marked three of us now." He commented lightly.

I said nothing.

"I can feel your emotions." He told me. "I know what you're feeling. You need to explain to me right this second."

My eyes burned. It would be okay if I cried, the rain was heavy enough. Right?

"This is all temporary." I waved my hand. "In a few weeks, I'll go back to my life and—"

"You think it's that easy?" Jae pushed his wet hair out of his face. "When this is done, you'll go back to your Fae master, and forget all about us?"

I wanted to nod, but I got the feeling that it would be a very bad idea.

"That man in there—" Jae flung his hand over his shoulder. "He needs both of us, and we're out here arguing because you can't bring yourself to feel for anyone but yourself."

"How dare you say that to me." I stepped forward with

clenched fists.

Jae closed in on me. "These bonds happen for a reason. They're permanent, and you can't even bring yourself to speak to the people that you've connected with about them." Jae's eyes narrowed, accusing.

My hand whipped out before I could control it, connecting with Jae's cheek hard enough to throw his head to the side. Rain dripped from the ends of his straight black hair as his head hung. My hands pressed against my mouth, rocked to the core, I stepped backward. My mouth formed the words 'sorry' over and over, but I could not force myself to make a sound.

Jae's eyes were hard as his head tilted up. He reached up and gripped my throat, enough to still me but not enough to hurt. He held me in place, and cocked his head to the side, moving in close enough that I could feel his breath on the skin of my neck.

"I can't get attached," I whispered, my heart was breaking. "If I don't get close... It won't hurt when I'm gone."

Jae released my throat. His face turned blank with shock. "Mara..."

"I'm the last one, Jae." I raised my hand to catch a drop of rain. "I'm the only Nightmare left."

Jae repeated my name. A soft prayer. His arms outstretched as he wrapped me in his embrace. He was the same height as me, and my head sat on his shoulder. He shook as he held me close, and I could not tell if he was crying or not.

I didn't know why the universe had given me three soulmates. I wasn't worth it. They deserved better than me.

"Aren't you afraid of my darkness?" I said in a tiny voice.

"I like it. It's the same flavor as mine." Jae replied simply, pulling away. His nose brushed mine, and my lips parted as I wet them with my tongue. Jae's hand cupped my cheeks as he pressed his lips against mine, hard and demanding. Eyes closed and desperate. He tasted sweet. His lips were soft, and

316

thin, as he pressed his mouth against mine, urging us closer until we melted into each other and became one.

My stomach clenched, and my hands reached forward with the intent to push him away, but instead, my fingers tangled in the sodden fabric of his dress shirt.

Jae broke away, only to sigh my name like a prayer. The world sparkled, the rain no longer poured down but bounced off the air around us. Protected by his invisible wings. I closed my eyes, listening to my name in his delicate voice, I wanted to swim in it. Jae kissed me again, chaste at first but deliciously wicked. He pulled my lip between his teeth and teased his tongue against mine as if to ask permission.

Then he bit me.

I broke away, hissing in pain, and my tongue swiped against my lip only to be greeted with the coppery taste of my own blood. Jae's eyes sparkled with wicked triumph.

"Now, you have to keep me too." He smirked before he fell to the ground and screamed in agony.

Drama queen.

Chapter 20

The next morning, I sat in the Mess Hall. Wedged between Jae and Hart like the bacon in the middle of a sandwich.

The night before, I had to carry Jae across the K9 enclosure and back into Hart's office before anyone saw. For a slim, petite, man, he sure was heavy.

Hart had woken up in the early morning, next to a still unconscious Jae, and had looked like Christmas had come early. Typically the stoic mountain man would have shut down his emotions like a nuclear bunker preparing for attack, the second that I caught a glimpse of them. But something had changed. I was allowed a glimpse into the relief and vindication that Hart wore proudly.

Callum had been kicked out of his pack as a teenager, but I suspected that he had been an outcast long before then. His dreams were of being hunted. I knew the feeling well. Of never knowing what would happen when someone finally caught you.

All three of us had not said a word to each other since waking up, sore from sleeping on the scratchy carpeted floor of Hart's office.

I needed food and caffeine stat.

Every eye followed us as we had walked in together, and I wondered if the rest of the compound could see the invisible change that had overcome the unlikely duo and their newest addition: me.

Hart had already procured a bottle of Tabasco sauce before I even thought about the journey to the condiment stand. Jae had stolen another slice of bacon from the tray and slid it onto my plate—much to Gary's consternation.

Everything was normal. Except it wasn't.

We sat down, Hart unwrapped my cutlery, and Jae put sugar in my coffee. All without a word, the two men wore blithe happy smiles as if they were guest-starring in an episode of Sesame Street.

I slammed my open palms down on the table. Breaking the silence. "Stop," I demanded. "You're freaking me out."

"I can't help it." Jae's smile ticked higher.

Hart grunted and reached into his jacket pocket. He pulled out a mini bottle of vodka and moved his tomato juice onto my plate.

I eyed him quizzically.

"Bloody Mary," Hart explained, though his two short words didn't actually explain anything.

"How in *Lucifer's Anus* did you get vodka?" I lowered my head and hissed. Hart's lip twitched the betraying hint of a smile as he sliced his omelet and ate his food without reacting to my hysterics.

"Callum does most of the supply runs." Jae unscrewed the vodka and dumped it into the glass. He tucked the small bottle into his sleeve in a movement so swift that I wasn't sure it had happened. "And maybe lay off the Hell-swears. It makes you sound like a Demon."

I bared my teeth in a mocking grimace of a smile and turned to my bloody Mary. I drank it all in one go, and I did not say thank you when I slammed the glass back onto my tray.

"You're a sour puss today," Jae noted.

"Very grumpy." Hart agreed, not looking up from his breakfast.

"Anyone would think that you're scared of commitment." Jae sang, sipping his coffee.

I stuck out my tongue. One of the chairs opposite scraped across the linoleum, and I looked up to see Hugo and Remi had joined us. Hugo leaned over the table and greeted me with a kiss on the cheek, which made me feel warm. I counted three scathing stares from the peanut gallery. Chloe was one of them.

I wiggled in my seat, smug. Hugo Sinclair belonged to me.

"What are you two so happy about?" Remi wondered. He had dark circles under his eyes, and he looked like he needed coffee more than I did. I pushed my mug across the table, Remi sniffed it. "Salt?" He asked.

I answered him with a look that would have made Daddy Davenport proud.

Jae and Hart, in a move that I could only assume they had choreographed, pulled the collars of their shirts down. Each man had a Soulbond on the left side, over their heart. The burnt scars had turned to silver, looking like they had been there years. I tried not to flinch.

Hugo's eyes sparkled. "Welcome to the dark side."

Remi glanced over his shoulder, and I followed his gaze. Alicia sat a few tables over, staring at us with hatred in her eyes.

"You don't have to sit here. Not if it's going to cause trouble for you." I offered weakly.

Hart placed his fork on his tray. He opened his mouth to say something but decided against it.

Remi sighed. "She's just worried."

Jae and I shared a look but wisely said nothing. Hugo, sensing the tension, decided to change the subject.

"I felt some fear through the bond last night, but couldn't find you." Hugo's gaze was soft. "Why didn't you tell me that someone had trashed your room?"

I stabbed a sausage link and ate it. "It's not a big deal. I probably left the window open, and a raccoon got in."

"A raccoon couldn't open a drawer and shred all of your underwear." Hugo's voice grew hard. "You'd tell us if someone was causing you trouble?"

I snorted. "What? Apart from the Summoner, who wants to kill my host?" I said sarcastically.

Hugo's gaze did not waver.

"What's this?" Remi asked, his emotions carefully guarded. I explained about the state of my quarters and my anger at seeing Frankie's belongings destroyed. I stopped speaking when I realized that my voice had risen and attracted the attention of several people. Remi's eyes grew harder and harder with every word. Boiling with anger. Jae rubbed my shoulder, and Hart shoved a fork loaded with eggs into my mouth when I took a breath. It was like having burly mother hens.

"They even took my hairbrush!" I said, covering my full mouth with my hand.

Remi stood up abruptly. His fists were clenched. He excused himself with a few clipped words, before marching over to Alicia. He bent down and whispered something to her. A few seconds later, they both left the Mess Hall without another word.

"What was all that about?" I wondered.

Hugo, Hart, and Jae shook their heads, wearing identical looks of befuddlement. Shaking off the weirdness, I finished my food and shifted backward on my chair. Uncomfortably full.

"Three O'clock," Hart said plainly, and the other men tensed. I opened my mouth to inform him that it was still the morning when Gary approached our table. Red-faced and shaking, the canteen worker looked like he didn't know whether to shout or cry. He only had eyes for me, even though Hugo, Hart, and Jae watched him like a threat.

"What is your problem?" Gary demanded loudly, spit flew from his mouth and landed on my cheek. My nose scrunched as I wiped my face.

"Huh?"

"My room has been searched seven times!" Gary shrieked. His shrill voice made my ears hurt. "I know that you had something to do with it. Call off your dogs!" He waved his hand to towards my soulmates.

"I'm so confused right now." I turned to Jae, ignoring the hysterical man. "I thought *everyone's* room's got searched this week."

"They did," Hart answered instead, his eyes bored into Gary as if he wished the man would melt into the floor.

Gary swallowed, but then rallied. "Not seven times!" He bit back.

"Maybe you're just a shady character?" I offered, with a timid smile.

Gary threw his head back and shrieked before grabbing Remi's breakfast tray. He wrenched the yellow plastic away from the table, letting the bottle of blue Gatorade fall to the floor with a bounce. Gary swung for my head. I arched backward, but the edge of the tray still rammed into my nose.

Hugo wrestled the canteen worker to the floor. My upper lip grew moist, and I pressed my fingers to my mouth, pulling them back bloody.

"I'm bleeding," I said numbly.

Hugo had restrained Gary on the floor, the snarling man had gone limp and was shaking his head, claiming he had no idea what was going on.

Jae gripped my fingers and pulled me out of my chair. "Let's go to the infirmary." He suggested.

I began to protest, but Hart shook his head minutely and glanced at the Nephilim. Jae hid it well, but he was upset. If going to see Dr. Dan would make him feel better, I could make the small sacrifice. I craned my neck as we walked away; Hugo had zip-tied Gary's arms behind his back.

Hart reached into his pocket and pulled out a pack of Kleenex. He handed it to me so I could staunch the blood dripping from my nose. My eyes watered with the sharp pain before it melted away. Thank the Seven Hell's for Demon healing. I'd seen human-speed healing, and it looked tedious.

"How big are your pockets?" I asked in wonder. Hart shrugged. Jae surged in front of us, a man on a mission.

"Cargo pants," Callum grunted as he held the door open for me. A wave of cold air and the smell of medical disinfectant hit me.

I took the bloody tissue from my nose. "I'm good. Let's go."

Jae rounded on me with intense eyes. I had never seen him so serious. "You're seeing the doctor." He told me before his phone chirped in his pocket. He fished out the device and swore. "I have an appointment. Watch her." Jae told Hart, pointing at me like I was an errant child, before disappearing in a whirl.

I glanced at Hart. "What was that about?"

"His mother refused to go to the hospital when she got cancer." Hart watched Jae's retreating figure. "He takes his health very seriously."

"But his mom was such a..." I trailed off, searching for the word.

"Abusive, strict, unaffectionate woman?" Hart rattled off dryly, his jaw ticked.

"Yeah."

"Sometimes we love people that we really shouldn't," Callum said.

"Like your family?" I wondered. Callum gave a short imperceptible nod. "Are you going to tell them that you've found your wolf?"

Hart snorted, and that answer was enough.

Dr. Daniel rounded the corner of his office, snapping his gloves over his outstretched hands. His eyes scanned my body for injury before resting on my bloody face.

"Sit down." Dr. Dan said. No brotherly greeting. The man needed to work on his bedside manner. "Corporal Gardiner is a grown woman. She can be examined without an escort."

"You've got this?" Hart eyed the door reluctantly. I rolled my eyes.

"I'll survive," I said. I was rewarded with a tiny smile. When the towering werewolf was gone, Dr Dan started to clean up my nose and check for concussion and other human problems.

Without a word, he readied a needle and rolled up my

323

sleeve. I jumped a foot in the air. "What's that for?"

"Vitamins." He replied shortly, the needle was already halfway depressed and emptied into my arm when he grunted the word. A wave of dizziness made my head swim as I stood up.

"You're good to go." Dr. Dan had already turned away, more interested in his computer screen than watching me leave. I thanked him with a salute and was on my way. Frankie's brother needed to get laid.

I'd gone back to my room to change clothes, but instead I passed out on my bed. Mouth open wide, drool, and everything. I startled awake when someone brushed my hair away from my face. I batted them away like a cat playing with a laser.

Remi chuckled as I rolled over and stretched; the sound was a deep rumble that I wanted to wrap around my body like a warm blanket.

"I like that." I smiled sleepily with my eyes closed

"Like what?" He asked, sitting on the end of my bed.

"When you laugh."

Remi sobered, his hand twitched before he pulled it slowly away from my face. "Good sleep?" He asked.

I shrugged. "No dreams."

"Is that strange?"

"For a nightmare demon? Yeah." I sat up and rubbed my head. Remi winced when my hand caught in a tangle. I swore.

"Let me," Remi sat up and reached into his pocket. He positioned my head and began to brush and section my hair.

"You found my brush!" I bounced before Remi put his hand on my crown to keep me still. "Where was it?"

Remi did not answer my question. "What have you been doing to your hair?" He started to tug and braid my hair

324

away from my face.

"You're really good at that," I said.

"I have three younger sisters. They have hair similar to yours."

The repetitive movement of his fingers against my scalp was comforting; before long, my eyes dropped closed again and I had to fight to stay awake.

"Where did you go at breakfast?" I asked sluggishly.

Remi tied a braid. "Nowhere important."

Calling his fiancée unimportant didn't sound conducive to a happy marriage, but what did I know?

"Did you want to talk or something?" I offered lamely, as Remi braided my hair and hummed to himself. His lips pulled into a slow but bright smile.

"Mara, I'm okay. I swear."

I didn't know what I wanted. Some deep part of me whispered that I should wrap him in my arms and kiss him until we forgot our own names.

"All done." He patted my head, still smiling indulgently. I wiggled around so that I could see the results in the mirror. It looked good.

Frankie had hair that bordered on dry and frizzy but still managed to curl into loose waves. It hovered on the threshold of Caucasian hair. Remi had managed to tame the mess. Every time I had looked at it, I had felt a surge of guilt towards my host for not taking care of her properly. It didn't matter that Frankie's soul had left its vessel weeks before, I still felt a sense of responsibility towards keeping it safe.

That was one of the reasons that I hadn't thrown caution to the wind and lost my metaphorical virginity.

I might have been a Demon, but forcing someone's body to have sex even when they weren't inside sounded pretty crappy to me.

"There's steam coming from your ears." Remi took the end of one of my Dutch braids in his hand and rubbed it between his index and pointer finger. "What are you thinking so

325

hard about?"

"Sex." I blurted out.

Remi slumped and let out a theatrical groan. "Mara..." He flung his arm over his face as he laid on the bed. "Don't. I've already had to listen to Alicia talk, at length, about how I am not to 'take a lover' while we are engaged."

"I could always kill her for you." I offered sincerely.

Remi, still prone on my bed with his eyes hidden, reached into his pocket and pulled out a small straw doll with no features. A band of straggly hair was wrapped around its neck like a collar, and I reached up to my own throat to make sure that my silver band was still in place. Remi pushed the straw doll into my hands without explanation.

I turned it over in my palms. "What's this?"

"A poppet."

I sniffed. "Coolios, I guess," I said before I tried to hand it back. Remi did not take it, but he eased his elbow away from his face so that I could see the tortured expression there.

"A poppet is like a western voodoo doll. Witchlings use them to focus malicious magic. They need a strand of hair, or drop of blood, to make one." Remi explained, glancing down at the straw doll.

"I feel like I am missing something." I cocked my head to the side. Sleep still fogged my mind, and I wanted nothing more than to curl up in bed next to Remi and fall asleep.

"Alicia stole your brush. She broke into your room and made a poppet so she could hurt you." His chocolate eyes narrowed and flicked away as if he couldn't bear to look at me. His jaw clenched. I shifted, crouching over and cupping his cheek.

"Remi," I repeated his name until his attention came back to me. Soft but steady. "Her magic can't hurt me."

"She wanted to hurt you." He said through tight lips.

I smiled sadly. "Yeah."

"How can you be so calm about this?" He sat up abruptly, his face only an inch from mine. I suddenly realized that I was on all fours, hovering over his body. It would have taken so little to move forward and feel his plush lips against mine. To see him smile and look down at me like he wanted me. That he was proud that we were Bonded.

Remi made a strangled noise in the back of his throat and pulled away, he gripped my shoulders so that I did not fall, as he lowered my body into a seated position. Remi stood and began to pace. Stopping once, he looked back at me and opened his mouth to speak, before shutting it with an audible click of his teeth.

He strode to the door, determined to leave before he slowly stopped and hung his head. "I came to see you because Team P has a mission. Davenport wants you at the SUV by twenty-three hundred hours." Remi tilted his jaw to speak and did not look at me as he said the words. I had no chance to ask any questions before he was gone.

"So, let me get this straight?" I said, turning to the back of the van from the passenger seat. "We're going to a duck pond, to hunt some deadly beastie."

No one said a word as they strapped themselves into the seats in the back.

"A duck pond?" I giggled incredulously. "Come on, guys, did anyone pack any bread?"

Only Jae snorted a laugh. Hugo rolled his eyes, and the others looked distracted. I turned to Davenport in the driver's seat as he adjusted his mirrors.

"Do you find me funny, Daddy Davenport?" I pouted. I saw every man in the back of the van perk up like a prairie dog, but they remained silent.

"Brat." Warren gave me his signature chiding look. I smiled and clapped in delight. His lips pulled into an easy smirk, arrogant and cocky, full of Davenport's trademark confidence.

The drive was short, and it didn't take us long to find the small park in the center of a cookie-cutter neighborhood on the edge of Maywood. I wondered why some Demon or Fae had decided to set up shop so close to the Hunters compound—but then I remembered that no one else actually knew where the compound was. The knowledge was carefully guarded.

Shielded from view by a concrete wall covered in graffiti, and a chicken wire fence with beautiful floral bouquets woven into the mesh, I paused outside of the entrance and looked at the rain-damaged photos of two smiling victims with the words RIP written in golden sharpie above their heads.

Everyone had loaded their weapons and readied themselves for whatever mission required our presence, except for me. I was unarmed and dressed in sweats. I had asked Davenport for a gun, and he had laughed at me until he looked like he was going to have a heart attack. The rest of the team had eyed him like he was having a nervous breakdown.

My only retort was a scathing look.

"Mara, you, me and Jae, will scout the west side of the pond. I want the rest of you on guard in case it goes south—Remi, stay by the car." Davenport threw his gun over his shoulder as he marched into the kiddie park like the terminator. He looked ready to throw down and seemed to be taking the entire mission too seriously. The backdrop of brightly colored monkey bars and a jaunty twirly slide hooked my attention long enough that I was tempted to ditch the Hunters and try out the equipment.

Jae put his hand on the small of my back, leading me back to the path. We fell into step behind the commander.

"What?" I asked innocently.

"You can play afterward," Jae assured me as Davenport walked from the path to the edge of a sizeable black space that must have been the pond.

Despite the assurance that it had once been a duck pond, there were no birds in sight. The reeds were still, and the water looked like glass.

Davenport and Jae clicked on their flashlights and began to shine them around, studying our surroundings.

They continued to walk at the edge of the water, utterly ignorant of the tiny ripples that had begun to spread from the center of the pond.

I stepped back and crossed my arms over my chest, content to watch the Hunters at work.

My presence was only required because Davenport didn't want me alone without Team P around to keep me in line. Heaven forbid that I TP his admin building—not that I had been tempted.

Davenport stepped towards the reeds, and my body moved so quickly that it shocked even me. One second I stood fifteen feet away; the next, I held the collar of a 6'1 man. Like I was a mother dog, and he was a naughty puppy.

Davenport stepped away from the edge and flashed his light into my eyes. "What are you doing?"

I jabbed my finger in the direction behind him. Not needing to say a word. Two shimmering pearlescent eyes glowed in the dark. The sleek equine shape of an almost blue horse, so dark that the creature melted into the night. It crept forward like the water was solid ground before the horse gathered speed as it cantered towards us. It made no sound as it moved.

"What is that?" Jae whispered in awe as he reached for the gun on the holster on his side. He did not take his eyes off the beast as he flicked off the safety and aimed.

"Kelpie." Warren and I answered in synch. "Jinx!" I blurted out. Davenport did not dignify my declaration with a reply.

"A Kelpie is a Fae water horse that drags people to their watery deaths, right?" Jae said, his gun was trained on the approaching creature.

"You guys have a lot of problems with the Fae, huh?" I tapped my chin. "Maybe it's time for a rebrand."

"Do you know anything about Kelpies?" Davenport asked, shining his flashlight at the ground. I shrugged. It was his show, not mine.

"Kelpie!" Davenport boomed, his voice echoed across the water, full of command. "You are in violation of 'section 2, subsection D' of the Fae-Human Realities treaty. Killing without the need for sustenance. You have been ordered back to Tír na nÓg to stand trial in the Summer Court."

The Kelpie tossed it's head back, but did not make a sound. The water at its feet began to shift and lap at its hooves.

"Kelpie—do you have the ability to create a portal, or would you like us to assist with your transport?" Davenport sounded like a very patient store manager. I bit back a childish laugh.

The Kelpie's eyes burned, and it began to shift on its feet. The water grew more tumultuous. I stepped back.

"He's not listening," Jae said. "He's scared and alone." The Nephilim would know, being an empath and all.

"He doesn't speak English," I said, waving my hand to the spooked water horse. "Most Fae speak Gaelic. All of them speak Fae."

"Do you speak Gaelic or Fae?" Davenport looked like he was about to blow a gasket.

"What do you think I am? The Duolingo owl?" I snorted.

Davenport's hand twitched, and he was either resisting the urge to press his fingers against his temple, or suppressing the desire to spank me. I couldn't tell which.

Jae's finger hovered over the trigger like a doomsday button.

"Okay!" I held my hands out, disarmingly, as the water from the pond began to recede. Mr. Kelpie was preparing for a mini-tsunami. Not good.

Both Hunters watched with interest as I reached up and unlocked my silver collar without a word. I threw it to Davenport.

"You could take it off at any time?" He growled.

"Shh." I hissed, closing my eyes. "I have to

330

concentrate."

It had been so long since I had accessed my *other* form that the transition was laborious, like swimming through syrup. Frankie's body dropped to the floor as I trotted forward on four legs, shaking the shadows of my mane.

"Is she a horse?" Jae said, trying not to laugh. Davenport did not say a word, but I felt his dark eyes as they followed my slow approach to the Kelpie.

My night Mare form was different than my true form, but was still a part of me.

I lowered my long snout and locked eyes with the scared water horse.

<You have killed> I said directly into his mind.

The Kelpie hung his head. *<Two children threw stones at my home. I defended myself.>*

I rolled my lips back, exposing my horsey teeth. *<You have been called back to Court for trial>*

The Kelpie threw his head back and let out a whinny. *<I did nothing wrong>*

<Above my pay grade.> I gave the horse equivalent of a shrug. *<If you don't go back to Tír na nÓg, those two Hunters will kill you.>*

The Kelpie reared up on two legs, and the water under his feet began to sink to form a swirling whirlpool. The Kelpie slammed back onto its front hooves, splashing.. *<May your rivers be clear and your tides strong.>* His words echoed on the air as he melted away.

I turned and trotted back to the edge of the water, sweeping back into Frankie's body like a rolling fog. I stood up and brushed the mud from my ass.

Everything was still. I'd taken care of the problem, and no one had gotten hurt. I spread my arms wide. "I accept praise in form of chocolate or tequila," I informed a shocked Davenport.

"Careful, War." Jae teased. "Don't get to close. She might not be stable."

Davenport broke out of his frozen state to groan at the terrible pun.

"Get it. *Stable*?" Jae threw his head back and cackled. "Because she's a horse."

I turned away and followed Davenport as he led us through the park and back towards the SUV.

I spotted Hart and Hugo by the drinking fountains. They jogged over when they saw us. Moving quickly and quietly for such large men.

"Mara's a horse." Jae blurted out with glee.

"I will rip out all of your feathers and use them to make a racially insensitive headdress." I bit out. The abstract nature of the threat made Jae laugh even harder as Davenport explained what had happened at the duck pond. All eyes shifted to me.

"I'm a night*mare*." I reminded them, emphasizing the last syllable.

"Yes, you are." An amused voice floated from behind us. Every Hunter shifted, and soon four weapons were drawn and pointed at the stranger's face.

"Ryn Cole." Hugo stepped forward, dipping his head. When everyone saw Hugo's lack of reaction, their trigger fingers relaxed.

"Hello, Mara." The Fae had his hands in his pockets. The picture of innocence, out for an evening stroll. Ryn's eyes did not stray from mine, none of the Hunters existed for him. His gaze unnerved me. There was no attraction there, just the same empty blankness that I often saw in higher Demons. Ryn Cole was the kind of man to start a fire just to see what would happen.

I would probably do the same, but I would try my best not to kill anyone. I got the feeling that Cole would not care.

Ryn Cole held a nondescript and water-damaged cardboard box in his hands. Small enough to be of note. He brushed the dirt from the top of the box before turning it over in his grip. "I found something interesting." Ryn lifted the box and shook it near his ear. It rattled. I perked up, curious.

Davenport stepped forward, his significant presence forced me to move back as the commander put himself in the line of fire.

"What do you want, Cole?" Davenport crossed his arms over his chest, his eyes emitted a soft glow.

Ryn eyed Davenport like a rattlesnake. "I come bearing gifts."

"At what cost?" Warren's voice was steel.

Ryn's eyes flicked to mine as I craned around Davenport's rigid frame. Davenport stepped forward, breaking his stare.

"No." Warren snarled.

Ryn smiled sleepily. "I have a question for the Drude. But one. If you agree to my terms, I shall impart my knowledge and be away." Cole rubbed his bottom lip with the pad of his thumb while he surveyed our group. "Surely one question is not too much to ask for such a boon."

I cleared my throat and raised my hand. "I want to know what's in the box."

"Me too," Jae admitted out of the corner of his mouth. Hugo stepped closer to my side.

Hart stalked forward, with no care for the growing tension. He sniffed the air once, saying nothing. It occurred to me very slowly that all my men had fallen into formation around me, like a star. Protecting me as the center of their group.

Ryn shook the box again. "One question."

Davenport glanced at me, and I nodded. "One." He agreed.

The bored expression melted from Ryn Cole's cherub face, replaced with shrewd happiness—the face of a creature that just got one over on someone. With a flourish, Cole opened the stained dirt box and showed us three rows of bullets. Dark, tarnished and uninteresting.

I feigned a yawn. "Boring."

Davenport ignored me. "Explain."

"It was a rare order. Iron wrapped in Devil's Silver. I

333

tracked the bullets, they were still active, none spent. They were buried in Queens, behind a suburban house." Ryn stepped forward, his arm outstretched to hand over the bullets. Hart intercepted and took the box.

Davenport's mind was going a mile a minute, I could almost hear the cogs turning. None of that showed on his stoic face.

Hart opened the box and showed us all the contents. Every bullet was accounted for. I had felt sure that Frankie had been shot in the leg. Each of the Fae had died so differently from the rest of their teams. The Ifrit had burnt out the Hunters from the inside, but the Fae had been killed by iron poisoning.

The only outlier was Frankie Gardiner.

Ryn brushed the dirt from his hands and put them back in his pockets. "It seems that your assassin procured the bullets but did not use them."

"Riveting," Davenport replied dryly.

Something else was killing the Fae. The bullets seemed like a good distraction technique. To keep us from looking at the actual weapon.

I, of course, said none of that. I was too busy shivering. The trees on the edge of the park provided little coverage from the wind.

Jae blew into his hands to warm them up.

I shrugged away from the center of the Hunters. "Your question?" I quirked a brow.

Ryn Cole cleared his throat and bit back a smile. "Do you remember?" He asked simply.

My brow furrowed. "Remember what?"

The Fae laughed bitterly, shaking his head to himself. "That's what I thought. You can't help me, Mara." He stepped back and melted into the darkness, bidding us all farewell with a solemn nod.

All of the Hunters turned to me.

"Was that the question?" I wondered, my head cocked to the side like a confused puppy.

"I honestly don't know." Davenport murmured in agreement.

The SUV was parked in the corner of the empty parking lot, furthest away from the street lamps at the edge of the concrete wall. Raised voices drifted across the asphalt from the second that we broke through the trees and left the path.

"Remi was meant to watch the car, right?" Hugo asked, pushing his hair out of his face. Davenport nodded wordlessly and continued his stride towards the hulking armored vehicle.

Jae reached into his pocket and pulled out his phone. Using the flashlight app, he illuminated the two dark silhouettes that appeared to be arguing by the side of the car.

Hart's lip hitched into a silent snarl. Jae rolled his eyes heavenward. Hugo slid his arm over my shoulder.

"Ms. Greenlea." Davenport greeted the hysterical redhead with polite indifference, only I could hear the rage building behind the surface. "You were not invited to this mission. Why are you here?"

Jae shone the flashlight on her beautifully made-up face. Her lips were curled back in anger, and Remi had been backed against the side of the SUV. I could taste the burning plastic of Witchling magic in the air, and I had no doubt that she had been able to drop a colossal spell. Remi plastered a smile on his face.

"It's okay." He assured us. "Alicia was just leaving."

Hugo clutched me tighter. To restrain me or to protect me, I did not know.

Callum stepped forward and brushed his fingers against Remi's temple. "You're bleeding." He stated plainly. "Her phone has blood on the edge. I can smell it. She threw it at you."

Alicia's face turned to stone. "Remington, it's time to go. I promised Daddy that we would come back to the estate to

335

check-in." Her eyes did not leave Remi's as they flashed with all sorts of veiled warnings.

Alicia Greenlea made my stomach feel like it was full of snakes. She made my skin itch. I wanted to peel her away from every facet of my life.

Every muscle in my body tensed as I processed Hart's words. Alicia had hurt Remi. She had made him bleed.

Remi pushed himself away from the car, following Alicia's orders to heel. I moved so quickly that Hugo's arm did not have a chance to hold me back. One second, I stood on the periphery, the next, I was in front of Alicia, chest puffed out, and fists clenched.

"No." I felt my eyes bleed into darkness. "You will not touch him. He does not belong to you." I told her. My voice layered and turned demonic.

Remi gripped my shoulder to pull me back. I would not be moved.

"Why are you here?" I cocked my head to the side, my eyes never leaving hers.

Alicia's jaw tensed. "Fuck you."

"Pleasant." I tsked. "Remi does not want you here. None of us do."

"He told me that he wanted space." Alicia spat. Waving her hand towards Remi as her face creased in disgust.

"You tried to use magic to harm my teammate." Remi's voice broke my heart. "That's not okay!"

"You're mine." Alicia hissed. "I can do what I like to make sure you understand that."

Remi stepped back, he began to shake his head frantically wincing like he had bitten into something foul.

Alicia tried to follow his steps, but I lifted my palm and pressed it against her solar plexus to halt her movements. She jerked away from my touch but recoiled when she met my black eyes.

"You will leave." Davenport enunciated clearly, speaking down to her like she was a naughty child. "I cannot

336

condone this kind of behavior."

"He *has* to marry me." Alicia smiled proudly. Deciding on another tactic to further her own ends. "We have contracts. He's signed. Remington belongs to me."

"He belongs to himself and the Balance." Hart pulled open the car door and nudged for Remi to step inside. For a second, he did not move, until Hart nudged him again.

Alicia tried to bypass me to get to Remi, I stepped into her path.

"Leave." I bit out.

"I'm not letting some tramp get her hands on my property." Alicia spat in my face, rising up, so her hateful eyes met mine. I caught the moment of horror when she saw the gaping pits of nothing that stared back at her. The Witchling flinched and wrenched herself backward. Alicia scrambled away, turning only once to shout a garbled and incoherent threat.

We all stood still, only our eyes followed the squealing wheels of her convertible as she did a tailspin out of the parking lot.

"She saw your eyes," Hugo whispered. "What if she tells someone?"

Davenport responded by pulling out his phone. "Ms. Greenlea is no longer welcome at the compound. I don't believe that will be a problem."

Chapter 21

We picked up takeout in Maywood and drove back to the compound.

Remi stared out the window for the entire drive and did not engage despite numerous attempts to catch his attention.

It was silently decided that we would eat at Jae's cabin, away from the listening ears of the other Hunters. Remi surged forward, the first into the cabin, as the rest of us followed. Davenport carried the unearthed box of bullets in his hands, delicately, like a baby bird. Hugo had insisted on paying for all of the food, and no one had argued. I felt like I had been included in a secret initiation rite. Hugo ordered the food on the phone as we drove, and he did not stumble once while rattling off a complex and extensive list of what the team wanted. He hadn't even needed to ask. I got a glimpse into their post-mission ritual, and I was all too happy that it included Kung Pao chicken and Chow Mein.

No one had asked for my order, but I had a sneaky feeling that the extra hot chili noodles had my name written all over them.

Hugo placed the white boxes onto the coffee table in the living room, while Remi reclined in the tub armchair and flicked through Netflix. The rest of the team dived into the food like ravenous animals. Davenport was the only person to get silverware and a plate.

Wedged in between Jae and Hart, I spooned noodles into my mouth and watched the silence slowly melt from tense to thoughtful.

Every so often, Davenport would glance at Remi to gauge his emotions. I could tell that we all wanted to bring up

Alicia's temper and her childish tantrum. I certainly wanted to talk about it. I wanted to shake Remi and tell him to ditch the witch.

I knew plenty of places to bury a body if she didn't get the message. Daddy Davenport and I shared a look, and I could tell that he was thinking the same thing. I stuck out my tongue. He clicked his chopsticks, threatening to grab it, even though I was across the other side of the room.

"Aren't we going to mention the horse in the room?" Jae said wickedly, spearing a piece of chicken into his mouth.

I groaned. Hart reached behind my back to smack Jae across the head. He darted out of reach, cackling.

Remi continued to flick through Netflix, silently perusing the movies, his food laid untouched on the floor by his combat boot.

"What's this about a horse?" Hugo asked innocently.

I swallowed a mouthful of noodles. "Nightmares can't change shape like Higher Demons, but we have more than one form. Most Demons do." I waved my hand dismissively. I dropped my voice, going for dramatic effect "Legend has it, that if you ride on the back of a Night Mare, you will see your own death." I said spookily, wiggling my fingers.

"Is that true?" Davenport quirked a brow.

"Who knows?" I blew a raspberry. "I can't ride on my own back, can I?"

"I'll ride you anytime." Jae's face was the picture of innocence.

"That's what Cole meant when he said stables," Hugo said without emotion.

"Yeah." I twirled noodles around my chopsticks. My nose burned with the spices. "The King of Greed, Mammon, collects rare creatures."

"And you're the last Drude." Hugo finished my sentence, but he did not seem at all happy.

"Most Demon and Witchling magic does not work on me." I shrugged. "I'm not worried."

Davenport eyed my collar but said nothing as he spooned one of his boring steamed vegetables into his mouth. Even with a plate on his lap, the man had impeccable table manners.

"My magic doesn't work on you?" If Remi's sudden decision to join the conversation startled any of my Hunters, they showed no sign of it.

"I guess." I winced. "Witchling magic comes from a Devil's bargain, and Lucifer's magic does not work on me."

"Including Devil's Silver?" Davenport sat forward, intrigued.

"I've never tried," I admitted. "Drudes have a collective memory. I can check back if you want?"

For once, Daddy Davenport looked stunned. Hugo perked up, eyes alive with interest.

"What does that mean?" Hugo asked.

"We share memories with our Cluster. If one Drude experiences it, we all do." I said.

"So you felt when all your family..." Hugo swallowed the lump in his throat, crunching his water bottle in his fist.

Davenport's face turned pale, and he looked sick all of a sudden. Sitting back, he took a swig of his water.

I stared down at my food, picking at the sauce-covered chicken. I didn't want to think about my kin.

Jae's finger drew patterns on my thigh. Even though I wore trousers, the delicate artwork of his touch made my skin tingle.

"Bullets," Davenport said, clearing his throat. No one said anything about his abrupt change of subject.

"Classic Red Herring." Jae sat back smugly.

Hart shook his head and snorted. "Not everyone reads as much as you do, Angel-face."

Jae looked contrite. "A red herring is—" He began to explain before Remi cut him off. The Witchling's eyes never left the TV screen.

"—it's a clue purposely meant to misdirect." Remi

interrupted. "The bullets were commissioned and planted so we wouldn't look at the true murder weapon."

"But there are no wounds." Hugo pushed his hair out of his face. "The only consistency is an elevated iron level in all of the dead Fae."

"Which was explained by the dissolving Iron bullets," Hart stated blandly. "Except that none of them were used."

"Is Ryn Cole the only supplier?" I yawned and slumped back, resting my head on Hart's shoulder.

Davenport scratched his stubby chin. "To my knowledge."

"Could an Ifrit kill a Fae with iron poisoning?" Remi asked, putting the TV remote down. Finally.

I chewed my bottom lip as I considered it. "Ifrits burn people out from the inside. They're primarily beings of fire. It's their calling card. Iron weapons tend to be more of a mortal thing."

"Initially, we looked into all of the proficient marksmen in the compound, but all of them had an alibi." Davenport took another sip of water. "How could someone use enough iron to kill a Fae, without wounding them?"

"Spinach?" Jae wiped his face on his sleeve and leaned back, full and sleepy.

Davenport rocked his head from side to side as he considered. "Feeding someone iron would be an effective poison and could take a few hours before it became fatal."

"Gary." I sat up. "It has to be Gary."

Davenport gave me his signature chiding look, and Hugo put his head over his hand and slumped down in his seat.

"It's not Gary," Hart stated plainly.

"It could be Gary," I argued.

"It's not."

I growled, sitting back on the couch with my arms crossed and my lip pushed out to form a petulant pouting lip.

Remi stood up, his food was untouched. He offered no apology as he moved towards the spare bedroom like a specter

341

and closed the door behind him.

"I'm worried," I said, eying Remi's plate of Chow Mein. He hadn't even picked up his chopsticks.

"He'll be okay." Hugo smiled, but it did not reach his eyes.

"You don't get it." I shook my head. "I'm a Demon. I don't worry. It's a pointless and tedious exercise. I am *worried* about Remi."

Each man looked at each other as they tried to decipher my words. When they failed, they turned back to me.

"He can't marry her." I hissed, lowering my voice to barely a breath. "She's a tyrant."

"She's a Witchling." Hart rubbed his head, mussing up his long hair. "They're all like that. Rich. Entitled. Powerful."

"And that makes it okay?" My tone was sarcastic.

Hart winced. "Of course not, but what can we do? It's his choice."

I thought about the wound on Remi's head. The defeated slouch in his posture. She had been in his life for a few weeks, and already she'd managed to lay a foundation of fear and rage as the bedrock of her relationship.

"He's mine," I whispered, looking down at my hands.

Jae's hand had never left my thigh, but he squeezed my leg to remind me it was there. "He's not, Mara."

I opened my mouth to argue.

Jae continued to speak. "The first thing Remi did when he found out about your bond was to ask how to get rid of it. You can't force this kind of connection on someone. It doesn't work that way."

I narrowed my eyes. "That's exactly what *you* did."

"But I knew that you wanted it. I *felt* it." Jae's eyes sparkled with mischief. "Besides, if we weren't meant to be, nothing would have happened."

I eyed the closed bedroom door. Thinking about Remi, alone, made my stomach squirm, but I remained on the sofa. Powerless.

342

Davenport stood up, taking his plate into the kitchen before he washed his hands and returned. He paused for a second and picked up the bullets. "We should all get to bed. It's been a long day."

Hart nodded, slapping his legs as he stood up. Subconsciously, as if the wolf was not aware of the movement, he pushed my braid to the side and nuzzled my neck, before drifting to Jae's room.

Davenport glanced at the door and then back again. "Mara, a word?"

Hugo grabbed my hand as I walked past, following on Davenport's heels, to steal a quick peck on the cheek.

"Visit my dreams tonight." Hugo Sinclair cupped my face, his words were a soft plea and a dirty promise.

I licked my lips, and I shook my head to clear it as I walked down the steps of the cabin. Davenport paced on the dirt path at the bottom of the porch steps. He looked wound up and ready to blow.

I steeled myself for a dressing down, but Davenport turned away and dropped his head like a man at a funeral.

"I shouldn't have collared you." He said. Warren's words were muffled as his chin rested on his chest.

I had nothing to say to that. I knew why he had done it.

"You did nothing to prove that you wanted to hurt my Hunters or me, and I treated you like a feral dog simply because you were a Demon." Warren continued, his voice was full of self-directed rage.

Unable to take his pain, I stepped forward and pressed my hand between his shoulder blades, rubbing his back through the material. His skin was hot, but he did not look up at me.

"You could have taken the collar off at any time." Davenport laughed bitterly. "You humored me."

I brushed my finger along the straight edge of the silver collar and smiled to myself. I *had* humored him.

Warren Davenport whirled around, his arms lashed out, and he gripped the top of my shoulders, holding me in

343

place. My eyes widened, but I did not pull away.

"I'm a strange man. I can admit that." Davenport's lips tightened, but I did not speak as his words rushed out. He was desperate to be heard. "I have command of everything in my life, and I like it that way. My Hunters. My lovers. Myself. I don't have command of you."

"And that scares you?"

"It terrifies me." He admitted, his smile turned self-deprecating. "You never do what I think you're going to do."

"I'm a Demon." I winked, extending my arms with a flourish.

Davenport did not smile. "You're more than that, Mara. So much more." His arms on my shoulders tightened, and with one swift jerk, my body was pulled to his, and his head was buried in my hair. Davenport was so much taller than my host, so he had to hunch over, but his arms wrapped around my body and held me in place.

"Is this a hug?" I asked, the sound was distorted by the fabric of his black tactical jumper.

"Yes."

I closed my eyes and focused on the feeling of his body wrapped around mine. Safety. Comfort. Love. "I like it," I admitted with a tiny smile.

By the time I crept back into the cabin, all of the lights were off, and everyone appeared to be asleep.

I went to the bathroom and did my business. I tried to be as quiet as possible, tiptoeing through the house. I failed spectacularly when I opened the bathroom door and found Remi taking up the entire doorway, his hand raised poised to knock.

I flew backward, with an impressive squeak, and bashed my hip into the side of the porcelain sink. It throbbed with the possibility of a large bruise.

Remi stepped forward, his large hand spread over my hip as he rubbed the area as gently as possible. "I didn't mean to startle you." He whispered, mindful of the quiet cabin.

I poked him in the middle of his chest and smirked when the big lug hissed in a breath. "Serves you right."

Remi glanced down the hall at the doorway to the spare bedroom. "Can I talk to you?"

"Always." I did not want to sound desperate, but I meant it. I would always have time for Remi.

The Witchling looked like he didn't know if he should be pleased that I had said yes. Every expression I had seen on his face recently was full of indecision and pain.

Jae's spare bedroom was painted a dusty pink, but the bedsheets were minimalist white, and the room was bare of any personal touches. I made myself comfortable on the edge of the bed, feeling dull wooden exhaustion begin to claim the muscles in my legs.

"What did you want to talk about?" I asked as Remi shut the door softly and leaned against it.

Remi rubbed his face, pressing his hand against his eyes and holding it there. When he spoke, he kept his hand in place like it was painful for him to look at me when he said the words.

"I don't know what to do." Remi's voice wavered. "I need someone to tell me what to do."

I sat up but restrained the urge to go to him. Part of me wanted to make a joke, and imply that he was asking the worst possible person for advice—but that wasn't what Remi needed.

"Tell me." I cleared my throat to speak around the awkward lump that had crept up.

Remi did not uncover his eyes. "I thought I could deal with it. Marrying someone that I don't know. Or love."

I said nothing.

"I can't do it, Mara." He whispered. "I'm not a person to her and her family. I'm a stud. The promise of powerful children. I don't have a lot of time. I'll live past thirty if I'm

345

lucky. If I use magic after that, I'm gone. I don't want to live my life like that."

My heart broke for him. "Remi, you won't die."

"You don't know that." His hand ripped from his face, and his eyes burned with anger. "I want to spend my life with someone that makes me happy."

"You came to America for her," I said softly.

"I came because it was what my family wanted." Remi corrected me. "I can't live for them. I have to live for me. I can't do anything about the color of my skin or my heritage. I shouldn't have to." Remi stepped forward, stalking closer until I found myself pushed back against the bed.

I wanted to tell him that he was immortal. That being my mate had freed him of his Witchling curse, and that his life was bound to mine.

Instead, I whispered his name. His lips brushed against mine. Tenderly as I was made of glass.

"I'm not going to marry her." He told me, speaking the words as if he couldn't believe he was saying them out loud.

His teeth were on display, proud, and happy for the first time since I had seen him with Alicia all those weeks ago.

"Is that what you want?" I asked tentatively. Remi rolled over onto his back, he gripped my forearms and pulled my body on top of his, so that I was straddling him.

"I want *more*." He whispered, looking up at me.

"I don't know how to offer that." My eyes dropped as I looked away, unable to hold his gaze.

"I want to be yours." Remi cupped my cheek. "Fate connected us for a reason."

I thought of the Balance and the shrewd and calculating intelligence that hid in the innocent eyes of a child.

I just hoped that the reason was a good one.

I dropped down until my cheek pressed against his heart and listened to the slow rhythmic organ. It was in that position that we both fell asleep.

Chapter 22

I stood in the hallway of my apartment complex in the east village, side by side with Remi, our hands entwined like a binary version of the shining twins.

We were in standard nightmare territory. The wallpaper had decayed and begun to peel, tiny flecks of old paint and glue floated into the air like dust motes dancing. The floorboards were visible in several places, and the carpet had worn away. The well-maintained building had been warped by the dreamscape, haunting the air with a delicious eeriness that made me feel at home.

My gaze roamed every facet of the entropy with wide-eyed awe.

Remi cleared his throat and moved to my side as if my incorporeal form could offer some protection. I did a double-take, staring down at our joined hands. If I squinted, I could see the red string of our Soul Bond tying us together, connecting our littlest fingers like a double-ended leash.

And we were touching.

I could feel Remi's hand in mine.

"Where are we?" Remi's chocolate eyes scanned the area, but he was relaxed, taking his cues from my own body language.

"This is the in-between," I told him. My voice was skittering leaves and rustling trees. My body was starlight and shadow. "Dreams and nightmares."

"Your home?"

"I have always straddled two worlds." I smiled lazily and jerked my chin to the door of my apartment. The brass numbers were gone, their nails had long since eroded away.

"That's my apartment."

"You have an apartment in the dream dimension?" Remi whistled, impressed.

"My apartment in the East Village." I corrected him. "This isn't *my* dream though." I tasted the air, noticing the delicate perfume of Hugo's magic. I turned away from my own door and strode across the hall, floating into apartment 36.

Remi followed, stepping over the debris as if it was really there. His caution was adorable. We found Hugo in the center of his bedroom, candles shining on every surface. His golden body was stretched out on his red silk bedsheets, and the iron lattice of his four-poster bed spoke of French brothels and red rooms of pain.

I loved it. Hugo's ice blue eyes flicked to Remi, but instead of jealousy, a lazy hooded smile swathed his perfect face.

"I must admit, it has been a fantasy since you marked him." Hugo smiled foppishly. "Is he a construct?"

Remi looked comically shocked. "That's Hugo?" His mouth snapped shut. "Quiet. Serious. Doesn't make eye contact. That Hugo?"

I rolled my eyes, gliding towards the half-naked man on the bed.

"I am an incubus." Hugo was amused.

"Everyone has a secret side." I reached out and stroked Hugo's face with a single finger, and then pulling his bottom lip away from his teeth. "Hello," I whispered, lowering my voice so only he could hear me.

A wide smile lit up his face. "Hello," Hugo replied equally quietly.

"I'm not wearing someone else's body," I said, innocently.

"No you're not." Hugo reached out, gripping my hip and pulling me onto the bed. He shifted over to make space, folding himself around my back. His hands skimmed the edges of my form, touching the undulating smoke. Reverent. I had never felt so truly seen. So beautiful, in all of my existence.

348

"We can touch you?" Remi asked, stepping forward hesitantly. His dark eyes fixed on Hugo's hand, skimming my shoulder, with thinly veiled interest.

"Yes," I whispered as Hugo's fingers brushed my collarbone. "I have a body here. I can be whatever I want. This is my world." With barely a thought, my shadows folded inwards and became clear pristine milk-white skin. Blonde hair and blue eyes. "Or, Brunette, if you prefer?" My form changed again.

Hugo's breath whispered against the shell of my ear. "We want *you*."

My skin turned dark as night, with shimmering diamonds again. I wanted to preen like a peacock.

I sat on the edge of the bed, my form becoming more human in shape as I responded to Hugo's touch. He hovered behind me, sweeping my skin with barely-there brushes. I arched my back and closed my eyes, reveling.

"Do you want to watch, Witchling?" Hugo purred. Glancing up from placing delicate kisses on the seam of my jaw, to tease Remi. My incubus's eyes glowed with lust.

Remi's responding smirk was one of confidence and daring. "I think we should teach our mate a lesson."

"Oh?" Hugo's brow quirked, but he did not stop touching me.

"No lessons." I protested. Panting.

Remi ignored me and knelt down on the floor, gripping my bare thigh and pushing it aside, so my legs parted.

"We belong to you." Hugo purred.

"We're bonded." Remi kissed the sensitive skin on the inside of my knee, his lips slowly peeled away, only to deliver another kiss. Each one was sensuously closer to my heated core.

I struggled to keep still as Hugo reached around my waist, looping my body to his with his arm. He smirked into my neck as he walked his fingers across my stomach, brushing the back of his hand across one nipple and then the next. Each time, innocently, as if by accident.

"What lesson?" I asked, breathy with need. Remi

smirked against the skin of my inner thigh. He sat up, only to command Hugo to get a gag. I straightened, opening my mouth to protest. Hugo's fingers twisted with a flourish. A master magician at work. He produced a gag from thin air, a round rubber ball with a hot pink strap.

I shook my head. "Nuh-uh."

Remi's eyed widened playfully. "Pretty please, Mistress Tequila."

"What does a big bad Nightmare have to fear from a tiny little gag?" Hugo tweaked my nipple, the motion bordered on pleasure and pain.

I gave them a look. "I'm not scared."

"Mara..." Remi sat up, his look was sobering. "We would never hurt you."

I chewed my bottom lip. "I know that."

Hugo swung the ball gag and clapped his hand over it. When his fingers parted, the shape had changed to reveal a small jeweled plug. "Better?" His pink lip quirked into a shy smile.

I nodded enthusiastically, sitting up. Both of the men laughed, and my chest inflated with a lightness that was foreign but not unpleasant. Hugo pulled his arms away, only to tilt my lips to meet his in a slow and exploring kiss that set my world on fire. While my mouth was occupied, Remi maneuvered my body with little protest until my bottom was tilted in the air, and my legs were spread. I felt exposed.

I had worn numerous bodies and been naked in dozens of ways, but none of those forms had been mine.

Remi slapped my butt cheek, gripping the rounded flesh with a small squeeze, further exposing my core. I felt the moisture on my inner thighs, proof of my arousal. Reality hurried to shape itself to my expectations.

Hugo continued to kiss me. His lips parted mine, and our tongues touched. He tasted like cherries and milk chocolate. Hugo's hand gripped the back of my neck, and I felt his magic roll over my body in hundreds of fluttering kisses. A single phantom touch rolled up my spine. I ripped my lips away from

Hugo's to bury my head in his neck, as I shivered and moaned. Turning to goo.

Remi brushed his thumbs across my inner thighs, parting my lips and dipping one of his fingers inside my core for just a second. He kissed the dimples on my back as his hand reached around and began to slowly tease my outer lips. He rolled his index finger around my clit, never touching it hard or directly enough to do more than make me twitch and beg for more.

Remi pressed the cool metal plug against my clit, warming the rounded edge against my hot wet skin. He dragged the toy down, through my parted lips, but never dipping inside, only to circle and return back to my clit with aching slowness.

I found myself opening my legs and wordlessly begging, like an animal in heat. Pushing myself back into his hand. Hugo stood up, pulling away despite my protests.

Remi touched the smallest edge of the plug against the muscles of my ass, just as Hugo lowered his trousers to reveal a curved penis—so perfect that dildo manufacturers would have paid millions just to mold it.

I smiled and licked my lips, my eyes fluttering closed when Remi twisted the toy and began to tease my behind. His fingers worked in time, rubbing my clit slowly before brushing against the inside of my pussy. Each movement was maddening. I needed more.

Hugo brushed his cock against my lips, smirking wickedly, his eyes glowed a soft ice blue as his inner Demon came to the surface. Lust continued to hang on the air like thick cologne, the Sin touching me in places that I did not know were possible.

I licked the head of Hugo's cock, biting back a squeak when I felt Remi's warm tongue begin to taste between my legs. Opening my mouth, I took the angry head inside my mouth and held it on the flat of my tongue. Tasting his skin, I broke free to lick the slit on Hugo's cock. Tasting his salty pre-cum. It was addictive, and I began to lathe him with my tongue. Hugo threw

351

his head back, his hips thrusting lightly into my mouth.

On all fours, my hands gripped the bedsheets as Hugo fucked my mouth, and Remi licked me from behind, working the toy further into my ass. With a tiny amount of added pressure, the toy popped inside, swallowed until the widened base stuck out, like a tail.

I moaned as it rubbed against my inner walls, making me feel fuller.

Remi straightened. "I think she likes the toy." He said smugly.

Hugo gripped the back of my head, but never forced my mouth further down, even when his hips began to rock with harsh and striking thrusts. I heard something unzip, and a few seconds later, I felt the blunt head of Remi's cock press against my empty channel. Wet and wanting, I rocked back, taking Remi inside of me. Just the head at first. He stayed still, allowing me to take my time, as my pussy slowly swallowed more of his length. With my back arched, I kept waiting to feel the rough brush of his pubic hair, only to throw my head back and laugh when I realized just how large his cock really was.

"Laughter is always a good sign." I heard the smile in Remi's voice. "But I think screaming is better."

Without warning, he bottomed out. Thrusting inside me until I felt his thighs against my own. I was so full. My eyes bulged, and I felt his head knock against my cervix. Just enough to add a bite to my pleasure, as Remi pulled away with a wet sound that implied that my body was reluctant to let his go. Remi continued to thrust, slowly at first and then building to a punishing tempo.

Hugo took his cue from the Witchling and began to take my mouth with vigor. His stomach tensed and I could sense that he was close. I wanted to look over my shoulder and watch Remi's body as he disappeared inside of mine, but seeing Hugo come undone with my mouth was just as good.

My orgasm build quickly and hovered like a raging forest fire, stalled by a river. Despite the tawdry wet sounds of

Remi's body slapping against mine and the taste of skin in my mouth, I could not reach my peek. I was held at the edge, like a woman strapped to a chair and tortured. I wanted to come so badly, but it was just out of reach.

Remi's breathing changed, and everything grew sloppier. His thrusts lost their rhythm and his body folded over my own. I felt him cum inside me. Grow larger somehow as he found his pleasure in me, Remi's moan threw me over the edge. I began to come. My body shook, huge full body jerks, as my eyes rolled into my skull, and waves of pleasure rushed over me. My toes curled, and I saw sparks.

Hugo thrust into my mouth, so deep that I tasted his seed on the back of my throat but not on my tongue until he pulled out, still spurting. Leaving a pearl of cum on my bottom lip for me to lick away. Hugo watched, with a fierce expression. My orgasm finished, but it held on for as long as it could, making my body tick like a slowly malfunctioning clock.

Remi did not pull out, but he leaned forward and wrapped his arms around me to give me a squeeze.

"That was worth waiting for." I breathed, sleepy, and spent even though we hovered in a dream of my own making.

I left the bed, in the early hours of the morning, to search for coffee. Davenport had returned and was sat, cross-legged on the floor, using the coffee table as a makeshift desk. An array of medical files were fanned out in front of him. Davenport did not look up from studying the manila folders, even when I sat down in the armchair with a mug of overly-sugared coffee.

I folded my bare legs under my bum. Dressed only in Remi's hoody. Looking over the rim of my mug, I starred at Davenport as I blew on my coffee to cool it down.

"The lab couldn't find any fingerprints on the ammo box," Davenport said, leafing through the pages, he pressed a single finger on top of a file and slid it across the table. "Can you take a few of these files?"

I put my coffee down. "What am I looking for?"

"We don't keep records of heritage. I'm trying to find anyone at the compound that may have Fae blood. Look for anemia." Davenport swiped my coffee and winced at the taste.

"Don't you have people to do these things?" I asked.

"My best Hunters are all currently asleep." Davenport glanced up past his deep-set brow. "I'm losing people left and right. Anyone that could help with this is already doing something equally important."

I shrugged and flipped open the file, eying the columns of numbers like someone trying to read a foreign language.

"Look for any hemoglobin levels below thirty." He advised.

The numbers seemed to shift and swirl in front of my eyes, but I wanted to at least appear to be useful. I turned the folder over in my hands and noticed the name on the front.

"This is Frankie's file."

Davenport did not look up, but he nodded as he arranged his paperwork. A thump came from one of the bedrooms, and it sounded like everyone was waking up.

"Corporal Gardiner consistently showed low levels of iron, after her physical last year, she should have been prescribed a supplement." Davenport sighed, rubbing his temples. I noticed the dark circles under his eyes for the first time. "The only reason she wouldn't have been given one was if her brother knew that she was Fae. Or had Fae in her bloodline."

My brow creased as I considered his words. Something at the back of my mind itched like a long-forgotten memory.

Remi swept into the room, his sweatpants hung low on his prominent hipbones. The Witchling was sans shirt, as I had stolen his hoody while he was asleep. He brushed his hand against the back of the armchair, dipping down to touch his lips to mine.

Davenport watched with interest. "I take it that the

354

engagement is off."

"I need to make a few calls this morning, but I wanted to say 'Hi' first." Remi turned to me, his eyes focused on mine like I was the only person in the world to exist for him. I was a cat, laying in a deliciously warm patch of sun. I wanted to bottle that feeling and treasure it.

"Hi," I whispered back.

Warren cleared his throat. "Have you been able to do any more research on the Ifrit?" He asked Remi.

Remi pulled a phone out of his pocket, swiped, and then turned the screen towards Davenport. "There was an antique listing a few years ago for something called a 'Genie cage' jewelry box. The rune on the side looks similar to the one that Mara saw on the security tape. I think that this box, or one like it, was used to trap the Ifrit."

"Dermot Dirk wouldn't provide the details of summoning?" Davenport's look darkened with storm clouds.

"Not unless we meet in person." Remi slipped his phone back in his pocket. "But, I'm confident that a brass box would hold an incorporeal demon."

"Can I see that?" I cleared my throat, gesturing to Remi's phone. Remi took the device out of his pocket and handed it to me. The two men continued to speak, theorizing about the Ifrit, as I stared at the brass box on the tiny phone screen. There was something inherently familiar about the box. I couldn't put my finger on it. My mind was racing with thoughts, but they hung behind a thick fog. I couldn't seem to form a coherent idea.

"Will the Ifrit turn on its summoner?" Davenport speculated. "Could we do something to make that happen?"

"All Ifrits turn on their summoner." I murmured, not taking my eyes from the screen as I studied the photo. "They help with the summoner's revenge, and when that's done, they feed on the summoner too. It's demonic karma."

"So, the Ifrit will eventually take care of our problem?" Remi perched on the armrest of my chair. "It's just a matter of time?"

Davenport's lip tightened. "And how many people perish in the meantime?"

Remi held up his hands disarmingly. "I want to catch this guy as much as you do."

Jae and Hart wandered into the room. Hart looked like he was ready for action, but Jae scratched his stomach and stretched, his shirt was wrinkled as if he had just rolled out of bed. They bid us all a good morning before Jae swiped my coffee and finished the dregs.

Jae smacked his lips in disgust. "This coffee is cold."

Everyone ignored him.

"Could we lure the Ifrit away with a new master?" Davenport slapped his file closed.

The men continued to think out loud, but their voices felt like cartoonish parodies as I tried to focus. *Womp womp womp*, like hearing someone talk while underwater. I had to make sense of what I was thinking. It was important, but paying attention to one thing for an extended period of time was hard. It made my chest feel itchy, and my head feel cloudy.

"Guys." I snapped. "I need a second to think."

Everyone stopped talking, looking at me like I had grown another head. I pinched the bridge of my nose and inhaled. Remi's phone sat in my other hand as I searched my mind for reference of a brass box.

Sifting through the collective memories of my Cluster, and then the residue from various possessions, I growled in frustration.

"Can we talk now?" Jae whispered. My eyes flicked open as Remi flailed his arms and put his finger to his lips.

"Is everyone alright? It just got really quiet!" Hugo froze in the doorway, noticing the tension.

"I've seen this box before," I said, brandishing the phone.

Davenport sat up. "Where?"

I wanted to throw the phone across the room. Remi

356

pulled it from my weak fingers before I could do so. "What is a supplement?" I asked, instead.

"What does that have to do with anything?" Davenport demanded. Jae reached over and touched his shoulder, shaking his head minutely.

Jae answered my question. "A pill you can buy over the counter. When someone lacks certain minerals and vitamins, because of their diet or a medical issue, taking a supplement helps."

"So, you'd take an iron pill for anemia?" I asked, my voice sluggish as I struggled to collect my thoughts.

"Or an injection." Jae supplied helpfully.

Frankie's file laid abandoned at my feet, the contents scattered like giant square confetti. "The injections aren't in there." I murmured to myself.

Someone put a hand on my back. I looked up to see Hart, leaning over and offering me comfort.

"Injections?" Davenport prompted, losing patience.

"Dr. Daniel gave me injections. Vitamins. Every time I've been in the infirmary." I said numbly.

Remi picked up the file and began to read, rearranging the pages. "There are no injections listed here. All of the other records are pretty comprehensive."

"Injections." Davenport echoed, without emotions. His eyes zeroed in on mine. "He's been giving you injections since you arrived."

I shrugged. "I didn't know what vitamins were. I was afraid to ask."

"Afraid to ask." Davenport enunciated my words as if he had trouble understanding them. I wondered if anyone else in the room could feel the burning heat that had begun to radiate from Warren's direction. The commander pulled out his phone and dialed the infirmary. He spoke a few words before hanging up and calling another number. We all watched without saying a word as Davenport's anger grew like a boulder gathering speed as it rolled down a hill.

Pacing the room, Davenport turned to us. "Daniel Gardiner left to go home for Christmas. I phoned the Gardiner's. He never arrived, and they aren't expecting him."

"Wait," My eyes widened, incredulous. "You think it's Daniel? Fae killer. Demon summoner. Master manipulator. Daniel Gardiner?"

No one spoke.

"Boring, white bread, no sense of humor, Daniel Gardiner?" My voice notched, as panic edged my words.

"Think back," Davenport asked delicately. "Where did you see the brass box?"

I gaped like a fish.

Remi exhaled deeply and closed his eyes as he tried to remember. "Dr. Gardiner had a brass box in his office. I told you off for playing with it. It looked like an old cigarette box."

"Right." Davenport nodded, repeating the word to himself. "If everyone could step out for a moment while I speak to Mara?"

Hart kept his hand on my back. "I think we're going to stay." His voice held no room for argument.

Davenport continued as if Hart hadn't spoken. "I have lost some of my most promising Hunters. Almost started a war with the Fae in the process. Used all of my resources and put several teams on finding the traitor in my camp—and you're telling me that he has been injecting you, since day one, with the very poison that has been killing the Fae under my care."

"She couldn't have known," Hugo whispered. Davenport threw up a hand to silence him.

"She damn well could have. He's been injecting her for God knows how long." Davenport snarled. "You've all lost your minds. Blinded by a Lower Demon that doesn't even have its own body!"

I recoiled, his words were a physical blow. Sinking down into the chair, I looked at the ground and folded inside my mind, focusing on the tiny place inside my mind that I used to protect myself when people hurt me. Surrounded by walls of solid ice, and beasts as large as skyscrapers, nothing could hurt me there. But somehow, Davenport's words continued to echo, as if he had wrenched my mind open like an oyster and spat inside of it.

"I can't believe that I entertained the idea of such a useless, selfish creature, working with us. She has the attention span of a five-year-old." Davenport ranted. "The Ifrit box was right there. Daniel has a history with the Blood Sidhe. They killed his birth family. They attacked him last year. I should have seen this. Why didn't I see this?"

"It's not Mara's fault." Hugo stood up, shaking with anger, as he got in Davenport's face. "Stop taking your frustrations out on her."

"Unless she had knowledge of medicine, she couldn't have known that many injections were unusual," Jae said, trying to soothe the situation. "Mara has never been human. She wasn't raised by them. She hasn't spent a lot of time around them. You're judging her by unfair standards."

"She's been distracting all of us." The commander's voice was menacing. "None of us saw what was right there."

"We don't have any solid proof," Remi argued. "I can do a Truth Amplifier. I'm going to the city to speak to my father. I'll get the ingredients. We find Dr Gardiner, and we get a confession. Then it's solved. Sorted."

I had folded myself into the smallest possible position I could find. I hid my trembling hands beneath my thighs

"Take Mara with you." Davenport turned away, dismissing us. "I don't want to look at her right now."

I watched as two raindrops raced each other down the car window, joining together at the last minute before the wind whipped them away.

I felt the same as I did when Dermot Dirk made a

comment or jibe about not expecting much from me. I felt untrustworthy. Worthless.

I hadn't expected the same words to come from Warren, which made it hurt more.

"Something is up with Davenport." Remi's British accent punctuated through my fog. "I haven't known the guy long, but he's always calm and rational. None of that was calm and rational."

I shrugged and continued staring out of the window.

"You didn't deserve that." Remi reached out and gripped my thigh gently.

"He's right," I mumbled. "I am useless. Stupid. I should have seen."

"I'm the one that found the box online. I'm the one that saw you playing with it." Remi admitted sheepishly. "I should have noticed it."

I shrugged. Davenport's gritted teeth and harshly flung words had carved out a gaping hole in my chest. I felt empty, the only thing that was stopping me from running away were the four threads of my Soulbonds.

"We're meeting my father at the Four Seasons." Remi continued. "He flew in as soon as Alicia called him."

"The Four Seasons, huh?" I finally smiled, thinking of Tony Salitari's failed gay orgy. The event that sparked my adventure with the Hunter's. "Sounds nice."

Archibald Weber looked nothing like Remi.

In a police line up, he was not who I would pick if I were asked who Remi's father was. Short with circle lenses that rested on the edge of his nose, he looked like a cross between Santa and a banker on Wall Street.

We sat at a circular table by the floor to ceiling windows, overlooking Central Park. Remi kept arranging his clothes, pulling his sleeves nervously, or re-buttoning his collar. It spoke volumes about his comfort level around his father.

The entire meal was spent in delicate but purposeful silence. Remi's father ate with tiny polite movements, and his only reaction was a small choking sound when I asked for hot sauce to go with my seafood pasta.

Remi had not stopped fidgeting. I placed my hand on his, but his father did not say a word. In fact, he hadn't said one word since we had sat down.

"This pasta is really great," I said enthusiastically, twirling my fork around. "I should go tell the chef how nice it is." Remi put his hand on my shoulder to stop me from sitting up and escaping.

Mr. Weber patted his mouth with a napkin. "Are you enjoying your brief sojourn with the Hunter's?" He did not glance at me once when he spoke to his son.

"I've learned a lot." Remi smiled. "They've needed my computer skills more than my magic, which is a pleasant change."

If that was a dig, Mr. Weber ignored it.

"Have you been taking the pills for your migraines?"

"Yes, father." Remi nodded, turning back to his food.

When the meal was done, and Archibald Weber sipped his wine, Remi finally blurted out what had made his body vibrate with tension for the entire meal.

"I'm not marrying Alicia." He said firmly.

Archibald rolled his eyes and took a sip of his red wine. "We've already signed the contract. The wedding is in six months."

"I'm not marrying her," Remi repeated.

"Alicia's father phoned me, most concerned. Naturally, I felt it best to come to talk some sense into my son." Mr. Weber's explained in a prim British accent. "Alicia claimed that your affections had strayed elsewhere." Not once did Remi's father look at me.

"Mara has nothing to do with this." Remi flushed.

361

Archibald folded his hands together, placing them on the table. "You are almost of age. Your magic is going to turn cancerous soon. All Witchlings have to make peace with this." He took off his glasses and pulled a cloth from his suit pocket. When Remi's father spoke again, his attention was fixed on polishing the lenses.

"Witchlings beget Witchlings." Archibald continued. "You are half Haitian Creole. Your children and your children's children will eventually breed out the curse."

"By that reasoning, I should be able to use magic after my thirtieth birthday without dying." Remi grabbed his napkin and snapped it passive-aggressively. Watching British people argue was like trying to translate another language.

"But why take the chance?" Archibald put his glasses on the edge of his nose and pushed them into place with a single finger. "What can Mara offer that Alicia cannot?"

"She's my Mate," Remi said quietly.

His father's eyes narrowed at the strange terminology.

"Mara is a Demon." Remi continued. "We have bonded."

Archibald Weber was struck numb. His mouth popped open, and his face turned a plumy puce. "Bonded?" He turned to me. "Does that mean what I think it means?"

I had no idea what Mr. Weber knew about demons, so I gave him a silly smile and a shrug, allowing my eyes to turn black. Remi's father's shoulders began to shake, and the man started to cry. Slow tears leaked from his grey-blue eyes, and he took a handkerchief from his pocket and blotted his face. Weber glanced at his son and then back to me. Visibly relieved.

"Are you alright, Father?" Remi sat up, ready to help. Mr Weber shook his head.

"My boy." He whispered. The reaction was so left field from his demeanor during the rest of the meal that Remi looked concerned. Based on his reaction, Archibald Weber thought I had either saved or enslaved his son.

Remi turned to me. His expression clearly read: "*What*

362

the hell is going on?"

I took my opportunity, seeing no better time to tell him.

"Your dad just found out that you're immortal," I said breezily. "Your life force is linked to mine, so..."

Then I had the experience of watching a 6"4 African British man stand up to bolt before fainting—dropping to the ground like a lead balloon.

Chapter 23

The cabin was full of delicious smells, chili strong enough to make my eyes water, and the tempting scent of seared beef.

I gravitated towards the kitchen, a wrinkled plastic bag wrapped around my wrist, containing all of the ingredients for Remi's various spells.

Jae raced around, frying brightly colored vegetables, as well as meat. Tiny bowls dotted the counter with pre-sliced ingredients. Jae's sleeves were rolled up, as he dumped a handful of chili peppers into the wok and was immediately rewarded by the roar of sizzling food. He did not look up as he rushed around, cooking the same Korean food that his Omma had probably taught him in her Formica kitchen all those many years ago.

Hart sat at the table, his tablet laid face up on top of a pile of old books. He visibly relaxed when he heard the rustle of my bag. "Did you find all the ingredients?" Hart asked.

Remi followed on my heels. "Tracking and Truth amplifiers. Have you managed to find anything?"

Hart rubbed his face, exhausted. "All Hunters are fitted with a tracker. Small as a grain of rice, in the skin of their arm. Daniel Gardiner didn't have a tracker. He wasn't a Hunter."

Remi made a thoughtful noise. "I've set up alerts for all his credit cards and his phone. So far, no activity."

"The commander is furious about all this, isn't he?" Jae cut in, finally taking a breath to wipe his hands on a cloth. "He's put everyone on it."

"All of the non-combative contractors have been called in to be fitted with trackers. The infirmary is packed." Hart continued, lifting the tablet. "And Riley Fisher is missing."

"Missing?" I blurted out, stepping forward. Worry seeping into my tone. "Do you think the Ifrit got her? We should do something. I like her."

"Her tracker implies that she hasn't left the compound, but she hasn't signed in to any building, room, or facility in the last forty-eight hours," Hart said, ignoring my hysterics. "We have to consider that she may be working with Dr Gardiner."

Jae turned to the cupboard and grabbed a pile of plates. Remi joined Hart at the table, as he looked over some of his abandoned books.

"Where's Hugo?" I asked.

"Sinclair and Davenport are searching the apartment in Maywood for anything we might have missed." Hart murmured, scrolling on his tablet. "Warren's got everyone on this."

I laughed softly. "And you guys are all sitting around eating dinner and reading dusty old demon texts?"

No one said a word.

"Wait? Why are you all here? If you're his best Hunters, you should be out there trying to find Daniel and his Ifrit." I waved my hand in their direction. Hart's face creased in a guilty expression, which said it all.

"He doesn't trust me anymore." I surmised through numb lips, slowly the cogs of my mind realized what was happening. "You're my babysitters."

Jae stepped up and flicked one of my braids. "Doesn't most pornography start with a horny babysitter." He winked.

"Or a pizza guy." Remi supplied helpfully.

I unwrapped the plastic bag full of ingredients from my wrist and thrust it into Jae's arms. "I'm going to bed," I said.

"Don't you want dinner?" Jae asked, helplessly. Hurt shone in his eyes. Guilt wormed into my chest, an alive and writhing being. I ignored the emotion to wallow in my own self-flagellation.

"If I'm asleep, I might actually be of some use." I stormed off into the spare bedroom, leaving the three men to share looks of pity at my departure.

As I sat on the edge of the bed, Davenport's words continued to haunt me. He'd called me useless, and he was right, but I couldn't stand to bear the brunt of his anger.

I had always viewed Warren as part of my troupe, as Daddy Davenport, but perhaps he couldn't truly come to terms with my demonism. Being a Demon was something I could never change.

A firm hand and punishment sounded good in theory when they were BDSM play tools—but I felt like I had been relegated to the sidelines of something that I was somehow crucial to. Then, punished when I didn't understand what was happening.

Hart found me an hour later, staring into space. "Warren's more angry at himself than you." He said as the door closed softly behind him.

"I don't know what you're talking about." I lied. My voice was muffled by my arm.

"The commander shouldn't have taken his anger out on you." Hart continued, perching on the bed. "Are you okay?"

"Peachy."

"Do you want dinner?"

"No," I said.

Hart moved, shifting until his head was against the pillow next to mine. He stared at the ceiling. Content to let me wallow. His presence was enough to ease part of the empty feeling in my chest. When Callum felt my shoulders relax, he reached over and rubbed circles on my back, content to offer his silent support.

"I never said thank you," Hart said softly after what must have been an hour of silent reflection.

"For what?" My voice was hoarse.

"You found my wolf. You found me." Hart sniffed, and I rolled over. He rubbed his eyes, but I caught a glimpse of a tear stuck to his russet lashes. The stoic and silent man gave me an uncharacteristically watery smile.

"Callum..." I murmured.

"I never told you how happy I am to be yours." He cupped my cheek. Both of our heads rested on the pillows as we studied each other. "I've never met someone like you before."

I opened my mouth to make a self-deprecating remark. Still hurting from Davenport's outburst.

"Don't." Hart put his finger to my lips. "That's not you."

"How did you know what I was going to say?" I narrowed my eyes.

Hart chuckled. "You're hurting. Warren is blaming himself but taking it out on you. The chances are, he already wants to apologize but hasn't had a chance yet."

"I don't want to talk about him."

Hart tweaked my nose. "Of course. Do you want me to continue telling you how brilliant you are?"

"I know how brilliant I am." My chin jutted out. "But it's still nice to hear."

"I've never met someone who loves life as much as you do." Hart's marmalade eyes glowed.

"Don't forget. I'm also a snack."

"I love you." He told me softly. My eyes widened as I blinked. Taken aback by his proclamation.

I opened my mouth to reply.

"Don't say it unless you mean it." I had never seen the burly man look so vulnerable but determined.

"Callum..." I whispered, gripping the front of his flannel shirt, I used it to pull him towards me. His lips met mine. Our kiss was sweet until it began to border on obscene as the heat grew. Soon, my chest heaved, and every inch of my body ached to rub against his. My fingers trembled as I undid the buttons of his shirt, skimming my hands against his hard stomach and the trail of coarse hair that led down to his prominently hard cock, still encased in his worn jeans.

The kiss ended slowly, and I kept my eyes closed even after his lips left mine. "Why did you stop?" I asked breathily.

He gave me a look. "Mara, you're wearing someone else's body."

I laughed to myself. "Yeah." I was glad that I didn't have to have the same conversation again. Hart understood. He had known Frankie when she was alive. Somehow using her body in that way felt disrespectful. I wriggled forward until my cheek pressed against Callum's chest. His arms wrapped around my shoulders.

It was in his arms that I fell asleep.

My dream was darkness filled with the sound of sobbing. An inhuman wail, so distraught that it sounded like an animal dying.

As I stepped forward, I realized that the darkness was fluid. It was made of thick smoke. Unable to find the source of the scream, I turned in a circle, completely alone.

<*Mother?*> The Cyclian words were guttural and harsh, spoken from a throat not intended for speech. <*Save me. Save me. Save me. Save me.*>

I whirled on the spot, only to be greeted by two static burning eyes, hovering in front of me. The smoke wrapped around me, cradling me like a child. It brushed against my being with a sense of kinship that I had not felt since the death of my Cluster.

The Ifrit was calling out in pain. It reached out, begging and pleading to be saved. Smoke began to fill my mouth and nose, racing down my throat until it felt like millions of fire ants were crawling into my chest.

My lungs were too large for my chest, hindered by my

rib cage, and unable to fully inflate.

I couldn't breathe.

I woke up, alone, to find the world on fire.

Flames licked the ceiling, a wall of heat that made my eyes sting, and my heart seized in fear.

For a long second, I considered leaving Frankie's body behind and floating away to safety, but I heard a cough from the other bedroom. I was not alone. Trapped by roaring fire, threatening to swallow my host in horrid pain, I surged forward. Dizzy and unable to breathe.

Someone called my name from the hallway, but when I put my hand on the doorknob, it melted my skin like taffy, leaving a sticky residue on the metal, and the scent of pork fat on the air. I cried out, cradling my defunct hand against my chest.

"Callum? Where's Callum?" I sobbed, my voice was weak and scratchy.

"Window," Remi shouted from the other side. "Jump out of the window."

I didn't need to be told twice. The flames had spread across the room, eating up the wooden floorboards and the edge of the unmade bed like one of the Shayati.

The latch on the single pane window was stuck, old and disused. With a growl, I pulled my unhurt fist back and punched through the glass, clearing the window, before crawling out in a smear of my own blood. With minced hands, my lungs seized as I felt my demonic healing try to battle with the smoke inside my host's body.

I tumbled to the ground, and into a thorny bush. Remi, Jae, and Hart had all made it out. Somehow that made it easier to forget my injuries.

Hart dipped forward and held me, pulling me from the foliage with muscular arms, but I could not say a word of thanks. Hunched over, wheezing, and coughing, black sludge coated my lips. Everything hurt.

Jae watched his home burn without emotion, staring at

370

the front door and the roaring flames visible through the tiny glass pane. Remi pulled out his phone to call Davenport.

Slowly, as if drawn by a trembling hand, words appeared, burnt into the wood of the door.

Sayve mi plees.

The Cyclian runes appeared below, to reinforce the message that the Ifrit had tried to convey.

Save me. Please.

Chapter 24

I was the only one admitted to the infirmary for smoke inhalation, despite my advanced healing. Everyone had come to visit, playing unfamiliar card games and then complaining when I cheated.

Davenport did not come.

The smell of disinfectant made me uncomfortable. Dr. Daniel's absence was a heavy cloud amongst the staff. The knowledge of his possible betrayal had circulated the compound and gained speed. Riley Fisher still hadn't been found, and while it had been speculated that she might have defected to his cause, the strongest theory was that Riley had been killed and her body, still in the compound, hadn't been found yet.

It would have been so easy to leave my host behind. To be free of pain and the shackles of the responsibility towards the Hunters that time and proximity had foisted on me.

I didn't want to think about the Ifrit's pain. Trapped and forced to do someone else's bidding. I sympathized in a small way. I often felt chained to Dermot Dirk because he had saved me, made to do things that I did not want to do. My wishes disrespected and pushed to the wayside.

Jae was on babysitter duty, keeping me company on my hospital bed. He had pulled the chair up to the rail on my bed and hopped up to fetch me water whenever I cleared my ravaged throat.

After several cups of tepid water, I stilled his hand as he tried to pour it down my throat.

"What are you doing?" I asked, my voice barely a whisper.

Jae gave me a stern look. "Helping you."

"I expected a dirty joke about my hospital gown, not a

nursemaid," I smirked wickedly. "Can I have a sponge bath?"

"You need to rest your voice." Jae's lip twitched before it began to shake. "I was so scared. We couldn't get to your room. I thought that you—"

"Jae." I reached out and put my hand over his mouth. His violet eyes bugged. "I'm immortal. I could have floated away any time I wanted to. I didn't want to leave Frankie's body behind."

He squinted, still gagged by my palm.

"If I see danger, I run," I told him. "Don't worry about me."

Jae finally nodded. "I'm sorry. It's because of my Omma—"

I interrupted him again. "I get it. I do."

He exhaled deeply. "I shouldn't feel so heartbroken because of a damn cabin, but I've lived there for years."

"Was there anything irreplaceable?" I asked.

Jae smiled sadly. "Only people are irreplaceable."

We talked for a few hours, about everything and nothing. Jae joked with the nurses and tried to convince them to let us order pizza. I put tongue depressors under my top lip and pretended to be a walrus. Overall, being a hospital patient wasn't the most depressing experience because I had Ahn-Jae Lee with me.

When Jae had fallen asleep in the chair by my bed, and the only light came from my reading lamp, I tried to make sense of a Sudoku puzzle and failed miserably. Instead, I drew a dick inside every box in place of a number, and one poorly rendered bunny rabbit.

Even though I had tried to put Davenport's comments out of my mind, I couldn't. The accusations of my selfishness and failings circled in with the fevered pleading of the Ifrit.

I swung my legs off of the bed, determined to do *something*. Anything.

Dr. Daniel Gardiner's office was locked and dark, but it was one of those locks that functioned barely. Easily thwarted with a nickel.

The doctor's office was as stark and boring as Daniel's personality, except the decorative brass box on his shelf, which was missing. The photo of Daniel and his birth parents smiled back at me. A picture-perfect redheaded trio of humans. No picture of Momma G and Arthur, and none of Frankie either.

I searched his drawers, but found nothing. I glanced at his bathroom door and the various knick-knacks around the room. Slouching down into the expensive leather office chair behind Daniel's desk, I worried for a second. Had I pointed Davenport and his Hunters towards an innocent man?

It was a few injections. He was a doctor, and that was what doctors did. It wasn't a crime to have an antique.

Riley's disappearance had thrown me too. Her partner, Harvey, had died with the first team, there was no possible way that she would be working with Dr. Dan.

I tapped my fingers on the desk, lost on my own thoughts when I felt a prick in the back of my neck. It must have been a biting insect. A mosquito or something. Slapping my hand against my throat, I noticed that the movements were sluggish. My vision had begun to tunnel.

My body dropped to the floor, sliding out of the chair and falling in a lump. My eyelids were too heavy. A pair of booted feet stepped into my vision, and then everything went dark.

I recognized the concrete basement cell. It was the same layout as the seamless room that Davenport had kept me in once he had found out my true identity.

The floor was clean if a little dusty. Across the empty room, a brass cigarette box sat ominously in a ring of salt. A dog cage, big enough for a wolf, sat in the corner. A hunched over figure laid behind the bars, shivering but not making a sound.

I tried to move my arms, but a loud clunking noise alerted me to the iron shackles wrapped around my wrists. As a Demon, iron did not burn me, but they were substantial enough that I felt the skin on my wrists chafe as I moved.

As before, the door was unseen. Locked away with magic that obscured the senses. The floor was hard, and I shifted positions when my legs grew numb. Sitting still was difficult for me, it was one of the reasons that I did not inhabit bodies for long. It was always obvious that I was inside if you knew where to look. The constant clicking and tapping that Dirk had often chastised me about.

"Will you stop that?" It was a question and demand at the same time. Why did humans never explicitly say what they wanted? A female voice, weak but fierce.

"I'm hungry," I said blithely, staring at the ceiling and the florescent strip lights. "How long have you been here?"

"Frankie?" Riley Fisher hissed, pushing herself into a sitting position, her head brushed against the ceiling of her small cage. "What are you doing here?"

I shrugged, wondering if Dr. Daniel was listening and if it was wise to inform Riley that I wasn't Frankie Gardiner, but a Demon wearing her body.

"Why are you here?" I waved my hand, but the movement was restricted by the heavy shackle. "Do you have Fae blood in your family tree?"

Riley shook her head. "A hundred percent human." She sat up, alert. "Is this about the homicides? Is that why we're trapped here?"

I had forgotten that I had told Riley about the possible traitor and his desire to kill the Fae living in the compound.

"Did you see who took you?" I asked.

Riley shook her head. "I was jumped outside the Mess Hall."

The light flickered, and the box shook before settling down.

"Have you seen what's in there?" Riley's eyes were full

375

of fire. "It's a damn genie."

"Ifrit." I corrected. "But they do grant wishes."

"How did you know that?" She squinted.

I glanced around for a camera, but could not see one. I allowed my eyes to bleed into black for just a second before blinking the dark was away. Riley swore and sat up, wrapping her hands around the mesh door of her dog cage.

"I don't even want to know." She shook her head to herself. "Has anyone been looking for me?"

I winced but said nothing. The box rattled again, but it stopped before the salt line, locked in place by the simple anti-Demon ward.

The door appeared like someone took a marker and drew the threshold, sliding open to reveal a tall, dark figure.

I knew that hair, unruly, and curled at the ears. The three-day-old scruff and dark eyes that were full of past pain and new punishments. The bottom lip of his mouth was plumper than the top, curled into a harsh smirk.

Warren Davenport.

I didn't want to believe it. My heart stuttered and shattered. All of the energy left my body and turned my limbs to wood. Inside, I grew cold.

Angrier than I had ever been, I remembered every close moment that we had together. Had it all been a lie to get closer to me? What had been the purpose? My world had folded itself inside out, and nothing made sense.

Then his skin melted, dissolving and rebuilding like wax until the much shorter, freckled face of Dr Daniel Gardiner stared back at me. He stepped into the room, his clothes hung from his body, much too large.

"You're a Dead Ringer," I whispered.

Dr. Daniel smirked for the first time since I had met him. "Got it in one, sis."

Dr. Dan's arms spread wide, he looked the most relaxed I had seen him in months. "Any last words?"

I jerked against my shackles, but they stubbornly stayed

in place. "You're Fae."

Daniel looked down his nose at me as if I was dim. "Yes. Unfortunately."

"What does that even mean?" Riley interjected. Dr Dan raised his leg and slammed his steel-toe boot against the bars of Riley's cage, startling her backward with the aggressive display.

"Don't you remember?" Daniel's smile turned bitter. "Your kind did this to me. Made me this way."

He was looney tunes, as he approached the salt line and looked down thoughtfully.

"The Fae killed my family. They took my humanity from me. You all need to pay." He continued, not looking at either of us as he spoke.

"You realize that Riley isn't Fae, right?" I asked carefully.

"She's here for a different reason." Dr. Daniel reached into his pocket and pulled out a handkerchief, dabbing his brow. "And you're here to die, sister."

The brass box shook, scraping against the concrete floor as if to punctuate his point.

"You have to be born Fae," I told him. "You can't make someone Fae."

Anger cracked across his face like a slap. He turned to me, eyes bulging. "Liar!" Daniel shrieked. His abrupt shift made me jump like a twelve-year-old playing a horror game. "You're a damn Blood Sidhe, Frankie! You did this to me, you damn half breed!"

"Fae can't lie." I countered smugly.

Daniel was red the face and heaving with rage. He stared at me like he wanted to peel the skin from my bones. Without a word, Daniel marched back to the salt line and drew his heel through the circle, disturbing the ward.

He kicked Riley's cage once more and then left in a flurry of flaring nostrils and evil looks.

The brass cigarette box was so tiny, almost too small to hold a creature as powerful as an Ifrit. The smoke leaked from

377

the keyhole, and began to fill the room; I quickly recognized the creature from my dream. I struggled against my bonds, tearing my skin and coating my shackles in blood as I tried to get away. I debated gnawing my arm off like an animal in a bear trap, but instead, I squared my shoulders and met the glowing eyes of the Wish Demon that had burned through Davenport's Hunter's.

I nodded a greeting and spoke in the harsh sweeping tones of Cyclian. The language of Hell. <*Greetings, Demon*>

The burning eyes of the smoky demon did not leave mine as it ate up the distance between us and plunged into my body, tearing apart every tendon before snapping them back into place.

I shrieked, collapsing. Sobbing, with snot rolling down my lip, as I shook.

"Why?" I asked, reverting to English. "What did I ever do to you?"

The Ifrit glanced once at the box before the torture began anew. His touch felt like razor blades as my skin peeled away and folded back like a blooming flower.

<*I am as commanded.*>

I could withstand anything, I told myself. I had the collective memory of Ba'el's tortures burned into my body. My siblings had experienced similar, if not worse at the hands of the once King of Wrath.

I could withstand. I could hold the line.

<*I have long since grown tired of revenge. To stop me, you must kill me.*>

My mates would come for me. Their bonds were alive in me, reinforcing mind and stopping the pain from stripping away my sanity.

Daniel had to be near. As long as he was busy, in hiding, directing my torture like a temporary art exhibit, he was not killing Hunter's.

Hours passed.

Blood splatter and pain.

No escape.

378

Never-ending.

My men would come for me. Remi, Hart, Jae, and Hugo. Even Davenport.

They would come.

I knew it.

Chapter 25

Riley's swearing and shouting protests died after a few hours, a pleading protest to my metamorphosis at the hands of the Ifrit.

I had tried to connect to the Wish Demons fears, but there were none that I could exploit. Inside their mind, they burned with hatred for their master. Caught in an endless cycle of being trapped to a vengeful master, before fulfilling their revenge, and finally turning on their Summoner.

Their summoning was meant to be a gentle journey, ending in a shocking karmic slap. Something that Daniel had done worried the Ifrit. Its mind was full of bastardized runes trapping it into the bidding of a Mimic Sidhe, convinced that his heritage was the result of a random attack at the hands of the Fae.

The door swished open, the sound like a letter leaving and envelope. The Ifrit's smoke retreated into its box, waiting patiently as Dr. Daniel reinforced the simple salt ward around it.

Riley's cage had been moved. Blood painted the concrete floor, mixing with the dust to create gritty patches of red and black.

Dr. Daniel drifted into the room, looking at me like I was a mild inconvenience.

"You should be dead." He said, with a detached voice. "Why aren't you dead?"

I rolled my tongue around my mouth, wincing when I felt a loose tooth pull free from my host's shredded gums. I spat the molar onto the floor by his feet.

"Where's Riley?" I asked.

Daniel glanced at the spot where her cage had been. He

did not answer my question as he squatted down by my side and gripped my forearm. Careful not to touch the iron shackles, he turned over my arm to survey the pristine skin.

"Why are you immune to iron?" Dr. Daniel demanded, frantically turning my arm over again, almost yanking it out of the socket.

"Maybe because I'm not Fae." I laughed heartily. Even with my enhanced healing, one of my eyes had swollen shut.

"You're half Blood Sidhe, it should still work." He muttered as if I wasn't there. "It has to."

"Where's Riley?" I repeated, a heavy sinking feeling meant I almost didn't want the answer.

He ignored me.

"Why did you kill all Hunters with Fae lineage?" I asked as Daniel stood up and slapped the dust away from his hands.

"I wanted to." He said, his tone was bored. "I thought that it would help cover up your death."

"Sucks to be you." I coughed. "You know that the Ifrit will turn on you, right? Once your revenge is done, it'll swallow you whole and go back to Hell."

My smug smile slowly faded when Daniel looked unfazed.

"What did you do?" I accused, my voice still weak, and my lips covered in blood.

"Ifrit kill their masters," Daniel said flippantly. "As long as I transfer ownership to Miss Riley Fisher before my crusade ends, I shall live."

"And Riley?" I squinted, which was hard to do with two black eyes. Daniel shrugged. "You don't care. You've already killed so many people, what's one more?" I laughed without humor. "There is a special place in Hell for people like you. Stretched out on Lucifer's dining table, and taken apart piece by piece."

"If you believe in Hell." Daniel straightened the lapels of his shirt.

"You've literally got a Wish Demon on a leash!" I waved my hand towards the rattling brass box.

"He doesn't speak, how do you know he's a Demon." Daniel pointed out.

"You've worked with the Hunters for how long?" I asked rhetorically.

"This conversation is tedious."

"Damn right it is." I snarled. "Are you deficient in some way?"

Daniel's face rippled. The only sign that the mimic Sidhe was bothered by our conversation.

"You had no family growing up, right?" I groaned as I tried to sit up. My body was one big bruise. "The Blood Sidhe killed your parents in some war of the houses, and you had no one to teach you what you were. It's an unfortunate backstory. I'll give you that, but you can't just go on a killing spree."

"I can. I did." Daniel pointed out blankly.

I cursed, using some very creative anti-fae language. "Why are you torturing me?" I asked, imploring for a response from the sadist.

He didn't have an answer for me, and that was the scariest thing of all.

I drifted along the horizon of the Human Realities and the Dreamscape, like a girl on a rowing boat dipping her fingers into the water. The Ifrit had been caged since Daniel had come and gone from my concrete cell. I laid on the floor, bleeding, and in pain.

Even in shackles, I could reach up to undo my silver collar. I could escape whenever I wanted, but I had grown attached to Frankie Gardiner's body. If I left, she would die. Completely and finally. I did not know my host, but I had lived her life for a few weeks. I respected her enough to try and preserve her body for as long as possible.

I didn't know how long that I laid on the concrete floor, staring up at the fluorescent lights, when the seamless door pulled away, drawing away to show Daddy Davenport in all his glory. His dark eyes were alight with rage.

I turned away and continued to stare at the ceiling. "Nice try, Dr. Dan. You haven't quite perfected the brooding stare, though."

"Mara." Warren Davenport marched into the room, dipping down low to wrap his hands around the thick iron chains attached to my wrists. "What the hell happened?"

It was him. He was real. He smelled like cinnamon gum.

"Daniel found me." I pointed out. My facial expression clearly said that I doubted his observation skills.

He gave me his signature look. "Why didn't you escape?"

"I was waiting for you," I said simply, and it was the truth. "Where are my mates?"

"The Ifrit has set up some pretty comprehensive defenses around the building. I was the only one that could get through." Warren studied my chains and tested their strength. "We have to hurry. Daniel might come back at any moment."

"Don't tell me that you're scared of Dr. Dan?" I sassed, watching intently as the iron beneath Warren's grip turned burning red with heat before snapping in an array of sparks. Damn. Hot stuff.

"I'll shoot him on sight," Davenport remarked as he freed me from my shackles. "I would prefer not to."

I hadn't heard the door open again, but Davenport must have done, because he stiffened, his hand twitched as he reached for his holster.

"I have no qualms with shooting you, commander." Daniel drawled. I shifted, seeing that the short doctor stood behind Warren with his arm extended and a pistol in his grip. Daniel's hand did not shake as he unclipped the safety.

"Dr. Gardiner." Warren addressed him formally. "We can talk about this. Find a way to deal with this."

Daniel clicked his tongue against the roof of his mouth. Blood hit my face in a fine spray, Davenport slumped, the back of his head was gone.

I couldn't move. I couldn't blink.

He'd killed Warren.

Daniel Gardiner had killed Daddy Davenport.

Bang. Gone. Dead.

I froze. Struck numb as I stared down at Warren's body.

Then, the Mimic Sidhe laughed. Daniel Gardiner chuckled like he had heard a benign joke on TV or something. Not like he had killed a man. A man that I loved.

My vision went red. I leaped up and wrapped my hands around Dr Daniel's neck before he could blink. Roaring in his face, I took us both to the ground. His head bounced against the concrete and tears dripped down my face as I slammed him down. With sure hands, I gripped his red hair and began to pound it into the concrete. Determined to make him pay. To make Daniel's head look like Warren's did. There was nothing behind Daniel's eyes. No human empathy.

Daniel laughed, his teeth were red with blood. "If you kill me, Riley dies next."

I let go, my lips curled in disgust.

"I don't have to kill you," I informed him delicately as my eyes turned to black oil slicks. "But I can make you wish that I had."

I laid, hunched over Warren Davenport's cold and still body, unable to pry myself away. My shoulders shook, and each breath was harder to take than the last.

There was so much pain that I wondered how humans

could live with such an emotion. I felt like I had been gutted and left hollow. All I could think about was Warren's angry face as he had shouted and called me useless. Were those his last thoughts of me? Or had he seen something, something vital, which made him come to rescue me?

Maybe Warren Davenport was just a good person. Behind his cocky and grumpy exterior.

I had genuinely believed that Davenport would belong to me too.

I threw my head back and wailed, unable to move from the spot by his side. Unable to look at Warren's body either.

Daniel laid, trapped in his own worst nightmare, and unlikely to ever wake again, but I still did not want to leave Davenport to find the Ifrit.

Hands gripped my torso, dipping under my arms. I turned, scratching, like a feral cat.

"Mara!" Hugo shouted my name until my senses came back. When he saw recognition light up my eyes, Hugo gripped my body and pressed it against his, as if he was worried that I would slip away again. When he pulled back, I saw the rest of Team P had come to the rescue.

Too late.

Remi's eyes widened, and his face drained of color as he looked down at Davenport's body "Is that—?"

Jae cut in. "We need to move. Now."

"But Warren—" I argued through numb lips.

"We'll talk about it soon. I promise." Hugo gripped my shoulders and led me away from the room. Away from Warren. I turned, my feet stumbling as I tried to claw my way back.

"We can't leave him," I whispered. Hart stepped forward, and the door swished closed behind us.

"It's okay—" Hugo said, reassuring me. I batted him away and turned. When I spoke, it was in a dead voice.

"It's not okay," I said. "Nothing is okay."

Every step I took away from Warren, even surrounded by my mates, was like losing a limb. Bleeding out with no wound.

"I can't do this," I said, hollow. The emotions that came with being inside a human body were too acute. Too strong. I reached up with shaking hands and gripped the latch of my collar. "I have to—"

"Mara..." Hugo sounded like he was in pain.

"She's running away." Hart crossed his arms over his chest.

"I'm not," I argued weakly.

"She's taking the easy route." Hart continued as if I hadn't spoken. "She's running away."

"Mara?" Jae's eyes were wide.

I stood on the precipice of the being that I wanted to be, but I was just a Demon. A small speck in the grand scheme of things. They would be able to live without me. They would survive.

"I love you." I smiled sadly, taking in each of their faces for the last time.

Then I dropped to the floor, leaving Frankie's body behind to die.

Chapter 26

Davenport POV

I hadn't died since the eighties, but I remembered the pain well, like being burnt alive and then hit by a semi and dragged for several miles.

Such was the price of being a Phoenix.

The night sky greeted me as my body rebuild itself from the ashes, the grass behind my back began to crisp and die as my fire consumed and birthed me anew.

Jae leaned over my face, his face was devoid of his usual sense of amusement and set in stone instead. He tossed a pair of cargo pants into my chest, with more force than necessary. I sat up and noticed Mara laid unconscious by my side. Her body was still warm, and her chest rose and fell with each breath.

I reached over to touch her face. To make sure that she was okay after seeing my death, and to find out what had happened with Daniel, my most significant oversight and biggest regret.

"She's not in there," Hart said from across the clearing. His head was in his hands.

Hugo's head snapped around, and he paused his pacing. "She wouldn't leave us." The incubus snapped.

"Sinclair's right." Remi rubbed the back of his neck.

I sat up, wincing in pain. "What happened?" I demanded, staring each of my men in the eye.

Only Jae looked at me. "Mara left Frankie's body behind."

"Why?" My voice was a harsh crack, but he did not flinch.

"I don't know," Jae admitted.

Hart stood up and advanced, his eyes looked dead. "She said that she couldn't do it anymore."

"I don't think it means what you think it means," Hugo said weakly.

Mara had run away? Had she abandoned ship to save her own skin?

We were gathered in a clearing to the side of the detainment building, a decent distance away, but even I felt the wave of heat when everything shattered. The unearthly keen as the Ifrit swirled into the sky, tangled in glittering smoke. We all watched in awe.

Mara ducked and dived, clinging to the Ifrit. Only able to battle the Demon because she had no body. As a hole tore into the Ifrit's darkness, Hart looked at his shoes, tears in his eyes before he stared at the sky, and watched with us.

"She's..." Hart was unable to finish his thought. Guilt and grief mingled on the set of his lips.

Our Drude expanded, swallowing the Ifrit, folding in on herself. There was no sound. A vacuum. No fireworks or grand finale.

None of us moved. Unsure of what had happened. My fingers twitched, aching to reach out to catch the rainfall of diamonds, as the sky turned to light and then dark.

For the longest time, we waited for Mara to come back, but there was no smoke, no darkness like our little nightmare. The sky was still.

"No," Hugo whispered, his voice a cry. "No. She's coming back. She has to come back."

We waited and waited. The air fogged our breath. Riley Fisher batted her way through the underbrush and collapsed in a heap, dirty but otherwise unharmed. Hugo raced over to support her body, wrapping her in a blanket as the fire raged from the building behind us.

Riley's teeth chattered. "S-She said that it was the only way." She whispered. "I don't know what she meant."

Everyone turned to the female Hunter, she looked so fragile. "She said that it wanted to die. She said that he begged for death."

Frankie's body began to stir. Relief filled me like an intoxicating drug. Sinclair's smile was radiant. Jae's was cocky. Remi's worried, and Hart's was unsure. Her eyes fluttered open, and she sat up, looking around like the world was new.

I found myself swaggering over, wanting to see her face when she realized I was alive. All that greeted me was a blank look.

"Mara?" I smirked, crouching down. "That was quite a show."

Mara blinked slowly, before cocking her head to the side. There was no life bursting from the seams of her body.

There was no manic energy, no random thoughts, and bratty behavior that she saved just for me.

Mara was gone.

Frankie Gardiner had woken up.

Chapter 27

Mara POV

I stood in the night sky, in the space between celestial bodies as I watched the stars being born, and then their slow descent into death. The balance was by my side, much larger than her childlike vessel had led me to believe.

I lived between the stars in the darkness. The Balance was the force that held the planets in place.

I finally knew who I was.

"When Nova sent her devouring beasts to kill you, she did not realize that such a feat was against the laws of existence." The Balance said gravely. "God sought only to destroy Death. She did not realize that to kill her sister was to kill part of herself."

"If I am Death, why can't I remember?" I wondered.

"You are many. Surely you can think back far enough, and remember." The Balance told me. "All Drudes are part of your being. Scattered after the Devouring beasts razed your home and ate your Demonic children."

"I am the last one left."

"You are all, and all are one." The Balance said as we drifted through the stars.

"Why am I here?" I asked.

"You are Mara. Goddess of Death, Rebirth, and Dreams. Sister to Nova, God of Life, Birth, and Creation. It was time for you to come home."

The swirling colored gases expanded further across the cosmos. Planets flourished and died in front of us.

"What about my Mates?" I asked.

"Each replaced something that you had lost to the devouring beasts." The Balance informed me.

I thought about each one of my Bonds. Hugo was my restraint. Jae was strength in the face of his past. Remi was compassion, the only person to be kind to me even when he didn't even know me. Davenport represented leadership and Hart, kindness. Qualities that I had lacked before.

"Demons do not require Balance." The universe continued. "Humans do."

"I am neither."

"You are the mother of the Demons." She said.

"But I'm dead."

"Millenia have passed since Nova released the Bhakshi and the Shayati unto Hell—killing the first Demons and scattering Death and all of her facets into the shadows." The Balance explained gravely. "Gradually, Hell regrew. Demons were reborn. Created when Sin evolved."

"Did you do all this?" I wondered.

"I cannot interfere with the Human and Demonic Realities." The universe said, but I had a feeling that she was lying.

"What do I do now?" I asked.

"You are the Goddess of Death, Rebirth, and Dreams." The Balance laughed. "I need you to whip those Hunters into shape. They'll be the only thing that saves the world when the end comes."

Chapter 28

I watched the compound from the top of a tree, as my memorial service took place in the K9 yard.

My human shell was easy enough to create once I had woken from the cosmos. I had chosen a form close enough to my true one. Wearing the dark shimmering skin of shadows, and eyes wholly swallowed by oil slicks. My hair was made up of tendrils of smoke, curling in the air as if underwater. The only difference was my ability to interact with the Human Realities. Touch, smell and taste. Power boiled under the surface of my being. I had been reborn.

Davenport stood in front of a group of Hunters. I was unable to move as I studied him, looking for the telltale signs of Dr Daniel's mannerisms. Warren's jaw gritted as he stared out at the crowd. It was only when his fingers tug his dark hair away from his face that I saw his hand tremble.

Warren Davenport, my Davenport, was alive.

Jae, Hart, Hugo, and Remi made up the front of the crowd with their hands folded in front of them. Tears rolled down Hugo's face, and his shoulders shook. There were no photos and no coffin. Scores of flowers lined the podium. I didn't need to read the cards to know who had given which bouquet. Red roses from Davenport. Tiger lilies from Remi. Daisies from Hugo. Peonies from Hart and Azaleas from Jae.

I could feel their emotions, resonating in my chest as if they were my own. Each bond flared to life as I leaped from the tree, floating to the ground.

Remi turned first, our bond coiling tightly to bring us together. His brow furrowed as he searched the surrounding area for something, unable to find me until I made myself visible. Jae felt the bond next. His smile was blinding as his entire body unfolded from grief. Hugo stopped crying, his brow furrowed in confusion. Hart was last, rubbing his chest, but otherwise not reacting. His expression stoic as he stared forward.

Davenport was unaffected. Our bond hovered, incomplete. Two frayed edges, drifting through the ether.

The other Hunters—few that I knew and many that I didn't—began to whisper, confused as I parted the crowd and made my way to my Soulbonds. Allowing everyone to see me in my true form.

I looked more Demonic than ever, despite my divinity, but my cloak was white. The smile on my face was radiant, but cocky, as I felt the true extent of my power rolling through me. Woken by The Balance, to retake my throne as Death.

The crowd became a roar of activity. Weapons were drawn, and commands were barked. They parted like the red sea, revealing my Mates. Feeling the tension, I reigned in my shadows and made my skin more textured, affecting a human facade.

"Everyone, quiet!" Davenport barked, his voice echoed over the clearing. "Stand down." His lip twitched, showing a hint of his arrogance.

Hugo stepped forward first; his pale blue eyes were wide, and his grin was silly as he ran towards me. Hugo Sinclair, my incubus, flung his arms around me and held me tightly. His shoulders shook with the overwhelming emotion of our reunion.

I began to cry and laugh at the same time. Huge embarrassing hiccoughing sobs.

His hand tangled in the back of my hair as he pressed me to him. "I knew you would never leave us," Hugo whispered. "But don't ever scare me like that again."

"How long have I been gone?" I asked.

Hart answered for him. "Three days." I craned my neck around Hugo, to look at my mountain man. Callum reached forward as if he wanted to touch me, but his hand faltered at the last second.

"I'm sorry for doubting you," Callum whispered. His eyes burnt with the desperate need for me to hear his apology

393

and for it to be accepted.

I smiled, and Callum's stance relaxed for the first time since I had seen him.

Jae and Remi approached next. Remi went for a hug and a playful shove, telling me off for throwing myself into danger. Jae pressed a hard kiss against my mouth before breaking away with a wink and a subtle demand for information (later).

Then came Davenport.

His long legs ate up the distance between us, like a man on a mission. I wanted to ask what kind of creature he was, but I should have seen it before. His team were called Team Phoenix for Hell's sake.

I expected the commander to begin to rip into me for taking down the Ifrit and putting myself in danger, possibly for getting him killed, or maybe for some other slight that was human in nature and therefore unfathomable to me.

Instead, Davenport dipped down and used his weight to leverage my body over his shoulder, his arm wrapped around my thighs just under my bum.

The crowd that had started to disperse began to pay attention once more, as Davenport carried me away, with the rest of my Mates following.

Warren Davenport led our group past the condemned shell of Jae's old cabin, and down a narrow path until he found what he was looking for.

I arched my back to try and see where we were going, only to receive a harsh smack on my butt.

"What was that for?" I laughed despite the stinging pain.

"That's for running off and sacrificing yourself when we could have found another way to handle the situation."

Davenport snarled.

I propped my elbows up and put my face in my hands. "Did you miss me, Daddy?" I pouted.

Davenport muttered to himself like a grumpy bear. The group behind us snickered, and Jae raised his palm for a high-five.

"If anyone deserves to be punished, it's you." I pointed out. "You let me think you were dead."

"I *was* dead." Warren's voice was dry.

My brow scrunched in confusion. "He's a phoenix, Mara," Hugo interjected helpfully.

"And you knew?" My eyes widened.

"We had to get out of the building. Once we were safe, we were going to tell you." Hugo dipped his head, hiding behind his bangs.

I jabbed my finger at each of them. "You're in my bad books!"

Hart stepped forward, his expression was pointed. "Don't deflect. You took on the Ifrit, even though you knew it would kill you."

I opened my mouth to argue, as we rounded the path and stood in front of a newer but more boring version of Jae's cabin, hidden between the trees. Onsite housing.

"I had to," I whispered as Davenport took the steps two at a time. He hadn't even broken a sweat. I tried to wriggle out of his grasp as soon as we stood in the living room, but I received another spank for my trouble.

My Mates surrounded us, their expressions ranged from wicked and mischievous to tentative and unsure.

Davenport shifted my body until I was pressed to his front instead of over his shoulder. Both of his arms wrapped around my butt, hoisting me, so that I could look down at him.

"What's going on?" I whispered.

Davenport lowered my body gently, his eyes never leaving mine. "What I should have done on the first day I met you." He pulled his hunting knife from the sheaf on the small of his back and gripped my finger. I felt like sleeping beauty about to touch the spinning wheel. The sharp point of the curved blade hovered in front of the pad of my finger.

"Last chance to back out." Davenport's words were a dare.

"You wish." I blew a raspberry. "I'm going to make your life hell."

Warren gave a deep throaty laugh as he drew blood and dipped down, sucking my finger in a dominant and seductive display. I squirmed. When my finger left his mouth, it pulled down his bottom lip, exposing his teeth. Davenport did not collapse in pain like the others. The room grew hotter, as Warren dipped forward and took my mouth, punishing and delicious at the same time. His tongue plundered my mouth, and another set of hands gripped my wrists and pulled them behind my back.

"Now, for your real punishment," Remi whispered in my ear.

I jolted, pulling away from the kiss with a gasp. "I thought you were joking." My voice pitched, shrill as I jerked against his hold. Remi looked down, his front pressed against my back.

"You wish." Remi's eyes sparkled as he repeated my earlier comeback.

Davenport used the brief respite from our kiss, to shuck off his clothes, allowing them to drop to the floor without much care. Around us, Hugo's magic saturated the air, as the incubus lounged on the couch and watched as I was pressed between two men, his demeanor like that of a king looking down on his subjects.

Remi reached up and unclasped my cloak, allowing the material to fall to the ground like water as he revealed my nude body underneath.

My arms curled around Davenport's neck, and the light bounced off my skin and shone. I breathed in Warren's air, as I rested my forehead against his.

"I've learned my lesson." I murmured with a naughty

grin.

Remi gripped my waist and pressed his crotch into the curve of my ass. Davenport smiled wickedly.

"Can you be a good girl?" He asked.

I nodded.

"You're not allowed to come until I'm inside you," Davenport warned sternly, before he stepped away, leaving my body cold. Warren leisurely touched his cock, rubbing it from root to tip as he perused my body with darkened eyes.

Just as I was about to ask what was happening, Remi stepped away, and Hart took his place. Jae gripped the back of my neck and pulled me in for a kiss that conveyed enough that speech wasn't needed.

I was loved. I was wanted. I was missed. I *belonged*.

Hart's hand slipped between my legs, teasing the inside of my thighs before he found my core. He dipped one finger inside, before spreading the wetness around my clit, never directly touching the bundle of nerves. I twitched with the sensation, pushing back until my butt pressed against the distorted zipper of Hart's jeans.

Jae's hands grazed my breasts before he held my waist. His lips broke free from mine to layer kisses over the sensitive skin of my throat. My eyes fluttered open for just a second, enough to see Remi's hooded eyes as he watched my body being touched and caressed by two of his teammates from his position across the room.

I let out a low moan as Hart's slow torture drew pleasure from my body.

"You're not allowed to come." Jae reminded me, tweaking my nipple before taking it into his mouth and twirling it around his tongue.

My thighs pressed together. Hart's other hand gripped my leg, and without much strength, pried them apart. Exposing my center.

Jae's kisses led down my stomach towards my pussy and Hart tilted my head until his lips could reach mine. He swallowed the sound as Jae's tongue parted my lower lips and continued what Hart's finger's had started. I whimpered. Jae pulled away as his hand reached up and his fingers spanned my belly, still exploring my pussy with his tongue. With a gentle push, as I was still enthralled in Hart's kiss, they maneuvered me down onto the sheepskin rug on the floor. Flat on my back, Jae continued to feast, making my neck arch and my heart race. I could feel my body begin to tighten and my toes begin to curl. Jae stopped and waggled his finger. I growled as my orgasm crested the hill and rolled back down again.

Davenport continued to watch from the sofa, stroking himself slowly. Hart sat down by my side and tugged my wrist, nonverbally urging me to sit astride him. I felt the blunt head of his cock rub against my folds, but not going inside. Jae crept up behind, his movements slow and lazy like a cat. Jae pushed my hair over my shoulder and kissed the seam of my jaw. His fingers danced across the sensitive skin of my back.

I looked down at Hart, the moment felt pivotal. Life-altering. He rocked his hips upwards and dipped inside me, just enough to make me want more. I was so wet that the sound of his thrusts were sloppy and debaucherous. Jae gripped my waist and urged me to move, positioning my body to take Hart's cock. When I found Hart fully seated inside of me, my clit rubbing against the base of his shaft and the head of his cock rubbing against my cervix, I threw back my head and began to move in earnest. Riding my Mate with vigor.

Jae placed a hand on the small of my back, and I felt the smooth skin of his member rub against my butt cheek. Could I take two at once? I didn't know, but I wanted to find out. Jae pressed his thumb against the puckered skin of my ass, making me tense and relax at the same time. The hint of danger and the promise of being completely full made Hart's cock feel even better inside of me. Every inch of my body was flushed and begging to be touched.

Jae pressed the mushroomed head of his penis against my ass. "Push out as I thrust." He warned, his voice strained with arousal. I nodded frantically as Hart pulled out, leaving me empty.

The head went in first, followed by the slow procession of the rest of Jae's cock. Each inch was more comfortable and soon I was panting, begging for Hart to fill me too. He obliged.

Remi stepped forward, unwilling to be left out. With Hart below, and Jae behind, I was able to take Remi's cock in my mouth by leaning to the left. He was so big that my hand could not fit entirely around his girth, so I settled for licking the vein along the shaft. Remi fucked my mouth, as Hart and Jae filled my other holes. Waves of lust danced in the air, mixing with my darkness as Hugo's magic messed with my mind and made me want to scream.

"I'm going to come." I panted.

"Not allowed," Jae grunted as he thrust into my ass. I reared back to meet him, more friction, and I was about to spiral.

Just as my body began to tighten, Davenport cleared his throat, and suddenly I was left alone and shivering on the sheepskin rug

"Hey!" I protested, but Warren knelt down and kissed me, settling my back against the floor; he slid between my legs and thrust inside me, right to the hilt. My eyes fluttered closed, but I saw the circle of men around me, touching themselves to the sight of Davenport thrusting inside me and rubbing my clit with his thumb. My juices were still shining on Hart's member.

When Davenport tensed, and I felt him harden inside of me, I could not keep my orgasm at bay any longer. It washed over me like a tide, stealing my vision and clamping down every muscle in my body.

Davenport collapsed on top of me. Both of us shimmering with sweat. He pushed my hair away from my neck. "You have scars on your neck. The stars," Davenport whispered. "Does that mean you're a Hunter now?"

I laughed nervously. "I'm actually something else. It's a long story."

Hugo reclined back, his erection was an obvious pipe, visible through his trousers. My feet began to move before I had made a conscious decision. Swaggering to my incubus, naked with cum dripping down my inner thigh, I straddled his hips and brushed my hair over my shoulder.

"Howdy, neighbor," I whispered with a giggle. Hugo looked bemused as he brushed his knuckles against my cheek. "Get it? Because we're neighbors?" I added with a wink.

I rocked and seated myself on his restrained boner, getting comfortable. Hugo had frozen.

"What?" He blinked slowly.

"I'm your neighbor. Or I was. Number 35. You were 36, right?"

Hugo swore under his breath, and his eyes rolled to the ceiling. Jae burst out laughing, gripping his sides. Hugo let out a resigned groan.

"We had a bet going." The incubus explained. "I said my neighbor had to be a drug dealer. Davenport said, prostitute."

"What did Jae think?" I was confused.

The Nephilim gasped with his hilarity, and wiped a tear from his eye. Unable to speak.

Hugo ducked his head, all evidence of the confident and magic-drunk incubus was gone as he mumbled. "I don't want to say. It's so cheesy."

"You have to tell me!" I bounced, demanding with glee.

Hugo closed his eyes as if in pain. "You used to get a lot of packages. Jae and I opened one once." His hands gripped my waist, and his knuckles moved the underside of my breasts. "It was full of pornography and toys. Jae said that if I ever met the woman that made that order, we'd be a match made in heaven."

Magic trailed up my spine like a hot tongue as I threw my head back and laughed with abandon. "A match made in Hell, you mean." I said.

Epilogue

1 year later

The armored van swayed from side to side as it ate up the dirt path leading away from the compound. I pushed my finger into seam of my tactical vest, and pulled the heavy material away from my skin.

I had affected a human facade for the mission, wearing deep black skin, and dark eyes. My hair floated, but I was unable to control it; at least my team of newbie Hunters wouldn't shoot me on sight.

I sat in the passenger seat, swiping through the file on the specifics of the mission, my tablet jolted every time we drove over a bump.

Purgers, mindless scavenger Demons, who collected food for Beezelbub, had escaped through one of the Folds, and were running riot in Homndel Park, New Jersey.

Purgers were what humans would call *'not a dog'*. There was something strange about them. An off-ness that was hard to pinpoint. They might have four legs and a canine head, but it was only when you got closer than you realized that their skin didn't fit right (they often stole skins to wear) and their eyes were empty and hollow.

Beelzebub was the King of the Sixth Circle, of Gluttony and Excess. He was reed-thin, skeletal, and always hungry for food, sex and life. Purgers were his servants and they collected his sustenance.

How the Purgers had gotten into the Human Realities? Unknown. They were stupid on the best of days.

It was my job to open the planes and send them back to Hell. If they tried to hurt anyone? I had a semi-automatic rifle in the weapons trunk with a rude word painted on the pistol grip in lucid pink.

"I can't believe commander Davenport put *her* in charge of this mission." One of the Hunters whispered from the back of the vehicle. My senses had vastly improved since I had been gifted my powers again, able to pick up on the tiniest sounds even over the roar of the engine.

"I hear that she's fucking all of Team P." Another goaded, and the men in the van snickered.

"As long as we don't die, I don't care." One of the women snarled.

"She's only here because she's his girlfriend."

I lowered my head and smirked. The mission was going to be fun.

As we disembarked from the filthy van, each of the Hunters were covered in pieces of gore and wearing expressions of horror. We had taken care of the Purgers without an issue. I had made a competition of it.

My team was new. Green. Setting them loose in a forest teeming with a horde of beasts that wanted to drag them into Hell had been a good way to show them what being a Hunter was all about.

They were a little chewed, and only the female Hunter, Brandy, had managed to kill one of the Purgers. My new team had caught a glimpse of my true form. I decided, that as their commanding officer, that needed to fear me.

I turned to address the ragtag crowd with a stern expression. Wide eyes and fearful flinches greeted me.

"Good work." I quirked a brow. "Go shower."

A dog yipped in excitement as Hart rounded the corner

with Dixie. I squeaked with glee and bounced on my heels, my serious demeanor gone in a blink. Every Hunter looked on in disbelief as I raced towards Callum and threw myself into his arms. Dixie hopped up and tried to get in on the action as I planted a big wet kiss on his lips.

"How was your first mission?" he asked with a tiny smile as he glanced over my shoulder at the limping group of Hunters.

"They said I was only leading a team because I was sleeping with Davenport." My expression was wicked.

Hart's eyes widened minutely. "Is there any permanent damage?"

"All psychological." I said cheerfully.

Our fingers twined as we held hands and walked along the path, led by an enthusiastic Dixie. The trail was dark enough that Hart used the flashlight on his cellphone.

Floating lights shone through the gaps in the trees as Jae's cabin greeted us. Rebuilt after the fire, with extra rooms for all of us, the awning was dotted with hundreds of lights, slowly blooming and then fading like will o'wisps.

"What are those?" I whispered in awe.

"Christmas lights." If Hart was surprised by my question, he did not show it. "Do you know what today is?"

"If you're referring to the birth of Yeshua, we're going to have a philosophical debate that will just bore you." I grinned a toothy grin.

Hart chuckled and shook his head. "That's next week."

"Then I have no idea what today is." I chirped, glancing at the porch as Hugo peeked around the front door.

"It's Tuesday." Hugo said, absentmindedly. He shot Hart a look. "You're early."

"You're both acting very suspiciously." I stroked my imaginary beard, squinting.

Hugo blushed, taking the steps two at a time as he greeted me with a quick kiss. Hugo wrapped his arms around my shoulders and pulled me to his side. Dixie barked and pawed the ground, letting out a whine. Hart knelt down and pulled out a treat from his pocket.

"I was asking Mara if she knew what day it was." Hart said pointedly.

Hugo's lips parted in an O. He glanced at me but said nothing.

"What's going on?" I narrowed my eyes, still smiling.

"Jae is making Donkatsu, your favorite." Callum informed me, straightening from his crouch.

I did a fist pump as Hugo slipped his hand in mine. "Come on." He said as he tugged me into the cabin with excitement—which was weird because Hugo did not like spicy food. Before I could open the front door, Hugo slipped his hands over my eyes, causing me to jump.

"Don't peek." The incubus laughed through his command.

"Would I do that?"

Both me answered in unison. It was a resounding *yes*. They also voiced their chagrin when I jinxed them both.

Leading me into the cabin, Hugo kept close, and Hart followed on our heels as Dixie jumped around us excitedly. They led me through the foyer and into the living room, my body instinctively remembered the layout of our home. I did my best not to harness my magic and to reach out to feel for an unfair advantage.

Strange smells made my nose tickle. The expected scent of the Donkatsu pork cutlet and it's insanely hot sauce was just one of the many in the room. I could smell the pine needles and plastic that belonged to the Christmas tree, along with the smell of burning wax and chocolate. Hugo pulled his hands away from my eyes, but I kept them closed just in case. I could hear the breathing of each of my men, but they were being deliberately quiet.

"What's going on?" I whispered, as a tendril of fear wrapped itself around my heart.

Hart put his hand on the small of my back. I felt his

warmth. "Open your eyes, Mara."

So, I did.

Hugo and Hart walked around my still and shocked form, to stand around the card table in the center of the room. Black balloons were tied with shiny ribbons, and a happy birthday banner spanned the wall behind the couch. Davenport, Jae, Hart, Hugo and Remi all stood around an obscenely large chocolate cake, the dessert buckled under the abundance of colored candles that someone (probably Jae) had tried to cram onto the cake's surface.

Jae stepped forward, his hair was a mess and his jeans had a sauce stain, but I loved that he didn't need to wear a mask in front of us. We got to see his true face. Jae took both of my hands and brought them to his lips.

"It's been one year since you came back to us." Jae whispered, his violet eyes burned into mine. "Happy birthday, Mara."

Remi let out a whoop and nudged Warren forward, causing the man to stumble as he tried to rearrange his suit jacket. Davenport shot a stern look over his shoulder before turning to me. He reached into his pocket and pulled out a single feather, his cheeks flushed red and he walked away before I could ask what was happening. The feather was crimson, tipped with canary yellow. A phoenix feather.

"Birthday presents!" Remi announced cheerfully, and I rushed into his waiting arms to plant a kiss on his lips.

Even with my divinity, my demon lineage, and five infuriating supernatural mates, I had never felt more human.

And that was just the way I liked it.

Bonus Chapter

Remi POV

I had turned the laptop monitor away from the door, as I took the Skype call away from the prying eyes of my team. My sister Suzette glared at the boring wall behind me.

"I don't want to look at Uma Thurman's pouting face. I wanted some eye candy." She whined, gesturing with a limp hand towards the oversized pulp fiction poster amongst the rest of my classic film posters.

"That's my team," I said sternly before breaking into a smile. "How have you been? How's mum?"

"Missing you." Suz rolled her eyes. "Dad can't keep harping on about the Weber Witch that broke his own curse." She sounded exasperated, but at twenty-one, it was rare when she didn't. Suzette, or Suz for short, was the youngest of my three sisters. Suz looked exactly like our mum, umber skin, and beautiful natural hair. The only difference were the vivid blue eyes that belonged to our father. While they looked watery gray in his face, they looked striking against her classic Haitian roots.

"Mara says hi, by the way." I tacked on with a smile. Suz buried her head in her hands, no doubt reliving the first time they had met (via Skype) when Mara pranced into my lap completely nude and wanted to know if I was watching porn.

"How does that work, by the way?" Suz reached over and unwrapped a green lollipop, she popped it in her mouth and rolled the stick from side to side. "Do you all... Together? Or do you each get a day of the week?"

I didn't want to go into the details of my polygamous relationship with my theatre studies student, candy-loving, baby sister. Besides, our Quintet changed from day to day. Sometimes

Mara subconsciously drifted to one of us over the other, sensing that we needed her in some way. Other times, it was a free for all.

"Is that a cannabis lollypop?" I squinted my eyes and leaned forward to study the screen.

Suz smirked, showing a hint of lucid green candy from between her teeth.

I shook my head to clear it. "Why the sudden nosiness about my relationship?"

She shrugged. "It's Valentine's day on Friday. I wanted to know what you were doing."

I froze on the spot. Did Demons celebrate Valentine's day? Unlikely. I was English as well as Haitian, born and raised in Kent. Valentine's day wasn't such a big thing back home. Shops tried to sell the themed chocolate and cards, but most people stayed in to avoid being caught by the random price-hike in restaurants and bars.

"You forgot, didn't you?" Suz pointed towards me through the screen with her lollypop.

"Where did you even get a cannabis lollypop from?"

"Camden."

I exhaled in frustration. "Do you think Mara will want to celebrate valentine's day?" I wondered.

"Everyone likes chocolate and sex."

I quirked my brows. Suz held out her hands in a disarming fashion.

"Except me. Obviously." She made the sign of the cross. "Praise Jesus."

"Worried that mum can hear you from the other room?" I speculated in a dry voice.

"Of course." Suz looked over her shoulder. "I've got to go." We said our goodbyes and I love yous before signing out.

What would a Demon Death Goddess want for Valentine's day?

I hadn't told Mara where we were going when I invited her to drive into the city with me. Driving into NYC was a pain in the arse. I felt uncomfortable leaving my SUV in Coney Island and getting the ferry, but it was easier than trying to find a parking space.

I had made a reservation at an expensive restaurant on fifth Avenue and just hoped that Mara liked it.

Trying to get Mara to sit still was like trying to contain a bag of ferrets. As she sat in the passenger seat, every breath was accompanied by a tiny human movement. Tapping her fingers on her thighs. Opening the glove compartment. Pulling her bottom lip.

Her human mask had completely slipped away as it often did when she was alone with us. I preferred her in her true form. Midnight skin with starlight that shimmered as she moved. Completely black eyes, somehow more expressive than when she had been hidden behind a human host. Mara seemed to move easier, with less weight on her shoulders than when I had first met her.

She rested her head on her hand. "I didn't get a mission statement. Where are we going?"

"It's not a mission." My heart fluttered as I searched her face for a clue to how she would react. "We're celebrating valentine's day."

Mara's eyes widened in wonder. Her lips popped open. "Valentine's Day?"

She was beyond adorable. I nodded as a smile broke over my face.

"We get to kill a goat and everything?"

"What? No!?" I gasped through laughter.

A hurt look flashed across her face. "That's what the Romans did."

I quickly sobered. "Nowadays, we do fancy food and

candy."

Mara nodded slowly and turned to the window. "The Roman way sounds more fun." She mumbled.

I patted her thigh. "You'll have fun, I promise."

I just hoped I was right.

We pulled onto the boardwalk on Brighton Beach, ready to take advantage of the free parking before we caught the ferry over to Central Manhatten. I was following Davenport's instructions; he drove into the City enough to know the best way to go about it.

We stepped onto the sidewalk and into the crisp Spring air. Mara wore an ivory summer dress covered in flowers, the picture of innocence. Her face rippled, and her skin mattified as she began more human. It was fascinating to watch her power in action.

Thousands of rainbow umbrellas dotted the beach, and a monstrous Ferris wheel overlooked the sand, surrounded by spinning and whizzing rides. I gripped Mara's hand, ready to hail a taxi to the nearest ferry port, her fingers twined in mine, and she gaped at the slowly circling wheel arching into the sky.

"Remi..." She whispered in awe. "This is perfect." The lights of the amusement rides reflected back in her coal-black eyes. "Can we go on the rides?"

I thought about the reservation at Le Bain and decided that it could wait. I had front row seats to Mara's first time at an amusement park. The greasy food and sugary scents, and the squeals of children filled the Coney Island air. She tugged me forward, but I did not need much coaxing as I watched her trying to take in everything at once.

I reached into my pocket and pulled out my card, gesturing to the token machine. "What do you want to go on first?"

Mara started to jump and clap. "Bumper cars!" She said with a wide grin, pointing over my shoulder. She was utterly unaware that several people had turned to watch her.

I had forgotten that I was scared of heights until we sat at the top of the Ferris Wheel with my hands clenched around the safety rail in a death grip.

Mara eyed me with concern and tried not to rock the small cart. The sun had begun to set, and our reservation had come and gone. We'd spent the whole day laughing and eating as much junk food as possible.

"Look at all the lights." She whispered.

The entire amusement park was a kaleidoscope of colors. "We didn't have things like this in Hell."

Mara did not tend to talk about Hell with anyone but Hugo, they had a special connection born from their roots. It did not bother me much until she said things like that.

"What's Hell like?" I asked gently.

Her brow furrowed as her eyes continued to drink in the view. "It's never day or night. Always sometime in between. Every Circle is different. Every Demon is different. Sport is bloodshed, but it's still beautiful."

"Do you miss it?"

"My place is here." She whispered, taking my hand. "Maybe one day, I'll create a new world, and we'll rule it together. Our own bliss."

My human mind was limited in understanding her magic because I could not conceive of anyone being powerful enough to birth and kill an entire world on a whim. I had to remind myself that Mara was a bonafide goddess, even if she didn't act like one.

The Ferris Wheel began to descend, but I leaned forward and pressed a light kiss to Mara's lips. I hoped it conveyed everything that I wanted her to know.

That I loved her more than breath.

Mara had successfully foiled every one of my attempts to win a plushie for her. First she had squeezed my waist, making me jump. Then she had covered my eyes. Eventually her tactics grew more underhanded as my gun jammed, and when I finally landed a shot, none of the cans fell. I gave her a look, which told her that I knew she was using magic, but her answering grin told me that she had not been trying to hide it.

"Better luck next time!" the stall owner bellowed before greeting another couple. A single raindrop landed on my nose, and I glanced at the sky.

"It's going to rain," I said to myself.

Mara gripped my arm. "I know." She said, leaning into me. "Isn't it wonderful?"

I laughed with her as the sky's opened and the streets began to flood. People covered their heads and ran for cover, but my little Demon pulled us into the downpour. Within seconds, our clothes were plastered to our bodies with ice-cold rain.

I blinked water out of my eyes and looked down at my beautiful Mate. I pushed her wet hair out of her face and tilted my lips to meet hers. Her skin was warm, and she tasted like mischief as she pulled away with sparkling eyes.

She gripped my hand and began to tug me towards the car. I allowed myself to follow without any protest. "Where are we going?" I asked, laughing at her determined stride.

Her lip twitched. "You'll see."

Our car was one of many on the boardwalk. A dark SUV parked between two compacts and directly under a streetlight. The orange glow died as we approached, and I had a feeling that Mara was to blame. The rain had cleared the streets of people.

Mara pulled me into the backseat of the SUV, pushing on my chest until I hit the backseat, and she moved to straddle my hips. Even in the large vehicle, there was limited space. Her hair tumbled down on either side of my head as she leaned

411

forward with a wicked smirk.

"I've never fooled around in a car before." She whispered, licking her bottom lip. I brushed my knuckles against her cheek.

"Allow me to help with that, love." I arched my neck to meet her lips, parting them with mine. My hands slipped under her dress, bypassing her ass as I trailed my fingers up her spine. Mara shivered as the car began to fog with our body heat. Our kiss turned harder, more desperate and her hands tangled in the fabric of my shirt, exposing my abs. My hips rocked up, the action was beyond my control, as I sought friction against her heat. I could feel her core through the thin fabric of her lace underwear. My fingers drifted down her spine until my hand rested on the curve of her bum. She rocked her hips, seeking the same contact that I was. She whispered my name as her hands drifted to my zipper, and she pulled my cock free.

"Remi... I need..." Her voice was breathy as she gripped my cock and pressed it to her core, pulling her lace knickers to the side. It felt so illicit, hurried but passionate. We grasped at each other. Too overcome by our Lust to even bother to remove our clothes.

Her head flew back as my cock seated itself inside of her, choked by her tight channel. She felt like heaven and hell. Soft and hot in all the right places. Laughing with abandon, she rode me as I teased her breasts through the thin fabric of her sundress.

When we both came, we came together. Foreheads pressed together and grinning.

"Happy Valentine's Day." She whispered. "Though technically, it's in a couple of days."

"Better than sacrificing a few goats?" I laughed, still breathless.

"Much better," Mara said, as her hand drifted across my chest to rest above my heart, and the Soulbond scar that rested there.

The end

Thank you for reading.
If you enjoyed 'The Dead Ringer', please please please leave a review on
Amazon and Goodreads.

Reviews can make or break and indie author, and every single one counts.

Love,
Michaela x

Keep reading for the first chapter of 'Red City' a MFM menage romance!

Welcome to the Red City.
You belong to the demons now.

Prison has not been kind to the girl who could paint the future.
When Doe is given the opportunity to serve the rest of her life sentence in the
confines of the Red City, without bars, she does not hesitate.
Demons rule the walled city, and humans are for food, pleasure or servitude.
When Doe is purchased at an auction by the Pink Sector, the sordid territory of
the Incubi and Succubi, she is thrown into a world unlike anything she has ever
seen.
Her new master hates her, without reason. The harem is full of beautiful
viperous women.
There is an insane Demon in the wine cellar of the mansion, who claims that she
is his soul mate.
Something deeper is going on, and snapshots of the future won't help.

Can Doe stay alive or will the Demons chew her up and spit her out like so many
before her?
Will the Wilde brothers, her new masters, be enough to save her from herself?

Red City is a standalone paranormal ménage romance novel
**Contains #whychoose, MFM, sexual themes, bullying and
violence**

Red City

Chapter 1

The runes that decorated the outer wall glowed in the twilight. Big hulking letters that spelt out words in an ancient language that I shouldn't have been able to read. My heart sank as the coach lurched forward. I gripped the worn vinyl of the bench in front of me, but it did little to stop my body from swaying side to side.

There was no other clue that we had approached one of the Red Cities. No *'Welcome to'* sign. Just concrete walls, marked up with magic, and border patrol for miles.

I rubbed the inside of my wrist as it prickled, reacting to the magic around us. The rest of the coach full of criminals did the same. A sucking sensation gripped my chest like the city wanted to vacuum me up and swallow me whole. The feeling made it hard to breathe, and a drop of sweat rolled down my forehead, leaving an itch behind as it dripped off my nose.

None of us wore cuffs. The mark on our wrist had many ways to subdue and harm.

"Everyone, border patrol is coming on board. Shut up. Be smart. And for God's sake, don't try and jump anyone." The guard at the front of the coach called down the benches. "These guys deal with Demons every goddamn day. Any bright spark that thinks that skipping the border might save them? Think again."

I shivered and looked out the window. Curious at the number of poor souls that had tried to run away at the last bastion of humanity. We were at the entrance to Hell on earth.

Abandon hope, all who enter here.

As our coach crawled past the first concrete wall, a gush of oxygen pushed from my lungs. Every other prisoner on the bus seemed to exhale in time as the pulsating magic rushed

417

over our bodies. A phantom gripped my wrist, and a deep foreboding feeling told me that no one with a mark like ours would be leaving the city alive.

The dark ink that the prisoners wore was a runic symbol like the ones on the outer wall of the concrete rings. Branded onto our skin and down to the bone. The circular loops crossed each other, forming small planets, with harsh guttural lines. Cyclian runes from the bowels of hell.

H'carykhut

The demonic language for trapped. Imprisoned.

The coach slowed to a stop in front of another checkpoint. The space between the concrete rings was a barren wasteland, empty of all but pockmarked dry mud. The new ring, closer to the city, was taller and ringed with barbed wire. A faint throb of magic, enough to rob me of my breath, but not enough to feel like my lungs were trying to hack up a blood clot.

If that was how I felt at the border, I didn't know how we would make it to the city.

A glance to my fellow prisoners told me that they weren't feeling much better. Sweat rolled down clammy foreheads. Una, one of the women that had been by my side at intake, held her stomach with tight fingers as she struggled not to moan in pain.

The driver stood up without ceremony and left the bus; he walked to a black painted door, spray-painted with the word 'border patrol' in white stencilled letters. The prison guard at the front stood up and rested his hand on the baton on his belt loop. His eyes were hidden behind aviator sunglasses, but the lines around his mouth hinted at his age. The word *Closter* was stitched to his breast pocket, which I took to be his name.

"Right, inmates. Get up." He barked. We all paused, unsure and scared. With a quick and practised movement, Officer Closter held his baton in his hand, slamming the heavy club against his open meaty palm. "Now." He added unnecessarily. All of us had rushed to our feet when the weapon had come out.

418

I swayed and grabbed the bar at the edge of my seat. I knocked into another prisoner and flinched as I waited for the pain of a hit or a shove. None came. Everyone was struggling just as much as I was to remain standing. Caught on the edge of cage that wanted to swallow us whole, I could feel the magic pinging back and forth between the concrete outer rings.

I shoved my fist to my mouth and bit down on my knuckle. The sharp slash of pain helped just enough for me to gain my feet and step forward. I kept my head down as I trudged past the guard, in line like a good little girl with the other prisoners.

A yellow line, stencilled and painted on the floor, told us which way to go to be processed. It was in the opposite direction to the door the driver had disappeared into. The red-painted door had no word on the outside to signal what laid behind the cheap metal.

Officer Closter passed all of us with an unhurried gait as we stumbled down the line. He pushed open the unmarked door and waved his baton to usher us through.

"Line up against the wall," The guard said lazily as he strode in behind us and joined another border patrol agent behind the desk.

Our group was a mix of both men and woman. Large, small, Black, White, and Asian. I recognised some of the other girls from the corrections unit. Una, the redhead, still clasped her stomach. I only knew her name because she was a loud personality. Una worked in the prison library. She'd once folded down a page in a romance novel and winked when she passed it to me, telling me to enjoy.

Bethany, who I only knew as a quiet woman, stood nearest the door. Ratty hair hung around her shoulders, stringy and matted. She wore the same black baggy clothes that we all wore, but hers hung off her. Beth was a junkie, and from the dark circles and trembling limbs, I would hazard a guess that it had been a while since her last fix.

Stepping through the metal door had washed away the

sickness that radiated from our marks, but my stomach squirmed at the thought of what awaited us closer to the city.

"You're all here because you're scum." The new guard stood up and began to pace the line of convicts. "The Demons need food, and you're it. You've signed away your rights for the chance to live without bars in a Red City. I want you to remember that."

Bethany started to shake her head, her hands boxed in her ears, and her mouth moved. No words passed her lips, but even we could see her soundless movements were pleading and begging.

Officer Closter pushed his substantial body to standing and walked around the table, his baton hung from his fingers. "What did you say, Miss O'Hallohan? You want to go first through the door?"

Bethany folded in on herself; her body began to jerk with the force of her shivering. *"No. No. No. You can't make me. I don't want to go."* She whispered to herself, repeating the words until they became mulch between her teeth.

"O'Hallohan. Stand up." Officer Closter demanded. "Get your ass up. You're first out the door."

Bethany began to rock but her head tilted and her wild eyes flung around the room, unable to gain purchase on anything. Her mouth never stopped moving; it took a second for me to realise that the words streaming out of her mouth were the Lord's prayer.

Closter palmed his baton as he moved closer, but with unexpected strength, Bethany jumped to her feet like a newborn giraffe and darted under his arm.

"You can't make me!" She screamed as her body slammed into the locked metal door that led to no man's land. "I don't want to go! God will forgive all sinners! Even those that repent in the last hour. He'll forgive me!"

"God ain't here, rat." The newer guard grunted, but Bethany was too far gone. Her shrieks had risen in pitch; she no longer formed words.

420

We all watched, in silence, as the stringy girl flung herself against the door. Her waiflike body was too light to make a sound.

A sharp crack rang out through the room, but the concrete walls swallowed the sound. Bethany's head slammed into the door; her body began to slide, leaving a trail of blood as it went. She did not make a sound. Her begging and pleading had been silenced. Half of her head was missing.

Officer Trigger-Happy pushed his gun back into his holster and brushed his hands together. "Fucking hate to lose a bright spark like that. Demons love a good crazy."

He wasn't wrong.

"Alright, single file." Closter snapped his fingers and pointed to the door on the other end of the room. "We've gotta walk you through the next checkpoints."

I forced my eyes to leave Bethany's mangled head and her awkwardly sprawled limbs. Unable to sum up any emotion, lest I unleash a torrent. That was the only way that I would survive. I had to be numb.

It worked in prison. I only hoped it would work in the Red City.

The exit swung open with a creak and a harsh bang. The bright sunlight lit up the stark terrain until my vision was almost white.

"Behind the line," Officer Closter called out as we began to file out. Without words, every other prison pressed their back against the concrete wall and waited for Officer Trigger-Happy to back up the line. He didn't. The office must have been his station. At least we wouldn't have to worry about a bullet to the skull. Closter had a baton, which was bad enough, but somehow a bullet seemed scarier. Zero to dead in one second.

"I'm going to activate the path in a moment. This section is filled with landmines. Deviate from the path, and there won't be enough parts to identify your corpse." Closter's tone was bored as he walked to what I had thought was a fuse box and scanned his retina.

The lid of the box flipped up; Closter programmed in a code word that I was too far away to see. A whirring motor began to chug, a high pitched whine filled the air. The path lifted off the ground, leaving huge chunks of the terrain below.

"Hurry up, inmates!" Closter's shout snapped my spine straight as I darted forward to the raised ledge. I put both hands on the platform and pulled myself up, crawling forward before I could stand. I did not look back as I began to navigate the nonsensical pathway to the next concrete ring. Grunts and groans of the other prisoners sounded out behind me, but otherwise, we all moved in silence. I concentrated on the sharp turns and trying not to think about O'Hallohan's pulpy brain matter or the ichor confetti that would scatter the ground if one of us fell off the ledge.

I saw a black stain a few feet away, past the edge of the path, and a large crater. The only evidence that an unlucky soul had slipped and been blown to pieces. Closter wasn't bluffing.

I was the first to reach the next inner wall, but I was hesitant to walk to the door without an instruction.

Closter had proved that everything was dangerous unless you had the right instructions, and I liked my body in one piece.

I began an orderly line, and soon, the other prisoners joined me. Someone tapped my shoulder, but I did not turn.

"I know you," A male voice badgered. "You're the Prophet. Aren't you?"

I shook my head and kept my eyes trained forward.

"Everyone in C wing was talking about some chick who looked like the girl from one of those old Japanese horror movies." He nudged my shoulder to try and get my attention. "They said you painted the fire before it took out the main office." He huffed a quiet laugh. "I bet my commissary that you set that fire."

I lifted one shoulder and shrugged.

"It's your fault we're all here."

I said nothing.

"Mr Willows!" Closter barked. "Flirt as much as you want once we get to the city, but if you say another word, I will leave you between the rings."

Willows snapped his mouth shut as Closter opened the door and began to usher us through. Another stark office. One blue line and one pink. The universal symbols for male and female on each side.

"Line up, inmates!" Closter's words jolted the drifting young adults into action. Una lifted her hand to ask a question.

"The sex you were born with, Una." Closter's voice softened as he gestured for her to join the line behind the symbol for male. "It's for credits. You won't need the feminine hygiene ones, that's all. You'll still get your HRT."

Una's turned on her heel and sauntered over to the other side of the room, to join the blue line.

Closter marched to the front before taking a sharp turn to the previously hidden door on the right, at the front of the men's line. He did not instruct us to stay still, but none of us moved.

As soon as we were alone, Willows turned towards me. "Psycho bitch," He hissed. "You killed five people, did you know that?"

Una jabbed him in the stomach, before flipping her long red hair over her shoulder. She said nothing before facing forward.

Closter came back only seconds later, holding two guns with a hollow plastic tube at the top. They looked like nail guns from the hardware store and the sight of them filled my stomach with squirming insects.

"Left arm out," He didn't look up as he began to load a capsule into the empty tube the first gun. "For those fools who don't know their left from their right, it's the arm without a mark on it."

Closter moved down the line. When he stood in front of me, the gun hissed and whirred as it shunted something under

423

the skin. After he walked down the line, I rubbed the sore spot. Something the size of a grain of rice rested under the surface.

The mark on my other arm didn't burn or throb, so I could only assume that whatever was in the implant was medical, not magical.

Once Closter injected all of us, he made his way to the front again.

"Those implants are your identity." He told us. "Your money, your ID. Your CV. Everything."

I rubbed my thumb over the tiny incision and noticed that a few of the others were doing the same.

"The city operates on a credit system. Women will get an extra five credits once a month for feminine hygiene products." Closter informed us.

Some of the men started to gripe. Willows was one of them.

"If you start bleeding from *your* pussy, Mr Willows, you can have some extra credits. Until then, shut your hole." Closter snapped.

"Can't they just like... Hold it in?" One of the men at the back whined.

Closter pinched the bridge of his nose. "The next person to say something stupid is gonna get a whack."

That shut the moaners up.

Closter raised his hand in farewell to whoever stood unseen behind the frosted glass window past the line of male inmates. He pushed open the door and tilted his head. We all filed out, the action more natural as we became accustomed to what was expected of us.

My stomach flew to my throat when I caught sight of the terrain behind the door.

A jagged scar on the landscape. A deep fissure that seemed to have no visible bottom, the edges sparkled pink and white. It smelt crisp. I could only guess at the material that lined the chasm. Salt? Crystal? Quartz? I didn't know. All I knew was that the air buzzed with magic.

424

It was on the other end of the spectrum to the spells that guarded the outer wall. An absence that told me that magic wouldn't work between these rings. The chasm had to be physically crossed, without preternatural help.

Closter strode over to another fuse box, the same procedure as before. Retina scan and passcode. A metal ladder emerged from the wall and fell across the chasm.

I closed my eyes and took a deep breath as I imagined crossing the chasm using only a steel ladder. I didn't want to do it, but still, I found myself in the queue of inmates waiting to reach the other side.

Willows was at the front of the line, muscular and physically adept, he had no issue traversing the crossing. Followed by Una, who moved with confidence. I was next. My hands trembled as I wiped my clammy palms against my baggy uniform.

I couldn't empty my brain of all thoughts. Bad things happened when I did that. But I had to find a way to cope with the chasm. I had discovered something new about myself, I was terrified of heights.

The words to the alphabet song ran through my mind; I sang my ABCs three times before my feet found purchase on the other side. I rushed over to the concrete wall and pressed my hands against the rough surface. The solid ground soothed the rolling waves of vertigo that washed through my body.

Closter was the last person to cross, and thirty seconds after his feet landed on the other side of the chasm the ladder swung up with a hinge and slowly crept back into its notch on the wall.

"What do you think's down there?" Una whispered as she sidled up to my shoulder.

I squinted at the glittering rock face and shrugged. Unable to answer.

Closter stepped to the front of the line and cleared his throat. "One more barrier before we reach the edge of the city." His booming voice warned. "This one's easy as pie."

Somehow I didn't believe him.

Closter opened another unmarked door and gestured for us to step through. No one moved until Willows straightened his shoulders and swaggered past the guard. His smirk was the epitome of smug.

"Not long now, ladies. Almost to the city of Sin." Willows laughed heartily, winking. He stepped over the threshold to the office and jerked as if he had been struck with a thousand volts of electricity.

I watched him fall to the ground with a groan. His hands clenched as if reaching for something. He curled into the fetal position. His arrogance washed away and left nothing but a scared child inside a man's body.

"Willows!" Closter barked, unsympathetic. "It'll stop hurting the closer you get to the entrance. Now move!"

I swallowed around the lump in my throat and stepped forward before my fear could catch up to me. My mark began to itch. The inside of my skin felt like ants were crawling over my every nerve ending. I gritted my teeth as I followed Willows, stepping over his inert body, and past the invisible line in the office.

The air was thick. Cloying. Stagnant with abundant magic. It raced through my veins, spreading out from the mark that they had burnt into my skin when I was asleep.

My thoughts swam away on a sea of pain, but I forced my feet to keep walking. Then, like a popping balloon, the pain was gone.

I belonged to the city now.

I didn't need to test my theory. I could feel it in my bones, the same way that I knew I had two arms and two legs. If I tried to cross over the barrier and back the way I had come— the magic would kill me.

Chapter 2

Closter walked unimpeded through the rolling and groaning bodies that littered the floor.

I was the only one that had managed to keep my feet, barely. With one arm propped against the peeling paint and another on my knee, I noticed the pain was gone, but my body was still weakened by it.

Closter took his baton and slammed it against the metallic table at the front of the room. The sound echoed out like the crack of a gunshot. Bethany's exploded head flashed behind my eyelids again; I drew my shoulders back to give the guard my full attention.

"Last hurdle, inmates," Closter warned. "I won't have time to go over these basics once I push you through the gate, so listen good and listen hard."

A surge of relief that we were nearing the final ring was quickly wiped away by whatever news that Closter was going to deliver as he took off his mirrored sunglasses and put them in his breast pocket. The guard made a point to meet all of our eyes as he rested his hip against the table.

"First things first," He sighed. "You're going to the meat market."

Horrified silence solidified the air of the room until it was almost too thick to breathe.

"There are two types of Demon." He continued. "Dæmons. Corrupted humans. They were once like you or me. Don't know how they changed. Chances were they made a deal with the Devil. Don't know. Don't care. They might have been like you or me once, they ain't anymore. Do not count on their sympathy or kindness. A Daemon feeds on human emotions.

427

Touch mainly. Stay too close, and you might find that you're walking a fine line between life and death."

Rita, a small girl at the back with tufty blonde hair whimpered.

"Then you got your Purebloods." Closter carried on, crossing his arms over his chest. "These are Demons direct from Hell. These can be anything from Imp to Drudes, aka Nightmare Demons. Kitsune. These don't bother humans much. They feed on Sin, they pluck it right from the air."

Closter took a deep breath. His eyes hardened. "You see a Pureblood, you run. Far and fast. The only time you would see one is if it wants something from you. Just because it's doesn't need to touch you to feed, doesn't mean that it's not one of the most dangerous things to walk this godforsaken earth. We clear?"

Everyone stayed silent.

"We're clear." Closter nodded to himself before heaving his rotund body to standing. He turned to the door, before clicking his tongue against the roof of his mouth as if just remembering something. "Red eyes means they've killed an innocent. It means that at some point, they killed someone for the fun of it. Demons typically have their own moral code. Red eyes don't. With a typical Demon, you smart back then you're fair game. Red eyes mean that a Demon has hunted someone who's done nothing to them but exist."

Una raised a shaking hand. "Why do their eyes turn red?" She whispered.

"Fuck if I know." He grunted. "I just know that a Demon that kills for sport'll have red eyes."

Willows raised his hand with a confident swagger despite the fact he had almost pissed himself not five minutes before. "What's the meat market?"

Closter pinched the bridge of his nose and sighed. "Meat market is where you're gonna go."

"But what is it?" Willows repeated.

"Daemons are separated in Families. Each Family

stems from the original Pureblood that created the Demons." Closter shook his head. "Families are complicated as shit, but the gist of it is... Say, you have a Pureblood named Jeff. Jeff corrupts five humans. Those humans corrupt ten more. Every human that is connected to Jeff belongs to that family. You get me?"

We nodded. Willows raised his hand again. "There are Demons named Jeff?" He chuffed.

Closter had moved before anyone had a chance to react. His baton landed sideways into the centre of Willows's gut. The inmate wheezed and hunched over. No longer laughing. Closter gripped his throat and raised Willow's head until their eyes met.

"You're a fool, Willows." Closter snarled. "I hope to God some Leviathan bitch makes a pretty slave of you."

He let the bulky young man without warning and Willows tripped over his feet. Closter dusted his hands and turned back to the line of prisoners.

"You're going to get chosen for a Sector. Don't know how the Families choose, but they've got a system." Closter informed us. "Its called the meat market because it's an auction. You might be bought to become a prostitute in the Pink Sector or a pit fighter in Black one. If you're lucky, you'll be passed over and chosen for grunt work."

My knees buckled, but I remained standing. It felt like a hand had reached down my throat and twisted my stomach.

Before my body had communicated with my mind, my shaking hand rose.

"What is it, Doe?"

"You said that we would be free." My tongue smacked against the roof of my mouth. My words croaked out as my throat was too dry to carry them.

Closter narrowed his eyes. "We said there would be no cages." He turned to scrutinise the Hodgepodge of failed humanity that stood, awkwardly, in front of him. "You all signed a contract for time served. You belong to the Red City now."

The water was cold as it thumped against my back like razor blades. It crossed over my filthy body in rivets, changing from clear to murky brown, before swirling down the drain. Behind the turquoise shower curtains, I could hear the other inmates enjoyed their showers simultaneously.

Naked, and without a towel, I kept my eyes straight ahead as we were herded through a glowing red tube, it was tall enough that I could walk through unimpeded. A wave of warmth dried the remained specks of water from my sun-deprived skin. I felt my now clean hair lose its weight as it dried, long and straight down my back.

Another set of cotton scrubs were shoved into my hands. Crimson this time. I clasped them to my stomach until the rest of the inmates filed through the dryer and they instructed us to dress.

The clothes were loose, and not made for someone of my pitifully short stature. I had to roll the waistband over a dozen times before the trousers were no longer a trip hazard.

There was a long dotted line that led around a dark corner. The corridor was narrow enough for one person to stand in, but the ceiling was high. An unknown guard waited at the mouth of the pathway.

Our group stood in the cement maze of paths hidden away in the final wall of the outer rings.

A hushed reverence had fallen over the rest of the prisoners as we had entered the final hurdle.

Whatever snark that had started to creep through from familiarity to Closter had bled away, leaving only fear of the unknown behind.

Closter had done his best to inform us of what was to happen. I suspected that he had done so to prevent another

430

incident, like Bethany's.

Closter had bid us farewell when we had passed the final barrier into the Red City.

At the lip of the dark path, above the guards head, sat a traffic light with only two colours. Red and green. We all stood, faces lifted and bathed in the red light as we waited for the colour to change. The minutes seemed to stretch and warp to hours. My hands twisted together, clammy with sweat.

Una stood in front of me. She gasped for breath and leant over with her arms wrapped around her stomach. "I don't think I can do it." She sounded broken. "I don't want to be a whore. I just wanted to get out."

I forced my eyes back to the glow of the light and tried to put her mutterings out of my head.

She heaved another gulp of air. "I'm going to be sick. *Fuck. Fuck. Fuck.*"

I reached forward and put my hand on her back. I did not let my eyes drop from the light above my head.

"Do not give them a reason to shoot you," I whispered. "Stand up straight."

I hated myself for uttering the words, but when the guard's dispassionate eyes roamed over our crew, my fingers twitched; I knew I had done the right thing. Una trembled, but she pulled her shoulders back.

"Thank you," She whispered but did not turn around.

I could not think of an adequate response.

The light turned green; the line began to trudge into the darkness, like cattle to the slaughter. The far-away roar of excited voices grew slowly, as the path twisted and turned. The guard at the front did not look back once, assured of our submission.

The low hum of the crowd had grown exponentially as the darkness abated. The chattering and laughing banter was an odd juxtaposition from the solemn faces of my fellow prisoners. Trading one Hell for another.

The promise of freedom. A life without bars had tempted each and every one of us, but none of us had known

431

what that had meant.

Each of the inmates in my group was young. Early twenties at the oldest. Good looking. They each had that something about them that drew others in, even if they also carried an edge of danger. Before we had left the bus, I had feared the prisoners that walked by my side. Unsure of their crimes, but guaranteed they were terrible if their sentence was long enough to want to trade it for time served in the Red City.

The music stopped; a hush fell over the crowd, hidden behind the door at the end of the corridor.

The line drew to a halt; I tripped into Una's back before I could stop myself.

The guard turned, silent, appraising. He said nothing. I heard the booming enthusiastic voice of an announcer behind the door, amplified by a microphone.

As if propped into action by some unknown cue, the sour-faced guard opened the door and pushed us through. Straight onto a stage.

My vision turned white with the lights overhead, and I pressed my forearm over my eyes to cover them. It took a few seconds for my eyes to adjust.

We were stood behind a white silk partition. The crowd chittered behind the separating wall like baying hyenas. I could feel the crackle of magic on the air, raising the fine hairs on the back of my neck. I was confident that the monsters in the audience could see our shadows through the flimsy fabric. A fact that seemed to only excite them.

"Fresh meat!" The female announcer boomed into the microphone. The audience roared. Some stools hit the floor as I heard people jump to their feet and stomp as they echoed the words back to the stage. *Fresh meat. Fresh meat.*

"Our first item to the docket is Mr Henry Willows. Twenty-one years of age. Convicted of death by dangerous driving, Mr Henry Willows spent eighteen months in The Allhallows Prison before being released on parole." The crowd was silent as they listened to the announcer as she spun her tale.

432

"Mr Willows was released, and yet sentenced to life in prison only a year later for murder. Come out here, Henry!"

Willows looked back at us once, and for the first time since I had met him, he looked green with fear. The trembling man pulled back his shoulders and stepped around the partition as if he had the world at his feet. His pale face gone and arrogance locked into place.

I could not see the crowds reaction, but the whispering grew louder. More frenzied.

"Who did you kill, Henry?" The announcer sounded positively delighted.

"My girlfriend." His answer was short. Clipped and no emotion.

"Why?"

The silence was long. I did not know if Henry didn't want to talk about it, or if he was searching for words. Either way, I struggled to find sympathy with a murderer.

I clutched the fabric over his chest as I recalled his earlier threats. I hadn't taken them seriously. I had thought Willows was bluster and testosterone. I sincerely hoped that his placement was far away from where I ended up.

"Stacey had cancer." He croaked. "I didn't want her to be in pain anymore."

There was stunned silence from the crowd.

"The capacity to love someone enough to kill them, folks! A rare find! Who wants to find a home for Mr Willows?" The announcer started the bidding, but as I had no frame of reference for the credit system, I did not know if it was a small or large amount that afforded Henry Willows to his new demonic master.

A few more inmates took the stage; the announcer lamented their stories and encouraged the crowd. Arson. Robbery. Murder. Rape. The crimes were severe.

"A rare item!" The announcer preened. "Born male, but now living as a female. Una Imari."

The redhead in front of me shook her hands as if that

433

could stop them trembling. With a deep breath, she pushed forward and past the partition to face the crowd.

"Hello, Una!" Someone cheered from the back of the room, followed by a wolf whistle.

I found myself praying that Una wouldn't be bought by some pervert.

"Una Imari is twenty-five years old and is a skilled pianist. She studied at Cambridge University and has a bachelor's degree in Mechanical Engineering. Una was arrested for first-degree murder. What happened, Miss Imari?"

Una cleared her throat. "My stepdad abused my sister and me." She thundered; without hesitation.

"It says here that he was bludgeoned with a claw hammer." The announcer replied, jovially. "A revenge story, my beautiful Hellions. What a treat!"

"What can I say?" Una's voice was dry. "I'm passionate."

The crowd roared with laughter; the bidding started enthusiastically. I kept an ear out for who eventually won, remembering Closter's words about prostitution in the Pink Sector. Una was ultimately won by the Purple Sector, which the announcer informed Una was pride.

Once Una's footsteps disappeared down the other end of the stage, it was my turn. Only a handful of other prisoners stood behind me. My shoulders hunched in a subconscious effort to appear smaller than my very petite five foot nothing. I knew that I could not wait any longer. The crowd hovered with bated breath for my arrival, stirred up by the frenzy of bidding.

My breathing faltered, and my feet dragged as I walked to the front of the silk wall and across the polished chestnut stage. The lights burned hotter than before without the partition's protection; I bent my neck so that my hair acted as a curtain. My eyes faced down, so I could watch my careful footsteps. I did not look up, even when I reached the small masking tape dot that told me where to stand.

"Jane Doe." The announcer humphed, I heard the

paper crinkle as she turned it over. "There isn't much information about Miss Doe. Only that she is a skilled painter with a penchant for disturbing imagery."

The crowd whispered, disappointed.

"Miss Doe is serving a life sentence."

"For what?" Someone called from the back of the room, and the audience laughed.

"It doesn't say." The announcer was confused. I blinked and raised my head, tilting my chin in the direction of the voice that had been entertaining the crowd.

The announcer was human. Long blonde hair and a body built for Sin. Breast implants, and a tiny waist.

I did not judge her for her part in the meat market, but I judged her for enjoying it.

"Miss Doe, why don't you tell us about yourself?" The announcer smiled brightly and hooked one hand on her hip. The other she swept out theatrically towards the audience.

For the first time since I had taken the stage, I allowed myself to peek at the crowd of evil that had chosen to participate in a human auction.

Each table had a tarnished silver candelabra, the tapered candles were white, but their flames glowed different colours. One pink, green, yellow. So many colours cast a soft light; I could only guess that those tables were representatives for various Sectors.

Some of the tables were behind a railing, hidden in the autonomy of darkness.

I hated talking about myself with a passion, and with the pressure to sell myself to a room full of demons, the desire to flee was even more prominent.

"I don't want to," I said.

I raised my chin, ignoring the way that I felt it tremble. My ratty midnight hair parted in the centre; the light hit my eyes, so I squinted. My stance was defiant despite every instinct inside my body screaming for it not to be.

All of the monsters in the room turned to each other

435

and began to whisper amongst themselves. Beautiful daemons or twisted Purebloods—I couldn't tell.

"One million credits!" A booming voice whipped out from the darkness of the VIP lounge. The words wrapped around my neck and jarred my spine straight. They echoed in my ears like a song I had always known but couldn't remember the name of.

"We have a winner!" The announcer cried out, bouncing on her heels and clapping. "Sold! To the Wilde Family."

Red City is available on Kindle Unlimited now

Books by Michaela Haze

Daemons of London

The Bleeders
The Human Herders
The Purebloods

The Devil's Advocate

The Devil's Advocate
The Devil's Lullaby
The Devil's Equal

Standalone Novels

Red City
The Dead Ringer

Coming Soon

Fire Heart (Feb 2020)
Underdog (June 2020)

Join my ARC Team!

I am always looking for beta and ARC readers for my books (I literally have no one, and do it all by myself). Check out my facebook group: Michaela Haze's ARC team, to get in on the action!

You can also follow me on instagram and twitter @michaelahaze

A Map of Hell

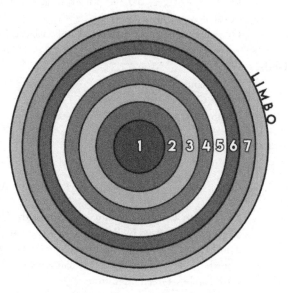

1.PRIDE & LIES   5.GREED
2.WRATH   6.GLUTTONY
3.SLOTH   7.LUST
4.ENVY   LIMBO

Glossary

The Fae (Sidhe):
A being that originated from the dimension of Faery.

- Mimic Sidhe – A shapeshifting fae
- Blood Sidhe – A fae that uses blood to create various treasures
- Fae Lord – A very old and powerful fae. Typically part of the Royal Court.
- Dragon-Blooded Fae – A cursed and enslaved Fae.

Gods:

- The Balance (The Universe)
- Nova (God) - Light
- Death - Dark

Kings and Queens of Hell:

- First Circle – Pride: Abaddon (Originally ruled by Lucifer)
- Second Circle – Wrath: Faith – Queen of the Valkyries (Originally governed by Ba'el and then Dahlia)
- Third Circle – Sloth: Belphegor
- Fourth Circle – Envy: The Leviathan King
- Fifth Circle – Greed: Mammon
- Sixth Circle – Gluttony: Beezlebub
- Seventh Circle – Lust: Asmodeus
- Limbo - Charon

Demons:
A sentient being with access to Hell magic.

- Daemon: A human that has been turned immortal by ritual. They are supernaturally strong and feed through touch.
- Pureblood: A creature born in Hell.

- Drudes – Nightmare Demons
- Incubi/Succubi – Lust Demons
- Ifrit/Dijinn – Wish Demons
- Leviathan: An Envy Demon (serpentine)
- Shax Demon: A snake-like demon (vermin) that feel from the discarded skin of the Leviathan.
- Kitsune: A Japanese fox Demon. A mischievous and tricky spirit.
- Baphomet-kin: Both beast and man. Sons of Baphomet, Duke of Lies (First Circle, Pride)

The Hunters:
Beings (both human and other) chosen by The Balance to act as her will in the Human Realities and to police the forces of Hell and Faery in relation to Humans.

Hellhounds:
First Circle lower Demons. Typically servial.

The Bhakshi and the Shayati
Devouring beasts created by Nova (God) to destroy Death.

Angels:
The Lord's Chosen (Seraphim), with golden wings and angelic magic, each of the Lord's Chosen has a title and runes that have been gifted to them by 'The Lord'.

Made in the USA
Monee, IL
01 February 2025

11403870R00243